The Uncles

◆

To Donald Reisman
a mensch
DMacrov
2009

The Uncles

◆

David Macarov

Writers Club Press
San Jose New York Lincoln Shanghai

The Uncles

Writers Club Press
an imprint of iUniverse.com, Inc.

For information address:
iUniverse.com, Inc.
5220 S 16th, Ste. 200
Lincoln, NE 68512
www.iuniverse.com

ISBN: 0-595-18945-8

Printed in the United States of America

Contents

◆

The Locker Room

◆ ────────

I grew up in the locker room of the Atlanta Braves. My Uncle Phil lived near the third base line; I had friends living in both right and left field; and we all went to school near home plate. In those days, which was before the Atlanta baseball team got into the big leagues and became polite, they were called the Crackers. The term "cracker"suggested a swaggering, illiterate, tobacco-spitting roughneck, and the baseball team adopted that name as a kind of macho symbol. It was also a tongue-in-cheek gibe at Nawtheners, who saw all Southerners like that. Later, "crackers" was supplanted by "rednecks," until gentrified by Governor Gene Talmadge into "good ole' boys."

All this symbolism was lost on my grandparents. They didn't know or care about Crackers, Yankees, Giants or Dodgers; crackers, rednecks, or good ole' boys. If I had come home excited about the Yankees winning the pennant, they would have thought it must be something good for the Jews. My grandparents were new immigrants, working hard, trying to get along, taking advantage of every opportunity, striving to make it.

If there was anything unusual about our family, it was the fact that when my mother's parents came from Europe toward the end of the last century (now the century before last), they didn't open a grocery store, a candy store or a dry-goods store, like most of their contemporaries. They operated a permanent poker game in their house on Washington

Terrace. The house had a front door, two side doors, and a back door—not to speak of the cellar entrance (which they didn't)—and lots of closets, which may have helped them stay out of trouble, although I do seem to remember uniformed policemen coming to the front door from time to time, and leaving without even entering the house. Indeed, Washington Terrace became a choice post for policemen, who vied for the assignment. Decades later the whole area was condemned and razed, and the Atlanta Stadium was built over what had been our neighborhood. As close as we can figure, our house was where the locker room is today.

As their children were born, my grandparents found it harder and harder to run the poker game and take care of the children at the same time. So they opened a laundromat on Georgia Avenue. With customers constantly coming and going, it was easy to turn it into the headquarters of the local numbers racket. It goes without saying that most of the proceeds went to the Southern version of the Mob, but my grandparents got their share. They never got rich, but they never had to go on welfare, either. And just when some of the children reached the point where they could support their parents, legitimately, death took grandpa and grandma in rapid succession.

I remember the day my grandfather called me into the room where he was bedridden with the cancer that would kill him. After talking to me a bit about life and death, about what I was reading and what I thought about it, how I was doing in school and how I saw my future, he turned very serious and said, "Because you are the eldest grandchild, and because of what I see in you already, I am appointing you the Joseph of the family."

He didn't explain, and I didn't know what he meant. All I remembered about Joseph from Sunday School was that he was sold out by his brothers. Thinking that my grandfather didn't trust my siblings to be nice to me didn't make me exactly happy. It wasn't until I was older that I understood. He was expressing a great deal of trust in me. He meant that no matter what they did, it would be my job to keep the family together; to keep in touch with whomever moved away; to know who was related to whom and how; and to corral whatever help was needed for family members in trouble. As I grew up I took the charge very seriously, but it didn't turn out to be easy. I was still young when my Uncle Sam suddenly disappeared from Malmo. Nobody in the family got upset, because they didn't even know he had disappeared—in fact, some of them didn't even know where Malmo was. And when Uncle Bernie put a lot of people in jail (including me) and then dropped out of sight, there was a lot of excitement. Still, all of this was within the family and we tried to keep it very confidential.

But when Uncle Eddie divorced his wife of twenty-five years and ran off with a mud-wrestler, the family really became upset. There were big headlines in the tabloids and people wanted to talk about it wherever they went. Uncle Leo becoming a Catholic priest certainly didn't do anything to damp down the excitement, nor did Uncle Buck help by trying to revamp the prison system—from the inside. Cousin Cat's ouster from the State Department as a communist was also hard for the family to swallow, and when he was decorated by the Russian government they didn't know whether to be proud or ashamed. Perhaps all of this made them more of an American family than they realized, but they never thought of it that way.

While I was making my own way in the world I tried to keep tabs on the family as best I could, but when I retired I decided to take my grandfather's charge seriously and become the family historian. Since Uncle Bernie affected my life more seriously than any of the others, I began with him.

Uncle Bernie

◆

UNCLE BERNIE

My Uncle Bernie put a lot of people in jail—including me. He wasn't a law-enforcement official or anything like that, but we ended up behind bars just the same. Finally, so did he, but I never thought that made us even.

I grew up in Atlanta, and when my mother died, it was her sister, my Aunt Sophie, who took care of me until I was old enough to live on my own. Uncle Bernie showed up one day from nobody knew where and simply swept Aunt Sophie off her feet. He was a calm, deliberate man who spoke slowly, had a sense of humor, and was always willing to compromise rather than to argue. He was also good looking. The only thing that could be said to mar his good looks was a small blood spot right under the end of his moustache, and most people never even noticed it.

Aunt Sophie, on the other hand, was not exactly the belle of the ball. To be honest, she was rather plain looking, somewhat heavy, and a terrible dancer. As a consequence—despite the fact that her father had left her very well off—she hadn't been at all popular as she grew up. No wonder everyone was delighted when Uncle Bernie began a whirlwind courtship. The whole family liked Uncle Bernie, and they were as sorry to lose him as they were to lose Aunt Sophie when he took her off to Columbus, Georgia.

Nobody really knew what Uncle Bernie did. He would leave suddenly, be away for a while, and return, usually sporting signs of wealth. He almost always brought gifts for everyone. Once he brought Aunt Sophie a really handsome diamond ring, and once every man in the family received a pair of very expensive imported shoes. When asked, he just said he took care of property and investments. Since Aunt Sophie was obviously so happy with him, that was enough for the family.

It was when I was twenty-one, working in a shoe store, that I went to Columbus to visit Uncle Bernie and Aunt Sophie. Columbus was smaller than Atlanta, I didn't know any other people of my age, and I got bored pretty rapidly, so when one day Uncle Bernie said, "Want to go to an auction?" I was practically out the door before he finished speaking.

We went to Fort Benning, that enormous infantry training camp outside Columbus, and Uncle Bernie began inspecting army surplus—stoves, heaters, typewriters, miles of electric wire in coils, spare parts, and junk. The material was in numbered lots, and as we walked around Uncle Bernie made notes on what he found.

Looking around, I saw another five or six men in civilian clothes who seemed to be doing the same thing. Uncle Bernie filled one small notebook and handed it to me to hold while he began another. I looked at it, but couldn't make heads or tails of what I saw. The various numbered lots seemed to have coded information written next to them, and I couldn't figure out the code. While I was holding the notebook and staring at it, one of the other men sidled alongside me and said, very quietly, "Where are you from?"

I replied that I was from Atlanta, and the man looked at me oddly and said, "Isn't that a long way to come just for an auction?"

Thinking of how bored I had been, I replied, "I thought it might be worth my time."

The man stared at me again, and then said, "I guess it will."

Just then an officer entered and bidding on the material, by lots, began. There were usually three or four bids on each lot before it was sold ("knocked down" was the phrase used) to the highest bidder, and everyone present seemed to buy at least one lot. Each winning bidder paid cash for his purchase, and usually had two or three men waiting outside in a truck, ready to carry the material out. At one point Uncle Bernie asked me to bid in his place, signaling me each time what to do. When I won the bid, Uncle Bernie gave me the cash to pay for the purchase, which was carried to his truck.

When the sale was over Uncle Bernie and I drove off, but to my surprise we did not go home. We went to an apartment over a store, and when we entered, I was again surprised to see all the other bidders present. They all sat around a table, on which there was coffee, tea, Cokes, and three kinds of cake, and then bidding began again for the same lots. This time the bids all seemed to be much higher, again paid in cash, and when they ended, one man who had been keeping a record of the bids did some calculations, and said, "Two hundred dollars each."

At which point he handed each person present, including me, two hundred dollars in cash. I started to protest, but Uncle Bernie motioned me to keep quiet. On the way down the stairs Uncle Bernie asked me, "Did you enjoy the auction?"

"Boy, did I? Two hundred bucks! I'm ready to go every day."

Uncle Bernie smiled, and explained that such auctions were held twice a year. The bidders were all in cahoots, of course, and at the second auction they bid what the goods were really worth, in contrast to the low prices they had paid the army. The difference was divided equally between them. "They're all a bunch of crooks," said my uncle jovially, "so I let them think you were a dealer from Atlanta. Do them good to get gypped themselves once in a while."

"But why did you tell me to bid?"

"So they'd think you were a real dealer, instead of just a visitor."

"Oh. Well, here's the receipt for the payment."

Uncle Bernie looked at the receipt, and stiffened. "Why did you give your real name?"

"Why not?"

"Oh, shit, I forgot to tell you to use a false name. Okay, I guess it will be all right."

"I don't understand. What's the problem?"

"Nothing, nothing. Tell me, what are you going to do with your share?"

"I don't know. Haven't thought about it. Maybe save it for a rainy day."

"Don't be stupid. It's easy money. Get drunk, get laid, have yourself a ball. In Atlanta, of course—not here."

But, somehow, I didn't feel like celebrating. It had never occurred to me that I would cheat my government. In fact, I had always thought of myself as a good citizen, who paid his taxes and stayed out of jail. I began wondering about Uncle Bernie, and, of course, about Aunt Sophie. Uncle Bernie must have sensed my feelings, because he said, "Look, these things happen every day. Getting the best of the government is part of business. Nobody pays more taxes than they have to, and everyone looks for loopholes and escape routes. T-men look for tax evaders, and businessmen look for ways to beat the T-men. It's a game, and everyone in business plays it. You'll find out when you become the owner of a business."

Back in Atlanta, I thought that maybe I could overcome my bad feeling by following Uncle Bernie's advice—I got drunk and I got laid, not once, but several times. And, to tell the truth, I pretty much forgot the episode, especially when I bought a tuxedo with the money I had left, and didn't have to rent one every time I went to a formal affair. The biggest formal affair was on Valentine's Day, of course, and I not only wore my new tuxedo for the first time, I sent my date an orchid, and I bought myself a pint of Old Crow.

It was while I was nursing a mild hangover the next day that two well-dressed men came to see me. They identified themselves as Federal investigators, and told me that they had known about the conspiracy to cheat the government for some time, but didn't have the proof. As a first-time offender, with no previous record, they said they were prepared to grant me immunity from prosecution if I would name and testify against the others. I acted as though I thought they were crazy. "What are you talking about? I haven't done anything. I'm not part of any conspiracy. I went to an auction, that's all. Is that against the law?"

"You were part of a group offering false bids on army surplus; you made a successful bid yourself; we have a copy of the receipt you were given; and the major in charge says he can identify you. Mister, I'd say you are looking at twenty years in the pen. Do you want to talk and walk, or do you want to be silent and serve?"

I was the classical innocent bystander. I hadn't intended to do anything wrong, and in my eyes I hadn't even done anything wrong. But I also knew I could never identify my uncle, not the least because of what it would do to Aunt Sophie. And I didn't even know the names of the other dealers. I squirmed, and I pleaded, and I begged, but I was caught, and there was nothing I could do about it. In the end I pleaded guilty but refused to name the others (in any case Uncle Bernie was the only one I knew). In view of my age, my confession, and the fact that I was a first-time offender, I drew only a year and a day. I don't imagine that I suffered more than most prisoners, and less than some, since I was not only unmarried but didn't even have a steady girl-friend. The prisoners in my section were all there for white collar crimes: income tax evasion, stock market swindles, using the mails to defraud, and so forth. I had no contact with prisoners for crimes against persons, which was a minor blessing. In order to protect Aunt Sophie's feelings, I told the family I had inadvertently bought a stolen car, which was why I was in prison.

I wanted to work in the prison library, but I found that was the hope of every white-collar prisoner, so I ended up making toys that went to children's institutions for Christmas. The work wasn't hard, the regime not too demanding, and the food was decent, if monotonous. Nevertheless, I became depressed every time I realized that I was in prison for nothing that I had done with intent to commit a crime. Often I wondered what would have happened if I had given the others away.

But I knew I couldn't have done it—not only because of my uncle, but because the whole community would have despised me for saving myself by putting several husbands and fathers in jail.

Ours was a minimum-security prison, so I had the chance to meet a number of fellow prisoners. I asked Robert, a small, quiet man, what he was in for (the question most asked by and of newcomers).

"Aiding and abetting customs evasion," he said, "but unlike most of the fellows here, I really am innocent. Okay, I know everybody says that, but in my case it is true."

Since I felt that I was innocent also, at least of intent, I asked him for his story.

He told me about a man who went to Belgium, loaded up on expensive diamonds, and when he got back to Idlewild (which is what JFK was called then), went right to the red line—"Items to be Declared"—threw open his briefcase of diamonds, and asked, "How much do I owe?"

A resident gem expert was called in, the diamonds were examined and appraised, the Customs Inspector did some arithmetic, and said, "Sixty-eight thousand dollars."

The man actually reeled in surprise. When he recovered he said, "I was told by the dealer in Belgium that the customs would be ten thousand dollars at most. I haven't got sixty-eight thousand dollars. What can I do?"

The Customs official said, "You can leave the diamonds here while you acquire the money, you can take them back to Belgium, or you can abandon them. If you abandon them, they will be sold at auction."

"Wait a minute," said the importer. "I am going back to Belgium next week. Can the diamonds be kept here until then? I'll just take them back to that crook in Belgium."

"If you will pay for the storage and insurance, they can be held for you here, but you must either take them back out of the country, or pay the customs."

So he left the diamonds at the airport and showed up a week later with a ticket to Antwerp. The diamonds were taken from the safe, examined, and receipted, and the importer took his briefcase full of diamonds towards the Sabena check-in. As he walked toward the check-in counter with his briefcase, a small quiet man fell into step with him.

"Who are you?" asked the importer.

The man silently produced an identity card and a badge, marking him as a member of the Custom Department's security force. It didn't take long for the importer to realize that the man was not there to protect him or his diamonds—his job was to see to it that the importer actually took the diamonds out of the country, rather than passing them to someone else, or perhaps, leaving without checking in. At the check-in counter the importer reached into his right pocket and produced his ticket and passport. The quiet man stayed next to the importer while the ticket was processed and stayed in step with him through passport control, boarding procedures and entry to the plane. Just before he sat down, the importer turned to the quiet man and said, "I know you were here to watch me, but in any case you made sure nobody robbed me, so take this with my thanks." He pushed some bills into the man's breast pocket.

"No way!" expostulated the quiet man, speaking for the first time. "I don't take money for doing my job." He pulled the bills from his pocket and thrust them at the importer, who took them back without changing expression. The quiet man walked out of the plane, looked back once and disappeared down the corridor.

Consequently, he did not see the importer call the stewardess, reach into his left pocket, and show her a passport. "I notice that my passport has expired," he said. "I hope I won't have trouble when I get to Antwerp."

She grabbed the passport, studied it, and called the chief steward. "How did you get this far with an expired passport?" he demanded.

"I don't know," said the importer, innocently. "Will I have trouble in Belgium?"

"I'm sorry to tell you, sir, that you will not be going to Belgium. You cannot enter a foreign country without a valid passport. You can't even leave this country without one."

"But what am I to do? I must go to Antwerp!"

"Sorry, sir. You cannot board this plane without a valid passport. Please return to the passenger lounge and deal with it there."

Since he was going out with his briefcase, and not coming in, there were no security or document checks to pass as the importer left the airport. Nobody challenged him. In fact, he heard two officials arguing about who was responsible for letting an expired passport through.

"I was the quiet man," said Robert. "In the investigation that followed, a small diamond was found in my breast pocket. The rest, as they say, is history."

"That story is too fantastic to be made up," I said. "I take it they didn't catch the importer."

"No, but I have a clear image of him in my mind, and if I ever do see him…"

"What did he look like?"

The small blood spot at the edge of the moustache clinched it for me.

The only consolation I could find was that Aunt Sophie really loved that diamond ring.

Uncle Bernie never visited me in prison, and given Robert's presence, it was good for him that he didn't. Indeed, I was told that he was first in Brazil and then in Mexico. I realized that these were places with no extradition treaties with the United States, and I also realized that he was taking no chances on my having second thoughts. "Ungrateful bastard," was all I could think.

When I was released from prison there was a decorous welcome-home party for me. Nobody mentioned where I had been, just how good it was to have me back. Aunt Sophie, in particular, hugged me for so long I didn't think she was ever going to let me go. As she did, she whispered, "Oh, how I have missed you. But, thank God, Bernie was here most of the time. In fact, he is here tonight."

And sure enough, there was Uncle Bernie at my "coming out" party, jovial as ever. I avoided him, of course, but when the party began to run down, he approached me and said me he'd like to talk to me in the next room. I went with some misgivings, because Uncle Bernie no longer seemed to me the companion that I would have chosen for myself. When we entered the next room, all I wanted to do was to turn around and run. Sitting around a table, on which was tea, coffee, Cokes, and, this time, four kinds of cake, were all the bidders from the famous auction. Before I could react Uncle Bernie said, "We owe you." Heads nodded around the table.

"We know we can't make up the year of your life you lost..."

"A year and a day," I interrupted.

"The year and a day you lost, but we have agreed to try to help as much as we can. We are prepared to back you financially in anything you want to do. You want to start a business? Fine. We'll put up the money. You want to go to college? We'll support you for as long as you go. You want to take a trip around the world? We'll pay for it. Just tell us what you want, and you got it."

"Within reason," added a short man with a goatee.

Uncle Bernie glared at him. "Anything at all," he insisted.

I thought about it. With a prison record, I would never be able to work for any government agency. I would not be able to become a lawyer, a banker, or an accountant. I couldn't run for public office. And wherever and whenever I would be someone else's employee, I could always be fired without notice and without compensation, on the basis that I had withheld my prison record from them. I was not an intellectual, and had neither taste nor aptitude for an academic life. About all that was left was to own my own business.

I had enjoyed working in the toy shop, and found that I had a certain aptitude for tools. I also knew that a business recession was beginning, and one of the earmarks of a recession is that people start making their own home repairs, when necessary. So after a while I got in touch with Uncle Bernie, and told him I wanted to open a hardware/do it yourself store, and that would require fifty thousand dollars. I think he was surprised at the modesty of my request, but I didn't really want to have to feel too grateful to him.

Very shortly afterwards Uncle Bernie showed up with a briefcase full of cash—fifty thousand dollars. He explained that this was the money put up by the members of the syndicate ("conspirators," I corrected him mentally). That was a lot of money in those days, and I was able to start off with a bang.

The store was an instant success. I named it the U-Do store to indicate its emphasis on do-it-yourself supplies and equipment. During the first five years the U-Do store was expanded several times. I was interviewed on the radio and in the newspapers. Do-it-yourself became a fad. Our advertising was clever and widespread, based on various scenarios—U-Do this, and U-do that. The only fly in the ointment was that Uncle Bernie insisted on hanging around. He didn't do anything; he didn't even get in the way; he was just there. Sometimes he would make a note in his little notebook, and when I once asked him what he was writing, he said, "Just some ideas that I think would improve the business. I'll share them with you when they have jelled."

And sure enough, one day Uncle Bernie said, "I'd like to talk to you about the business."

I was wary, but listened. "You were right," he said. "You were smart enough to foresee the trend. And now you have to stay on top of the trend. This is a good store, and a big store, but very soon now someone is going to open a string of such stores—one in every new neighborhood. Look how Atlanta is spreading out to the suburbs. People are not going to drive to another side of town, or even downtown, if they can get what they want close by. In addition to this one big store, you should think of a chain of small shops. You can still buy in bulk, and you can supply from one store what another temporarily lacks, and even if business gets bad, you can close little stores and still keep the big one."

I had to admit it made sense. But there was one problem. "Will the 'syndicate' finance such expansion?"

"That group no longer exists," replied Uncle Bernie. "One went bankrupt; one is being bankrupted by his third wife; one has retired to fish in the Gulf; one works in a junkyard; and I don't even know where the other one is. You realize that after your little, uh, unpleasantness we couldn't continue to deal in surplus materials."

"So where is the money to come from?"

"I'll make you a proposition."

I felt my hackles rise.

"No, no, just listen. I know how you feel about me. I've seen it on your face now and then. But listen: I've done well in the stock market, but I still can't finance a string of stores, even small ones. But I've got enough for the initial investment necessary for expansion. You'll keep the big store—sole owner, no strings, I have nothing to do with that business. I'll incorporate the small store operation into a separate corporation. It will be completely separate—separate offices, separate staff. You'll own twenty-percent of the shares, I'll own thirty-one percent, and forty-nine percent as a stock offer will bring in the capital we'll need. You'll get twenty percent of the profits with no investment and no risk."

"I don't understand why you don't open the string of stores without me."

"I need your advice and I need your know-how. In addition, you have credit with the suppliers, and the name of your store is well known and well-trusted. If we can't use the name U-Do for the little stores, the deal is off. The name is the most important thing."

I analyzed Uncle Bernie's proposition for some weeks. I didn't trust him, but I couldn't find any way that he could cheat or exploit me. I didn't see any way I could get into trouble. As just a stockholder of a corporation I wouldn't be liable for anything. The only weak point that I saw was the "credit with the suppliers" bit. I decided I would not buy for the small stores, but would recommend extending credit to Uncle Bernie, "without prejudice," as they say. I was still debating Uncle Bernie's proposition when I saw a new do-it-yourself store opening very close to my home. That settled it for me.

The operation went just the way Uncle Bernie said it would. The string of little stores kept expanding, and the name of our store was accepted as guaranteeing quality. We took back purchases without asking for a reason, and refunded cash—not credit slips. We stocked all the latest gadgets—even those just being mentioned in *Popular Mechanics* and elsewhere. We not only gave service, we gave instructions, and when someone couldn't follow instructions we would often do it for him or her. In short, we were a success.

The small store operation was kept completely separate, just as Uncle Bernie had promised. Each of them was a replica of the big store in appearance, but financially and administratively they were distinct. There was one difference. Whereas the big store had a massive safe, the small stores had only cash registers. Their safe was in the home office of the corporation of small stores. (Individual safes in each store were too expensive and unnecessary, explained Uncle Bernie).

Then something happened: There was a series of break-ins in the small stores, with the cash registers taken. The burglars seemed to know exactly when to come and where the money was, which mystified the police. Uncle Bernie seemed very perturbed. Of course, the buildings and stock were insured, but it was hard to get insurance on cash. What worried Uncle Bernie was that all of the robberies occurred on Saturday night, after the stores were closed. Saturday was the big day in all of the stores, and the amount of cash kept overnight until the banks opened on Monday was, in total, considerable.

His solution was to have the office manager/bookkeeper of the corporation, a young man named Morris, make the rounds of the various stores late Saturday afternoon, picking up the bulk of the cash, and bringing it to him in the office to be put into the safe. Of course, the office manager would not ordinarily have been working on Saturday afternoon, but when Uncle Bernie mentioned the idea, and indicated how much he would be willing to pay a trusted employee for this service (a very nice sum, indeed), Morris volunteered. In addition, Uncle Bernie bought Morris a Reo Flying Cloud in which to make his collections, had it registered in Morris' name, and gave Morris the use of it in his spare time. No wonder Morris worked on Saturday afternoons.

During the next few years I got married, and my wife and I had twins. The store continued to do well, and the income from my twenty-percent of the small stores helped, although considering how many there were, it was surprising how much more the big store continued to make.

One spring afternoon my secretary told me that there were two men who wanted to see me, and she handed me a card. The names meant nothing to me, but the words, "Internal Revenue Service" sent a jolt into my gizzard. The two men were almost identical to the two who had come to see me so many years ago, although they were, in fact, not the same men. They informed me, softly, that they were going to conduct an audit of my books; that it would be illegal for me to remove them from the office or to alter them in any way until they finished; and that my accountant could be present while they worked.

I had complete faith in my accountant, who had been in high-school with me; and I felt that both the business and myself personally had paid all the taxes due when due. Nevertheless, I felt my hand sweating as I picked up the phone to call the accountant. As Manette in *A Tale of Two Cities* went back to shoemaking when made to recall the past, so I had visions of making toys again.

The audit took several days, and when it was over, one of the men said, "Congratulations, sir. Your books are in excellent order and we have no tax claims against you." I tried to keep a straight face as I felt the stone that had been on my heart fly off, and offered them coffee.

As they were drinking, one of them said, "We see from your books that there is no connection between your store and the chain of like-named stores in the city. Do you have any personal connection with them?"

"Only as a stockholder. I own twenty-percent of the stock, as you've seen in my tax return, but I have nothing to do with the management. Why do you ask?"

"Well, from their tax returns they don't seem to be doing as well as you. Why is that, do you think?"

"I've noticed it myself. I guess it is just the difference between a big operation and a series of small ones. To tell the truth, I've never thought much about it one way or another."

When they left, my accountant looked puzzled. "That was almost a breach of professional confidence. They had no right to tell you how well another operation is doing, even if you are a stockholder in it."

The mystery was solved about ten weeks later. The audit of our books had evidently been just to get some comparative figures. Uncle Bernie was charged with tax evasion and falsifying records. The gist of the matter was that he had been "skimming" the cash proceeds. The cash brought to him on Saturday night for years had been reduced by ten percent before being deposited on Monday—an amount that aggregated to over two hundred thousand dollars. The difference was hidden in inventory losses, bad debts, and falsified sales figures.

Uncle Bernie declared himself ignorant of any such shenanigans, and accused Morris of skimming the money before turning it over to him, and, as office manager and bookkeeper, falsifying the records. It would have been Uncle Bernie's word against Morris', but Morris had signed receipts when taking money from the stores, and had received no receipts when turning the money over to Uncle Bernie. However, the fact that probably swayed the jury more than anything else was the Reo Flying Cloud which, according to the records, Morris bought as soon as he started collecting the money, and which he could not have paid for out of his salary.

Immediately after Morris was imprisoned, Uncle Bernie disappeared. I received a frantic phone call from Aunt Sophie, who was distraught. It didn't seem that an accident had happened to him, for he had taken all his clothes—and all their money. Despite the police and private investigators, we were unable to locate him. I was well able to support Aunt Sophie by this time, and I did, but she remained disconsolate.

Morris received five years as a first-time offender, which meant that he would be out in about three years if he behaved himself. I visited him several times and found that he was working—in the toy shop. When Morris was released, I hired him as chief cashier, which gave him access to all the money that came in. He realized why I was doing it, and it gave him back a lot of the self-confidence he had lost when he was railroaded to prison.

Once Morris was knowledgeable about the business, my wife and I decided to take the twins on a long-deferred vacation to Biloxi, where I intended to do some deep-sea fishing. I was reasonably well-off by now, and sometimes even fantasized about retiring from the business and studying, or writing, history—something which had always fascinated me. I eventually did it, but at this moment all I thought about was reels, lines, bait, and boats.

On the dock where boats were rented there were several old codgers sitting in deck chairs with fishing lines in the water. As I passed them, I heard someone call my name. I peered at the faces, but had it not been for the goatee I would not have recognized one of the "syndicate." He gave me a bigger greeting than I was prepared to give him, and I tried to get rid of him, but he wanted to talk. "I've been watching what you've done with your stores. You are really a bright young man. I figure that ninety thousand dollars that you started with must be worth ten times that by now."

"Ninety thousand dollars?"

"Yeah, sure, you remember. Fifteen thousand from each of us six. I gotta tell you, son, it was well worth it to me. I wouldn't have survived a month in the clink."

I felt my bile rise again. Uncle Bernie had given me only fifty thousand dollars—which was ten thousand from each of the other five. In his usual manner, not only had he not contributed anything, he had also skimmed five thousand from each contribution, making twenty-five thousand for himself. I must admit that this knowledge ruined my fishing trip. I remembered the famous phrase, "If a man fools me, shame on him. If he fools me twice, shame on me." What a gullible fool I had been!

Sitting in the office one day I had a visit from someone who introduced himself as Roy, a distant cousin. We delved back into the family tree, insofar as we remembered it, and I found that he was related to me through Aunt Sophie's grandmother. It was a rather far-fetched relationship, but he seemed like a nice person, and I enjoyed talking to him. Eventually, of course, one of us mentioned Uncle Bernie.

"That bastard," said Roy.

Just to draw him out, I asked why he felt that way.

"In a way, it is because of him that I am here. You see, Aunt Sophie felt that you might give me a job. To tell you the truth, I am just out of jail, and given your own experience, Aunt Sophie felt that you might be willing to take a chance on me."

"What were you in jail for?"

"Customs evasion."

"And I bet Uncle Bernie had a hand in it. Want to tell me about it?"

It seemed that while I was in prison Uncle Bernie had come back from South America. He invited Roy to visit him in Columbus, and while Roy was there, asked him if he wanted to go to an auction in New Orleans. Roy had never been to New Orleans, and the idea of a trip excited him. He was bored in Columbus. (I had a feeling of *deja vu* as he talked).

The auction of unclaimed imported items was in the customs shed, and Uncle Bernie showed no interest until an unusual lot was announced—1000 imported shoes. All for the left foot. They had been addressed to someone in Gulfport, at an address that didn't exist, and were never claimed. Bernie asked Roy to do him a favor and bid a hundred dollars for the shoes.

"All left shoes?" remonstrated Roy. "What good are they?"

"I have a connection at the Veterans Administration," said Bernie, "and I can get a list of veterans with only one leg—the left leg. Those poor guys have to buy pairs of shoes in order to get one to wear. If I can sell them left shoes only, I can help them save money. And if I sell them only ten shoes at ten dollars each, I'll have my money back. I'm willing to take a chance on that to help veterans out."

Roy thought it was altruistic of Bernie, but asked why he didn't bid himself.

"I told you," said Bernie. "I have a connection at the VA. I don't want them to know that I am doing this. I get embarrassed when they send me letters of appreciation, and honor me at public functions, and all that junk. They won't know you, so go ahead and bid."

Roy bought a thousand imported left shoes for a hundred dollars, no one else bidding on the lot at all. He and Bernie had a good time in New Orleans, visiting the shops on Bourbon Street, listening to jazz in Preservation Hall, and drinking sazeracs in the Court of the Two Sisters.

It was about a month later that Bernie asked Roy if he'd like to go to Savannah. In fact, he pretty much insisted that he needed Roy to help him. Savannah sounded tame after New Orleans, but Roy was game, and went.

To his surprise, after they had visited the ante-bellum mansions that had been restored, and seen the lovely squares at every cross-street, and eaten in the famous De Soto Hotel, Bernie suggested that they attend an auction. Again, the auction was on behalf of the customs authorities, and again there was one lot of unclaimed imported shoes being auctioned.

They had been addressed to a person and street at Isle of Hope that didn't exist. And to Roy's amazement, these were all shoes for the right foot.

Bernie explained that so many veterans had bought the shoes for the left foot, and that since there was now a set for right feet, he would like to help them, too. Again he had Roy do the bidding.

"Would you believe that I was so stupid that I didn't put two and two—or, right and left, I guess—together? I even admired him for his concern for veterans. I kept admiring him until the sales records came together somewhere—perhaps in Washington—and someone realized that I had imported a thousand pair of shoes, paying two hundred dollars customs, instead of the ten thousand dollars that was due.

"The shoes had been sold to a number of shoe stores, and were irretrievable, but my name was on the customs records. Uncle Bernie disappeared again, and I got three years. It wasn't too bad—I worked in the toy shop—but with a prison record, it's hard to get a job. Can you use me?"

I hired Roy at once, of course, and put him in charge of our import department.

When computers became cheap enough for individuals to buy them, I decided to add that to our line, and we opened a computer section, handling both hardware and software. I was fascinated by computers, and had one on my desk in the office, and one at home.

One day, while still discovering what computers could do, I saw an ad concerning an electronic bulletin board, and I subscribed. Among other things, the bulletin board distributed a kind of newsletter called Pat's Patter. It contained recipes, personal advice, singles ads, and amusing feature stories.

On a dull Saturday morning I called up Pat's Patter on the monitor, more to kill time than anything else. In the gossip-cum-joke column something caught my eye. It was just a sentence: "The cognoscenti are talking about something good and big happening at U-Do stores—remember, Pat told you first."

This really had me puzzled. We were in an in-between season; no big promotions were in the pipeline; and if there were, how would this mysterious Pat know about it? During the next week I got some clues. U-Do stock, which was traded over the counter, began to rise. Having started at twenty dollars a share, which was its nominal value, it went up to twenty-two, twenty-eight, thirty-five, and almost to forty. I had my stockbroker make some inquiries, and he reported that the stock was being sold in small lots, and that there seemed to be great demand for what little there was for sale.

The phenomenon meant nothing to me personally, since I was neither buying nor selling, but such a surge of activity in U-Do stock was unusual. A few days later my stockbroker called to tell me that the bottom had fallen out of U-Do stock; a big block had been sold at the top price, and the value was falling rapidly. When the stock reached the position of sellers only, with no buyers, I began to have my suspicions.

After that I read Pat's Patter assiduously, and about once every two months or so there would be a reference to some business or some product that would, in effect, change the world. I found that these references were always for companies that were financed by shares traded on the Exchange, and the value always went up after the mention by Pat.

Oddly, Pat never mentioned a stock that would go down, nor was the subsequent fall in value of each of the stocks mentioned ever referred to. Ordinarily, I would think this was none of my business, but since U-Do stock seems to have been the first one mentioned, I decided I would look into the matter.

I found that Pat operated out of Ty Ty, Georgia, of all unlikely places, which is an indication of how electronic media have erased geographical importance. I decided to go to Ty Ty, which wasn't too far away, but the Feds got there before me.

Pat, who turned out to be a nice-looking middle-aged woman, protested that she hadn't made any money out of these stock market tips—she just passed along what her advisor told her. Unfortunately, she couldn't produce her advisor, who had disappeared. From her description, I had no doubt as to who he was. Again, the jury might have believed her if the prosecution hadn't turned up a twenty-thousand dollar savings account that she claimed she knew nothing about. The money had been deposited almost simultaneously with her arrest, and the jury evidently thought that she was trying to hide her proceeds in that way. She got three years imprisonment and ten years probation, with the money confiscated.

When Pat got out of prison, Robert, Morris, Roy and I went to see her, and we all compared notes. We agreed that we would have to take care of Bernie, but the first job was to find him. It took us eight months of following false clues, and three private detective agencies, but we finally located him in Memphis.

Bernie was living with a widow who owned a chain of paint stores. Morris' eyes glazed over when he heard there was one main store and several branches, and he wondered out loud what kind of car Bernie had bought the pickup man. We puzzled for awhile as to how we could use the paint stores to fix him.

"Paint is pretty," said Pat.

"Paint is movable," said Morris.

I remembered working in the toy shop, and the precautions they had taken about paint. I saw Morris looking at me, and I looked at Roy, and I realized we were all thinking the same thing.

"Paint is highly flammable," said Morris and I together.

We made our plans. Morris called three insurance companies, and—as Uncle Bernie—arranged for large policies on one of the small paint stores. We sent the premiums in cash, by messenger. The next day Pat called Bernie, cried about how much she missed him, swore she forgave him, and asked for at least one more night together. She also mentioned that she had found some old stock certificates that had been in the family papers for many years with no one paying any attention to them.

They seemed valuable, but she needed Bernie's advice. They made a date for Saturday night.

On Friday morning Roy, without his habitual glasses, wearing a wig, with a false wart on one cheek and walking with a limp, bought a can of paint, paying cash. On Saturday morning he took it back, said his wife didn't like the color, and got his money back. He carefully put the can back on the shelf from whence he had taken it. He didn't see Uncle Bernie on either occasion.

Uncle Bernie came to Pat's motel room, as arranged, on Saturday night at eight. When he saw Pat he turned on his old charm, but when Robert, Morris, Roy and I came out of the next room his face dropped and he turned toward the door. Morris got between him and the door, and I said, "Not to worry, Uncle Bernie. We have a very promising proposition in mind, and we need someone with your experience to help us pull it off. We all have jail records, and we need someone clean, who is not too scrupulous. None of us like you very much, it is true, but this is a very, very profitable scheme and it can't work without someone like you to front it."

Uncle Bernie looked from one of us to the other, his suspicions not allayed. Pat said, gently, "Bernie, you're not afraid of us, are you?"

That got to him. He had bested us before and he was sure he could do it again. And the idea of a swindle, and himself as the only one who could front it, tantalized him. Morris took some diagrams out and spread them over the table, and Pat brought coffee and cake from the kitchen. We all huddled over the table like old friends, and Roy spun a long cock-and-bull story about an illegal gambling operation which, if swindled, would not even be able to go to the police. The story was very long, and very detailed, and full of holes. When he finished, Uncle Bernie began pointing out the fallacies, and we argued about each of them.

We had, in the meantime, stopped twice for refreshments, and with each of us going to the bathroom in turn, and with some time out for long fictitious phone calls, it was almost midnight when Uncle Bernie turned to us, and with his usual understated charm and good humor, said, "You are a bunch of hopeless amateurs. I'd be crazy to get drawn into something like this. Frankly, I think you're trying to con me. Don't you know you can't con a con man?"

We all tried to look contrite, like children caught with their hands in the cookie jar, and he laughed out loud. As Uncle Bernie buoyantly left, he said, "See you in jail."

Not one of us cracked a smile.

The paint store had started burning at about nine o'clock, and burned for several hours. The police picked Uncle Bernie up in the morning on the complaint of the three insurance companies we had used, and one from whom Uncle Bernie had—unknown to us—also purchased a large policy. Uncle Bernie protested that he didn't even know that there had been a fire, since he hadn't been home all evening.

Pat, Robert, Roy, Morris and I waited in Memphis until the police finished interrogating us about Uncle Bernie's alibi that he had been with us from eight to midnight. We each explained that the five of us had been playing penny ante in Pat's room and that we had neither seen anyone else nor talked to anyone else all evening.

As they took him away, Uncle Bernie looked at us and said, sadly, "Arson? That was the best you could do? Arson? You people have no class."

It would be a nice touch to be able to report that during Uncle Bernie's twenty-year term he worked in the toy shop, but he didn't. With his usual charm he got to work in the library. He died in prison, after a stroke.

I wasn't quite sure how to break this to Aunt Sophie, who was now quite old and frail, but still in good health. At last, I held her and said, "Aunt Sophie, I don't know how you feel now about Uncle Bernie, but I must tell you that he passed away."

She unconsciously played with the diamond ring on her finger. "That charming rogue," she sighed. "He could talk the rattles off a snake. Well, we had good years while they lasted and I'm grateful to him. By the way,

I've been meaning to tell you this for a long time—you really shouldn't call him Uncle Bernie. To tell you the truth, I could never get him to marry me. But never mind—if you want to continue calling him Uncle Bernie out of respect, I'll understand."

What can I tell you?

Uncle Eddie

◆

UNCLE EDDIE

When my Uncle Eddie divorced his wife of twenty-five years and married a girl twenty years younger than himself, all the women in the family put their heads together and went, "Tsk, tsk." When it turned out that his new wife was not only young, but pretty and rich, all the men in the family went, "Boy, oh boy," (but only to themselves). And when they learned that she was a mud-wrestler, nobody knew what to say.

Eddie had always been active. As a child, he never went out a door if a window was handy. He never walked—he ran. He just liked being on the go; he had no *sitzfleish*. Eddie's hyperactivity helped him in athletics, though. He was on the track team, played basketball (baseball seemed to entail too much waiting around) and tried to introduce soccer into his high school. Consequently, when he grew up everyone thought that Eddie would marry someone like himself, and when the family matchmakers suggested a girl to him, it was always a sporty type, an athlete, a go-go girl, in a way. But somehow it never seemed to "take." It wasn't until he took a job in a summer camp that he fell in love with Sylvia, who was the exact opposite of all the girls thrown at him.

He had come from Atlanta to the camp in Wisconsin a day early to check the sports equipment and to begin to get things ready, since he had been hired as the sports instructor. The rest of the staff was due the next day to begin a three-day staff orientation period. The director asked Eddie if he would hang around the office building to receive the staff, show them their quarters, help with their luggage, etc.

While waiting, Eddie began mowing the high grass that had grown up over the winter around the office. One by one the staff showed up, some knowledgeable from previous years, some quite new, and Eddie did the necessary. By the beginning of evening, all of the staff except the dietician had shown up. Actually, "dietician" was a misnomer. She not only planned the meals, she was in charge of the kitchen, including the cook and his helpers; and the dining room.

Eddie waited impatiently on the porch, since it was already too dark to continue cutting weeds, and at last a taxi from Webster showed up. Eddie moved to open the back door for the passenger, and a very self-possessed young lady opened the door for herself and got out. Eddie said, "You must be the dietician."

She looked him up and down, grass-stained overalls and no shirt, bandanna around his neck, baseball cap worn backwards, mirrored sunglasses, a wild rose he had found stuck over his ear, and sandals, and said, "And what might you be?"

Eddie was delighted with the "what" instead of a "who" and certainly instead of "whom" so he grinned, took off his hat, and gave a cavalier's flourish. "Your obedient servant, m'am," he said, knuckling his forehead.

She watched him as he moved to the trunk of the cab and said, "Let me get your bags out."

She gave him a suspicious look and said, "No, thank you. I can manage."

With some difficulty she lifted out two obviously heavy suitcases, a pocketbook, a light coat, a thick novel, and an umbrella.

This nonplussed him a bit, but he recovered and said, "Let me carry some of that."

She tightened her grip. "No, thank you. I can manage."

Now he began to get stubborn. "Let me show you to your room."

She looked at the map of the camp prominently displayed on the porch under the light, saw the spot marked, "You are here," and said, "No, thank you. I can manage."

This began to nettle him. He took a ring of keys out of his pocket and shook them. "Do you want me to come open the door for you, or do you want to manage entering through the locked window?"

She thought about this for a moment and said, "You can come and open the door—but don't you try to come in!"

Now he was furious. He stalked down the path not waiting for the dietician, who was almost staggering under the weight of her luggage. He threw open the door, leaving the key in place, and bowed deeply. He said, "Please do not thank me. I can manage," and ostentatiously retreated several feet from the door.

Back in his bunk, which he shared with Pete, the colored waterfront director (as Blacks were then called), he said, "Wow, the most peculiar creature has just been dumped on us. Be careful of what you eat," and he repeated what had just happened.

"Man, this I want to eyeball myself," said Pete, and was out the door before finishing the sentence.

He was back in record time. "That must be the snottiest, snootiest, most stuck-up, high-falutin' kitchen help that ever scrambled an egg. Looks like we're going to be up to our eyebrows in caviar and eggs Benedict. What say we lay in a supply of soul food, or at least some hawg jowls and black-eyed peas?"

Eddie added, "And maybe some chitlin's and collard greens, just to be sure?"

They both howled.

During the orientation period Eddie deliberately dressed as sloppily as he could, to maintain his image before Sylvia. He found that she was not as prim as she looked, for when she realized that he was putting on an act for her, she made some suggestions that would have made his costume even more outlandish, like a cummerbund over his overalls and an ascot tie worn without a shirt. However, he found that she was—in contrast to him—rather placid. She said little, and accepted what was said by others without comment. She began to get the kitchen help in order without much fuss, and when crises occurred she was almost unflappable. In fact, he began to think of her as almost bovine in her lack of excitability. He found he liked it.

On the last night before the campers were to arrive, the staff decided to celebrate the end of their comparative freedom with a costume party. The theme, related to the beginning of camp the next day, was, "In the beginning." Eddie didn't know what to portray, but finding himself walking alongside Sylvia impulsively said, "Let's go as Adam and Eve."

Sylvia lowered her eyes in mock modesty and said, "But I don't have any fig leaves."

"That's just the point. We'll be Adam and Eve before she ate the apple—we don't have to wear anything. Are you game?"

"Are you willing to walk into that party stark naked?"

"Sure. Are you?"

"Okay. I will if you will. Come by my bunk and escort me in. Nine-fifteen, okay?"

Eddie was staggered. He never thought she would agree. Then he was delighted—to see Sylvia nude! Then he thought about all the other males in camp seeing Sylvia nude. That bothered him. His next thought was about himself. Seeing Sylvia nude would certainly give him an erection. In fact, just thinking about seeing Sylvia nude had already given him an erection. He tried to picture himself walking into the group, many of whom he still knew only slightly, stark naked, preceded by his outstretched penis. He knew he couldn't do it.

At nine-fifteen Eddie appeared at Sylvia's door wearing the same crazy outfit he had worn the first time he saw her. She was wearing her dietician's white uniform with a gold halo stuck in her hair. She didn't seem surprised. "I'm going as an angel. I take it you are going as the caretaker of the Garden of Eden. Not bad."

"You knew I wouldn't go as Adam?"

"I didn't think you had the balls for it. Or, if you did, that you would let everyone see them. Let's go."

Eddie began to look at Sylvia in a new light.

At the end of the party several couples that had already been formed decided to go into Webster to look for a bar with a dance floor. The camp director had no objection, but insisted that everyone be back in camp by one in the morning, in order to be in reasonable shape to receive the campers the next day.

In the bar, Eddie had trouble dancing with Sylvia—or, to be more precise, Sylvia had trouble dancing with Eddie. As was his nature, he didn't glide, he jumped; he didn't turn, he pivoted; he didn't swing her out, he twirled her around. After a bit of this, Sylvia suggested that they go for a walk.

"Oh, boy! I know what leaving a dance for a walk means in my Southern culture. Does this also have a different meaning in the North?"

"Yeah. It means going for a walk. Are you on?"

He had a hard time slowing down to her pace; she had a hard time keeping up with his pace. "You know," she said, "I think we are basically incompatible. You are fast, and I am slow. You are active, and I am passive. You are a sportsman, and I am not even a willing spectator. So why do I like being with you?"

His heart jumped. "Because opposites attract. Because we complement each other. Because I like being with you."

She sighed. "This is going to be a very difficult summer. But don't worry—I can manage."

"Let's make a pact. You will never, ever, say 'I can manage,' again."

"And what will you do?"

"I will never, ever, go to a costume party naked."

"That's as one-sided a pact as I have ever heard. Kiss me to seal the deal."

Would surprises never stop? He kissed her with passion, and was rewarded with a chaste peck. He looked forward to an interesting camp season.

Eddie was using the bathroom in Sylvia's hut one day when a teenage girl camper who was to help in the kitchen came in and apologized to Sylvia for being late.

"I fell off the roof," she said.

Eddie was first incredulous, and then furious. What was a camper doing on a roof? Was it a prank? Was she a peeping Tom? In any case, the danger of climbing onto a roof was obvious to him, so he came charging out of the bathroom. "What were you doing on a roof?"

The camper took one look at him, turned red, swallowed hard, looked to Sylvia for support, and bolted out of the hut. Sylvia, for her part, was sitting on the edge of her bed rocking back and forth with laughter. She was holding her stomach to keep from exploding.

Eddie was bewildered, and when Sylvia stopped laughing she said, "Men are so stupid. And Southerners are the stupidest of all."

Eddie didn't get it.

Sylvia continued to laugh as she explained.

"'Falling off the roof' is a euphemism for the beginning of a menstrual period. How you embarrassed that poor girl!" And she was off in gales of laughter again. It was the most emotion Eddie had ever seen her display. He decided he wanted to marry her.

When the camp season ended Eddie accompanied Sylvia to Milwaukee and there met her mother. As Sylvia introduced them she said, "Ma, I think he wants to marry me and take me to live in Atlanta."

Eddie was staggered by the assumption, and fearful of the reaction. He expected her mother to say, "Who is he?," or "Why Atlanta?," or even "Why so far away?"

Instead of which, Sylvia's mother smiled sweetly and said, "My dear, a wife goes wherever her husband goes."

"Then I guess that's settled," said Sylvia to her mother. "Do you have any preference as to a wedding date?"

And they began to discuss the details of the wedding while Eddie stood by in shock.

Eddie wanted their arrival at the church to be on horseback, and Sylvia wanted to come in a comfortable limousine, so they compromised on a beautiful horse-drawn buggy. For their honeymoon, Eddie wanted to go to Pamplona to run with the bulls, and Sylvia wanted to take a tour of the stately homes of England, so again they compromised and went to Club Med, where Eddie participated in all the sports and programs, and Sylvia sat in a deck chair and read.

Once back in Atlanta, Eddie was sports instructor at a high school and refereed professional basketball games for extra income. Sylvia was the dietician in a local hospital until their first child, Donny, was born. They didn't get rich, but they weren't poor. They met the mortgage payments on their house, had a new car and an old car, and had a daughter three years later.

Eddie not only kept up his sports activities—tennis, squash, and bowling—but jogged in the mornings. He worked out at the high school gym whenever he could, and swam throughout the winter in an indoor pool.

The term "couch potato" hadn't been invented then, but it could have been devised to fit Sylvia. She indulged Eddie's restlessness, encouraged him to participate in all the sports that interested him, but didn't join him. When he was in competition, she came to cheer him on, but she preferred reading, watching TV and knitting, or working on the New York Times crossword and double crostic puzzles.

One summer evening, when their son was six years old, they were preparing to attend a performance at his school. Eddie was ready early, but Sylvia was still putting on finishing touches, and their son, who was eager to get to school and take his part in the play, said he'd wait for them downstairs. As usual, Sylvia said, "Be careful," and Eddie said, "Don't go out into the street."

But the ball that he was bouncing against the house eluded him and went into the street; he followed it; and a car that was not speeding, but also not crawling, hit him as he darted out. He was knocked against a parked car. The driver slowed down after he heard the crunch, looked around and saw no observers, and picked up speed as he left the neighborhood.

Donny was in critical condition. The chief doctor, an older, usually comforting person, always looked somber as he reported on the latest developments. He was factual. He offered no encouragement, but he didn't seem to be preparing them for the worst. Donny's case was touch and go for five days, but then it seemed clear that his life would be saved. After another two weeks it was clear that he might walk with a limp, and have to be extra careful of his back, but eventually, he would be okay.

The convalescence was hard for everyone in the family, but the day came when Donny went off to school, although he had to drop back a class for missing so much. The next day, when Eddie started to go jogging, Sylvia said, "Wait for me. I'm coming with."

Eddie saw with amazement that she was outfitted in a classy blue gym suit, and was wearing new white sneakers. "What the hell…?" he asked.

"I'll tell you while we're jogging."

"Talking while jogging is not easy, nor is it recommended. Tell me now."

"When Donny was hit…" She started over. "While he was in the hospital…".

Eddie made her sit down and talk. "I made a deal with God. I said that if You let him live, I'll do the thing I most hate in the world as repayment. And that, my dear sportsman, is to exercise. So I am going to jog with you every morning."

Eddie was very touched, but he became every bit the professional coach. "Jogging is not as simple as it seems…," and he was off on a complete run-down concerning jogging. He suggested shorts and T-shirt instead of a gym suit, and shoes made especially for joggers, rather than the simple sneakers she was wearing.

Sylvia came back from the first morning, flung off her clothes and headed for the shower. "I really hated that," she said as she came out, toweling her hair.

"You know, you really don't have to do it."

"Yes, I do."

"For how long?"

"Forever."

"That's a long time."

"I hope Donny will live a long time."

He had no answer to this. He wanted to say something about superstition taking the place of religion, but since he was far from religious, restrained himself.

Sylvia jogged with Eddie every morning. At first he deliberately cut his distance down, but after a while he didn't have to. When she sometimes pulled ahead, he reminded her that jogging wasn't a competition, and that jogging wasn't running. Maintaining the proper pace was important.

One morning a couple of years later Eddie had a suddenly upset stomach and decided not to jog that day. Sylvia said she'd go alone. She was gone much longer than their usual time, and he was beginning to worry when she came in. She explained that she had been thinking about something, and hadn't realized how far she had gone. She had almost doubled their usual route. The return trip made it even longer—it was much further than they ordinarily went. "But I'm not tired," she said.

Again Eddie explained to her that jogging was in order to keep fit, and that too much could be worse than too little. Without thinking, he asked, "Do you still hate it so much?"

Sylvia looked surprised. "I don't hate it at all. In fact, I enjoy it. I'd miss it if I didn't do it."

"Thank God, or whoever is in His place, for that. Jogging for punishment is one thing, but jogging for pleasure is another."

"But there is a problem."

"That it is no longer punishment?"

"No. It isn't enough for me. I think I need to run as well as jog. I feel the need for more exercise. You know what—I'd like to run in a marathon."

The coach came to the fore again. "Hey, wait a minute. Even if you decide to run instead of jog, a marathon is an endurance contest, not a race. You'd have to change your style, train for months, and accept the fact that you won't be near the winners."

"Okay, coach. Prepare me for a marathon."

Sylvia did, indeed, become a marathon runner. She never won. She didn't always finish. But she got better and better. She began to chase marathons whenever they were within reasonable distance, and even subscribed to a marathon runners' paper.

Little by little, Sylvia's interest in sports grew and widened. Part of it was to defeat the middle-age spread that was beginning to show, and part was to be with Eddie, but part—a big part—was that she enjoyed sports, win, lose, or draw. So she went bowling, and began playing tennis, and discovered squash at Eddie's high school.

And then an unfortunate thing happened. She began to outstrip Eddie. The first few times she beat him at bowling they both acknowledged that there was a lot of luck in the game, but when it became almost habitual, that excuse didn't hold. She ran faster than he did for short distances, and finished ahead of him in most marathons. He kidded her that she was two years younger than he was, but they both knew two years wouldn't make much difference. They played tennis, squash, ping-pong and touch football. When he offered her advice, or even supported her, her habitual response was, "I can manage." The first few times they laughed at it. Then they discussed it. In the end, Eddie was forced to realize that this was a response dating back to childhood, and Sylvia could repress it only with deliberate conscious effort. In the heat of a game, it came out unconsciously, and if she concentrated on with-holding it, her competitive effort was harmed. Eddie stopped complaining about it, because it had become a source of contention, but to him it was like chalk screeching on a blackboard.

Sylvia slowly began to beat Eddie consistently at most sports. Eddie was able to defeat her handily only in squash, and that gradually became the only game in which they competed with one another. Eddie stopped entering marathons for which Sylvia had signed up, he went bowling with other fellows, and he found a quasi-permanent tennis partner.

This situation was not uncomfortable, and time passed quickly. Over the next ten years Eddie was hired as a coach by a professional basketball team which, fortunately for him, won a lot. Although the job paid much more than the high school job, he continued refereeing. Sylvia got tired of dietetics, and took a couple of short courses and became a practical nurse. She worked only private duty, which not only paid well, but allowed her to take off any time she wanted to for participation in sports events.

Over time, of course, they both changed somewhat. Sylvia became concerned that her diet keep her fit, and gradually became, not a vegetarian, but a naturist. She bought food only in health food stores, and was a semi-expert on the use of sprays, fertilizers, and insecticides. Her training as a dietician gave her a good background for this. Eddie maintained his usual diet, but—as many new converts do—Sylvia kept trying to convince Eddie, covertly and overtly, to change, while he resisted. Some friction developed around this, particularly when Eddie wanted to go out for a fancy meal, and Sylvia didn't want to eat what would be served.

Eddie realized that Sylvia didn't do things half-way when they ended up with three goats, several chickens, some fruit trees, some nut trees, and a herb garden in what had been their backyard, in order to safeguard Sylvia's diet. He found the noise of the goats and chickens offensive—not to mention the smell. They bickered about it.

Sylvia also developed some habits that bothered him. Any time she didn't understand something, in the newspaper, in a book, in the course of daily activities, she would invariably precede her comment with, "This is the funniest thing...," and then outline the situation. The phrase bothered Eddie out of all proportion, and he mentioned it to her several times, but she was unconscious of using it, and it continued to slip out even when she tried to control it. It actually reached the point that Eddie found himself stiffening and already angry when he heard, "This is the funniest thing..."

Other things began to annoy him. Sylvia developed the habit of twirling her hair with her fingers when she was deeply engrossed in something, whether it was a conversation, a book, a telephone call, or many other things. She also made notes to herself of things she wanted to remember, but she made the notes on whatever paper was handy where she happened to be, using a different pencil each time, so Eddie would sometimes wander around the house picking up pencils from bedside tables, coffee tables, shelves, kitchen cabinets, and other places, including the top of the toilet. He occasionally found that a note was on the back of some paper that he considered important.

They began to bicker more and more. For example, one of them would suggest going to see one of the children, and the other would say they had just been there last week.

"Once a week isn't a lot."

"We don't want them to think we are crowding their lives."

"Once a week isn't crowding."

"Some people might think so."

"You might think so, but I don't."

And so it would go, more and more often.

One day Eddie was lying in bed, watching Sylvia dress for a tennis match, when he suddenly realized that she had become very muscular. Her forearms, her upper arms, her legs, all seemed to be expanding her skin. He had a sudden thought.

"Are you using steroids?"

"Only before matches. Why?"

"Why? First place, it's illegal. Second place, it's dangerous. Third place, it's ugly."

"Oh, everybody does it. You wouldn't have a chance to win today if you didn't use steroids."

"Is winning so important?"

"As the baseball coach said, 'Winning isn't the important thing; it's the only thing'. And I win more often than I lose."

Eddie lay back on the bed and reflected. He felt that somehow an era in his life had just ended. Placid, bovine Sylvia was now the ambitious competitor and overactive sportsman Eddie was the weekend athlete.

Ordinarily Eddie, as a referee, did not go into locker rooms after ball games—there was too much chance of recriminations and even violence. One evening, however, he wanted to visit an injured player who had not returned to the court, and when he came out, he found a young lady waiting outside the door. The gym was not in the most savory part of town, so, ever the gentleman, he asked if he could help her. It seems she was waiting for the injured player. Eddie gave her an update on his condition, and started away, when she said, "Look, I know this is an imposition, but I'm not allowed in there. Would you take him a message for me? I'd really appreciate it."

For the first time Eddie really looked at her. She was young, and truly beautiful. Not beautiful just because she was young, but with an open, innocent, choir-boy look that he found, well, interesting. He took her message to the injured player, which was that she couldn't wait any longer, and when he came out again she was a block away, walking rather fast.

He ran to catch up with her. "Don't you want to know his answer?"

"He sent an answer?"

"Yeah. He said you should go on—and that I should accompany you."

"He never did."

"Sure he did."

"I know better. He would never think of me or my safety. He is one of the most self-centered persons I ever met."

"Then why do you go with him?"

"I'm a sports fan. I admire him on the court. I can't really say I like him much off the court."

By this time they both realized that he was accompanying her. "You're the referee, aren't you?"

"The same."

"You run as much as the players do."

"Slightly more."

"Can I ask you a personal question?"

"You can ask. I may not answer. The question?"

"Don't answer if you don't want to. How old are you?"

"Why?"

"Why do you answer a question with a question?"

"Why not?" They both laughed.

"I'm ancient. Forty-four pushing forty-five. Why did you want to know?"

"I just didn't know at what age a man can no longer run like that. I guess forty-four pushing forty-five isn't the answer."

"Fair's fair. How old are you?"

"Twenty-four pushing twenty-five. Why did you want to know?"

"I just didn't know at what age a girl stops hanging around a basketball court." He was instantly contrite. "I didn't mean that. I was just trying to parallel your reasoning. It didn't come out as funny as it should have."

"It isn't funny. I am too old to be running after basketball players. But I'm twenty-four pushing twenty-five, unmarried, not engaged, I don't even have a steady boy friend. So what's wrong with me?"

"Oh, c'mon. With your looks you certainly can't lack for boy friends."

She stopped and turned on him. "It's always looks, isn't it? What's inside never seems to matter. Suppose I was ugly—would you have paid any attention to me? Jesus, looks are an accident but thoughts, ideas, character—they don't just happen, you know."

"Hey, wait," Eddie expostulated. "I didn't mean to insult you by calling you pretty. Can we have a cup of coffee while you tell me about your thoughts, ideas and character?"

"Okay, so now you're making fun of me. Why don't you just go your way and I'll go mine."

He was practically running after her now. He caught up, put his hands gently on her shoulders and looked her straight in the face. "I really do want to get to know you. Don't make it so hard."

Eddie realized that she was on the point of tears. "Let's have some coffee," he said, steering her in the direction of an outdoor cafe. Once there she began with apologies, and then tried to laugh it off, and finally said, "Oh, hell, I had to talk to someone. I'm sorry I picked on you."

"I'm not. I'm honored."

He wanted to stay in her company to continue looking at her, so he said, "What do you do when you are not watching ballgames?"

She bit her lower lip.

He thought it fascinating.

Then she took a deep breath, expelled it, and said, "Please stand up."

"Stand up?"

"Yes. Stand up."

"Why?"

"Because when I tell you what I do, you'll want to run, and I wouldn't want to see you tangled up in a chair."

"What in the world are you talking about? I just asked you what you do."

"I'll tell you one thing about myself, and then watch you take off. Ready? I am a female mud-wrestler in the Lakewood Luna Park. Barbara the Beast. I wrestle Betty the Beauty twice a week. You've probably heard of me. So don't bother with excuses—you can just go."

Eddie realized that she was on the point of tears again. "More coffee," he said gently, pouring her some.

"That must be a hard way to make a living," he said thoughtfully. "There must be lots of other things that you can do—and (hastily) I don't mean just because you are pretty."

"Pretty! Pretty! Pretty! Listen, all my life I've been told that I am pretty—'a pretty girl like you should do this,' or 'a pretty girl like you shouldn't do that.' I'm sick of being judged by my skin and my figure." Then, forcefully, "I will not, will not, will not make my way in life on my looks."

"Is that why you mud-wrestle?"

"It's the fartherest I can get from being judged by my looks."

Eddie was not a profound thinker, but he began to understand. "You mean you wrestle in the mud so you won't look pretty? So people will have to look under both the mud and the prettiness to see what's really there?"

"I do believe you are beginning to get it."

"And the basketball player? He sees what's under the mud?

"No. He likes to be seen with characters. He'd go with a fire-eater, or a well-known murderess or a movie star, as long as she was seen as different."

She didn't invite him in when they reached her house, nor did he expect her to. But at the next game his eyes searched the stands until he found her, and she saw him doing it. Over coffee after the game he asked her if she would like to bowl, or play tennis.

"I'm strictly a spectator," she said. "When I feel the need for exercise, I sit down until it goes away. I've been going to sporting events because that's where the men are—lot of good it's done me. I'm a clinical psychologist. There is no end of professional literature to be read—literally, no end. And I enjoy it. But I do like to watch a rousing match. I really do empathize."

"Would you like to watch the semi-finals of the men's bowling tournament? That's Friday night."

"Are you a semi-finalist?"

"I have that dubious honor."

"Then I'll come—but only if you'll come to see me mud-wrestle."

And that's the way it started. Eddie started going to mud-wrestling shows. And that's what they were—shows. They weren't contests, and everybody but the most innocent spectator knew that. Barbara was billed as the Beast because she was pretty, and the other wrestler made herself up as ugly as she could, and was therefore called the Beauty. This was part of the show atmosphere. Barbara was a good actress and had the crowd shouting, stamping and clapping. Eddie was a bit embarrassed to be in the group, and more than a little sorry that Barbara felt the need to grapple and grope in the mud because of her hang-up about being pretty.

When she came to basketball games to watch him referee, it took Eddie back to the early days of his marriage, when his wife either stayed home, or came to cheer him, but wouldn't touch physical exercise with the proverbial ten foot (vaulting) pole. Now she was not only better than him, but away from home for long periods as she chased marathons around the world. Lately she had become interested in tricathalons, which added to her absences.

Eddie was flattered to be found interesting by a beautiful twenty-four year old. He was proud when they went to a cafe or restaurant and heads swiveled. He began to look forward to their after-game meetings. He tried mentioning to Sylvia that he was the only referee he knew who had a fan, and a female fan, at that. She replied, "That's nice for you. I do wish you wouldn't put your sweat socks in the washing machine after a game. They smell up the whole bathroom."

"I have to put them somewhere. I thought the washing machine was for things that need washing."

"Why can't you hang them outside first? Then put them in the next day."

"I need a routine to get socks washed?"

And they were off again.

Eddie began to realize that he was always tense when Sylvia was in the house; relaxed when she was away; and happy when he was with Barbara. He wondered whether this was what was meant by the phrase mid-life crisis, and he even tried to read the book, *Life Begins at Forty*, but it didn't seem to apply to him.

This situation continued for several months. He saw Barbara regularly, didn't try to keep it a secret, and found he didn't feel guilty.

Barbara raised the question first. "What's going to be with us?"

Eddie gave her an out. "Forty-five is pretty old, isn't it?"

She didn't parry. "Not for me."

"Are you serious?"

"You know I am."

"Barbara, you're twenty years younger than I am."

"I know it."

"When I'm sixty-five you'll be my age now."

"Sounds pretty good to me."

"When you're sixty-five, I'll be eighty-five."

"Stop stalling. Do you want to marry me or not?"

"I do. Oh, how I do."

"Then let's."

"Barbara, I think Sylvia will divorce me, or let me divorce her, but I may be wrong. It may be long and messy. In any case, she'll need all we have to get along financially. I won't fight her about that. I'll have nothing, and even my earning power is diminishing. Coaches, trainers, and sportsmen have a short half-life. I don't see how I can offer you that."

"If I thought you were marrying me for my money I'd stalk out. But I am more than fond of you; I think you feel the same way about me; and I want to marry you. May be I haven't mentioned it, but I'm wealthy. I'm not Croesus, but if you give your wife everything you have, we'll still be able to live well."

"I think we ought to make this formal. Barbara, will you marry me?"

"Idiot. I love you. When you are free I'll marry you. Now that we've settled that, could we go to bed?"

"Barbara, understand me. I have never been unfaithful to my wife. When you are my wife I will never be unfaithful to you. I don't want to bed you until I can do it legally and morally. Does that sound too Victorian to you?"

"The Victorians were a helluva lot more sexy than you think, but I kind of admire your misplaced morals. I will control my lust for you until it is legal lust."

Eddie didn't know when or how to broach the matter of a divorce to Sylvia, so he waited until an evening when they were both home. The basketball game he was to referee was called off due to an electrical failure in the neighborhood of the gym, and Sylvia was preparing her clothes to take off for Israel for the Tiberias marathon.

"Sylvia. I guess it is no secret to both of us that we haven't been getting along very well lately. We get in each other's hair. What would you think of a separation?"

She looked up from the suitcase. "Why not a divorce?"

With nothing to lose, he said, "Okay, a divorce."

She thought a moment. "You are right. This is no good. But I want the house, the good car, and alimony."

"You got it!" he said, almost too joyfully.

"What's the weather in Israel now, do you know?"

None of either family came to the courthouse for the wedding. Eddie invited them all, and they might have come, but no one was ready for the publicity that the manager of the Luna Park whipped up. The headlines made every member of both families cringe. The worst headline was in a tabloid, and read, "Eddie the Coach to Barbara the Beast: Here's mud in your…eye?"

Barbara's parents weren't too pleased with their new son-in-law—a rundown sportsman, a divorced man, and so much older! He was, in fact, only five years younger than her father, and although her mother didn't want to admit it, as old as she was. Barbara said that not only was it her life, she also had no intention of becoming an old maid, and besides, Eddie was not too old to give them grandchildren. Her mother looked doubtful, but her father said, "Of course not!" Her mother shot a look at him and he wiped the grin off his face.

When they were married they honeymooned in the Rainmaker Hotel in Pago-Pago, Samoa. Barbara had been curious when Eddie suggested it, and he explained that he had grown up poor, during the Depression. Nobody knew anybody who had been abroad. Rich people who did travel used ships, which were not only horribly expensive—they were, after all, floating hotels with more than hotel rates—but the trips took a long time. Consequently, he had always fantasized about being able to visit some of the places they talked about in school and at university, and about which he had read or heard. Far-off places, romantic places, famous places.

Barbara's money came from a trust fund left her by her grandfather—a sum she had hardly touched in twenty-five years—and the income was sufficient for a good life, including travelling. She found Samoa boring, but Eddie found it thrilling. They stayed in a thatched hut on the waterfront, which was part of the hotel, rented a car to drive the island's thirty-four miles of paved road, had youngsters climb tall coconut palms and teach them to eat the green coconuts, and tried to imagine where Sadie Thompson had lived.

They flew over to Western Samoa, and found the drive from the airport to Apia the most beautiful airport drive in the world, as noted in their travel books. It went through palm forests, next to villages where daily life was carried on in wall-less huts, and ended at the rustic but luxurious Tusitala Hotel—"The Storyteller"—named after Robert Louis Stevenson, who was buried in the hills above the hotel.

As newlyweds, they made love almost nightly in the places they visited. In fact, their only stipulation when registering at hotels was for a double bed. Barbara badly wanted a child, so they took no precautions in their lovemaking, but nothing happened. In fact, Barbara's desire to get pregnant made her tense during lovemaking, and it wasn't the complete pleasure that Eddie had anticipated.

During the next five years they traveled a lot. Eddie made a list of names that intrigued him, and they planned their trips to include as many as possible. Samarkand and Singapore; Papeete and Papua; Delhi and Delphi; they hardly touched base with San Diego. Barbara got caught up in the fever, and her interest was rivers and seas, so they sailed the Amazon and the Brahmaputra, the Congo and the Danube, and continued down the alphabet to the Yangtze. The also managed to get in the Sea of Marmara and the Sea of Galilee; the Red Sea, the Dead Sea, the Black Sea, and the Yellow Sea.

They were planning to start collecting mountains when Barbara found she was pregnant. She didn't think that thirty was dangerously old to start having children, but she took no chances. Traveling ended as though a book had closed.

Barbara became a homebody, and spent more and more time with her mother. After the baby was born—her parents' only grandchild—it seemed that her mother was hardly out of their house. She seemed to neither like nor dislike Eddie—she tolerated him. Barbara's father sincerely liked Eddie, but had to be careful not to show it too clearly when his wife was around. Barbara was very protective of the baby, hardly allowing even Eddie to pick it up. He wondered whether she thought he had forgotten how to handle a baby, but decided not to ask. He wasn't sure he wanted to hear the answer.

A next-door neighbor introduced Barbara to bridge, and she began to play regularly, but always at home. She would not leave the baby. Her mother played canasta and mah-jong, but Barbara stuck to bridge. Eddie tried his hand at bridge but it didn't entice him, and he began to feel like a fifth wheel around the house. He found that fifty was too old to start again as a referee, nor did he find any coaching jobs open.

However, his name was still known around town, so more to pass the time away than anything else, he began selling advertising items—engraved pencils, keycases, pocket diaries, desktop items —to be given out to customers by sports fans who owned businesses. He liked being back in touch with sports, and began to pal around with other fans like himself—old-timers who knew the names and records of long lists of players. He bought season tickets to the basketball, baseball and football games, and found he liked being a spectator. He even did some mild betting from time to time, and found that his background knowledge paid off.

Eddie's now-grown son and daughter thought it charming to have a half-brother who was an infant, and showered him with gifts. Sylvia sent Eddie a printed congratulations card from Tokyo, where she was participating in a tri-cathalon.

Eddie and Barbara tried to have more children—that is, they used no contraceptives. When after two years they hadn't succeeded, they went for fertility counseling. After the requisite tests, they were told they were both perfectly healthy and capable of having children, and to just relax and keep trying. But they had no more children.

When Eddie spoke to Barbara about sports, he found she had told him the exact truth. She had been interested in sports, but more interested in getting married. Now that she was married, and had a child, her interest in sports receded.

Eddie didn't mind that at all. He didn't want to begin to compete with his wife again, not even in discussing sporting events. As he became more and more secure in the knowledge that Barbara wasn't interested in sports, he became more active. He found that his bowling just needed some practice; he could play tennis well with people of about his own age, and sometimes with someone younger; but he didn't want to exert himself as much as squash required. Then Eddie discovered golf. How it had eluded him all these years he didn't know, but he realized he had found his metier.

Gradually, he became a sportsman again. He bowled some, he played some tennis, but mostly he golfed. Again, it was not just the skill and the score that interested him, it was the camaraderie that he had always associated with sports—the pre-game joshing, the locker room gossip, the drink after the game. He found that he was perfectly content. He again had a homebody wife who took care of the house and the child, and he had a pleasant, leisurely life-style among buddies.

Consequently, it was the men in the family who put their heads together and said, "Tsk, tsk;" and the women who said, "Ah, ha," when Barbara left him, taking the boy with her.

Her parents had moved back to Boston, which was her mother's original hometown, and Barbara and her son had gone with them. Eddie came back from the Rose Bowl game in Pasadena and found a note, with no explanation or excuse, saying that they had left and wouldn't be back.

He called, he wrote, he visited, he threatened, he pleaded. He simply didn't understand. At last Barbara's father took pity on him and told him that Barbara had always wanted to be a mother. She had been fixated on having a child, long before Eddie married her. She had even threatened to have a child out of wedlock if she couldn't find a man to marry her. Eddie had come along just as she was getting desperate. She probably did love him, but when the child was born, it was all transferred to the baby, and Eddie was just a hanger-on, in the way.

"I'm sorry," said the father. "I don't imagine you can understand this. I have a hard time understanding it, although I've lived with it for a long time. But that's the way it is—she just doesn't feel she needs you."

Barbara left Eddie the house and all the belongings, and a guaranteed income sufficient for a modest life. She never wanted to see him again. She wanted a divorce, and would give him generous visitation rights, but if he didn't grant the divorce, she would take all the belongings and the income, never let him see the child, and fight him tooth and nail. Eddie gave her a divorce, more for the visitation rights than anything else.

The empty house was lonely, and Eddie stayed away as much as he could. He began to let golf fill his life. He played mornings and afternoons, and sometimes drove golf balls under lights at night. He traveled to tournaments, some to watch and some for participation. His game began to improve. He became a middle-ranked golfer in the club that he joined. He had no particular playing group—he joined whoever invited him, or he filled in a threesome or a foursome.

About three years after Barbara left him, he was waiting to tee off in Lake Tahoe as part of a foursome, and watched the women's foursome ahead of them start their round. The third member of the group took her stance, took a couple of practice swings, and then hooked the ball badly into the trees. She looked at her partner and said, "This is the funniest thing. I did everything right and look what happened." Eddie didn't even have to walk around to see her face to know that it was Sylvia.

Sylvia spotted him just as he recognized her, and both foursomes had to wait until the greetings, and questions and answers, were over. At the nineteenth hole they both talked so fast that it was almost a comedy act. Sylvia had been expelled from the Olympic tryouts and put on indefinite probation when a urine test detected steroids. She had gone through a bad time, including a descent into alcoholism. She had joined AA, and not only sworn off liquor but off all sports, until she discovered golf. She was still a duffer, but improving.

Eddie recounted his past, and when he got to the part about Barbara walking out on him, she said, "Oh, Eddie, that's awful. Is there anything I can do?"

He was very touched by her evident concern, and without thinking said, "No, thank you. I can manage."

A slow grin came across her face, and when he saw it, he realized what he had said. They both burst out laughing.

When Eddie and Sylvia were remarried, all the women in the family put their heads together and said, "She's crazy."

All the men in the family looked at each other and said, "He's crazy."

Eddie and Sylvia said, "We know we're crazy, but what the hell? We can manage."

Uncle Willie

◆

UNCLE WILLIE

My Uncle Willie decided to become a sociologist while he was on the island of Tarawa. It wasn't that he was interested in the natives—there weren't that many on Tarawa. And it wasn't that he found the American Army a great sociological laboratory—for him it was normative (to use a sociologists' phrase). And it wasn't because he thought of himself as a scientist or a scholar. He was just bored.

Uncle Willie had landed on Tarawa after the fighting there was finished, and since he was in the quartermaster corps, he had little to do but make sure that not too much beer was stolen. So to pass the time away he started taking the correspondence courses that the army offered through the United States Armed Forces Institute.

The only introductory course that he had trouble with was math. The test, when he got it, proceeded from simple to more complex problems. It was sent to and administered, as were all the tests, by his commanding officer. When Willie was ready to take the test he sat in one corner of the office working on it, presumably being monitored by his commander, while normal army activity went on around him.

However, during a lull, the commanding officer picked up the last page of the test and looked at it. The final problem had to do with the height of a tree growing on a steep slope, as determined by the position of the sun, the distance from an observer, the angle of the slope and the length of the shadow of the tree. He seemed fascinated by the problem, and called his adjutant over. The two of them put their heads together, and after two more officers came into the office for various reasons, there were four heads bent over the problem, and four voices vociferously explaining why the other three were wrong. Willie had little trouble with most of the problems, some trouble with the later ones (he did some guessing), and he didn't attempt the last one—which he didn't even understand.

He sat listening to the argument when he finished writing his other answers, but even when three of the four agreed on the solution, with the fourth vigorously protesting that they were wrong, he hadn't the slightest idea how to approach the problem, but perversely, he went with the minority opinion. He not only got a 98 on the math test—the scorer returned his paper with the comment, "Excellent!" He never told his commanding officer that his solution had been wrong—Willie might not have known math, but he wasn't stupid.

For some reason, however, Willie liked the soft sciences, and particularly sociology. He thought of some of the groups he had seen at home—Blacks, Hispanics, Jews, Orientals; new immigrants and old Americans; poor people, newly rich people, and the rich from inherited wealth; and found that some of what he was reading made sense.

When Willie decided to go to college on the GI Bill, he decided to go to New York, where there were many universities, rather than to any university in Atlanta, or even in the south as a whole. He was somewhat bored with what he saw as placid, unexciting places. He found a one-room apartment in the Village with the bathroom down the hall and a hotplate for a stove, and enrolled in NYU, because it was easy walking distance.

Willie came to love New York. He often said that it was a great place to live, but he wouldn't want to visit there. He knew that visitors touched only the surface of the world's greatest city, but he explored local folklore, byways, history, rites, and locations until he felt that whenever he left New York, he got withdrawal symptoms.

Willie was particularly fascinated with Greenwich Village. He loved the ethnic trinket shops and the ethnic food stores. He discovered artists' bars and poets' cafes; gay bars and transvestite coffee shops; Italian bars, Irish bars, Puerto Rican bars—there was no end to the variety. He visited the various art galleries as they opened and closed, and watched the shills enticing the rubes into the Three-Card Monte games on the street corners, which closed in a rush when a blue uniform was spotted in the distance. He learned to avoid the dog poop on the streets—well, most of it. He went to classic movies and blue movies and ate food ranging from Albanian to Yemenite (he looked for but couldn't find a Zulu or a Zaire restaurant). He went with many girls and slept with a few. But he discovered that the thing he liked best in all the Village—and maybe in all the world—were the cheeseburgers at the Nedicks on his corner. He could never get enough of them. In between all this, he went to classes.

His class in Introduction to Zoology was hardly a class. It was held in an auditorium with four hundred and fifty freshmen in attendance, and was a straight lecture course. During the first session the professor announced that the grade would be based on a term paper. At the end of the semester Willie realized that he didn't even knew what a term paper was. There were no advisors or counselors in those days, and he felt stupid asking other students about something that seemed so obvious. So he went to the library and took out zoology books. Whatever he read, he realized the professor already knew, and possibly had written the book himself. He couldn't figure out anything to write that the professor wouldn't know, and didn't see any sense writing things that the professor did know. In fact, the only thing he retained from the whole semester was that the thyroid secretion is so powerful that it has an effect even if diluted to one part in a million parts of water (or was it ten million?). Even that he wasn't sure about. So in the end he never turned in a paper, and he got an incomplete in the course.

He did better in his other courses. He took a course in Freudian psychology, and liked it so much that he couldn't decide between sociology and psychology. When he learned that there were social psychologists, he decided that was what he wanted to become. Of course, it might be that he liked the psychology course so much because there was a blonde with the exotic name of Vasilly sitting next to him. The fact that she was both Southern and Jewish intrigued him, too. He had never known there were Jews in the South. Growing up in Utah, he had never met a Jewish girl—nor, for that matter, many people from the South.

One day she appeared in a long, old-fashioned skirt, with her hair in a bun, and he whispered to her, "Mother fixation."

She looked at him in surprise. One day she was dressed in pants and a man's shirt, and he whispered, "Penis envy."

She smiled. When she marked her place in a book with an unused bus transfer, he said, quietly, "Transference."

She tried not to giggle, and he said, "Repression."

She took the transfer out and gave it to him, saying, "Counter-transference."

"No, no," he wrote on it, 'counter-transference' is when you sell me your restaurant, lunch counter and all."

She waved that one away. The next day he handed her a small onion roll, wrapped in paper on which he had written "Dr. Freud" many times.

"The psychiatrist's role," he explained.

Soon they were leaving class and having their mid-morning snack together—always cheeseburgers for him. On a snowy winter day they headed for his favorite Nedicks. She skirted a snow-covered lawn while he cut across it through the snow. "Rigid," he said to her.

In reply, she lifted her foot and showed him that there was a hole in her shoe. "Reality therapy," she said.

On another occasion he walked her past two drugstores to a third in order to buy some aspirin. "Do you always buy here?" she asked.

"Always."

"Now that's really rigid. We passed two perfectly good drugstores."

He held up the Green Stamps he had just been handed, and said, "But they don't give Green Stamps. Situational differentiation."

He steered her toward his room.

"Hey, aren't we going back to classes?"

"No. Going back is regression. I'd like to make you half-way happy."

"What the hell does that mean?"

"Freud said that the way to happiness is to love and to work, didn't he? I don't want

to put you to work, so how about we make love?"

"Whoa, Buster." She stopped in her tracks. "You want to have fun together, I'm willing. But I'll tell you something even Freud didn't know. I'm saving my virginity for my husband. I don't usually talk like that, but I don't want there to be any misunderstanding."

"Is that a proposal?"

"No. And it isn't a challenge, either. I like being with you. I like your sense of humor, I find you interesting, and you are not bad-looking— maybe your eyes are a little too close together, but I'm willing to make allowances. If you ask me out, I'll go. But you will not, repeat not, get into my panties. Any questions?"

"Yeah. Wanna see a movie tonight?"

Despite what Vassily said, he found her a challenge. She was willing to neck, and responded to his kisses with passion. Under the proper circumstances, she would let his hand into her brassiere. Once in a while he was able to loosen her brassiere and fondle her bare breasts—but that was the end of the line.

All of this was within the context of doing many other things together. They studied together, and he often felt that she was smarter than he was. They went to movies, to cafes, to the Washington Square outdoor art exhibition, to block parties, to the beach, and—of course—to Nedicks. They laughed a lot, and quoted a lot, and punned a lot. They had fun together.

Once in a while he would feel he couldn't stand it any longer, and would start going with another girl, with sex the major aim. When Vassily saw him with another girl, she would nod her head understandingly, which infuriated him. Each time he decided he wouldn't have anything further to do with Vassily, and each time either he would call her to say something innocuous, like "I hear you got an A on your economics paper;" or she would call him, "Did you find a copy of Hartley and Hartley in the library?"

And they'd be off and running again.

It was almost a year after they had first met, and Willie didn't know how much longer he would be able to stand it, when one evening Vassily was lying on his bed reading. He made a shaker of sidecars, sugared the rim of the glasses, and handed one to her. She sat up, tasted, and said, "That's good. What is it?"

He explained how it was made, and she took another sip. "Why haven't I ever had one before?"

"I don't know. I didn't know you'd like it. I used to drink these in the army whenever I got to a place that served more than beer."

She finished her drink and said, "I don't feel anything. Are you sure it's alcoholic? I usually get sick from liquor, but this is more like a soft drink."

Hope stirred in his heart just as sex reared its head in his trousers. "Here. Let's finish these."

When she put her glass down she lay back down to read, but in a moment put the book aside and looked at him. "I think I've been had. I feel that I'm floating. No, don't quote: 'Candy is dandy but liquor is quicker.' Now I know it."

He leaned down and kissed her, and her arms went around his neck. He unzipped the back of her dress, unsnapped her brassiere, and pulled them both down to her waist. She writhed and twisted in his arms, and began to suck on his lower lip. When he made to take off the rest of her dress, together with her panties, she lifted her hips to assist him. As she lay nude on the bed, her eyes closed, he hastily began to undress. Just as he stepped out of his pants, the telephone rang.

He ignored the phone, but she opened her eyes, turned her head, and looked at the ringing phone on the night table.

"Forget it. Let it ring. We won't answer," he whispered, as though the phone could hear him.

But she reached one hand out, put the phone to her ear, and said, "What? Emergency? Okay," and handed the phone to him.

He was shaking from longing when he took the phone, and almost dropped it. "What emergency?"

A laughing voice said, "It isn't really an emergency, but I only have half-an-hour between trains, and didn't want to miss you. You will never, ever, guess who this is. Boy, are you going to be surprised!"

"Look," whispered Willie, "I'm in the middle of something very important. I can't talk to you now. Call me back."

"Don't you want to know who it is?"

"I really can't talk now. Call me back."

"Okay. I've only got half an hour, but I'll call you back just before the train leaves. Boy, oh boy, are you going to be surprised."

Willie figured that half-an-hour was time enough. In the state that he was in, five minutes would be more like it. He slammed down the phone, and turned to find an empty bed. From the doorway of the bathroom Vassily, wrapped in a towel, said, "That was close, wasn't it? Are you sure those are called sidecars—they felt more like Mack trucks. And who was your gallant friend who rode to my rescue?"

"I don't know," said Willie, "but when he calls back I'm going to find out who he is and kill him."

The mysterious caller never called again. Vassily thought it might have been an angel, and Willie thought it might have been the devil, but they never knew, because for the rest of their lives they never met anyone who mentioned calling Willie on his way through New York.

Willie didn't feel he could go on like this, and began proposing marriage to Vassily. Every time he did, she would become very serious and say that they were very young, and simply thrown together at the university, and that they didn't know what they wanted to do with their lives—in short, that they should wait until they were at least university graduates with some sense of direction.

They broke up, they came back together, they quarreled, they made up, they got angry, they got over it, they went with others, they came back to each other, they went on separate holidays, they couldn't wait to get back together. They explored New York from the Cloisters to Staten Island, from Montauk Point to Bowling Green. They saw the Rockettes and they skated at Rockefeller Center; they stood up at the Met and the New York Opera; they went to open rehearsals at Julliard; they roller skated in Central Park and danced at Roseland. They had four marvelous years at the university, while Willie kept trying to sleep with Vassily, and she kept resisting.

Willie couldn't wait to graduate, which for him meant marrying Vassily. As the end of the year approached, he began to make his preparations. At one point, however, when his credits were being evaluated, it turned out that he was two points short of graduating. He slapped his forehead when he remembered that incomplete in zoology. He went to see the head of the department—in vain. He offered to write the term paper. Too late. He offered to take a test. Not done. In the end, he had to take a summer course in zoology, which not only made him give up a promised camp job, but put his wedding off. And he still didn't know how powerful thyroid secretion is.

On finally graduating, Willie got a job with the State Civic Research Association as a research assistant, and Vassily became a junior aide to a New York City Council member. They figured they could manage on both salaries, and got married in the fall.

Their honeymoon was very short—a long weekend, in fact—since the Council member was in the midst of an election campaign, and the SCRA was making a major presentation to their managing board. They picked the St. Moritz for their honeymoon because Willie thought he might like eating at Rumpelmeyers and Vassily liked looking at the windows of Bergdof-Goodman. After several meals at Rumpelmeyers though, Willie decided he was really a Nedicks cheeseburger freak.

Willie wasn't sure reality could live up to expectations after four years of waiting, but he wasn't completely disappointed. Vassily said nothing the first time, when she experienced pain, but after the second time she said, "How long has this been going on?"

"We could have had this four years ago if you hadn't been so stubborn," ventured Willie.

"Yeah? And now you'd be married to some Boston debutante and I'd be standing with those girls around the corner on Sixth Avenue."

On the way home from the St. Moritz, in a cab, Willie was startled to see tears begin to roll down Vassily's checks. "Vas, what's the matter?"

"We haven't said anything to each other for the last three blocks. Now that we are married we have nothing to say to each other."

Willie burst out laughing. "I've heard of post-partum psychosis, but I never heard of post-marital nuttiness. Wait until we get home, Vas. I'll do something better than talk."

Willie went shopping that afternoon for some of the things they needed in order to live together, and when he came home, Vassily's first cooked dinner was waiting. "I know how much you like cheeseburgers, so that's what I made you."

Willie said nothing, and sat down at the table. He managed to down two of the underspiced, overcooked cheeseburgers—made with Swiss cheese instead of cheddar—while Vassily fussed over him like a mother hen. It wasn't until the next morning that he said, gently, "Vas, everyone has their specialty. Cheeseburgers are Nedicks' specialty. Why don't you develop your own?"

She said, "I think there is a message there. I get it loud and clear. Okay, I'll make you anything but cheeseburgers."

In the two years that it took Willie to get his masters in social psychology they had their first child. At the end of that time, it was clear to both of them that he would need a doctorate if he was to make a name for himself, or even amount to anything other than someone else's assistant. Since they needed both salaries to manage, Willie had a hard time finding a school that did not require full-time studies for two years.

At last Willie made a deal with the New York City branch of Continental Technical University. Most people didn't even know that Con-Tech, which was basically an engineering school, had a social psych department. He could do his first year on a half-time basis—taking two years—but they made it absolutely clear that he would have to attend full time for the second year of studies, that is, the third calendar year. However, since the social psychology department of the New York branch was very small, Willie figured that by the time he had studied there for two years, knowing all the faculty, and making sure that they all knew him, his family and his situation, they would make some arrangement for the third year—in short, that he would be able to con them into something agreeable.

During the first two years of his studies Willie managed reasonably well. The SCRA was helpful in letting him do his research during odd hours, and he got very interested in his studies. He and Vassily were expecting another child and needed larger quarters, of course. Rental apartments were expensive and hard to find, but when a faculty member of the school died, it turned out that he had been living for years in an apartment originally purchased for visiting faculty. Since by this time Willie had created the kind of relationships at the school that he had envisioned, they were kind enough to allow him and Vassily to rent it. It was a large, old-fashioned apartment between Riverside Drive and West End Avenue in the Sixties; the kind of apartment that Marjorie Morningstar might have lived in, thought Willie. He hated to leave the

Village and Nedicks, but there wasn't a chance of finding an apartment like that anywhere downtown. Anyway, there was a Nedicks on Broadway, not too far away.

Vassily gave birth to a girl in Riverside Hospital. After seeing her there once, Willie was visited by two friends from Orange who had come to New York on business. They were young men who also knew Vassily, so they accompanied him on his second visit to see her and the baby. After the conventional remarks were exchanged there was an uncomfortable silence. The two young men didn't have much more to say to a woman who had just given birth, and both Willie and Vassily realized they were looking for a polite way to leave.

"Why don't you go with them and show them some of the sights of New York, Willie," said Vassily.

"Oh, that would be nice," said one of the visitors with evident relief.

"Well, I thought…"

"Oh, go on. I have to nurse the baby soon anyway."

On the way out Willie said, "What would you like to do?"

"We've got to take the train back in an hour and a half so we can't go far from Grand Central. What is there to do around mid-town?"

Willie thought of Forty-Second Street. "Schlock shops, hookers, and blue movies."

"You mean like a burlesque show?"

"Migawd, I haven't been to a burlesque show since I was a teen-ager and lied about my age. As a matter of fact, one of the few burlesque houses still in business is on Eighth Avenue. Man, that would take me back to my youth. Wanta go?"

So the three of them very self-consciously bought tickets to the burlesque. It was a rather tawdry theatre, with all the drawbacks of a dying business—it showed long boring films between performances, so as not to keep the "actors" busy for too long (and to keep from paying them too much); had long "breaks" when popcorn, Cokes, and all kinds of minor put-ons were sold: "With this genuine, sparkling, first-quality

zicron-diamond ring we will give you—this time only—a box of genuine Atlantic City saltwater taffy, and in each and every box you will
find a prize, which might be a wristwatch, a patented three-color flashlight, or a leather-covered wallet. Who'll be the first to take advantage of
this one-time exceptional bargain? You, sir? And what is the prize in
your box of taffy? A wristwatch! Will you hold that up, please? Who else
wants one of these zicron-diamond rings and the box of saltwater taffy
with a prize?"

When they went to the burlesque, the visitors knew that they would
have to leave early to catch their train. First they saw the film; then there
was an acrobat; then the interval with the sales pitch; then a comedian;
and just as they announced the stellar stripper—"Down to the bare
skin, if not more"—Willie's friends had to leave to catch their train.
Since there was no sense in wasting all the tickets, Willie stayed until the
end of the stage show.

When he saw the bored, mostly ugly, strippers, he was very embarrassed for them, and ashamed of being there. He thought of Vassily and
their new baby and wished he hadn't come.

The next time he saw Vassily in the hospital she said, "For someone
who had the hots for four years, going to a burlesque show when your
wife has just given birth is probably the most stupid thing you could do."

"Vas, if you had only seen those strippers, you'd know that the very
thought of them would keep me from getting it up. Seeing them was
probably the smartest thing I could do while you are still hors de combat. As a matter of fact, I didn't really want to go and didn't enjoy it
while I was there."

"What horseshit! You couldn't wait to get there, and enjoyed every
minute of it."

"How do you know how I felt?"

"I've lived with you long enough to have developed some empathy. I
usually know how you feel."

He realized that at this instant, Vassily really thought she knew how he felt, and that she was dead wrong. It made him began to question the phenomenon of empathy, about which he had never thought. He stored the question away for future cogitation.

As Willie had planned it, by the time he finished going to the university for two years, he knew all the faculty and all the few social-psych students. All the faculty had been in his house, and the head of the social psychology department held him in high esteem. Willie was trying to decide on the best approach concerning dividing the next year into two when he got a letter on the stationery of the university. The letter was terse:

"Due to financial reasons, the Board of Governors of Continental Technical University has decided to close the social psychology department in the New York City branch as of this date. Students desirous of transferring their credits to the Denver campus may do so. We trust this does not inconvenience you."

"Inconvenience me!" exploded Willie. "It kills me. Why didn't anyone tell me? Christ, for two years I built up my relationships in order to con them, and now look what they did to me!"

"The best laid plans of mice, men, and especially would-be con men…We'll work it out, dear," said Vassily.

But they didn't. In the end, Willie had to take a year's leave from his job and go full-time to Lever College to finish his doctorate. It was a good piece of work, and just before his dissertation defense he was approached by the head of the psychology department who asked him if he would like to join the faculty when and if his dissertation was accepted. He nearly knocked the man down saying yes.

Dissertation defenses were technically open to the public, and anyone who wanted to was entitled to ask questions. Ordinarily, however, only the dissertation committee was present. Willie had followed up his questions about empathy and done a study of it. He found that some people understood the word to mean reading non-verbal behavior; to others it meant giving off a feeling of caring; and to still others it meant sharing someone else's feelings. He had studied all the literature on the subject, and the results of all the tests of empathy. He had also devised and given some tests, and in the end concluded that although the first two definitions were acceptable, there was no proof at all that one person could really experience the feelings of another, or—more exactly—that anyone could know if he or she was experiencing the same feeling as another.

As he entered the room to defend his dissertation, he was disconcerted by the fact that in addition to the committee, the room was full of people. He had no idea that empathy interested so many members of the faculty, and he anticipated not only technical questions, but political attacks and personal biases on the part of some of the other people present.

He summarized his research, which the committee had read, and waited for questions. One member of the committee felt he hadn't put enough emphasis on ethnic differences; another felt there should be more concerning kinesthetic empathy; the chairman, on the contrary, felt that both areas had been adequately covered. One member of the committee kept asking questions that other members answered without giving Willie a chance. It turned out that he had not even read the dissertation. When these questions were answered, the chairman asked the audience if there were any questions.

Willie waited with bated breath. Not a hand was raised. The chairman looked puzzled, and again explained that the audience had the right to ask questions. There was no response at all. The chairman shrugged, and asked Willie to leave the room. In a few moments, he came out and said, "Doctor, will you come back in, please." Willie felt a surge of exultation, and couldn't wait to call Vassily and tell her that he was now a Ph.D.

The mystery of the audience took a bit longer to solve. It seems they were a trade delegation from Bulgaria who had wandered into the wrong room. They spoke not a word of English, but thought they were in the right room, and kept waiting for the translation. Their host and translator, next door, had finally given up and gone home.

Although Willie was a very junior member of the faculty, he loved academic life—he was an inventive researcher and a gifted teacher. As the first step of his career up the academic latter, he published his findings concerning empathy in a scholarly journal. He was surprised at the controversy he had created. The article caused consternation among many psychologists and social workers who felt that they empathized with their clients to the extent of sharing their feelings—and, indeed, that this was their major treatment tool. The resultant spate of letters and counter-articles spread his name in scholastic circles—one journal calling him an expert on something that he didn't believe existed—and resulted in clarification of the term empathy, and more caution concerning its purported use.

In three years he was given tenure, which caused him to sigh in relief and allowed him to begin the kind of research he wanted to do, instead of things which would result in several quickly published papers.

As one of the more junior members of the faculty, Willie was asked to take on a number of thankless jobs, including housekeeping committees, library supervision, and so forth. One Thursday he received a call from the chairwoman of the Alumni Association. She told him the annual dinner of the Alumni Association was being held on Sunday, and they would like him to be the main speaker.

He was somewhat startled: "You are inviting me on a Thursday to speak on Sunday?"

"I'll be perfectly honest with you. We had a speaker, but he cancelled this morning, and it was suggested by the dean that you might do this for us."

Before he could answer she said, "There'll be a fee for this, of course. Would $50 be all right?"

Willie figured that if the dean wanted him to speak, he could show good will, and since fifty dollars was more a gesture than a fee, he indicated he would speak for free. The chairwoman was most grateful and told him that he would be allotted forty-five minutes. He prepared himself thoroughly.

On the day, he found himself on the dais with a number of other people. The meeting opened with an invocation that went on for so long that the program chairwoman leaned over to him and said, "I see we are running quite late. Can you cut your remarks a little?"

Willie said, politely, "It's your affair. I'll be glad to oblige."

The meal was served and eaten leisurely, with people table-hopping to greet old friends.

After the dinner, the chairwoman introduced everyone on the dais, at length and profusely; she explained the meaning of the Alumni Association, at length and profusely; and she introduced the president of the Alumni Association, at length and profusely. The president spoke, at length and profusely. Whereupon the program chairwoman leaned in Willie's direction again and said, "We didn't plan for this. Could you cut your remarks to half an hour?"

What could he say? He agreed, of course.

The chairwoman began an introduction, and Willie began to psyche himself up for his speech when he realized that she wasn't introducing him. Instead, the past president of the Alumni Association was introduced, at length and profusely; and she spoke, at length and profusely. When the program chairwoman leaned toward him again, he knew what to expect.

"Could you possibly confine yourself to fifteen minutes? We are running so late, and have so much more to do."

"Look," he whispered back, "if I speak for only fifteen minutes it will be just an outline—no instances, no stories, no examples, no explanations. It will be extremely boring."

"Fine, just fine," she reassured him. "We only want the simple facts. Fifteen minutes."

Well, as he had said, it was their meeting and—as she had hinted—he was there at the request of the dean, so when his turn came, he spoke very quickly, very briefly, and—there is no question—very dully. The audience listened and duly gave him a polite smattering of applause.

Then he saw the chairwoman brighten up, turn to the audience with a broad smile, and say:

"And now, friends, the event we have all been waiting for so patiently. Marian Greensleeves and her guitar!"

There was a swelling roar of applause, and a young lady put her foot up on a chair, supported her guitar, and began singing. She sang Greek songs; English songs, including Greensleeves, of course; an Irish lullaby; some American folk songs; and some Negro spirituals. Each rendition was greeted with a roar of applause. Then there was a pause, and she said, "I know that the language of this song will be difficult for some of you, but the content will be familiar."

So she began to sing "My Yiddishe Mama." The group nodded their heads in rhythm, and every one had a broad smile on her face, except the chairwoman, who took out a handkerchief and began sobbing. The program chairwoman leaned over to Willie and confided that the chairwoman had lost her mother during the year, and it was very appropriate for Marian to sing this song for her.

The folk-singing went on for forty-five minutes, and there was great reluctance to let Marian Greensleeves go. She had to give three encores, but finally packed up amid wild applause. "Wasn't she splendid?" asked the program chairwoman of Willie.

"Yes, she was very good," said he, politely. "Tell me, did she also donate her services?"

"Oh, no! She's a real artist. We wouldn't even ask that of her. But with the addition of the fee that you donated to us, we were able to get her to come. She was the highlight of the program, wasn't she?"

Willie nodded agreement, but made a mental resolve that any time he was asked to speak in the future, he would ask who else would be on the program, and if it were a folksinger, comedian, or other entertainer, would ask for ten dollars more than whatever their fee was to be.

Lever University had exchange agreements with a number of foreign universities, and one of the perks of the faculty was to accompany these groups on short summer courses. Although Vassily couldn't leave the children, Willie managed to wangle a trip to Italy, and while the students were taking capsule courses in English concerning Italian history, art, and so forth, under the watchful eye of a fellow faculty member, Ron—who had been in Italy before—Willie was exploring the country. He saw the opera in Verona, the flea market in Luino, Isola Bella, Capa de Monte in Naples, and the grotto in Capri. He went to the straw market in Florence and rode a gondola in Venice. He packed a lot into his two weeks, practically running from place to place. He was looking forward to sleeping all the way home, with Ron, his co-leader, taking care of the group.

In the Rome airport, on the way home, Max, the only economics student in the group, asked Willie, "Will they take American dollars at the tax-free shop here?"

Willie was amused at Max's naivete and amazed at his ignorance of the simple facts of economics, so he simply said, "Try them."

Their charter plane was a small one, and so touched down in London, and Max asked,

"Will they take American money here?"

Willie said, "Try them."

They took off for Iceland, and on landing Max asked, "Will they take American money here?"

Willie, a little annoyed at this point, said as usual, "Try them."

When they left Iceland everyone settled down to sleep, but in a few hours they landed—back in London. It seems there had been a mechanical malfunction, and the decision was to return to London rather than continue to New York.

At Heathrow they did not go through passport control and customs but were herded into a small transit lounge. There Max approached Willie once more, and before he could ask, Willie—knowing that Max was an economics student—said, "Max, of all this crowd people like you should know something about money. Yes, they'll take American currency here."

Max looked at him queerly, seemed on the point of saying something, changed his mind, and said, "That wasn't what I was going to ask you. You see, I'm out of American money. Could you loan me some?"

Some economist, thought Willie, but he said, "Okay, I'll be your Shylock. How much do you need?"

"Never mind," said Max, and turned on his heel.

"Wait," said Willie. "Do you want the money or not?"

Max kept walking, and didn't answer him.

Willie was puzzled, but soon let it go.

At the beginning of the next school year Willie went over his class list and asked each student to stand as his or her name was called, in order to begin to identify them. This was, for Willie, one of his most difficult tasks, for he taught four sections, each with about thirty students, and putting more than a hundred names to as many faces each semester—which meant twice a year—was never easy for him, and usually not completely successful.

On the fifth name that he called, a young lady stood up and without prompting or provocation said, "I'm a lesbian."

Both the class and Willie looked at her curiously, because he had not asked the students to introduce themselves in any way. Each time after that when the student spoke she introduced her subject, "As a lesbian, I feel…".

It began to get annoying, both to the other students and to Willie. At last he called her in and said, "I realize that being a lesbian is important to you, but isn't there anything else in the world that interests you?"

With asperity she said, "If you were Gay you'd realize that it is the whole meaning of your life. And don't tell me you can empathize with me. I learned from your own article that you can't."

This began Willie on a series of investigations concerning flaunting and hiding homosexuality, and he eventually published a long article on some social-psychological implications of homosexuality. The article was published in a second-level psychological journal, and Willie felt he had added one more item to his curriculum vita.

However, the article was picked up by a West Coast Gay journal, with a bitter attack on its contents. *The Village Voice* picked up the article in turn, and published a rebuttal. *Commentary* then wrote an article about the article and its attackers, and Willie found that he was in the middle of a controversy that was no longer academic.

The result was that the Dean of the University told Willie, effusively, that he had the highest respect for academic freedom, and did not want his comments to be misconstrued, and that Willie was free to research and write about any subject he chose, but .. . The Gay Movement had become powerful, and the Board and other supporters of the university didn't like controversy of any kind, and…

Willie's first impulse was to make an issue of the academic freedom involved. After all, he had tenure, and couldn't be fired for what he wrote. On second thought, he realized that he wasn't that interested in homosexuality as a subject, and if he fought, he would be almost compelled to continue writing about the subject as a matter of principle, so he indicated that he understood, and the matter was dropped.

With time and with aggregated publications, Willie was promoted, and one day was able to hear himself referred to as professor. He was very proud, and he and Vassily had a small party for the faculty and some graduate students.

When a new Department Head was to be appointed, Willie felt that he might well be in line for the job, but he wasn't even put on the short list. Some time later, chatting with Ron, who had since become Dean of the University, he mentioned how he had fantasized about becoming the Department Head. Ron took it very seriously. His face became grave, and he said, "You really were in line for it. But some of the alumni said that judging by your speech at the annual meeting, you weren't suitable. Forgive me, Willie, but they said it was both short and dull, as though you were contemptuous of what the alumni thought of you. And one of our Gay trustees had read some of the comments on your article about homosexuality, and said anybody but you. The funny thing was that he had never read the article, because I asked him, but he wouldn't budge. So there were two strikes against you from the start. I am sorry about that."

Willie took his non-appointment with good grace, even though he realized how unfair life is.

It was around this time that Willie realized that he was teaching from textbooks that were becoming outdated. Theory was moving faster than practice. He didn't have the patience for writing a textbook himself, so he decided to prepare some teaching material for his own use. He looked for an overall theme on which he could hang a number of psychological and sociological concepts, but had difficulty deciding on one. In the meantime, he read some anthropological studies of cargo cults, and thought they might make excellent teaching material.

Cargo cults, as he understood them, arose after World War II on some of the South Pacific islands and in Africa. The arrival of soldiers in airplanes, bringing with them strange artifacts like Coca-Cola, wireless sets (and cheeseburgers, thought Willie), and so forth, set in motion religious beliefs concerning a future return of such gods from the sky, with priceless treasures for the people. If they would just behave properly and pray properly, cult members believed, these gods would return.

Willie wrote of an imaginary island group that worshipped an airman who had crashlanded and been killed, and whose father and mother had come to reclaim the body. They liberally rewarded the natives who had been helpful to them. Since then the natives had waited for the next coming of an airman, and had begun to emulate the behavior of the father and mother in order to hasten the event. Both men and women in the group wore solar toupees, as the father had done. Every morning and evening they faced the sun, from which direction the airman had come and would presumably come again, holding their topees over their breasts, as the father had done when he found his son's grave. Twice a year, presumably on the anniversary of the son's death, they fasted, and on the anniversary of the day when his body was dug up and taken away by the parents, they feasted. They broke their fast by marching up to their high priest and drinking a cup of tea, and they began their feast the same way, as legend said the mother had drunk tea on each occasion. The symbol of their group was a propeller, and each person had a small propeller in the house, to which he or she paid homage.

Willie asked his students to find in this teaching record evidences of social psychological and psychoanalytic processes, and to compare them to the daily behavior to which they were accustomed. The students were amused by the record, and some of them turned in highly imaginative but serious papers. Willie was very pleased with himself and with them.

Consequently, he was quite unprepared when he was again called in to see Ron. It seems that some students who were amused by the record had shown it to others, and one had shown it to her father, an Anglican clergyman. He, in turn, had circulated it to other members of the clergy, and the result was that the university in general, and Willie in particular, were being seriously accused of holding Christianity up to ridicule and indoctrinating the students with irreligion.

Willie had not even thought about the parallels with Christianity when he wrote the record, although he realized later that his own unconscious was probably more potent than he thought. In any case, he explained to Ron that there was no malicious intent in the teaching record, and since it had not been published anywhere, and was of no scholarly value, he did not object to withdrawing it. But life isn't that simple. The university chaplain felt impelled to attack the record in a sermon, which drew faculty who were jealous of academic freedom into the controversy. The fact that there was controversy was enough to interest the local press, and that impelled Willie to defend his right to use the record.

The controversy was unpleasant, but as such things do, it faded in importance with the advent of other events. However, Willie felt that his standing at the university was now that of a controversial figure. He decided that he would not use the same record the following year, but went back to the usual textbooks.

For the next few years Willie steered clear of controversy, but was then enmeshed in something much more serious. His daughter noticed black and blue marks on Vassily's arms, and called them to his attention. He tried to make light of it: "Vas, I might beat you once in a while, but at least you could wear long sleeves."

The joking ceased when Vassily was diagnosed as having leukemia. There followed the experience which has become all too familiar in many families—the disease, the remission, the disease again, the series of painful and disfiguring treatments, the denial, and the final sinking into a coma. Vassily died at age fifty-eight, with both children married, two grandchildren, and a husband who could not stop grieving.

With the passage of time Willie learned that one may learn to live with the loss, but the loss never goes away. He threw himself into his work, teaching, lecturing, writing, going to conferences, and taking on jobs in the university and in professional associations.

When he was sixty-five, and internationally recognized as a scholar in his field, he again realized that textbooks had not kept up with him. His own insights were not properly reflected in them. Again he thought of writing a textbook, and again rejected the monotonous work, consisting of the proposal, the acceptance (perhaps after some rejections), the library research, the actual physical writing, the rewriting according to someone else's editing, the footnotes, the references, the indexing, the galley proofs, the page proofs, and the invariably "balanced" reviews. He just wasn't willing to undertake it. So, very carefully, he decided to write another—this time non-controversial—teaching record.

He had fun writing it, because it was totally imaginative, and he could foresee students enjoying learning from it. This time he wrote of an imaginary group discovered by astronauts on a distant planet. They lived in small groups, and each group had their territory marked out by a string that went around their area. In order to make the string visible, colored rags were attached to it, each group having a different color. Within their own territory, groups had wide freedom of action, but once outside their territory, or in that of another group, behavior changed drastically. In that case, they were not allowed to pick up anything that was lying down; could walk only two hundred steps; and they could not wipe the sweat off their faces, no matter how hot they were. Incidentally, if the string around their territory broke, they were presumed to be outside the area, or in another group's area, which was terribly dangerous.

Although the climate was hot, they wore only heavy red clothing, since that is what their mythical ancestors presumably wore. They were obsessed with sex, and felt that uncontrollable lust arose from the sight of ears, fingers, and ankles. Consequently, they wore a kind of headphone on their ears, gloves at all times, and elaborate wide ankle bracelets made of leather and silver. They were evidently also concerned about homosexuality, since two men were not allowed to be alone together—either a woman, or a third man had to be present at all times.

They worked only in the morning, and their definition of work was very strict. Anyone doing anything that could be construed as work in the afternoon was ostracized and sometimes expelled. For example, they could not read in the afternoon, not only because they might read professional literature—which would be work—but also because turning pages was considered work. They used considerable ingenuity inventing things to turn the pages of books—that were obviously just comic books—so they could read without sinning. Sometimes a member of another group who was present could be induced to undertake the job of turning pages, but only if he were asked to in pantomime.

The kept their chief idol in a wooden box, and nobody but the high priest was allowed to see the idol itself. The others worshipped the box, dusting it gently whenever they walked by, and putting smaller copies of the box on their tables, where they dusted it before and after eating.

Every person was compelled to read a portion of their epic poem—dealing with a presumed world to come—every day, starting it again when the end was reached. On the night of the full moon the entire poem was read over and over throughout the night.

Once a year the group made a sacrifice. The women shaved off their hair, and the men shaved off the beards that had grown all year, and with much work the hair was woven into a net that was immediately thrown into a fire when it was completed. When men reached the age of twenty, one ear was nicked slightly and after that could be exposed, to indicate that the man could now control his lust.

Willie traced out for himself the concepts that he had built into the teaching record, as a basis for grading students in their analysis of the record. As he had anticipated, the students were already grinning before they got to the second sentence. He liked them to enjoy their studies.

It was almost two months before he was formally asked to see Ron, the Dean, again. As he entered, he was surprised to see three men, all dressed in heavy black clothes despite the heat, each clutching either a box or a book (he couldn't see which), and each with a beard, leaving the office. He felt that had they worn red, they might have come from his mythical planet. Consequently, he was not prepared for the gravity—indeed, almost the anger—with which he was greeted.

"That," said Ron, waving at the departing backs, "was a delegation from the New York Board of Orthodox Rabbis. We—you—are being accused of anti-Semitism. That is a charge that even academic freedom cannot condone. In addition to which, some of the most important members of our Board of Trustees are Jewish, as are some of our largest contributors. I would think that you had learned to be discreet by now—or are you really an anti-Semite? And don't tell me that some of your best friends are Jews—that's the sure mark of an anti-Semite."

Willie was frozen. "I don't know what you are talking about. Never, in all my career, have I ever said anything that could be remotely considered anti-Semitic. Don't you know that my wife was Jewish—at least technically? None of my best friends are Jews—in fact, I don't think I even know *any* Jews socially or personally. And if I do, their Jewishness has nothing to do with it. What the hell is this all about?"

"Are you trying to tell me that you didn't deliberately make fun of Orthodox Jewish practice in your teaching record?"

"I haven't the slightest idea of what Orthodox Jewish practice is—or any other Jewish practice, for that matter. I've heard of a Seder, I know what circumcision is and I know what a bar-mitzvah is, but that's about the extent of it. How did this start?"

"Do you know a former student named Max?"

"Max? Max? There was an economics student on our Italian trip named Max. What's he got to do with this?"

"He is the one who complained to the rabbis. He says you made some anti-Semitic remarks to him on that trip."

"I? Me?" Willie tried to remember. "He was the only economist in the group of sociologists. All I said to him was something like, 'People like you ought to know about money.' My God, I meant economics students—did he think I meant Jews? I didn't even know he was Jewish. Oh, hell, I also said I'd be his Shylock and lend him money. I guess that can be construed as anti-Semitic, too, can't it?"

The Dean appeared mollified. "Willie, you are in very hot water, and it isn't only Max. It is those teaching records. The first was construed as anti-Christian, and the last one is seen as poking fun at Jewish practice. I'm not sure I can save you this time. This matter will be all over the Jewish press in a few days, and it will become a national matter very quickly. You know you have an excellent reputation. It would be a shame to have it all end this way. Can you think of any way out?"

They both sat and looked at each other. Then Willie said, "Look, suppose I pre-empt their attack by saying that their comments have made me very interested in Judaism. I realize that I should know more about it, and am resolved to study it."

"Good, but not enough."

Another pause.

"Suppose I take a trip to Israel to try to study it first hand."

"Not bad."

"Let us ask them," he waved in the direction that the delegation had taken, "to put me in touch with the best rabbi in Israel to teach me."

"Better and better."

"And let it be known that I will not return until I am thoroughly versed in Jewish thought and practice. That should get you off the hook, don't you think?"

"That should do it. But Willie, are you sure you want to do something so drastic?"

"I had a friend who volunteered and died in the Israeli war of independence. Many of our students spend periods there. I'd like to see what it is that gets people so passionate on one side or the other. From a social-psychological point of view, it should be interesting. And to tell you the truth, we have so many Jewish students I really should know more about their religion."

So Willie informed people that he was entering a new area of study—the social-psychology of comparative religions—and was going to Israel to learn about Judaism first hand. At his bon voyage party all three of the rabbinical delegation were present, each giving him different advice as to where to study and with whom. He noticed, incidentally, that they didn't eat anything.

Uncle Willie never came back to the States. Five years later I went looking for him. I found him in an unheated room on a side-street—really an alley—in a neighborhood that looked like something I had seen in pictures of pre-war Polish villages. He was dressed all in black, and had a long beard. He wore a skullcap, and hanging over the top of his trousers I saw the fringes of the undergarment that all Orthodox men wear.

When he saw me he put down the enormous volume he had been holding, and gave me a smile. "Ah, a searcher for true knowledge," he said.

"Not really. I was trying to find out what happened to you. What did happen to you?"

"As you can see, I am studying Judaism."

"Okay, you are studying it. And you have been for the past seven years. But do you have to practice it?" And I pointed to the mezuzzah set in the doorpost, and the fringes of his arba kanfot and the skullcap on his head.

His voice took on a curious singsong: "We are told, in *The Ethics of the Fathers*, 'Do not throw a stone into the well from which you have drunk'. That's good advice. I've learned a lot, and there's a lot yet to be learned. Although there are things I could complain about, and even make fun of, I won't."

"And how much longer do you intend to study Judaism?"

He grinned and held up his book so I could see it. He wasn't reading from it, he was writing in it. I could make out the title: "A Social-Psychological Interpretation of the Lubavitcher Chassidic Movement."

I was almost frightened for him, again creating a controversy. "Do they know that you are studying them?"

He lifted his head proudly. "The Rebbe himself wants to read it when I am done. Do you know what an honor that is?"

"Uncle Willie," said I, "how much longer are you going to keep this up? You're not going back to the university—you are well past retirement age. Any controversies have long since died out. I know how you have always loved New York, and especially the Village. You don't have to do this any longer. C'mon home."

"What have I got left in New York, son? My wife is long dead and my children are self-sufficient. It is true that here there are some inconveniences"—he motioned to the skullcap and fringes as symbols of other things—"but what do I lack?"

"For one thing," I said, smiling, "cheeseburgers. Because here they are *treife*."

He seemed to be looking into the past, and said, nostalgically, "Yes, they are."

"Cheeseburgers," I said again.

"It has been a long time," he said, almost to himself.

"At Nedicks," I added.

He looked shocked. "Nedicks? Are they still in business? Really?"

"Yep. On the same corner, in the Village."

He sat thoughtful for a long moment, saying nothing.

"A Nedicks cheeseburger. With a malted milk," I added.

His fingers drummed on the table.

"On me."

He sat silent for another few moments, then slowly stood up, took off his skullcap, laid it on his book, and put his arms over my shoulders.

"That," he said, as we started for the door, "is the most attractive offer I've had in the last seven years."

Uncle Buck

◆

UNCLE BUCK

My Uncle Buck had some very sound ideas about prison reform. They were intended to make prisons more efficient, more humane, and easier to govern. His ideas came from a lifetime of living in large social groups—summer camps, the Civilian Conservation Corps, the American Army, and the Peace Corps. His ideas about prison reform made sense, but he could never get them implemented, or even listened to.

My Uncle Buck had always loved camping. The first camp he went to was a Fresh Air Camp for poor children sponsored by a local charity. His family wasn't that poor, but as a city boy he wasn't a member of the Four-H Club; he was too young to be a Boy Scout; and private camps were for very rich kids. So he wangled his way into the charity camp. He loved it. He liked being with other kids, he liked sleeping in a dorm, he liked the high-jinks that went on at lights out, he even liked the food.

He could hardly wait to become twelve so he could join the Boy Scouts and from then on he went to Boy Scout camps. He tied knots, built fires with only one match instead of two, cooked in a tin can, went skinny dipping, and learned to tell the leaves from the trees. He loved it.

At age fourteen or thereabouts he discovered girls, but since he was invariably in a boys' camp, he—together with the others—just talked about girls, fantasized about girls, and pretended that their pillows were girls. At sixteen he and a friend found that they could make dummies in their beds with pillows, sneak out after hours, and walk two and a half miles to the nearby Girl Scout camp and, since it was long after lights out in the girls' camp, too, hope to see a girl in her nightgown or pajamas on her way to the john. In fact, they often saw two girls, since girl campers invariably went to the john in pairs—a phenomenon he could never understand.

At eighteen Buck became an assistant scoutmaster, and could use the camp jalopy to drive the two and a half miles to where girls of his own age held equivalent rank. He never could decide whether or not to call them assistant scout mistresses, but decided he might be misunderstood, so didn't. Most of the nocturnal visits involved marshmallow roasts, or cocoa, or both, with a lot of giggling, hints, allusions, and occasionally a couple slipping out of the room.

Buck's turn came one night when it was cool enough to require blankets around the campfire. He and Sissie shared a blanket, and as his hands explored her, she kept talking steadily about the camp—how bad the food was, how strict the discipline was, how shallow the riverbed was, how stupid the director was. Buck thought she was talking so no one else would realize what was going on under the blanket.

She didn't run out of talk while Buck took off her halter top. She redoubled her talk as he reached his hands into her shorts and under her panties. When he started to pull these down, she said, "Let me prove to you how uneven the tennis court is," and got up with the blanket wrapped around her.

On the tennis court she put the blanket down and lay down, slipping off shorts and panties at the same time. All this time she was telling him an incident about a visiting parent, and as he entered her she continued the story without a break. She climaxed before Buck did, while continuing to describe the visit to him. Buck began to realize that she was one of those girls who do not let their top half know what their bottom half is doing. In her mind, she was probably still a virgin, since the portion of her that was copulating with vigor was not something that she acknowledged as part of her body. Her conversation was part of her self-deception—that she was just talking to Buck, and doing nothing else.

He decided he was right when he realized that she was a conversational prude—she blushed at sexual allusions, and changed the subject when he tried to talk about sex. But sign language, in a manner of speaking, was something that she readily understood and accepted. Buck began to think he liked Girl Scout camp even better than Boy Scout camp.

During Buck's last season at Boy Scout camp he was assistant to the director. He found that with his experience, he was able to make many useful suggestions to improve the camp. Among other things, he suggested visiting the parents who had questions or comments about the camp, rather than just acknowledging these with letters. One mother, who lived in the town adjacent to the camp, told Buck during his visit that the only thing she wanted from the camp was that her twelve-year old son, Marvin, would learn to eat.

Buck thought she meant table manners, but she insisted that she meant what she said: "I can't get him to eat a thing. I cook everything I think he'll like, and he doesn't touch it. I argue with him about it all the time—I guess I even yell at him. I can chase him around the table with a spoonful of food, but I can't get it into him."

By chance, Buck had just been reading a psychology-made-easy book—a popularization of the subject—and came to an immediate decision that what was being described was typical adolescent revolt. Marvin was using food to fight his mother, thereby asserting his independence. Buck felt that if she would refuse to fight, Marvin would probably eat food but refuse to do something else that she wanted. So at camp Buck got hold of Rube, Marvin's counselor, and said, "I don't want you to pay any attention to Marvin's eating habits. Whether he eats or not is none of your business. Don't mention it, don't pay any attention to it, just ignore it."

Three days later Rube came to Buck. "Look, take Marvin out of my bunk, will you? I can't stand it. He doesn't eat a thing. His plate remains empty no matter what I say to him or what I try to put on it."

Buck said, quietly but vehemently, "I will murder you! Don't you dare talk about his eating, or pay any attention whatever to it. In fact, I won't murder you—I'll fire you."

It was about two weeks later that Buck suddenly remembered Marvin. He had heard nothing in the meantime, and had a sudden panic that maybe Marvin had starved to death. He got hold of Rube and asked, "How is Marvin?"

"Marvin? He's fine. Why?"

"Is he eating?"

"Eating? That little horse! He can't get enough on his plate. I have to make him leave some for the others."

"How did you do it?"

"I did exactly what you said. I didn't pay any attention to his eating, and the others kids were happy with his not eating—they got more, especially desserts—so they didn't say anything. And little by little he began taking some food, always looking at me and the others to see how we were taking it. And we paid no attention at all. Every time it happened I got the others kids interested in talking about something else. That's all."

"You know, I don't think I'll fire you. In fact, we may hire you again next year."

Marvin went home when his session was over, and as Buck handed him over to his mother, she took one look at him and said, "You look great. How much did you gain?"

He didn't answer her, so Buck said, "About eight pounds."

"How did you do it?"

So Buck had Marvin join some other kids who were waiting outside, and explained to Marvin's mother that food was the weapon he was using to assert his independence, as all adolescents must, and that if she would ignore his food habits as they had in camp, he might find some other area to assert himself, but he would eat. She thought that was marvelous, and assured Buck that she would follow his advice.

When the next camp session of the same summer was over, Buck dropped in to see Marvin's mother as he was leaving.

"Oh, I'm so glad to see you," she enthused. "I don't know how you did it, but I can't get Marvin to eat. I've tried everything, and ended up chasing him around the table with a spoonful of food again. How did you do it?"

Buck prided himself on understanding that the food fight was as much the mother's need as Marvin's, but he didn't feel he yet knew enough psychology to give advice, so he just excused himself and left.

This was the year that Buck graduated high school, and finding a job was a bummer. It was the middle of the Depression, and millions of people were out of work. When he heard about the Civilian Conservation Corps, it seemed made for him. He joined the CCC immediately, and was sent to a camp in Pennsylvania. After being there only a few days he approached the camp director and told him that he thought he could make some suggestions to improve the camp. The director was a bit skeptical, but listened. Among other things, Buck suggested that rather than lay out paths, and then put up fences to make sure people stayed on the paths, it might be better to wait and watch where people walked, and then put the paths down there, obviating the need for fences. His other comments made equal sense, and as his experience as a camper made itself felt, he was appointed a group leader, although many of the participants were older than he was.

Buck knew that in the CCC he wasn't getting anywhere in life, but he was enjoying it. Sometimes they were really in forests, felling trees, making fire lanes, and cutting away secondary growth. Sometimes they were clearing fields or deepening riverbeds. This was camping for real, and as usual, he loved it.

When he had some time off, Buck was at loose ends. Finally, he made it his business to find out where Sissie was, and wrote to her, asking her to join him on his next leave. Sissie replied that she was trying to write a novel, and needed some local color, so a visit to Pennsylvania might be a good idea. She was there for five days of his seven-day leave, and they hardly left the hotel room.

She discussed her ideas for the novel—the setting, the characters, the action, the style, the possibilities of publication—straight through the wildest lovemaking Buck had ever fantasized. She was willing to do anything, as long as she didn't have to talk about it, or even to acknowledge that it was happening.

Buck prepared for her leave-taking with real regret, and as they were waiting together for her train, he asked, smiling, "Did you get as much local color for your novel as you wanted?"

She replied seriously, "I can describe a typical American hotel in great detail. The furnishings, the service, the food—yes, it was a worthwhile visit. Thank you for inviting me."

Buck re-enrolled in the CCC twice, and each time he was in a new camp, he made suggestions to improve the setting, some of which were accepted.. About the time he got out of the CCC, he heard reverberations of a posssible upcoming war. He decided to enlist, which he did. He was a new recruit in the regular army, and one of the missions of the old-timers was to make life miserable for new recruits. His bed was short-sheeted, he was sent for left handed wrenches and polka-dot paint (he knew better, but didn't let on, feeling it was better to be laughed at than to be thought a wise-guy). He was also a bit of a curiosity, because he didn't bitch about every aspect of army life, which was expected of newcomers.

Actually, Buck became a problem to the army. When he was put on KP, he scoured the cooking pots so well and so quickly that the sergeant had a problem finding something else for him to do. When he finished washing all the windows in the mess-hall and so reported to the sergeant, the latter thought and thought, and then said, "Do them over." Buck was not stupid—he got the message: In the army, whatever job you are doing takes up all the available time. (This was long before Parkinson said the same thing more elegantly about all jobs).

As usual, Buck wanted to make some suggestions to improve the camp, but found that getting to the commander of an army camp was somewhat more difficult than getting to a summer camp director. However, he persisted, and when he finally got his interview and made his suggestions, they were dismissed out of hand. And then three of them were implemented during the next few weeks.

With time, Buck made sergeant, and then tech sergeant. When put in charge of sanitation, he knew exactly where to look for leaks, blockages, and unsanitary latrines. When his assignment was in the office, he handled the paper work efficiently and excellently. When he was drill sergeant, the new recruits drilled until they were perfect. However, he knew that drill day after day was one of the more monotonous aspects of army life. He couldn't reduce or abandon drilling, so took the other route. He asked for volunteers to learn a new, additional, method of drilling. A few curious soldiers took him up on it, and he began training them in what was called the "monkey drill."

He taught them very intricate movements with and without their rifles. There was, for example, the Queen Anne salute, which involved twirling the rifle 360 degrees and going down on one knee with the rifle still at "port arms." There were other movements that were almost ballet-like in their execution, and the participants not only enjoyed them, but took pride in being able to carry them out. That pride, and an exhibition of the monkey drill, led to others volunteering for this additional drill period. Buck's superiors had a hard time believing that soldiers were actually volunteering for extra drill, and Buck added another improvement to his mental list of successes

Three days after Pearl Harbor Buck was shipped to Officers' Training School. He had opted for infantry, so he was sent to Fort Benning.

There he found that it was no summer camp. The training was arduous, but his past experience was useful. He had also become army-wise enough not to volunteer suggestions for improvements. When he received his brass bar as a second lieutenant, he was called into the Manpower office. There a lieutenant colonel had his file on his desk, and informed Buck that he was to be an officer in the Military Police. No response seemed to be expected, so Buck made none.

Buck learned his way around from the MPs in Fort Benning, and then was sent to Fort Lee. He became a first lieutenant before being shipped overseas to England, where he found himself near Canterbury, in Kent. He liked army life generally; he liked life in camp; and he liked the camp in Kent. He found that as an officer who was not preparing to lead troops into battle, his task was easier in some ways and more difficult in others. He decided to keep his suggestions for improving the camp to himself until he was more firmly into things.

In any case, he found enough time to tour around Kent, insofar as wartime transportation was available. He began to read English history, and as a consequence decided to visit each of the Cinque Ports; to see where Dickens wrote; to examine the old forts which still dotted the countryside; and to learn all that he could about nearby Canterbury Cathedral.

He was fascinated by the two Thomases—a Beckett and More. He tried to put himself in their places to see how he would have acted. He also found a good version of *The Canterbury Tales*, and found that being on the spot made it a good deal more meaningful to him.

On one of his visits he saw a sign on the gate of a seaside house that read "SPQR." He couldn't figure out what it meant. While he was pondering, he noticed a very attractive female officer—actually, a major—who glanced at the sign and then looked thoughtfully at the house. He decided to ignore the difference in their ranks, and asked her, "Do you know what that means?"

"Oh, yes. That is an indication that this is the property of the Roman Empire—'Senatus Populusque Romanus'—but I can't figure out what it is doing on the gate of a house on the bank of the English Channel, particularly since insofar as I know there is no Roman Empire left."

The upshot was that Buck and Major Wilkins went to the local library where the librarian was eager to tell them that this marked the spot where Caesar first landed in England.

They parted at the SPQR sign after exchanging names.

In the mail one day there was a personal letter addressed to him. Marvin, the problem eater, was now with a government agency (he didn't specify which) and coming to England. He knew that there were many shortages in England, and since he intended to visit Buck, asked him to specify what he should bring as a gift. In fact, he said, "You know that I wouldn't come without a gift for you, so if you don't want to get something you don't need, tell me something you do need."

Although England was a land of shortages, American army personnel didn't suffer. In fact, they were the source of supplies for the families of many girl friends. So Buck looked around his office, slapped his pockets, and tried to think of something he needed. Playing with his keycase, he noticed that it was worn—the edges were scuffed, and one of the hooks was bent out of shape. So when he wrote Marvin telling him how to locate him, he added, "If you must, bring me a new keycase."

When Marvin arrived, it turned out that he was with the Adjutant General's office, on an inspection trip. He was, of all things, an expert on nutrition. And, to Buck's surprise, despite his youthfulness, he was a full colonel. They had a pleasant reunion, during which Marvin ceremoniously handed Buck a beautiful keycase with his monogram on it. Buck was impressed with the concern that had evidently gone into preparing his gift. Marvin left the next day to continue his inspection trip.

The Military Police generally dealt with minor crimes, and only those in the army—the British Constabulary took care of non-army offenses. Occasionally the crime would be major—there were murders, rapes, mayhem, and even—once—a kidnapping. The Military Police's job was prevent crime if possible, and to apprehend the criminal if necessary. Judgement, sentencing, and punishment were not their concerns, these being handled by military courts.

Thus, Buck's job was mostly routine—record-keeping, making sure that supplies were adequate, personnel matters, and so forth. He handled it all adequately, and with time became a captain. But one day he had a caller from the WAC (Womens Army Corp), who turned out to be Major Marjorie Wilkins. He was delighted that she had found his number, and even more that she was calling him, but the thought died away as she explained she was calling on business. She told Buck that one of her soldiers had been raped by an army truck driver.

The story, as it unfolded, was that Shirley, the girl soldier, had been in London, and having missed the last train to Canterbury, was hitch-hiking together with three other girl soldiers heading in the same direction. An army truck picked them up. One girl left the truck at Rochester; two others got off at Faversham; while Shirley was to continue to Canterbury. On the way the truck driver said he was sleepy and needed a cup of coffee, and since he had a furnished room off the base, which was on the way, would she mind if he stopped for a moment? She agreed, and when they got to his house, he invited her in for coffee, to which she also agreed. Once in the house, he forcibly raped her, bundled her into the cab of the truck, dropped her off at the gate to the camp, and threatened to kill her if she reported him.

She was understandably hysterical, and almost in a daze, but she retained enough presence of mind to note down his license number. She was frightened, humiliated, and in pain, and she tried to hide her condition from her hut-mates. They finally wormed the truth out of her and reported it to the major. She wanted to know what steps to take.

Buck had no question. He called the motor pool and asked for the name of the driver of the indicated truck on the said night. They said they would check the license number and get back to him. Buck explained to the major that in the meantime it was imperative that the soldier swear out a complaint and agree to testify. The major took this as her responsibility, and said she would see to it.

It took three days for Buck's MPs to find the name and army address of the truck driver, plus his trip card which showed a trip only as far as Faversham. Getting the girl to agree to identify him and testify proved more difficult, because not only did she not want to have to face him again, but she was afraid of his threat—especially once he learned her name and location by her testimony. However, the major and her hut-mates convinced her that it was not only her duty to punish him, but to protect other girls.

Buck had him picked up and jailed the next morning, on her sworn complaint. The truck driver immediately denied rape, and said she had asked to accompany him home, and she had voluntarily undressed once there. A trial date was set, he was assigned a lawyer, and he was held in the stockade in the meantime.

A week later Major Wilkins again contacted Buck and said, with some repressed anger, that the girl had withdrawn the complaint, and would not say why. The major came over and showed Buck a copy of the signed form withdrawing the complaint, sent her by the truck driver's army lawyer.

Buck went to see Shirley, and found her alternately stubborn and withdrawn. He drew on his experience with campers and didn't mention the case to her, but asked her about her school, her post-school experience, her family, and other non-threatening subjects. Finally, he had a bit of luck. Her brother had been in the CCC. Buck talked about his experiences there, and she mentioned things her brother had said, and Buck at last felt that he could simply ask her why she had withdrawn her complaint.

Shirley explained that a secretary from the American Embassy in London had heard about her case and had come to see her. The secretary had explained that the Embassy knew about every American who was in trouble abroad, and it was this secretary's specific job to deal with all rape cases. But since as a civilian she had no standing in the army, she couldn't do anything about this case. However, having heard the story, she had come on her own to give her some personal advice, woman to woman.

The secretary said that in her job she had unfortunately had lots of experience in handling cases of American girls raped in England, and although she had no doubt that the soldier had been raped, she also wondered whether she knew what was in store for her. The truck driver's only defense would have to be that she had consented to, or even requested, sex.

Nor would it be her word against his. He would bring witnesses—friends of his, or paid witnesses—who would swear to the jury that they not only had slept with her, but that they had paid her for it. In other words, they would brand her a whore, and he would claim that her complaint arose from the fact that he refused to pay her price. She would obviously have no witnesses on her side. In addition, the British yellow press would love a story about an American girl soldier who was whoring on the side; and this would certainly be picked up by the American press, and get back to her parents.

At this point Shirley broke down and cried, and repeated that she wanted the complaint withdrawn. Buck didn't dare comfort her by holding her, and he just sat until she calmed down a bit. Then Buck said he understood her position and sympathized with her, but she should understand that both she and the truck driver were in the army. This would not be a civilian trial, but a court martial. There would be no jury. There would be no publicity. This would be a closed trial. And if the driver brought witnesses, their story would be checked as to dates, places, other witnesses, and so forth, so that they could all go to jail for perjury—and he would make sure they knew it in advance. He asked her to think about it for a few days, and to talk it over with the major once more. She agreed.

As he told her good-bye he asked, as though in an afterthought, for the name of the secretary who had come to see her. She said she hadn't asked, but, unexpectedly, she said she did know the name of the lawyer. It was Peterson. It seems that not only had the secretary come to see her, but she had persuaded her to go to the lawyer's office, in an army camp near Deal, to sign the form withdrawing the complaint.

Back in the office, Buck called the American Embassy. They were aghast at the idea of a secretary whose job it was to deal with rape cases. In any case, they knew nothing about this incident. Buck thought about this for a long time, and finally went to Deal to see Peterson.

Peterson had been a criminal lawyer in civilian life and evidently thought he had an airtight case. He greeted Buck very confidently. Buck explained that he was not part of the judicial system. His job was to investigate, charge, and arrest. And he was investigating a case of judicial fraud, suborning witnesses, impersonating an official of the United States Embassy, and threat. He felt that the lawyer's confidence was quickly evaporating.

Buck had thought very carefully about what he was going to say next. "I have all the evidence that I think I need before turning it over to the Judge Advocate's office, except one thing: Did the accused truck driver send the woman to impersonate a member of the Embassy staff, or did his lawyer? On that issue stands the question of who will be accused of these crimes."

Peterson evidently decided to try a bluff. "It is a lawyer's professional duty to try to defend his client with every means at his disposal. That's what I am doing. There may not even have been an impersonation. The girl soldier might have made it all up."

"Counselor," said Buck equably, "not only was there an impersonation, but I think I can easily put my hand on the one who instigated it. I am sure you are an expert in civilian law. I am not sure you understand military law. Three officers of the United States armed forces will decide this case—not a jury of twelve civilians. And those three officers will not decide on the basis of technicalities, but on what they believe to be the truth. Tell me, counselor, if the truck driver in the stockade raises the question as to how in the hell he could have contacted the bogus secretary, provided transportation to your office, and had a withdrawal of complaint form ready, while he was behind bars and only allowed visits from you, who do you think those officers are going to believe? By the way, if you give me the withdrawal of complaint form so the young lady can destroy it, you will be obviating a lot of complaints other than rape. What do you say?"

Peterson looked at his desk for a long moment and then said, "What you are saying isn't true. And even if it were, you couldn't prove it. The girl is lying and now she has no choice but to keep on lying. Unfortunately, lies go up the elevator while truth climbs the stairs. Since you are a Military Police officer, your very accusation that I tampered with witnesses is enough to destroy my career and ruin me as a lawyer both in the army and out, regardless of how the case comes out. But I have a duty to my client, to the law, and to myself. I'm not giving you the form."

"It doesn't really matter, counselor. She has agreed to testify that she signed the form in error, under coercion, or as a result of fraud, and the case will then go to trial. And your court-martial will follow. You lose either way. However, since you are a warrant officer, you have the opportunity to resign and at least avoid your personal unpleasantness. If you do not resign, I promise you that I will have you broken to buck private with a dishonorable discharge."

Peterson fiddled with his letter opener for a long time. Eventually, he sighed and said, "Okay, you are right. I lose either way, because the court will undoubtedly accept her word over his. She will appear as a lonely, frightened, away-from-home young girl, and he will be judged as a burly, experienced truck-driver. And you will then carry out your threat against me. .Nevertheless, as a matter of personal integrity, I'm keeping her waiver."

The truck driver appeared at the court-martial without a lawyer and drew only three years, since Shirley admitted that she had kicked off her shoes before doubling up her legs and sitting on them while drinking coffee. None of the presiding officers had daughters young enough to realize how common this had become, and thought the truck driver might have been a bit misled by this "undressing."

Buck looked back on this case as the most interesting incident that happened to him as an MP officer, and he was pleased with the way he had handled it. He credited himself with having understood the psychology of both Shirley and Peterson.

Major Wilkins thanked him profusely, and on impulse he asked if he could come over to her base and talk to her about it. She replied, very coolly, that he could come to her base, and they would talk, but she wasn't sure the case was all he had in mind. He congratulated her on her perspicacity.

Over time they found that they enjoyed each other's company, and it was clear to both of them that this was edging over from a purely platonic relationship. However, logistics was a problem. She lived in officer's quarters on her base, as he did on his, and privacy was almost impossible. Time became a problem, as she was scheduled to be shipped to a camp near Patrington, in Hull.

At last, he managed to get a room in a small hotel in Herne Bay. He registered, took the key, went to the nearby pub where she was waiting, and told her the room number. He then went back to the room, and she joined him there. They spent the weekend together, and she left on Sunday afternoon for her base. He wandered along the waterfront until evening, and checked out.

A few days later Marvin was again announced into Buck's office, but this time he came striding in, stood in front of Buck's desk, and demanded: "What did you do to me with those damned key-cases?"

Buck had no idea what he meant, and said so. Marvin explained. "When you wrote me to bring you a key-case, I assumed they were in short supply in England, so I bought eighteen key-cases. They are light, not expensive, and not dutiable. As I have been visiting around, I've been giving key cases to people that I want to impress, or to become friendly with. And, invariably, people look at the key-case, look at me, and say 'Thanks,' rather weakly. In fact, I began to feel ridiculous. Now I find that you can buy a key-case at almost any luggage store, department store, or even drug store—excuse me, chemist shop. So what was big deal about key-cases?"

Buck stopped laughing long enough to explain why he had asked for a key-case, and Marvin began smiling. He dropped six key-cases on Buck's desk, one after another, and with each one he said, "Stick this one up your ass." With that they went off to the officers' mess for lunch.

Despite the food shortages in Britain, American army officers ate well. In fact, the officers' mess in Kent had been an exclusive country club, and was still staffed by those workers who were too old for the army. When they began to order lunch, Buck was impressed with the way Marvin discussed dishes with the elderly waiter, who, in turn, seemed delighted to be serving someone who knew something about food. Marvin chose carefully, and he and the waiter discussed timing, sauces, and methods about each dish.

Waiting for the food, Buck said, "Marvin, I hope you won't take this too personally, but I remember when you weren't such an expert on food. At home you didn't eat anything, and at camp you ate like a horse. Of course, I understood the psychology of the situation, adolescent revolt and all that, but it is interesting to see how you still overcompensate."

"Buck," smiled Marvin, "you were a good camp director and you are probably an excellent MP, but as a psychologist you stink. My mother was not only the world's worst cook, she was also a health food addict before there were health foods. She served the vilest concoctions of herbs, barks, soybean curds, and other junk you can imagine. She was a divorcee and I was an only child, so I was the only one she could experiment on. I finally left home the day she served a conglomeration of leftover experiments, and when I asked what I was eating she said, in some exasperation, 'Call it hotsy-totsy. Put enough ketchup on it and you can eat it.'"

Buck began to wonder whether perhaps he should have studied some psychology before trying to use it.

When the war ended Buck was a major, and while waiting to be shipped home, wrote a long treatise on how the Military Police force could be improved. He never knew whether anyone even read it. Before leaving England, he decided to jump over to France to see his brother Leo, who had been in some of the heavy fighting and had a number of decorations. He pulled some strings to locate him, and when he did, he was astounded.

His brother had become a Catholic priest. In fact, he was so interested in meeting with some Polish nuns that he had no time to talk to Buck when he arrived. Leo wasn't interested in any form of religion, so it shouldn't have mattered to him that his Jewish brother had become not only a Christian, but a member of the clergy—but it did. He was surprised at his own reaction.

Once back in the States, Buck had no idea what he was going to do. He finally decided that having become so interested in English history, he would use the GI Bill to go to university. Before he got around to doing anything about it, though, he heard about the Peace Corps. That seemed made for him.

Marvin was now the head of Peace Corps recruiting. He didn't even look at Buck's record, lying on his desk, but said, "You'd be wasted out in the field, teaching Nigerians to grow better crops. We need you as part of the staff."

Buck explained that he did not want an office job, did not want to live in Washington, and preferred to be out in the field—the further out the better. Marvin refused to accept this, and spoke at length about the multiplier effect—that Buck's knowledge and experience could be spread through many volunteers, rather than being concentrated in one geographical area.

In short, he offered Buck the position of head of training. Again Buck explained he did not want an office job in Washington.

Marvin thought about that and said, "We are a new agency. We have much to learn

and much to do. I think we need some sort of training camp for volunteers before they go overseas—preparation for the various kinds of jobs they may have to do. Would you agree to set up such a camp and direct it?" Buck didn't hesitate a second.

Despite Buck's reluctance to do an office job in Washington, it was almost six months before he actually found himself directing a training camp in Louisiana, near Alexandria. He felt very much in his element, and put his experience to good use. He immediately put into effect some of the improvements he had learned in the Boy Scouts, the army, and the CCC.

One of Buck's tasks was to recruit staff for the camp, and among others, he interviewed a young man named Gus. Gus was big, both vertically and horizontally. He had been to social work school and knew all the jargon. He was very much at ease during the interview. He sat with his chair tilted back against the wall, with the front legs in the air. Buck found him acceptable, but before confirming it said, "Is there anything else about the job that you want to know; or is there anything else about yourself that you think I should know?"

Gus smiled, and said, "Well, I do think you should know that I have some trouble handling my feelings about authority."

Now Buck knew that as good psychological practice he was supposed to respond, "Now that we have both acknowledged your problem, we'll work on it together." He also knew that having said that, his authority would be nil. Gus would do whatever he wanted to, and explain everything away with, "I told you I had trouble accepting authority."

So instead Buck said, "And just what do you plan to do about your problem?"

The legs of the chair came down to the floor with a crash, and a less-at-ease Gus said, "I guess I'll try to handle my feelings."

"You'd better, or you'll be outside this camp on your ass."

He had no trouble at all with Gus, and he wondered if even a trained psychologist could have handled the situation better.

Although Peace Corps volunteers were interviewed in their home communities, Buck met with each of the volunteers as they came to the camp to try to determine their skills, weaknesses, desires and needs. One of his first interviewees was a young woman, rather heavy, dressed roughly. As he interviewed her, he became less and less impressed with her potential. At last, as a method of rejecting her gently, he said, "Tell me. If you were me, how would you describe yourself?"

She said, "Fat, sloppy, not very good-looking and only reasonably intelligent."

Buck couldn't believe how easy this was going to be. "So why should I accept you over a candidate who is trim, ambitious, hard-working and smart?"

"Because I am completely honest. I tell the truth as I see it and I don't make excuses."

"Delighted to have you with us, my dear," said Buck.

Among other candidates that Buck interviewed was a slight young man from California, named Gene. Everything seemed okay, and Gene was assigned to his dormitory, but that evening the person in charge of the dorm, Ernie, asked Buck to come over. Buck knew Ernie as a very solid, down-to-earth older man who usually handled all problems without needing help, so he went right over.

This is the story as Ernie related it:

The group in the dorm had gone for their first orientation session and after they left for their respective dorms Ernie checked around and in the meeting room found Gene still sitting there, strumming on a guitar, his luggage around him. Ernie asked him why he hadn't gone out with the rest of the group, and he replied that he had special permission to go to the dorms later. Could happen, so Ernie thought nothing of it.

However, after a few minutes the young man left, leaving his guitar behind, but came back half-an-hour later. When Ernie looked in on him, the fellow was picking at his guitar, but openly crying. As a very experienced housefather, Ernie went in and asked the boy if he could help him. At which, the boy began speaking broken German phrases. As Ernie tried to speak to him, the boy kept speaking a broken German—not only broken but, as Ernie, who knew German well, could ascertain—thoroughly mistaken. Suddenly, the boy grabbed his guitar and made for the door, saying—in English—that he was taking the train to New Orleans. As he said so, he broke out in loud sobs, and disappeared. At that point, Ernie decided he had better call Buck.

It was late afternoon, and the last train for New Orleans was about to depart, so Buck rushed to the station and went through the train, checking the faces of each passenger. His boy was not among them. There seemed nothing else to do, so, after notifying the police and the hospitals that he was the proper address if the boy turned up, Buck began a rather worried night.

Gene showed up the next morning, as normal as a sunrise, and Buck and Ernie decided to say nothing about the incident, that might have had to do with a girl or with parents, but to keep an eye on Gene.

A week later Ernie told Buck that he thought there was something wrong with the boy. Buck asked why, and Ernie said that at every meal Gene took off one shoe at the door of the dining hall, and came in wearing only one shoe. Wary of trying to understand psychology again, Buck said that maybe Gene's shoe hurt. Ernie replied perhaps, but in the middle of the meal, he goes to the door and puts the shoe on, taking the other one off. That, Buck agreed, might be construed as slightly odd.

In addition, Ernie said that when the boy was assigned to work in the kitchen, he simply walked out of the kitchen every time he was told what to do, returning in a quarter hour or so. This happened every time he was assigned a duty. Buck opined, like Alice, that it got curiouser and curiouser.

Buck asked Gene to come in to see him, and when he did, asked him about his trip to New Orleans.

"Oh," he said, "that was a mistake. I didn't take the train to New Orleans—I took the bus. When the bus stopped at Baton Rouge I started drinking a coke. At the next table I saw a colored man drinking beer, and since I've heard how colored people are discriminated against in the south, I decided I would show him we are not all like that, and that I would pay for his beer. However, I had heard that all colored people carry switchblades, and are very proud, so I was afraid that if I paid for his beer, he would be insulted and would kill me with his knife. The thought of being killed in a restaurant in Baton Rouge by a colored man was so sad that I started crying, and he came over and asked me what was wrong, and could he help."

Buck was amazed that Gene didn't even see the irony that climaxed his story—of the colored man offering to help him, instead of the reverse. Anyway, it seems he paid only for his coke and took the bus back to Alexandria.

"And what is this business about leaving the kitchen every time you are asked to do something?

"Oh, that is very simple. You see, they are testing me. They want to know if I will take orders from a woman, or whether I am the strong manly type who won't obey a woman's orders. So whenever a woman tells me what to do, I walk out."

Gently, gently: "Why do you think they are testing you?"

"Why, to see if I am the Adolf Hitler type, who won't take orders from a woman, or whether I am the Jesus Christ type, who is kind and meek. I think I like being Jesus better."

Easy, easy: "Have you had these feelings of being Hitler or Jesus before?"

"Sure, that's why I was in therapy."

"You were in therapy before you joined the Peace Corps?"

"Sure."

"Why didn't you tell us?"

"You didn't ask." (Again, an improvement to be made).

"What did your therapist say when you talked about joining the Peace Corps?"

"He thought it showed great strength on my part." (I'd like to meet that therapist some

day, thought Buck).

Very softly, carefully: "Tell me, how would you like to get out of all this—the kitchen, colored people, the Peace Corps—and go back to your therapist?" (He very carefully did not say "to your parents").

"But nobody should know."

Great relief: "Oh, no, no. Nobody will know. We'll say you are going to bring the next group back here."

"Hey, that would be great, wouldn't it?"

So Buck and Ernie escorted Gene to the plane for California. He balked at the last moment, but the comment that his psychiatrist had been alerted and was waiting for him was enough to overcome the problem.

Buck mentally wiped his forehead and waited for the next problem to arise. It came in six weeks, with the next group to arrive.

The housemother of a girls' bunk asked to see him. She reported that on an unannounced visit to the girls' area, she met one of the girls coming out of the shower room with a young man, both of them sharing one bathrobe.

Now this was in the early sixties, before the days of "doing one's own thing," and of personal morals being no one else's business. As the person in charge of the camp, Buck was responsible for everything that went on there. Newspapers were hungry, and parents were fearful, of sexual escapades in the camp, although the male and female sections were quite separate. This was not a prison camp, however, and there were no barbed wire or other kinds of fences.

So Buck invited the young lady in question to come to his office, and she showed up with her paramour. When Buck told her he wanted to talk to her alone, she said, "Anything you want to say to me, he can hear."

Buck said, "No. If you want to let him hear anything you say, that's your business, but I have the right to choose my audience."

Well, eventually he left the room, and before Buck could say anything, the girl exclaimed: "You've got nothing to say about it. We were married, and can do what we want to."

"You were married? When, where, and who was the minister?"

"Not by a minister. He is part of a group that doesn't believe in being bound by any religion. In his sect you just say to each other, 'I marry you,' and that's all that is needed."

"My dear," he said gently, "I'm afraid someone has been misinforming you. No matter what the cult believes, marriage in the United States must be preceded by a license, and then registered."

"Well, I don't care. If we're not married, then I'm going to marry him."

"Okay, that's also your right. Is your mother coming to your wedding?"

"She isn't going to know anything about it. We'll get married here and tell her later."

"How could you do that to your mother? You know she'll want to be present at her daughter's wedding."

"I don't care. We'll be married here."

"But, look. Here you'll go to the courthouse, and someone will say a few words that you won't understand, and you'll walk back out onto the street. There's no dignity, no joy, in that."

"I don't care. That's what we are going to do."

"But think. If you go home to get married you'll be married in a church. The church will be decorated with flowers, and you'll come down the aisle…"

"I don't care about all that formality."

"…and your friends will be there to kiss you and wish you well…"

"Doesn't mean a thing to me."

"...and in the next room there will be shelves and tables filled with the beautiful and expensive wedding presents that your relatives and friends have brought..."

"You know, maybe you're right. Maybe I shouldn't do this to my mother. I won't get married until I get back home. And I'm sure he'll follow me!"

"I truly hope so," said Buck, and with that the wedding plans were literally shelved.

Ben, one of the group leaders on the boys' side, was a solid citizen. He was built solidly, walked solidly, talked the same way, and didn't indulge in histrionics. So when Buck got a message from him that said, "I think you better come over here as soon as you can," he didn't hesitate. If it was a situation that Ben couldn't handle, Buck decided he'd better know about it.

When he got there, Ben told him that the group had arrived on time and settled in nicely. However, one young man had been unaccountably delayed, and arrived two weeks after the rest of the group. The next day a member of the group confided to Ben that he couldn't find his wallet. The next day one of the boys reported his watch was missing.

"What would you like me to do, Ben?" Buck asked.

"Oh, there's nothing for you to do about that. I took care of the matter. I handled it like we did in the Marines."

Migawd, thought Buck, he's probably declared "Code Red" on him. "And how's that?"

"I waited until three o'clock in the morning, then I came into the living quarters and ordered everyone out on the lawn, in their nightclothes and bathrobes—carrying nothing. I searched thoroughly, but found nothing. Then I invited the natural leader of the group into my room, and asked him pointblank if he had stolen the wallet and watch. He was shocked, and said of course he hadn't, and I told him I was sure he hadn't, and let him go.

"Then I invited another boy in, and asked him the same question, and he also said of course not, and I let him go. You see, I knew that as soon as they came back to the group, everyone would ask what happened, and they would say that I had simply asked them if they had stolen the material, and when they said no, told them they could leave.

"Then I invited the newcomer in. He came in very relaxed, sat down with one leg over the arm of the chair, and waited for my question. I said, 'You son of a bitch, I know you stole that wallet and watch, and I'm going to break every bone in your body until you tell me what you did with them.'

"He was scared to death, and told me he had hidden them down by the trees. I went and found them, and gave them back to the owners."

Buck was impressed. "Well, Ben, it sure looks like you handled it. Why did you need
me?"

"What should we do with the thief? He acts as though nothing happened. Everybody knows he stole the wallet and watch, so I told him he couldn't remain as part of the group, and he really seems to be puzzled by it. He doesn't seem to understand why he can't stay in this group."

At that point Buck knew he didn't have to be a psychologist to realize what they were dealing with—a real, classical, textbook kleptomaniac; someone who stole with no sense of guilt, of having done anything wrong. They would, of course, have to send him home, but until they did, where should he be? He couldn't stay with the group that knew about the incident, since everyone knew that he was a thief. Ben felt that they should persuade another Peace Corps training camp to take the kleptomaniac until they could arrange his passage home, and that's what they did. Buck simultaneously began the procedure to discharge the fellow and send him home—to California, of course.

While Buck was making these arrangements, Ben got a call from the other camp. Two transistor radios and a flashlight were known to be missing so far, and all members were making inventories of their personal possessions. They refused to keep him any longer.

There was a small hotel near downtown Alexandria, and Buck checked the boy in there. The owner of the small hotel had accommodated emergency situations for Buck before, but two days later she was close to hysterics. What he did with the sheets and pillowcases they never found out, but they finally shoved him aboard a plane headed directly for Los Angeles—without telling the pilot to count the wheels. And during the entire time, little innocent blue-eyes kept telling them he didn't know why they were doing this to him. And the tragedy was that he didn't.

This incident would have remained in Buck's memory for what it was, even if there had been no aftermath. But after the young man was returned to California, a wire was received by the national headquarters of the Peace Corps informing them that they were going to be sued for breach of contract in sending this boy home. On investigation, it turned out that he was known to his family as a kleptomaniac, and his father had deliberately sent him to the Peace Corps so that they would "make a man of him." Buck began to feel that there were vagaries of psychological defenses and reactions that even he didn't comprehend.

After these shocks, Buck felt that he was due a little luck, but he didn't believe it when Sissie turned up as a volunteer. He was torn between his professional self as director of the camp, and his personal self as a former lover of Sissie. He rationalized that if Sissie were a camper he had never known, he would leave her alone; but since they had a previous relationship, all he had to do was to be discreet.

He couldn't visit Sissie's bunk; he couldn't have her spend the night, or even any length of time, in his house; he couldn't be seen going out with her. So he fell back on time-honored methods, and took a hotel room—but far from Alexandria. They went to Natchez, whose name and history had always intrigued him. It turned out that Sissie knew a good deal about the War Between the States, and as they made love she talked them from Fort Sumter past Little Round Top to Appomattox Court House. He learned a lot on both counts.

Their next date was on a long holiday weekend, and they flew to Hot Springs, Arkansas, since it was a famous spa in those old days. Sissie talked about geology, marl, tectonic plates, aquifers, and artesian springs. Buck wished she would keep quiet for a little while, but when she stopped talking she also stopped making love, so he encouraged her to talk.

Once Buck thought he saw a familiar face in Hot Springs, but it was gone before he realized it.

He asked Sissie about her novel, and she said she really needed to know more about the Southwest, so on their next holiday they went to Houston, which Buck found just like any other big city, but Sissie spoke of Sam Houston, the Alamo, the Mexican War, and other lengthy topics—and Buck appreciated the length.

In Houston, too, Buck thought he glimpsed a familiar face, but thought little of it.

Buck had headed the Peace Corps training camp for four years, sending in reports on how to improve the Peace Corps every six months, when he was visited by the local sheriff, Noah Peterson. Thinking back on his own years as an MP, Buck was curious as to what the sheriff wanted. The name also had a familiar ring. When Peterson came in, complete in uniform with pistol and handcuffs, Buck recognized the lawyer from Deal.

Peterson looked at Buck for a long time before he said anything. Then he said, "I want to tell you something. That girl Shirley was lying. Because you saw her as almost one of your campers, you believed her and felt you had to protect her. She went with that truck driver willingly. She started undressing before she was through the doorway. She practically raped him. She asked him to come back to see her.

"Only when she missed a period and thought she was pregnant did she put on that rape act. She didn't intend to be an unmarried mother who had been dishonorably discharged; and she couldn't get an abortion in the army. So you and that major bought her story. Hell, you didn't even have a doctor examine her. And my client was in jail on her word.

"Then she got her period. It was just a few days late. So she withdrew the complaint. But that you wouldn't buy. So she made up the secretary story and the trip to my office, to support it. But you, on your white horse, insisted on coming chivalrously to the rescue. Well, she wasn't going to admit her fakery, especially under oath. She was ready to sacrifice both the truck driver and myself to stay clean. And she did.

"She used you. She understood your psychology so well that she played you like a fiddle. Like that 'brother in the CCC' twaddle—she doesn't even have a brother. I don't know whether you were playing along with her or not, but she used you. And the two of you ruined me. Instead of being a corporation lawyer on Wall Street, I bought a hardware store here in Alexandria. I piddle along. Sheriffs are elected locally, and the office isn't important enough to dig up a candidate's past, so what happened to me in the army doesn't matter to anyone any more. Except to me."

Buck had listened intently, but couldn't let himself believe what he heard. "And I suppose you have proof of this fairy tale," he said.

"I have," said Peterson. "The truck driver got three years, with a third off for good behavior, and the pre-trial time taken off, so he only served about eighteen months. Shirley visited him in jail to apologize and explain, and they eventually fell in love. She waited for him, and married him. He understood that she couldn't have admitted what she did without going to jail herself and he loved her, so he didn't complain. They have twins."

He took a picture out of his briefcase and laid it before Buck. He recognized both Shirley and the truck driver. The twins were gorgeous.

"Jesus," he began. "I didn't know…I mean, I'm sorry but…Oh, brother!"

"I believe you are sorry, but you are going to be more sorry. More sorry than you have ever been in your life."

Peterson took out some more photos and laid them on Buck's desk. Buck and Sissie checking in at the hotel in Natchez; Buck and Sissie coming out of the baths in Hot Springs with one towel between them; Buck and Sissie coming out of their hotel room in Houston, with the rumpled bed visible through the doorway.

"When I found out that you were heading the camp here I nearly went bankrupt tracing and trailing you. And it finally paid off. The Peace Corps is not going to continue using a camp director who sleeps with his campers. But that isn't the snapper. The Mann Act is still in force. It mandates twenty years in prison for anyone taking an unmarried female across a state line for immoral purposes—even if she consents. As an ex-lawyer, I tell you, you haven't got a chance. By the way, would you like to see Shirley's waiver? I have it right here."

When I visited my Uncle Buck in prison he had been there a year, and he said he had some good ideas on how to improve the place, but the warden wouldn't listen to him.

Uncle George

◆

UNCLE GEORGE

My Uncle George grew up poor. He scrabbled for a living for years. But then he found a money machine and became a millionaire. A rich millionaire. But, as everyone knows, money can't buy happiness.

Uncle George came to the States as an orphan refugee from Greece when he was just thirteen. He grew up with his adoptive family—my grandparents and uncles—during the Depression, and like the rest of the family, had to hustle to make a living. I don't mean hustle in the negative sense; I mean he really worked his butt off. He sold *Liberty* and *Saturday Evening Post* from door to door. He had a newspaper route. He sold white linen caps in the summer time, carrying a big box of caps on his back and going into garages, pool parlors, and anywhere else that men congregated. Of course, a lot of them thought the caps were just a cover (no pun intended), and that he was selling rubbers. A surprising number asked for rubbers. Nobody in those days said condoms. Maybe a doctor or a professor would use words like that, but rubbers were rubbers—Trojans, Pyramids, or any other brand. In most states it was illegal to sell them, which made them reasonably hard to get, and George could probably have made a living peddling rubbers, but he was not only basically law-abiding; he was afraid to be anything else.

George also found a wholesale house that sold sox, and always had a supply of "seconds", i. e., defective sox. He would buy these pretty cheap, and then put up a cardboard box on the sidewalk in the blue-collar part of downtown on Saturdays, when people got paid, and peddle them. He never claimed they were perfect.

However, on the Saturdays when there were football games (college teams always played on Saturday afternoons—there were no professional teams then) George closed the sock stand and sold "colors." These were badges with the teams' names, and short ribbons in the team colors, attached. Some of the badges had small tin footballs attached to the ribbons—these were more expensive, of course. The hawkers made wooden frames covered with cloth and pinned the badges to the cloth. They hung around hotel entrances, the parking lots and gates of the stadium, and other places where football fans might be found. The ideal customer was a well-dressed young man who had already had a few pre-game drinks, escorting a visiting girl from a hotel lobby. He could be shamed into buying the colors she supported, and overcharged without mercy, since he didn't want to seem a cheapskate.

George also sold fireworks. It was a custom peculiar to the South that not only were the Fourth of July and New Years' Day celebrated with fireworks, but so was Christmas Day. Knowledgeable young men like George would get a supply of fireworks on consignment from a wholesaler before each of these holidays, and sell them from makeshift stands for whatever the traffic would bear. They paid the wholesaler his price, but kept all profits for themselves.

These activities did not make George rich, of course. They simply helped himself and his adoptive family to get through the bad times. And these really were bad times. Whenever George and his friends would happen to see wealthy people they would conceal their jealousy by assuring one another, "Well, they may be rich, but I bet they aren't happy."

At the end of high school, when most of his friends were looking for and taking jobs, George enrolled in the state university. Not many young men in his position could do so, but he had it figured out as a business proposition. Not only did he enroll in the university, he also joined a fraternity—an expensive business. As a fraternity brother, he quickly got the laundry concession from all the fraternities and sororities on campus, making a commission on every load the local laundry handled. He also became the agent for the pin and ring company that made the required items for fraternities and sororities, and he became the campus representative for a number of magazines—mostly Esquire and similar journals. Before graduation each year he rented all the gowns and mortarboards available, and in turn rented them out at a somewhat higher rate.

He introduced pizza, which was just becoming popular in America, to the campus, opening a pizza stand that became the "in" place to go. He hired university students to work in the stand, getting a percentage of their tips (he paid no salaries—indeed, some students paid him for the job because of the tips involved). For a short time he became a bookmaker on college sports, off-loading the bets to an off-campus syndicate and only making a percentage. But he didn't like the looks of some of the members of the syndicate, and since bookmaking was illegal, he dropped it.

He became the editor of the yearbook, getting a commission from the photographer and a kickback from the printer. He was instrumental in having the "beanies" worn by freshmen changed, since he held the agency for the manufacturers of the new type. Enormous belt buckles with the university's insignia on them became the rage, after all the members of George's fraternity started wearing them. They received them free, of course, since George had the exclusive agency for all the others sold.

Strangely enough, George also found time to study. He attended classes sufficiently, if not religiously, and read the assigned material. He was fascinated by history, and began to focus on modern European history, and—naturally—Greek history, which is hardly a "snap" subject.

He also began to study Greek, since he had forgotten most of what he knew when he came. He had a problem when, after six weeks, he found he was studying ancient Greek literature instead of modern Greek language, but he eventually found the right class.

When the United States entered World War II, George was a junior and deferred as a college student. He had no objection. When he graduated, however, he did not opt for graduate school and continued deferment, but allowed himself to be drafted, because by this time George had become a Greek patriot, and earnestly hoped to be sent to Greece. Unfortunately for his dreams of liberating Greece from Hitler and Mussolini, he was sent to Alaska. The American army never set foot on Greece.

When the war ended the human situation in much of Greece was desperate, and Greek War Relief came into being. This was a humanitarian organization to raise money and material to relieve suffering in Greece. George applied for a job with the organization, and was assigned to Long Island. He didn't want to leave Atlanta, but there weren't enough Greeks concentrated in any one place in the south to make fund-raising efficient. His office was in Mineola. There were Greek-Americans scattered all over Long Island, and his responsibility was Nassau and Suffolk counties.

He had an office and a secretary, got reimbursed for his travel costs, and made a modest salary. He traveled over his two counties, making contact with people who came from Greece, or whose parents came from Greece, soliciting donations in cash and in kind for Greek war orphans (at least, they were his major pitch). In time, he found that non-Greeks could also be approached on a purely humanitarian basis, and he concentrated on manufacturers, wholesalers, and others who might be inclined to give material more readily than money.

George found a furnished sub-leased studio apartment on Clinton Street, complete with a security door and an intercom system to each apartment. He particularly liked the small balcony, although it looked out over the parking lot. He didn't think he could afford the rent being asked, but applied anyway, in hope. The owners—a middle-aged couple—seemed

delighted to see him. He later learned that they had seen a steady stream of
what they considered undesirable tenants, including a teen-age unmarried
mother, a jazz musician who seemed stoned when he talked to them, a gay
couple who had a nasty argument in front of them, a Polish refugee whose
English they couldn't understand, and a coarse-talking woman accompanied by her parole officer. Consequently, when George told them he could-
n't afford the rent they were asking, they reduced it immediately. All the
details were settled and George asked when he could move in.

"We're going to Florida two weeks from today. You can move in the
day after."

"Oh, no. I can't wait two weeks. You see, I've been living for almost a
month now with a girl cousin in her one-room apartment. We both
find it most uncomfortable. I just can't continue to do that for another
two weeks."

"But we don't plan to leave for two weeks."

"I didn't realize that. I assumed from the ad that the apartment was
available immediately. I'm sorry—I just can't wait two weeks. If I can't
get the apartment within the next day or two, I'll have to look elsewhere. I can't live with my cousin for another two weeks."

They both looked at him. He was wearing a conservative business
suit and a quiet tie. His hair was not long, and he was carrying an
impressive-looking briefcase. They retired to the kitchen to discuss the
situation. When they returned, the man said, "Okay. You can move in
day after tomorrow. We'll go live for two weeks with a cousin of ours."
Which proves that, in a way, everything is relative.

In his work George was constantly surprised, not by the fact that
many people responded generously, but by the kinds of things they were
willing to contribute. He accumulated a carload of wooden toilet seats,
since they were being replaced by plastic. The owner of a string of trick-
novelty shops offered him a supply of false moustaches and exploding
cigars. Dog food, cardboard cartons, plastic slip covers for furniture,
vases, and art deco bookends were among the items offered in quantity,

as well as more than one used station wagon. At first George was inclined to refuse useless items, but the home office instructed him to take everything. Anything useless in Greece could be sold for something, somewhere, somehow, and the money used for the cause.

George's first entry into the world of fund-raising was far from the field of history that he had studied, and he couldn't believe some of the things he encountered. During his second week on the job he visited a very wealthy Greek importer who had built a replica of the Parthenon on his estate on the North Shore. Mr. Grykos showed George around the estate, explaining in detail the construction of the replica. He also pointed out his small private zoo, in which he had most of the animals native to Greece.

When they returned to the house, George explained the situation current in the Greek villages, the devastation caused by the war, and the needs of the population. He concluded by asking for help for the children, since he had found that this was the most effective appeal.

Grykos replied, "Children, hum? Not very interested in children you know. My wife and I never had any children. But there is a zoo in Athens, isn't there? Tell me, do you think the zoo could use some help?"

"Mr. Grykos, I am sure everything in Greece today could use some help, but we are talking about children who will die of cold and starvation unless they get immediate help. Anything that you could contribute would be appreciated."

"Are you in touch with Greece?"

"My office is."

"Maybe you could find out for me what the situation is in the zoo. I wouldn't want the animals to go hungry."

George had been taught never to lose his temper with a contact, even if the answer was negative, but this time he could not control himself.

"Mr. Grykos," he said, "we will put the children in cages if that will induce you to help them."

"Oh, no, no. Wouldn't want to do that. But find out about the zoo for me, will you?"

When George reported this to the New York office his superior, whom he knew well, said, "Idiot! Get all the money you can for the zoo. And we'll send it to the zoo. And we'll get a receipt to show Grykos. And the zoo will give an equivalent amount for the children. These are called fungible funds."

George had never heard the term before, but he realized the office was right. He had a picture of the zoo sent to him, and with it he pried a sizeable amount of cash out of Mr. Grykos.

At one time George was told to concentrate on blankets—there was an urgent need for blankets as winter approached in Greece. George considered this no problem—one of the generous financial contributors was a manufacturer of blankets.

George made an appointment, and when he arrived made his pitch—the cold, the orphans, the winter, the poverty. He asked for at least a carload of blankets, and more if possible.

The blanket manufacturer listened politely, turned his cigar in his mouth, and said, "No."

George was used to first refusals, and repeated his pitch, with variations, including the fact that the man had given generously previously.

Again: "No."

"But Mr. Pappas, why not?"

Pappas thought a moment and said, "Because I think the government of Greece is leaning too far to the left."

"But Mr. Pappas, we're talking about human need, not politics. The poor and the children aren't responsible for what the government is doing."

"I'll tell you a story," said Pappas:

"Years ago Julius Rosenwald gave a million dollars to the University of Chicago, and they were not only grateful, but asked him if could induce his friend, Cyrus McCormack, to do the same. So Rosenwald invited McCormack to lunch in his private club atop a Chicago sky-scraper. The meal was sumptuous, and ended with apple pie topped with cheddar cheese, and coffee. Then Rosenwald said, 'Cy, I've just given a million dollars to the University of Chicago. I set it up as a foundation, so tax-wise, it cost me almost nothing. They're very grateful, and they've asked me to get you to do the same. What do you say?'"

"Without thinking McCormack said, 'Nope.'"

"Rosenwald said, 'Cy, why not? You're richer than I am; you're also a graduate of the University of Chicago; they really need the money; you can set it up so that it will cost you almost nothing.'"

"Again McCormack said, 'Nope.'"

"Exasperated, Rosenwald said, 'Give me one good reason why you won't do it.'"

"McCormack looked around the room, and then down at the table, and finally said, 'Because I didn't like the cheese on the apple pie.'"

"Rosenwald exploded: 'Cy, I'm talking about a million dollars for the University of Chicago and you're bothering me about the cheese on the apple pie?'"

"'Let that be a lesson to you,' said McCormack. 'When a man doesn't want to give, *any* excuse will do.'"

"So," concluded Pappas, "I don't like the policy of the government of Greece."

"I see," said George, chastened.

"But that's not why I'm not giving you blankets," said Pappas, smiling. "I just sold out to a conglomerate, so I don't own any blankets. But it was a good financial deal. I'll give you a check and you can buy blankets. I'll see that you get them wholesale."

After that, "the cheese on the apple pie" explained a lot to George as he continued his fund-raising activities. He wasn't making much, and he lived frugally, but he was happy. He believed in what he was doing, and he was doing it well. Although many of the people with whom he came in contact were well-to-do, and some were wealthy, he didn't think they were any happier than he was.

Among other potential contributors, George visited a Mr. Skouras, who owned a small—by Greek standards—shipping line; only twelve ships. As he waited in the outer office for his appointment, a woman whom he judged to be roughly his own age came out of the inner office. The secretary's back was to her, and to George's surprise, the woman stuck out her tongue at the secretary's back. She saw George watching her, and smiled.

"You're new here, aren't you? I haven't seen you before. What is your job here?"

George explained that he didn't work there, but had an appointment with Mr. Skouras.

"What about?"

"Well…", he floundered, "it's…, I really don't think I can discuss it before I see Mr. Skouras."

"I'm Mrs. Skouras. You can tell me."

He shot a look at the secretary. She was studiously examining her fingernails. He realized that there was a cue there, but he also didn't see how he could evade the question, so he tried to compromise. "I work for Greek War Relief."

"Oh, so you want a contribution. Believe me, friend, you've got your work cut out for you. He is tight. I'd help you if I could, but he's even tighter with me."

"Thank you, but I'll…."

"You're kinda cute. I tell you what. I'll try to help you. Where can I reach you?"

Before he could reply the secretary cut in. "Mr. Skouras will see you now," and she rose and opened the door, giving him no chance to do other than say good-bye to Mrs. Skouras.

Contrary to what Mrs. Skouras had said, George found Skouras quite receptive to the idea of helping.

When George rose to go, he said, in the way of small talk, "I met your wife outside."

To his surprise, Skouras' smile disappeared, and he seemed to swallow hard. "It was a pleasure meeting you," he said stiffly, "and I hope my contribution will be helpful. Good-bye."

That night George had a phone call: "Hi. I met you in my husband's office this afternoon. Remember me?"

"How did you get my number?"

"Easy. I called Greek War Relief headquarters in Manhattan. Are you busy? I can call back."

"No, it's all right. What can I do for you."

"I have two tickets to the opera Friday night. My husband finds unexpectedly that he can't go, and suggested that you might be interested, since the opera is *Medea*, and you are Greek. Would you like to go?"

"That's very nice of you and your husband, but I don't know much about opera."

"Then it is time you learned. Meet me under the marquee of the Met at eight Friday night. Oh, don't eat dinner beforehand. And this is not an opening, so formal dress is not required." She hung up before he could respond.

He wasn't sure he would recognize her again among the people waiting to meet others under the marquee, but he did. He had seen *Medea* many times as a play, and heard it read at poetry readings, but he was entranced with the opera. At intermission, she led him to the balcony dining room where she had ordered dinner in advance. The arrangement was especially for opera-goers—those who found it too early to eat beforehand, and too long to wait until it was over. The food was served with the assurance that they would not be late for the next act.

He was completely caught up in the story, and when she found his hand and clasped it during the tense moments, he found it quite normal. He joined in the cheering at the end of the opera, and walked out feeling he had discovered a new dimension to life. They had coffee at

Ballons. While they waited to be seated, he learned that her first name was Millie, and that she had also come to the States as a refugee, although from Holland. She was two years older than he was, and had never been to university.

He was surprised when she told him not to call a taxi to take her home, and he assumed she lived so far away that a subway or a bus, or both, were involved. However, she walked him across the street from Lincoln Center and through the lobby of One Lincoln Plaza. He didn't know whether to say good-night at the elevator, or to accompany her to her door, but decided the latter was probably indicated.

At the door, she said, "Please come in."

He looked at his watch and said, "But won't your husband…?"

"This is my home," she said, "not my husband's."

It took him a moment to catch on. "You mean you and your husband have more than one home?"

"No. Come on in, and I'll explain it to you."

He came in cautiously, nevertheless expecting to see Mr. Skouras looming in the doorway.

She was pouring drinks at the small bar, and without looking around said, "Ouzo? Or have you become too American for that."

"To tell you the truth, I don't like any of the drinks that come from anise. I don't even like licorice candy. If you have Scotch, that will do. If not, Bourbon."

She handed him his drink, kicked off her shoes, undid the two top buttons of her blouse, and curled her legs under her on the sofa. She patted the seat next to her. "Sit down. You look like you've been to a funeral, not to an opera."

He was bewildered, cautious, frightened—and interested. He sat down, keeping a decent space between them.

"My husband and I are separated," she said. "We have been for three years. He won't give me a divorce because then I'd get half his precious shipping line, but he supports me in a manner to which I've become accustomed. I am a free agent, and so is he. So stop fidgeting."

He wasn't aware that he had been playing with the coins in his pocket to relieve some tension.

"You're not married," she continued. "I found that out. You are the right age for me. You seem like a gentleman. I like being with you. I don't imagine you are a virgin. Finish your drink and let's go to bed."

He was surprise, flattered, a bit eager, and very surprised. But he went to bed with Millie.

The result left him vaguely unhappy. He was used to being the seducer, including the tentative moves, the explorations that went a little further each time, the feeling that he was succeeding in convincing her because he was irresistible—in short, a feeling of triumph. But she was both anxious and ravenous, and he felt he was being used for her needs, not his.

In the morning, as he was getting dressed, she said, "When shall we two meet again, my delightful stud?"

"I'll call you," he said.

"Ah. Post-coital guilt. 'Don't call me, I'll call you.' You'll get over it. And you'll call me. The number is on the phone." And she pulled the sheet over her face and turned away.

He didn't call her. Her reference to him as a stud particularly galled him. He decided that he really didn't like her.

The next day he was asked by the main office to go to a meeting of the United Fund budget committee in Hempstead. As a member organization of the United Fund, Greek War Relief received an allocation. The size of the allocation was decided by each local United Fund office, and hearings by the budget committee ostensibly decided on the size of the allocation. "Ostensibly," because in actuality the influence of big givers was considerable, and their favorite cause was often funded out of proportion to the actual comparative needs.

When George got to the meeting, he found that several other overseas relief organizations were represented. At the instigation of the Armenian representative, they all met before the meeting, and the Armenian pointed out that if they each touted the merits of their respective organizations, it would have limited impact, but if they all simply asked for more overseas relief, the cumulative impact might redound to everyone's benefit. Consequently, they all agreed that they would each talk about overseas needs, rather than their respective organizations.

Then came the question as to the order of speakers. Everyone wanted to be last. There was no question in anyone's mind that the last speaker would double-cross the rest. Once consciousness concerning overseas relief had been raised, he would plump for his own organization. They decided to draw straws, and George was selected as the first speaker. The Armenian, by some method that he never detected, managed to be last.

George made his speech to a largely apathetic audience, and resumed his seat at the long table. After the remaining overseas organizations had made their pitches, the Armenian rose and, as expected, launched into a spirited pitch for Armenian relief alone. As he did, someone sitting across from George slipped him a note, on which was written, "Are you the same George that I knew as a fraternity brother?"

George looked across the table and recognized the advertising editor of the yearbook. He nodded his head enthusiastically, and his friend motioned toward the door with his head. They went out together, arms across each other's shoulders. George shot a look at the Armenian speaker. He had halted in mid-address and was watching them, wordlessly. George chuckled inwardly. He realized, and the speaker evidently realized, that a friend on the budget committee is worth infinitely more than the last slot as a speaker.

When the greetings and reminiscences were over outside the meeting room, George said, "What are you doing now? Boy, you must be rich to be on the budget committee. Only big givers rate that privilege."

"Big giver? Hah! I'm taking a masters in social work at Adelphi University, and I'm observing the meeting as an assignment in community organization."

Let the Armenian dangle in the wind, thought George, as they went off together to the nearest bar. They had a few beers while they talked about college days, and then a margarita to finish off the evening. George decided to walk from Hempstead to Mineola, which was a long walk, but he figured it would sober him up, and he needed the exercise anyway.

When he got home it was almost one in the morning, and when he came in, he found the lights on. He immediately thought of burglars, but a familiar voice from the sofabed said, "I'm ready, willing, and able. Where are you?"

"Millie! How did you get in here?"

"I told the super that I was your sister; that you had given me the key; and that I had lost it. No problem."

"Millie, you can't stay here. You'll have to go. I'll call you a cab."

"You can call me anything you want to, but I'm not getting out of bed. Now come on over here and let's screw."

He was more astounded than angry. He had never heard a girl use that word. He thought they weren't even supposed to know it. It certainly didn't seem cute to him, but coarse. "I'm not coming to bed with you, and we aren't going to screw. You get out of here, or I'll call the police."

"What's the matter? Didn't we have fun the other night? Why are you being so sticky?"

"Millie, the other night is over. All our nights are over. I don't want to sleep with you. I don't want to see you again. Now get out of that bed and get out of here."

"No way, lover. You'll get over your hangup here in bed. C'mon, let's start."

"Out, Millie, out!"

"Not until you come to bed."

"Millie, I'm serious. You have to get out of here."

"No, I don't."

He felt ridiculous. He could just imagine the face of a policeman being ordered to get a woman out of his bed. He certainly didn't want to physically put her out in the hall—and he wasn't sure he was strong enough if she resisted. He thought of calling her husband, but rejected that out of hand. At last, feeling like a fool, he went into the bathroom and collected his toilet articles; went to the bureau and took clean underwear; and started for the door.

"Where are you going?"

"If you are staying here, then I'm staying somewhere else."

"Don't be stupid. Come on to bed."

He spent the night in a motel, and went directly to his office the next morning.

During the day he had a call from the national office. It seems that the Armenian organization had been in touch and suggested that perhaps they should combine efforts on Long Island in some way and pool results. George laughed out loud. The office wanted to know George's reaction, since the call seemed to be in response to the budget committee meeting. Controlling himself, George suggested they accept. If the Armenian succeeding in getting more money on the basis of being the last speaker and split it, then George meeting a friend would have paid off for his organization. His boss never knew the details, but assumed George had been instrumental in arranging the split, and that polished George's image a bit. Queens was added to his territory.

During his visits around the Island George had found that recent immigrants from Greece were too busy becoming Americans to relate to their Greek background. He also found that their children, who were still seen as Greek-Americans, were not very interested in Greece, or at least, not interested in being seen as interested in Greece. They were still fighting to maintain an all-American image. But the third generation were secure enough as Americans to be interested in their roots. He remembered Hansen's Law from his sociology classes: "What the grand-parents wanted to forget, the grandchildren want to remember."

He suggested to the office that a periodical about Greece, in English, might be useful. The third generation, who were beginning to take over from their parents, did not speak or read Greek as a rule. The bulletin could contain the kind of news that didn't get into the daily press, as well as the derivation of names, nostalgic bits about Greek cities, Greek recipes, and so forth. A representative of the national office explained to George that it was a good idea, but that Greek War Relief was a tax-exempt organization whose money could only be used for direct relief.

However, if George wanted to publish such a periodical, the office would make its mailing list available to him, and buy space to advertise the organization. George promised to think it over, and by the end of the day had already made some inquiries concerning printing, mailing and clerical costs. These would be his major expenses, and getting the initial money would be a problem.

When he came in that evening he went right to the super and told him that he was to let no one into his apartment, no matter what story they told. "Does that include your sister?" asked the super.

"I don't have a sister."

The super looked puzzled but George didn't explain. George tipped him to make sure he'd follow instructions.

He slept well that night.

His head was full of plans and questions about publishing when he entered the office. His secretary nodded toward his door and said, "Someone is waiting for you."

Millie was ensconced in his chair, fiddling with his letter opener. "I missed you. Why didn't you call?"

George took a deep breath, controlled himself, and said, "Millie, I am not interested in you. I do not want to see you. You must leave me alone. Can't you understand that?"

"I'm interested in you. I want to see you. I will not leave you alone. Can't you understand that?"

He sighed. "I am not going to let you continue to pester me. And I am not going to change my life to get away from you. I swear to you that no matter what you do, I am not going to give in to you. Now go away and let me work."

"I'll just sit here while you work. I like to look at you."

"Get out of my office! Do you want me to call the police?"

"I love it when you get mad. And it won't do you any good to call the police. They won't make me get out—they don't know who you are, who I am, whose office this is, nothing. They'll tell you they are not your employees. You'd have to swear out a complaint against trespassing before they'd do anything, and you wouldn't do that because you wouldn't want your fund to get that kind of publicity. So you see, I have the upper hand. You will eventually give in to me."

George turned on his heel and left the office. "I'm going to make some visits," he said to his secretary. "Take messages from whomever calls."

"What about her?" His secretary nodded toward his office.

"Forget her. She can stay or leave. As Rhett Butler said, 'Personally, my dear, I don't give a damn.'"

George's goal was Grykos' home on the North Shore. The organization had decided to raise money by holding an art exhibition, and wanted the use of a site that would itself be an attraction. George thought that Grykos might be induced to show off his zoo and—incidentally—let some art be hung.

As George mentioned showing off the zoo Grykos became excited, and readily agreed to let people take tours of the house, and see the art which would be exhibited there. As a preliminary, George asked if he could wander around and get an impression of what could be done where.

Since bulls figured prominently in Greek mythology, Grykos had several bulls, included some Brahmins, in the lower pasture. As George came by, he noticed what seemed to a child bundling hay into feeding troughs. When he came closer, he found that it wasn't a child, but a young lady wearing jeans, boots, and a workshirt. She was so thin as to seem delicate, and much smaller than George. He was surprised that Grykos would hire a woman, and particularly such a small, unmuscular woman to take care of his animals.

As soon as she saw him watching her, she stuck the pitchfork into the bale of hay and started walking away. He liked the way she walked, and he particularly liked the behind he saw in the tight jeans, so he called to her.

"Don't quit because of me. I'm just a visitor. I didn't mean to upset you." He caught up with her.

Her voice was so low he could hardly hear her. "I didn't quit because of you, and you didn't upset me. Those bulls eat less than people think they do, and I eat more than people think I do. It's time for my mid-morning snack."

He sat with her while she ate a sandwich, an apple, a banana, another sandwich, and a chocolate bar. He found out that her name was Lily, that she didn't like to be called Lil, and that she didn't work on the estate. She was the daughter of the gardener-cum-animal keeper, and was helping out that day because her father had to go to the dentist. He also found out that she lived in Alberton, which was almost walking distance from Mineola. She was a student at Hofstra, studying for a master's in special education, and was an amateur painter. He gave her a ride home, and she invited him in for coffee. He had coffee and a slice of carrot cake. She had three cups of coffee, three slices of cake, and some chocolates from a very fancy box. He felt very comfortable in her presence.

As they talked, he told her about himself, and even about the periodical he was planning if he could swing it. She said, "You'll need a printer who will give you credit. My younger brother Murray is just trying to start a printing business—maybe the two of you can work something out."

He was as delighted with her interest as he was with her advice, and went back to the office to start planning the art exhibition with a lighter heart.

When he walked in, his secretary looked up and motioned toward his office. He understood her to mean that Millie was still there. She was asleep with her head on his desk. He was in a quandary. He didn't want to involve the police, but he did want his office back. Then he remembered that the building had a security officer. The latter understood the situation to the extent that George explained it to him—that there was someone who wouldn't leave the office, and needed to be escorted out. The building contained a number of services whose clients sometimes became threatening, if not violent, and the security officer was familiar with such problems.

He came into the office with George, and turned to him in surprise when he saw that the offending person was a sleeping woman. But with George's reassurance he woke her, told her she would have to leave, and almost frog-marched her to the door. She made no resistance—indeed, one would almost think she was used to it.

If he could get credit from the printer, there remained the problem of money for postage and for getting the addresses typed. He hesitated to go to anyone he knew through the organization, feeling it would be unethical exploitation of his position, but he finally got so desperate that he asked his boss if it would be all right. He was told that as long as he made it completely clear that the organization was not involved, they would not object.

He decided on Mr. Pappas for his request, and Pappas was immediately amenable. George was curious as to why Pappas yielded so readily to his request, and asked him.

"I've watched you collect for Greek War Relief. I think you really care. And I think you are completely honest. I am sure you could make more money elsewhere, but you have chosen to do something you believe in. Look, I wanted to be a writer, but I didn't have the guts to go through the starving genius bit, so I went into business. I'm successful—I'm even rich, but I'm not sure I wouldn't have been happier as a writer— even an unsuccessful writer. So if I can help you do what you want to do, that's enough for me."

George felt more complimented by the comment than by the easily-acquired loan.

He turned his attention to the art exhibition, and found that he had taken on a full-time job of contacting artists, agents, and studios; insurance companies; cartage companies; and others. After surveying the enormity of the job before him, he made a decision. He called a number of art schools and explained that the organization was planning a benefit exhibition of never-shown artists —if students and alumni were willing to bring and mount their own work, and donate half the proceeds of any sales to the organization, they could place one item each. There would also be a prize for the work judged best. He thus reduced his own work to insurance, advertising, and collecting.

He felt good about his decisions until he walked into his house that night and found Millie sitting in the hall with her back against his door. "How in the hell…?"

"Oh, you're so stupid. That's why I like you. Don't you know that all you have to do in an entrance hall like yours is to ring all the bells? Someone is always waiting for someone, and opens the door without asking. Let's go in and talk about me and you."

"Millie," he shouted in exasperation, "there is nothing to talk about. Just leave me alone. Get out of here."

The upshot was that he again spent the night in a motel, and the next day he got in touch with the organization's lawyer. With some embarrassment he explained the situation and asked what legal remedies he had. The lawyer explained that the best thing would be to get a court order against harassment, but that he would need to prove harassment, and for that he would need witnesses. He counted up: The super, the secretary, and the security guard. The lawyer said it might be enough, but it would better if he could field about five witnesses. This made it a strategic problem. He never knew when or where Millie would show up, so he couldn't plant people to be witnesses.

Millie solved half his problem for him as he left his office with Lily's brother, with whom he had been discussing printing. She joined them and said, "My car is here. I'll give you a ride home." She pointed to a chauffeured stretched-out limousine that was obviously rented. George didn't introduce her to Lily's brother, and said, "Sorry. We have business to discuss."

"Oh, he can come, too. We'll drop him off wherever he likes."

"Millie, leave us alone. We don't want company."

"Well, he may not, and you may not, but I do. C'mon, get in, I won't bite you—not here, anyway."

Lily's brother looked bewildered at this exchange, and even more so when George hurried him across the street. When they had turned the corner and Millie was safely out of sight, George steered him into the Jack-in-the-Box on the corner and sat him down. He explained the situation, and told Murray that he might need him as a witness. Murray thought it awfully funny, and said that if he were a bit older, he might try to take Millie off George's hands.

"I wish someone would," said George, fervently.

"I don't guess you want Lily to know about this."

"On the contrary, I think she should. But I'd rather tell her myself."

George couldn't get Lily on the phone but understood from Murray that she was at Hofstra all day and at a painting lesson until nine. George knew that he could wait until the next day to call her, but suddenly realized he would like to see her as soon as possible, so he went to her house at nine and waited outside for her to come home. For a horrible moment he thought he might be acting like Millie, but banished the thought.

Lily was surprised to find George waiting for her, but when he said he had to talk to her, she opened the door. As he unfolded the story of

Millie, (leaving out the details of their night together) Lily was eating an overstuffed corned beef on rye sandwich and drinking a celery tonic. She took his story very seriously. "So you need one more witness? Wait a minute."

She went into the next room and George heard her telephoning. When she returned she said, "My father is coming by and will go home with you in case she is there now. If not, he'll meet you at your place every night for the next three nights."

"Your father? What must he think of me?"

"He thinks you're being victimized, although neither of us can figure out why. Want some ice-cream?"

When George and Lily's father got to the apartment, no one was there, and after having a cup of coffee, the latter got up to go. He looked toward the balcony door, looked again, and motioned to George. On the balcony a rocking chair was going up and down methodically, and in the chair was Millie. With Lily's father as his witness George found that she had used a light grappling hook on a fishline to pull the swing-ing end of the fire escape down, and a board to get from the neighbor-ing apartment's balcony to his.

He spent the night with Lily's father, and the next day had the lawyer ask for a court order to protect him from Millie's harassment. The judge wanted depositions from the witnesses, rather than appearances, and by running around all day, George got these together. The next day he was armed with a court order forbidding Millie to come within a hundred yards of him.

For the first time he was delighted to see Millie in his office the next day, and with both his secretary and the security guard as witnesses, handed her a copy of the court order. "I hope you realize," he explained, "that if you come within a hundred yards of me I can have you arrested and jailed. Now please get out and leave me alone."

"You are a stubborn bastard," she said equably, "but I am even more stubborn. I always get my man. You'll see."

He worked on both the art exhibition and plans for the new periodical that day, and for the first time was not worried that night about Millie bothering him. He went to see Lily to tell her of the new situation, and ran into a new complication.

Lily wanted to enter one of her pictures in the exhibition and to compete for the prize. George explained his quandary: If she won the prize, it would look like favoritism; if she didn't win, she might hold it against him. He found she could also be stubborn. It was her right to enter a picture, and he had no right to try to stop her.

He sighed, and agreed. But he wasn't sure he wasn't being disloyal by hoping she wouldn't win. She flourished the remains of an eclair at him in triumph.

The art exhibit was a success. Not a lot of money was made from sales of the paintings, although some of them seemed surprisingly good, but the organization garnered a lot of publicity, George was congratulated on his administrative skills, and the museum director who acted as judge bought one item for the museum. However, the nicest part was that Lily did win the prize, and even nicer was the fact that she had painted one of Grykos' bulls, which made him so happy he bought her painting. George was sure he could get another contribution out of Grykos, perhaps even directly for children this time.

The only fly in the ointment was that Millie showed up at the exhibition. She ostentatiously stayed far from George, running at full speed whenever he appeared, but waving wildly at him from the required distance. She attracted some attention, but George couldn't see that any harm was done.

The next morning when George took the Long Island commuter train from Mineola to Manhattan, he found Millie sitting in what had become his accustomed seat. "Damn it, Millie," he started to shout, until he saw other commuters looking at him.

"Don't you understand what that court order means?"

"Sure. It means I can't come near you. It doesn't say you can't come near me. I was here first. So sit down and relax."

He stomped angrily into the next car, where he had to stand all the way to Penn Station.

Using Murray as his printer and the money borrowed from Pappas, George got the first issue of his periodical out. He had decided to send the magazine itself, and not just an announcement, to everyone on the mailing list, at least for the first issue. The contents included mention of the Parthenon on Long Island (another link to Grykos), a short story George translated from a Greek periodical, the background of some Greek names, and other items, including a cut of the bull painted by Lily.

He waited impatiently for feedback, and was gratified the day the mail brought him his first eight subscriptions. The next mail brought twelve more. By the end of the month he had about a hundred and fifty subscriptions, which represented five percent of the mailing list. The auditor of the organization told him that five percent was about what they expected as responses to their mail appeals.

Before printing the next issue, George sent out announcements, including the proposed table of contents, and was pleased when the subscription list increased by fifty percent. He also began to get comments from readers, and answered each of these. It took three issues until George had paid off his debt with incoming subscriptions and began to make a profit.

In the meantime he saw more and more of Lily. He found her sedate—almost prim—except where food was concerned. Then she was voracious. After his experience with Millie, he liked being with Lily. She had little sense of humor, and he found he could tease her gently without her being aware of it. She took whatever he said very seriously, and thought before she answered. She was more serious about her art than her studies, and sported an artist's big print case. Since she was small and the case was large, she sometimes reminded him of a butterfly in a strong wind. He found he was very attracted to her.

Some of the correspondence from readers indicated an interest in more articles about business conditions in Greece, so George went to the Fifth Avenue library and browsed through business journals, including administration, management, and manpower. He found that few of them related to doing business abroad—cultures, manners, structures, government agencies, etc. He also found that some of the business journals charged what he thought were astronomical prices for their subscriptions.

He decided to take a chance, and in addition to the more general journal about Greece, announced a journal dedicated to persons doing business with or in Greece, or desirous of doing so. He took a deep breath and put the subscription price at a hundred dollars a year. In addition to the mailing list he was using, he went through the lists of colleges in the United States and mailed a prospectus addressed to the librarian of every one that contained a school of business or business administration, and then, as a gamble, he mailed the prospectus to a number of international corporations.

To his surprise and delight, he received subscription requests from many of the schools, and a number of businesses. He also learned that many such businesses had their own libraries for executives and other employees. Indeed, before he had even printed his first issue he had enough money to pay for all four quarterly issues. He banked the money in a savings account and went to work on the first issue. He had feared that he would have to pay for articles, but found that academics, in particular, were delighted to get another item on their curriculum vita. In fact, some journals charged for printing the articles they selected. George felt he was getting an education in the journal publishing business.

Millie bothered him only twice more. Once she came to see him in the guise of someone wanting to contribute to Greek relief, and when he tried to chase her out, she threatened to tell the organization that he was refusing her substantial gift. The blackmail didn't work—he was simply too busy to bother with her.

The next time he saw Millie she was again in his apartment. She had gotten hold of a mechanical skeleton key somehow—a gadget that moved back and forth in the keyhole, holding each of the tumblers back as they gave, until the key turned. He realized that by now she wasn't interested in him as such—she was just getting a kick out of outwitting him. He reluctantly called the police for a patrol car to oust an intruder, while she watched with an amused smile. When the police came, and tried to beg off from the unpleasant assignment, he showed them the court order. They not only took Millie away—they handcuffed her. He felt thoroughly ashamed of himself, but not enough to call them back.

The judge reviewed the file and told Millie he was keeping her in jail over the weekend for contempt of court, and that if she was brought back again for the same offense, she would get a much longer period of confinement. He also offered her psychiatric help, which she indignantly refused.

George proposed to Lily while visiting her on Grykos' estate. He said, "Lily, I love you and want to marry you, but before you answer you should know that I make a nominal salary, I live in a sub-leased studio apartment, and I have no great future ambitions or prospects. We'll be poor, but I think we'll be happy."

Lily thought before answering, as she usually did, and then said, "That sounds good to me, but you must promise that I'll always have enough to eat."

For a moment he thought she was serious, then he saw her hide a grin. George pulled her over and kissed her. He thought her response was remarkably chaste for someone who had just become engaged, but before he released her he realized that Grykos was standing near by.

"We're going to get married!" he informed Grykos excitedly. Grykos looked inquiringly at Lily, who thought a moment, and then said, "Yes, we are."

Grykos shook both their hands, and then—looking from one to the other—said, "How would you like to have the wedding here? It's where you met, and where you became engaged. Will it be big enough for the crowd?"

George thought Grykos was being sarcastic, but he saw that he was in earnest, so controlling his own amusement, he said, "I think we will manage."

And so it was arranged. As they left the estate that day, George looked back at the enormous building and said to the gardener's daughter, "Lily, someday we're going to have a house bigger than this."

Quite seriously, she said, "It will be hard to keep clean."

Compared to the art exhibition the wedding crowd was not large, but the wedding was according to bell, book and candle, and Grykos had laid on a magnificent spread. Lily did well by it. George gave up his apartment and went to live in Lily's, which at least had a bedroom as well as a living room.

On their honeymoon night Lily wore pajamas and George, as usual, was nude. When he took her in his arms, he found she was stiff. He assumed she was frightened, and said, "Don't worry, honey. We'll just lie here and hold each other as long as you like." After a while she relaxed, but when he tightened his arms, she became stiff again. Toward morning, not having slept at all, he said, "Lily, take off your pajamas and we'll hold each other."

She dutifully undressed and lay down, again stiff as a board. He hugged her to him, but made no further attempt to make love, and during the day he was very gentle with her. At night, he said, "Lily, I know this might be a frightening experience to think about, but believe me, it really is pleasant—at least, after the first few moments the first time. Give it a chance."

As usual, she was acquiescent, and although her body was stiff, she allowed him to engage in foreplay—which had no result on her—and then to penetrate her. It did hurt, as he had warned, but she found no pleasure in what followed. At George's urging she tried again, knowing the initial pain would not be repeated, but again she could not respond.

George was concerned, but said, "Well, let's give it a few more days for you to relax and get used to me, and to being married." The following nights were the same. George was unsatisfied and Lily was sympathetic. They discussed it, and came to the conclusion that Lily was frigid. He wanted to talk about the possible roots of her frigidity, but she said, with complete self-assurance, that this was not something for amateurs. She would see both a marriage counselor and a psychiatrist.

Neither course proved successful. After almost six months of this kind of marriage, Lily sat him down in the kitchen and said, "George, as you know, I don't enjoy it when we have sex. In fact, I feel terribly embarrassed—almost dirty. I'm not willing to undergo years of psycho-analysis to try to get at the root of it. I simply don't feel the need for sex, and could live the rest of my life without it.

"But I know you want and need sex. I don't want that to come between us, because I really and truly do love you, George. I've been thinking, and this is what I have come up with: You can have sex when-ever you want, wherever you want, with whomever you want—but I don't want to know about it. Never mention it, never allude to it, we'll never discuss it. It will be like some part of your business dealings that don't interest me. If you can't accept that, then I'm going to divorce you or let you divorce me. I can't live under the constant tension of your wanting sex and my not being able to give it to you. But we could be perfectly happy if sex were removed from our relationship."

George thought the proposal was monstrous. The upshot was that they agreed to separate for a month. During the first two weeks George chased every woman he saw, slept with several, and even had a call girl twice. Before the month was up he was back with Lily. "I love you, Lily. I don't want to live without you. I do need sex from time to time, but it's just like I need a beer from time to time. I'll treat it like any other appetite—satisfy it, and forget it. Can we be married again?"

And so they settled down to a married life that included separate bedrooms—to keep George from trying to give in to any impulses he might have. He found he was very happy, and without Lily's fear of sex hanging over them, they were very much in love.

Over the next few years the success of George's growing magazine venture tied him up so that he was relieved when the Greek war relief organization ceased operating. His activities were centered in a room in Murray's printing plant, since he conducted all of his business by correspondence.

As George added journals to his list, he found that he had uncovered a vacuum. Many enterprises were interested in doing business abroad, but didn't know where to turn or how to act. George branched out from Greece into periodicals concerning Turkey, then Yugoslavia, Italy, and Egypt. He would have loved to include Albania, but these were the years when that country was a closed enclave.

The journal business not only spread horizontally. George kept raising the prices of subscriptions, and found that some technical libraries, conglomerates, and government offices would pay whatever the cost to have complete coverage. In fact, the subscription list for each journal ranged from four hundred to six hundred copies, and subscription prices stabilized at around two hundred dollars each. It must be said that these were good journals—no longer light reading, but sound technical and business journals that threw insight on areas that were obscure in and from other publications.

George then found that he faced a unique problem. When the yearly subscriptions came in, he had an income from each journal of around a hundred thousand dollars. By the time he was publishing ten journals, he was taking in a million dollars a year. And he had nothing to do with the money. The journals were published only four or six times a year, and his expenses were spread out accordingly. He had stumbled into one of the few businesses in which the money comes in first, and the costs come in later.

Lily kept painting, mostly large pastel garden scenes. At one point five of her paintings were sold at an exhibition, and it seemed that she would become the latest rage, but it petered out with another sale. Lily didn't seem to mind—she painted because she enjoyed it

He met Millie only once again. Lily had hired the services of a firm of interior decorators whom she thought would best accommodate to her own ideas, and when he came home he found Millie (whom Lily had never met) and a young man discussing the decor with Lily. Millie smiled at him conspiratorially, and he found that he was sweating. While Lily was talking to the young man, with a buttered bagel in her hand, Millie managed to whisper to him, "You keep quiet and so will I." She lifted her eyebrow toward the young man, and George realized he had been replaced. He felt some sympathy for the young man, knowing what might be in store for him, but managed to squelch it before acting on it.

And the money kept coming in. Belatedly, he realized what he should do. He began investing the money as it arrived, selling stock only when he needed money for publication. George's list of journals eventually ran to thirty-three, which meant that he had about three million dollars to invest at the beginning of each subscription year. The income from the investments alone, leaving out the profit from the journals, was accumulating far beyond their modest way of life.

He moved into a luxurious suite of offices; Murray's printing plant used the most advanced technological methods; and Lily and George moved into a townhouse in the East Sixties. They traveled, bought a condo on Corfu, and visited mainland Greece at least twice a year. They attended La Scala during the fall opera season; went to Verona for the opera in August; to London in the fall; to the Edinburgh Music Festival; and, of course, to both the Met and the New York Opera. Lily suggested that they go to Vienna and Salzburg, but George explained that he could never forgive the Germans and the Austrians for what the Nazis did, particularly to his beloved Greece.

George learned to appreciate fine wines, and became a gourmet, ordering exactly what he liked cooked exactly as he liked it. Lily remained a gourmand. He investing a few thousand dollars in a Broadway show, and although it didn't last long, he enjoyed his continuing contact with show people (many of whom were trying to get him to invest in another show). George gave generously to Greek War Relief, and when that stopped operating, to various Greek causes. He met with Greek politicians, and was courted by journalists, businessmen, and would-be endowees, not only in Greece. In short, he enjoyed life

His presumed influence put a number of profitable business deals his way, and his wealth continued to grow. A rival journal company offered to buy him out for five million dollars, and he laughed and offered them ten million for their journals. It became a stand-off.

One day he said to Lily, "I think the time has come to keep my promise." She couldn't figure out what he was talking about, and said so.

"I promised the gardener's daughter that I would build her a house bigger than the house of the gardener's boss. And I want to."

So they built a mansion, with guest apartments, and private elevators to each apartment, and every detail figured out in advance, down to 110v and 220v outlets in the bathrooms for guests from abroad. Lily was fascinated with the architect's drawings, seeing in them works of art in themselves. She insisted on keeping them, and later framed them. They made a very interesting addition to the art gallery in the house.

Once the house was finished Lily traveled much less with George. She loved staying home, and particularly being in her atelier. Traveling became just a burden for her. She rarely even went to the City. George traveled widely, and often slept in the Manhattan townhouse that they had kept.

They had been married slightly more than fifteen years when a man who introduced himself to George's secretary as Mr. Bellows asked for an appointment. He said his business was private, and George agreed to see him out of curiosity. Bellows waited until the secretary had closed the door, and said, "I want to show you something."

He reached into his briefcase, and George realized with some fear that he had never taken any precautions against kidnapping, violence, or anything like it. To his relief, Bellows took some large photographs out of his briefcase and spread them on George's desk. They each showed a man with a woman—a different woman in each of the four photographs. In one the couple were kissing; in another they had their arms around each other, evidently in a nightclub; in the third, the woman—nude—was closing the door while admitting the man; and in the fourth, he was driving a car and she had her arm around his neck. George recognized the women before he recognized himself.

The man looked at him quizzically, saying nothing. George collected his thoughts. "They're not very good," he said, "but I guess that comes from concealed cameras. I'll take one of each, and two of the one in the car."

"Nice bluff," said Bellows, grinning, "but it's not the first time I've heard it. I want a hundred thousand for the negatives, and you'll have my word that you'll have all the copies."

"Wow," said George, amused. "Your solemn word, sworn on a Bible, with a lock of your mother's hair? That really convinces me. You know what you can do with these pictures? You can stick them up your ass."

"Okay," said Bellows, no longer smiling. "Then I'll send them to your wife."

"I've got a better idea. Come home with me and we'll show them to her together."

"You don't play much poker, do you?" asked Bellows. "You can't even bluff well."

George flicked his intercom on. "Have the car sent round, will you. And call my wife that I'm bringing a visitor, for whom she should prepare no refreshments at all." He turned it off. "Now let's see who's bluffing."

Bellows said, "I'll call you. I'd raise you if I could. Let's go."

Neither of them said a word all the way to the North Shore. George showed Bellows into the small dining room, where Lily was finishing a double hamburger, and said, "I won't introduce this fellow to you, honey, because I don't want to besmirch you. He has some pictures that he has asked a hundred thousand dollars not to show to you."

"Not to show to me? I don't understand."

Bellows said, "Last chance. Fifty thousand and I'll pack them up."

"Where are the pictures, please?" said George politely.

Bellows' face turned red and he bit his lip. "Are you sure you want to do this?"

"Show the pictures."

Bellows looked toward the door, then reached into his briefcase and slammed the pictures onto the table.

George watched impassively as Lily picked them up, one by one, examined them, and then looked at him. Bellows smirked.

"They aren't very good, are they?" said Lily. "What makes him think they are worth anything at all?"

Bellows looked as though he had been hit in the stomach. He dived for the pictures and snarled, "*The Daily News* will think they are good enough. Twenty-five thousand to destroy all prints and negatives."

"I think the *National Enquirer* is a better bet," said Lily, thoughtfully. "They have a bigger circulation, probably pay better, and this is more their style. What do you think, George?"

"Well, I've been trying to figure if they would fit into any of our journals, but I just don't think they are good enough."

George and Lily might have been discussing whether to buy some new silverware. Bellows looked from one to the other, incredulously.

Then he rammed the pictures into his briefcase and headed for the door. "See you in the newspapers," he said, nastily.

When he was gone, George said, "Lily, I'm sorry it happened this way. You know I didn't want to break our agreement, but a blackmailer never stops. He would have sucked us dry. Please forgive me."

As usual, Lily was thoughtful. Then, "There's nothing to forgive, George. I've always assumed you were satisfying your appetite for sex somehow, just as I satisfy my appetite for food. And I don't mind. Incidentally, they looked like nice girls. Not a tramp in the bunch. Now let's don't discuss it any more."

The four pictures were published in the *National Enquirer*. The results of the publication were that most people that George knew didn't read the *Enquirer*. He was kidded by some of those who did; some expressed envy; and there was a spate of letters, mostly from women wanting to meet George. He debating showing these to Lily, but decided the sooner the incident was forgotten the better. Only one letter made any impression on him. It was on the letterhead of an interior decoration firm, and said, simply, "Why not me?"

Lily and George grew old together. She stayed home more and more, and he kept traveling, mostly to opera sites. She did accompany him to Greece where he accepted an honorary doctorate from a Greek university, as a tribute to all that he had done for Greece. On the way home Lily had a heart attack, mid-way over the Atlantic. The crew was well-trained and did their best, but even landing in Iceland was too late. She was buried on the North Shore estate.

There was a large crowd at the funeral—larger than there had been at the wedding. Among others, Mr. Skouras, by now a very old man, was there. As they walked back toward the driveway together Skouras said, "How I envied you your married life. So peaceful, so serene. You, of all people, can guess what my married life was like."

"Yes," said George, "I think I can."

"Of course, it was partly my fault," said Skouras. "I knew she was a nymphomaniac, but I thought marriage would cure her. Well, as the Pennsylvania Dutch say, 'Ve get too shoon ould und too late shmart.' She's dead now, you know"

George was startled. "No. I didn't know. How, when?"

"She committed suicide when her last young man left her."

"Poor Millie," they said simultaneously.

When George reentered the house, he knew at once that he would sell it. He would sell the townhouse, and the house on Corfu. In fact, as he thought about it, he would liquidate all his holdings in the publication business and live on the interest from his stocks.

He found a very luxurious and very expensive retirement complex on Long Island, and bought in there. He played golf and tennis, chess and backgammon, and very intricate computer games. He continued his interest in operas, went to first-nights and art exhibition openings, and learned to folk-dance, which he enjoyed more than he thought he would.

I went to see him because I was not only his nephew, but he had appointed me the executor of his will, which he shared with me. I understood that having no children, he was leaving the bulk of his estate to Greek charities, but I was puzzled by some codicils, especially those dealing with lifetime support for four people whose names didn't mean anything to me.

When I explained my presence, he smiled. "Come, take a walk with me," he said. We walked in the luxurious garden, and he stopped by a woman who had leaned down to smell some lavender. "Join us, my dear," he said, and she did.

By the swimming pool he invited another woman to join us; another who had just come back from playing tennis; and a fourth who dropped out of a bridge game, to the consternation of her co-players. We all trooped up to George's apartment, and I got my first good look at the women. They were all about his age.

George said, "I'd like to introduce my nephew, who will be the executor of my will. If I predecease you—that's legalese for 'If I die before you do'— provisions are being made for lifetime support for each of you. That support will be generous, I assure you. Now if there is anything else that you want now, or want to be sure of in the future, my nephew will take care of it."

"Oh, c'mon, George," said a woman that was still a blonde, "who could want anything more?"

A dark redhead said, "Is there something wrong? Why start this now?"

The small brunette said in some alarm, "Don't you feel well, George? Is something the matter?"

A languid-looking tall brunette said, "We'll kill you if you die." They all laughed.

As I left the room I looked at my uncle surrounded by those women. He winked at me, and then turned back to them.

Everyone knows that money can't buy happiness. How can everyone be so wrong?

Uncle Leo

◆

UNCLE LEO

If a corpse can move, Uncle Leo must be trying to kick his coffin open. After being a militant atheist all his life he was buried with a full religious ceremony in a cemetery reserved for very devout Jews. It must be killing him.

Uncle Leo grew up in Moultrie, Georgia, the only child of the only Jewish family to be found there. Not only were there no Jewish institutions in Moultrie—his family were so busy trying to make a living they had no time for anything else. In any case, they considered themselves Reform Jews, and abandoned everything that smacked of Orthodoxy.

As a consequence, Leo received no Jewish education at all. Every *Rosh Hashonah*, the Jewish New Year, the family traveled to Atlanta, and went to the Reform service, which Leo found not too bad since it was almost entirely in English. Once he visited cousins in Augusta over *Pesach* (Passover) and attended a *Seder*. And that was the extent of his Jewish experience.

Leo was traumatized when he was not yet twelve and saw a Boy Scout troop marching in the Fourth of July parade. He was so impressed with kids wearing uniforms and marching in unison that he took the Boy Scout Handbook out of the local library and began practicing the Boy Scout Oath, learning to tie knots, and making a fire with two matches.

He could hardly wait until he was twelve to join, and only regretted that there were no Cub Scout packs in Moultrie for kids under twelve. Once he joined, he threw himself whole-heartedly into scouting. This was something completely American. So American that being Jewish didn't count. He began to acquire merit badges very quickly, concentrating on those that required outdoor skills, because Moultrie was that kind of town. He was handicapped somewhat by the fact that there were no forests around Moultrie, so he couldn't look for moss on the north sides of trees and things like that, but he managed in other fields. Scouting became his major interest. Even girls were peripheral, since the troops were single-sex, and in any case Scouts were to be pure in heart and mind, as well as honest.

With five merit badges he became a Star Scout; with ten, a Life Scout; and with twenty-one, an Eagle Scout. He was not quite sixteen when he became an Eagle Scout—the youngest Eagle in Georgia. When he graduated high school at eighteen he became an assistant scoutmaster, and at twenty he should have been the town's scoutmaster, but some of the preachers decided that having a Jew shaping the town's youngsters might be dangerous, and appointed one of the preachers as the nominal scoutmaster, although it was Leo who taught the scouts, took them on hikes, tested them for merit badges, and did all the other actual work.

Leo worked in the family store from the time he graduated high school to the day after Pearl Harbor, when he heard President Roosevelt on the radio, delivering his "Day of Infamy" speech. He enlisted in the army the next day, without even informing his family.

He did his basic training at Fort McPherson, and was a model soldier. From his scouting he was accustomed to sleeping in a tent, making his bed properly, keeping his mess-kit clean, and even marching. He was made a Private First Class in short order, and taught new recruits the basic elements of camp living. By the time he was sent to Fort Benning for infantry training, he was a corporal, and he finished infantry training a sergeant.

Leo never had any question about preferring the infantry. Outdoor living, physical training and using his own strength and skills seemed natural to him, but he was upset that he was retained at Fort Benning as an instructor, instead of going overseas where the war was being fought. His constant requests for overseas duty were met by his commanding officer by further promotions as sops, but he performed well in each of them and reached the rank of master sergeant.

In the spring of 1942 the Jewish Chaplain got in touch with Leo to help locate the Jewish soldiers on the base, in order to invite them to the forthcoming *Pesach Seder*. Rabbi Dubnoff was a Yankee from Connecticut, and his speech seemed somewhat affected to Leo, but he gave the rabbi a hearing. He agreed to allow an announcement to be put on the bulletin board of his unit, and not to assign duties to any solder that indicated that he would be attending the Seder.

"Sergeant Rabinowitz," said Rabbi Dubnoff, "it would be very nice if you would take an active part in the *Seder*. I think it would indicate something to the men."

"Take part, sir? What do you mean?"

"Oh, ask one of the four questions, or be one of the four sons, or read a bit from the *Hagaddah*, or even make the *kiddush*."

"Rabbi, I don't know what you are talking about."

Dubnoff looked at Leo for a moment. "Doesn't any of that ring any bells with you?"

"I went to a *Seder* once. Boy, was I bored! The food was good, though." He caught himself: "Sir."

Gently, Dubnoff inquired into Leo's knowledge, understanding, and experience, and at last realized that he was dealing with a Jewish *tabula rasa* for the first time in his career.

"Leo," he inquired, "do you believe in God?"

"Believe in God?" repeated Leo. To his mind came one of the Scout laws: "A Scout is reverent..." He had learned it, repeated it, taught it, but had never really tried to understand it. "I don't know, rabbi. I guess I never really thought about it. I really stay pretty busy, you know."

"Leo, will you read some things if I give them to you? And then maybe we can talk again?"

Leo's mind had already returned to duty rosters, weekend passes, replacements for staff shipping out, and what to do about a soldier whom he suspected of being queer. "Sure, sure, rabbi. Just leave it in my mailbox."

Dubnoff realized that he had lost contact for now, and said goodbye. He put a pamphlet called *What Jews Believe* in Leo's box the next day; and then a few days later, one entitled, *How Can We Know That God Exists?*

About ten days later Rabbi Dubnoff came into Leo's office. "Do you have some time, Leo? If not, I can come back."

"Sir, I never have enough time, but I have to make time for whatever is important. What can I do for you?"

"In the first place, you don't have to call me 'sir.' I'm an officer by virtue of being a chaplain, but I don't command troops, give orders, or make decisions. My job is to help. But the important thing is, did you read the material I left you?"

"Yes, sir, as a matter of fact I did."

"And?"

"And what, sir?"

"Please stop the 'sir' stuff. Call me rabbi if it will make you feel any better. What did you think of the material?"

"Rabbi, chaplain or not, you are still an officer and I am an enlisted man. There are things that I can say to other enlisted men that I can't say to an officer. Can we just stop this conversation right here?"

"Sergeant, I am going to call you Leo, and if you can't call me Al, just call me rabbi, but tell me, man to man, not enlisted man to officer, what is your reaction to what you read?"

Leo hesitated. "Man to man? No repercussions?"

"My word."

"I thought it was crap."

"Why?"

"Because it says nothing; it proves nothing; it is just superstitious nonsense. I don't have time for such stuff, and I'm not interested in it."

The conversation was not going the way Dubnoff had planned. These were not the responses he had learned to expect at the Jewish Theological Seminary at 3080 Broadway. But he had also learned that a Jew should not be allowed to simply drift away from Judaism. He tried another tack.

"Leo, do you believe in evolution?"

"From what I remember from high school, I do."

"Well, don't you think that if one thing succeeds another, if lower organisms become higher ones, if apes become men, that some power must have planned it that way?"

"Not necessarily. It might have happened naturally."

"But if you say nature, aren't you speaking of some plan, some power, some kind of order?"

"Rabbi, I don't want to hurt your feelings. You have your job to do, and for people that need you, that's fine. But I don't know how the world started, or how it will end, any more than you know what existed before God and what will be after God, so there is really no point to this discussion."

For Dubnoff, Leo became a test case, an indication of his own abilities, and at last almost an obsession. For Leo, the Chaplain was an annoyance at first, and then a challenge. For a high school graduate to best a rabbi who held at least a master's degree and maybe the equivalent of a doctorate began to seem like another, more difficult, merit badge.

The more Dubnoff discussed Judaism with Leo, the more it became a question of the existence of a transcendental power that had a pattern, a plan, a program for human existence, and for every individual in it.

And the more this became the question, the easier it became for Leo to deny such unproven claims.

Dubnoff at last reached the point where he felt there was no longer any point in being diplomatic. "Leo," he said at one point, "I am going to tell you a story: A man came to a noted rabbi and said, 'Rabbi, I'm a confirmed agnostic, and I want to debate the existence of God with you.'

"The rabbi was a kind man, and he accepted the challenge. 'Let us start with the Bible,' he proposed.

"'No,' said the man, 'I've never read the Bible.'

"'Well,' said the rabbi, 'let's approach it from point of view of the history of religion.'

"'I don't know much about history,' said the man.

"'Okay,' said the rabbi, 'perhaps your point of view stems from a sociological perspective.'

"'I don't know what that means,' said the man.

"At last the rabbi said, 'Well, maybe it is the psychology of the question that bothers you.'

"'No,' said the man, 'psychology is not my strong point.'

"'My friend,' said the rabbi, 'I have news for you. You're not an agnostic. You're an ignoramus.'"

"Leo, pardon me, but you don't know enough about Judaism to even have an opinion. When you've lived longer, experienced more, and learned more about your Jewish roots, you'll change your mind."

Leo wasn't offended. He had backed the rabbi into a position where he was just being dogmatic. "Maybe, rabbi, but I don't think so. Since we've begun talking, I've given it some thought—for the first time, I must admit.

"I don't think that there is any plan, any program, any goal, to mankind's life. There is no higher power that plans, controls, intervenes, rewards or punishes. We don't know where we came from; we don't know where we are going; we just are—and we have to accept that. We can't depend on anything other than ourselves and on other people.

Man made God in his own image, because he couldn't stand not having someone or something to blame for his own actions and inadequacies and plain bad luck. I think that living without God must be the most difficult religion there is for many people, because it deprives them of the crutches and excuses that belief in God offers, but as long as society continues to depend on God, blame God, and beseech God, there is no hope for us; when we begin to depend on each other, maybe we'll get along better. Or maybe we won't. But we are going to have to try."

Rabbi Dubnoff was awed. "Do you know what you have been saying?"

"I'm sorry if I hurt your feelings or insulted you, but that's the way I feel."

"No, no. Don't you realize that you have just verbalized Jean Paul Sartre's philosophy of existentialism? Where did you read that?"

"Never heard of him," said Leo, honestly.

Dubnoff would have continued his dialogue with Leo on other occasions, but Leo's orders to report to the Overseas Replacement Training Camp in North Carolina put an end to their relationship. Dubnoff came round to say good-bye before Leo left.

"Leo," he said in parting, "do you know what an oxymoron is?"

Leo didn't know whether to be insulted or not, but looked puzzled.

"An oxymoron is a description of opposites, like a square circle, or a memberless group, or a cold fire. You are an oxymoron; a religious agnostic—that is, agnosticism has become your religion. Or, to put it another way, you believe religiously in your agnosticism. But thank God, there is still hope for anyone who believes religiously in anything. I wish you well. Shalom!"

"Give up on me, rabbi. God knows I don't believe in God. And would you believe it? I may not know what an oxymoron is, but I know what shalom means. Shalom to you."

Leo went overseas in a convoy of troop transports. Later, the things he remembered about the trip were the smell of potatoes rotting in the hold; the constant crap-games that took place all over the decks during the daytime; and the constant rumors of spies on board, blackout violations, submarines in the vicinity, and other things that soldiers could not possibly have known with certitude.

England was hard work for Leo. He was stationed in the Midlands and had to get his unit back into fighting shape after the journey and after the simulations of battle conditions that made up much of the training, especially since everyone knew they were just simulations. But he felt pressure all around him, and on himself, and that pressure communicated itself to the men.

On a personal level, England was even harder on Leo. He was, after all, an American, and the tempo of life in Britain—even under wartime conditions—seemed strange to him. Englishisms bothered him more than they should, rather than seeming novel or quaint. He called a trash basket a trash basket, and not a rubbish bin. Napkins were things you put on a table, not something that women wear. If his back left tire blew out, he didn't want to have to report it as his kerbside rear tyre. And he was convinced that driving on the left side of the road was simply unnatural and, as such, should be illegal.

At one point in the dining room Leo felt that he was far from everyone else. They suddenly seemed physically very distant from him. He wondered if he was having some sort of mental breakdown, but as he analyzed it, he realized that he wasn't hearing them very well. In short, something was wrong with his hearing.

The next morning he went on sick call, and after waiting the usual time, saw the doctor, who was a captain. Leo told the doctor that he didn't seem to hear well, and the doctor looked into Leo's ears in a rather cursory way and said, "You have a cold in the head."

"Sir, I haven't been sneezing or coughing. My throat isn't sore and my nose isn't stuffed. I don't think I have a cold in the head."

"Soldier, you have a cold in the head. Next!"

Leo was a well-disciplined soldier, so he waited about six weeks, and since he still didn't hear well, went on sick call again. This time there was another doctor/officer on duty, and he also cursorily examined Leo's ears and said, "You have a cold in the head."

"Sir, I was here six weeks ago and was told that I had a cold in the head. Since that time I have not coughed or sneezed. My throat hasn't been sore and my nose hasn't been stuffed. I don't think I have a cold in the head."

"Soldier, you have a cold in the head. Next!"

In another six weeks Leo went on sick call again. The first doctor/officer who had examined him was again on duty, and he again gave Leo a cursory ear examination and said, "You have a cold in the head."

"Sir, I was here three months ago and you told me I had a cold in the head. I was here six weeks ago and another doctor told me I had a cold in the head. Today you are saying I have a cold in the head. In all that time I have not coughed or sneezed. My throat hasn't been sore and my nose hasn't been stuffed. I don't think I have a cold in the head. Sir, I don't hear well."

The doctor looked at him in disgust. "All right, I know what you want. You want an appointment with a specialist in the London hospital so you can spend a few days in the big city. Okay, but I warn you, I can't get you an appointment in less than six weeks."

Leo said, "Sir, I'm not going anywhere. I can wait six weeks."

So the doctor arranged an appointment in the London hospital for him, he waited the necessary six weeks, and woke up on the day of the appointment—with a terrible cold in the head. He didn't even bother to use his pass.

Life in England became easier for Leo when his brother, Buck, looked him up. As a military policeman, Buck knew his way around and made life in England more pleasant for Leo. He began to actually like the pubs that Buck took him to better than American bars, and he began to experiment with English food: ploughman's lunch, fish and chips, scones, Yorkshire pudding and the rest.

When Leo got orders confining him to camp he realized that the invasion must be near. Even as a master sergeant it was hard for him to invent an excuse to visit Buck,. But he managed. They embraced and Buck, in parting, said, "God be with you."

"I'd rather have a good rifle," laughed Leo, "because I can personally make sure that the rifle is with me when I need it. I'm not so sure about God. Anyway, if there is a God, surely he, she, it or they have disowned me by now."

Leo landed on Omaha Beach on D-Day, and his unit fought their way inland. They helped liberate Spa, in Belgium, and Maastricht, in Holland, and were caught in the Battle of the Bulge. Leo was lightly wounded twice, once a scratch on the back of his hand, and once a piece of shrapnel bit into the fleshy part of his calf, but he was with the troops that fought their way out, and was later awarded a Purple Heart (both wounds being considered as one), and a Distinguished Unit Citation, with an oak leaf to mark the battle.

He was not among the liberators of concentration camps, but got to one about two weeks after it was first discovered, and was so appalled by what he saw that he threw up for the first time in his life. For his remaining three months in Europe he tried to do what he could for and about concentration camp survivors, but he learned how little power a master sergeant really has, even in a victorious army.

On the other hand, his efforts put him in touch with other Jews (and a few non-Jews) who were trying to help the survivors, and he was mostly impressed by Palestinians who had either been in the British army, or in an all-Jewish unit that he heard about. They were dedicated and selfless; they never rested and they never gave up.

Nor were they all men. Among those who were trying to arrange for the refugees to go to Palestine were a number of women. In fact, all his activities began when one of them—Naomi—came into his office unannounced and without preliminaries said, "Rabinowitz, we need three large lorries, enough petrol to get to the coast, and papers. Can you get them for us?"

"Wait a minute, wait a minute," he said. "How did you know my name?"

She made a contemptuous gesture. "It's on your door."

"How did you know I was Jewish?"

"Oh, come on, Rabinowitz. We have no time for games. Can you get us the lorries?"

"No," he said, deadpan, "nor can I get you petrol. But if you want trucks and gas, I'll see what I can do."

Despite her urgent manner, a flicker of amusement crossed her face. "Rabinowitz, you can call them kiddy-carts and bug juice if you like, as long as you can furnish them. I'll be back in the morning."

He got up to open the door for her, but she stepped back. "Sergeant Rabinowitz, I am perfectly capable of opening doors myself. Please control your male chauvinism."

At first he was angry, then amused. After which he began to plan how to get the trucks and gasoline she asked for. Later he realized he had never even thought about *whether* he should do it. It meant ordering trucks and supplies for fictitious purposes, but he knew the equipment was now just sitting around rusting. It also meant falsifying papers, and that was serious. Leavenworth could be the result of that.

"You know I could go to jail for this," he said to Naomi.

"No matter how bad an American jail is, it can't be as bad as the concentration camps that we are rescuing these people from."

That shook him, and he knew he was hooked. From that point, he did everything he possibly could when asked, and didn't think about the possible consequences. Naomi was his usual contact, but she had little time or inclination for socializing. However, he was able to offer her coffee—a very scarce commodity in occupied Europe—when she appeared, and she sometimes seemed to show up for very minor reasons. He dared hope it was for himself, and not the coffee.

He hoped it enough that he found himself trying not to do things that to him were Southern courtesy, but to Naomi were evidences of sexism. Once he unthinkingly held up her coat for her to put on, and she snatched it from his hands and put it on without help. He finally realized that not only was he dealing with negative-sexism—he was experienced pioneer and collective values for the first time.

The early attempts to get Jews out of the concentration camps were relatively easy, but when the British learned that they were being prepared for and taken to Palestine, earnest efforts were made to prevent it. As one of the occupying powers, the British were able to control a great deal in Europe. The Americans, for their part, didn't much care where the refugees went, as long as it wasn't to the States.

Leo found helping Naomi becoming more and more difficult. There were more checks on documents, more roadblocks—physical and bureaucratic—and more British agents around. But the challenge had aroused him. Every truckload of refugees seen off to a ship was a personal triumph for him.

One evening Naomi came running in, a bit disheveled. She was carrying a big box, from which she began hastily drawing white and black clothes. Leo was astounded to see that she had a complete priest's outfit, and one for a nun.

"Put these on!" she ordered in what he had come to accept as her usual method of talking.

At the same time, she began to strip.

"Hey, what?"

"Fifty-seven nuns! The Magician says we are taking them from Polish convents to a hospital in Rouen. They've all been repeatedly raped by the Germans and need treatment. They are in such shock that they can't even look at a man, much less communicate. You're the Polish priest that speaks neither English nor French, and I am the Mother Superior who carries on all negotiations. Got it?"

"Who is the Magician?"

"One of the heads of our operation. That's his cover name."

"Wait! Why are we dealing with Polish nuns? I mean, they have my sympathy but…"

"Father Rabinowitz, you are still an amateur! These are Jewish women from Ravensbruck on their way to Palestine. The British are looking for them everywhere. They are in a church five miles down the road, and we have to get them out before the British come. Let's move!"

Leo was so confused that he didn't even realize that Naomi was in her panties and brassiere while talking to him, and she threw on the nun's outfit before he was able to enjoy it. Leo was arranging his cassock when they heard a car stop on the road, followed by a knock on the door.

"My God, the British!" breathed Naomi.

When Uncle Buck appeared in the door, he stared at Leo for a long moment before he broke into a smile. "Leo! Is that you? Boy, have I been chasing you. What's with the priest bit?"

Before Leo could respond, or even make a move toward Uncle Buck, Naomi stepped between them and said, "You must be mistaken. This is a Polish priest whom I know well. And we have no time to talk."

She moved to go around Buck. Leo said, "Wait, Naomi. You don't understand. This is my brother Buck. He's a Military Policeman from Britain. Didn't I ever mention him?"

Naomi looked at Buck suspiciously. "A policeman, huh? And from England? He's been chasing you? Rabinowitz, we can't take a chance on him." She produced a small pistol. "We'll lock him up until we get back. Then we'll decide what to do."

"But, Naomi. He's my brother."

Just then a small, dirty-faced boy slipped into the room and reported breathlessly: "They are in the village. The women said you must come at once."

He slipped out without looking back. Again Naomi started for the door, and Leo found himself following. "Buck," he shouted as he started for the garage, "Leave your address on the desk. I'll get in touch with you."

He saw Naomi locking the door before she joined him. They got the women out only five minutes before the British soldiers entered the church, but when Leo and Naomi returned to his office, exhausted, several hours later, they found Buck gone. Evidently his training as a policeman had included lock-picking. A note on the table said couldn't wait any longer, as his transport back to England was timed to meet his transportation to the States. He had left a note for Buck, saying, "I don't know why you did it, but I am sure you have your reasons."

Naomi was puzzled that Buck would question Leo's commitment to the rescue operations, but Leo knew that he would have some explaining to do after Buck reported to the family that he had become a Catholic priest.

The rescue work became more difficult as the British redoubled their efforts and as sympathetic GIs who had helped them were sent back to the States. Thinking about it, Leo had an idea. When Naomi showed up the next time, Leo had all the arrangements made. He showed her the papers, documents, rubber stamps, insignia and other paraphernalia that he had bought from the master-sergeant of the departing 47th Combat Camera unit for three cases of Scotch and a German Iron Cross. The unit was scheduled to be disbanded immediately on return to the States. She looked at him inquiringly.

"You are now the phantom master-sergeant of the 47th Combat Camera unit," he explained. "You can cut transport orders, type mission statements, order transport from motor pools, requisition gasoline—not petrol, because this is an American operation—and use all the American Army logistic support you need to smuggle refugees to the coast. Your people will be covered by American Army documentation, and the British won't be able to stop them."

"My God," whispered Naomi. "Rabinowitz, you are brilliant!"

The 47th became a legend in the rescue operations. Their cameramen had to be in the most unusual places at the most unusual times, and had the documents to prove it. Although ships were loaded with refugees in out-of-the-way ports, Hollywood might have been making an epic movie by the number of camera crews who were present. Strangely, nobody ever saw their films.

Leo didn't realize how much he had come to enjoy his contact with Naomi until he got orders sending him back to the States. This time he sought out Naomi and told her the news. With her usual directness she walked over to him and kissed him passionately, holding him tight. It took only a short moment before he began to respond.

She broke loose. "In another time, under other circumstances, we might have…Come to us in Palestine, Rabinowitz (she would never call him Leo). We need people like you."

"We?"

She came as close to being girlish as he had ever seen her.

"I."

She wrote her address on a scrap of paper—"Meshek Yagur"—and pushed it into his pocket. Then she pushed him away and said, "The lorries—I mean trucks—for tomorrow night?"

He left Europe without seeing her again.

When Leo was being prepared for discharge at Fort Bragg, the sergeant in charge of the unit made a short speech, which he had evidently given hundreds of times previously:

"You are entitled to a physical examination if you think there is anything wrong with you. However, I must warn you that there is a two-to-six-week wait to see the doctors, and you will not be allowed to leave camp during that time. Those that do not want a physical will now leave the room and be on their way home by morning."

The men in the room, many of whom were within a few hundred miles of the homes and families they hadn't seen for two or three years, rose as a body. Only Leo remained seated.

"Didn't you hear what I said, sergeant?"

"Well, since I don't hear well, maybe I didn't. But I'm not going until I see an ear doctor."

"Oh, shit," said the sergeant, seeing his own free time being cut down, "there's one in every crowd. Okay, go back to your barracks and wait to be called."

It wasn't in six weeks or in two weeks, but on the next morning that Leo was told to report to the doctor. "Bullshitting sergeant," he said to himself. The doctor could find no physical injury or trauma in Leo's ears, and wrote on the record, "Claims doesn't hear well," and dismissed him.

The first person Leo called when he got back to the States was the family matron, Aunt Sophie. "Leo?" she said. "The Catholic priest. Buck told us. How could you do such a thing? You've disgraced us all. It's true we are not very observant Jews, but converting to Catholicism! And then becoming a priest! Maybe you hope that someday you will also be called Pope Leo, but we don't want anything more to do with you."

Leo was laughing. "Aunt Sophie," he said, "let me explain."

"No. I don't want to hear about your theology, and I don't care if you had a vision. We don't want a Catholic priest in the family, and that's final."

He realized that she had not just hung up—she had slammed the phone down. It wasn't until he returned to Moultrie and told his family all about his adventures that they talked Sophie out of her pique.

Once in Moultrie, Leo realized that his parents had aged by more than four years during the same years he had been away. They still ran the store, with local helpers, but were delighted to have Leo back to take some of the burden off them. The town had grown and a number of soldiers had either married local girls and settled down, or come back to do so. Consequently, the store was busier than ever. Leo did what was necessary in a rather desultory sort of manner, but soon realized that he wasn't really interested in the store. He thought of Dubnoff; he thought of the refugees; he thought of some of the Palestinians he had met; and he thought of Naomi.

Leo still didn't hear well, so he went to Atlanta and saw an EENT specialist, who diagnosed otosclerosis. He explained that nobody knew what caused this spongifying of the "anvil" in the ear—it might be heredity, it might come from trauma, it might be caused by what the army called "wind and weather," or it might be from diet. In any case, Leo didn't have a cold in the head—he had a hearing loss, and needed a hearing aid to hear normally. Knowing that Leo was a veteran, the doctor recommended that he apply to the Veterans Administration for a hearing aid.

He gave himself a few days to think about what he wanted to do with his life, and to prepare his parents with hints and hypothetical discussions. Finally, he sat them down in the kitchen and said, "Dad, Mom, I can't keep working in the store. I've seen things; I've done things. I've got to get involved."

"Involved in what?"

So he told them what he had seen, and what he had done, and how he felt, and what he thought he had to do. When his father realized he wasn't going to take over the store, his whole body slumped, but his mother said, "Fish gotta swim, birds gotta fly. Do whatever you have to do."

In a few weeks Leo was in New York, taking over a small room on West 122nd Street, near Broadway, from an army buddy with whom he'd kept in touch, who had decided to go to that Mecca of the restless—the West Coast. One of the first things Leo did was go to the Veterans Administration office downtown, and explain about his hearing. There followed some very detailed examinations of his ear and his hearing, and in the end, he was declared a handicapped veteran, fitted for a hearing aid, and was told he was eligible for a small pension. As he got ready to leave, signing the final papers, the clerk looked at Leo's file and said, "Boy, do you have luck!"

On inquiry, the clerk explained that his condition was declared service-connected because on his discharge record it said, "Claims does not hear well."

"If you didn't have that on your record, the VA wouldn't have given you a thing," said the clerk. Leo mentally blessed his own stubbornness.

During this time, Leo went to the Jewish Agency on West 65th Street, and got referred from person to person as he told what he had done and what he was willing to do. He finally talked to Akiva, who probed many areas of his life, over several interviews.

At the end, Akiva told him that he could serve on one of the ships being prepared to take refugees from Europe to Palestine, although he had no training as a sailor; or he could go to Palestine and try to enroll in the underground *Haganah*; or he could go to a training farm and prepare himself for life on a kibbutz in Palestine; or he could possibly return to Europe and try to get re-involved in the activities that were not only still going on, but accelerating.

The thought of working with Naomi in Europe excited him, but he told Akiva he would think over the possibilities. The next morning when he came back, Akiva was waiting for him, and spoke before he got a chance.

"Leo, something has come up. As a master sergeant, you had to deal with administration, didn't you?"

Leo nodded.

"Can you type?"

Leo nodded again.

"Well, look. I know this doesn't sound glamorous, but it is important. We have a very secret set-up in this country to buy, stock and man the ships that are going to Europe to try to take the refugees to Palestine. The British are doing their damnedest to try to stop us, and we feel some American governmental bodies might be doing the same. But we are the beginning and the foundation of the whole operation—the infrastructure, so to speak. If we were to slow up or fold up, refugees might have to stay in concentration camps, or at least in the countries where they were held.

"The head of this operation is a Palestinian, and he needs an American assistant—well, not really an assistant, but an office manager, courier, jack-of-all trades. You'll launder money, bribe officials, contact sources, and cover his tracks. Are you interested?"

Leo said, "It isn't exactly what I had in mind, but if you say it is important…I know I'm not on the level to evaluate the various needs, but I do know how to follow orders. If this is the most important thing I can do, I'm willing."

"Great," said Akiva. "I'll put you in touch."

"On one condition," added Leo.

"Oh, oh. What is that?"

"That you find out for me what has happened to Naomi from Meshek Yagur. Where she is and how she is. Can you do that?"

Akiva sucked his knuckle for a moment. "It won't be easy, and I may not succeed, but I'll do my best. Is that okay?"

"Done and done," said Leo, using a phrase he'd heard in Britain.

The cover name of Leo's boss was Danny and he headed that part of the American involvement in the illegal immigration operation that was concerned with buying, supplying, and manning the ships. As Akiva had pointed out, this whole operation was a secret one, for the British were determined to intercept every ship, and if they could learn what ships had been bought, the travel plans of crews, etc., it would make their lot much easier, and that of the Jewish refugees much harder.

Leo's duties were primarily clerical, but he also participated (as a messenger) in laundering the money that was being raised so that it could not be traced back to its (usually) respectable source. Consequently, he would draw money out of one bank and deposit it in another; deliver money to a stock broker who would buy stock with it, and then pick up the proceeds from him when he sold the stock; take cash from one person and write a check to another, etc.

His duties also included visiting various Latin American Consular offices. He would ask for Mr. Lopez (that always seemed to be the name he needed), and when he appeared, Leo would put one hand behind his back and say, "Mr. Lopez, I have an envelope for you. Do you have one for me?"

Lopez would usually reply, "Give me your envelope and I'll give you mine."

And it was Leo's role to reply, "No, Mr. Lopez. You give me yours first."

When he did, Leo would examine the contents before swapping envelopes. Lopez' envelope was expected to contain the flag papers for one of the ships, registered in the name of his country, while Leo's envelope contained a bribe, usually of a thousand dollars or so. This was not only necessary to get the ship registrations that were needed quickly and quietly—it also put Lopez in a position where he could not then publicize the fact that such a ship had been registered by his country. Leo got to know a number of Senors Lopez that way.

The secrecy with which the operation was carried on was very important, although due to inexperience probably not as good as it should have been. However, not only were the British trying to deter the ships, but it seemed quite certain that the American intelligence services were cooperating with them. Whether this was to buy good-will for other operations, or for ideological reasons, or as deliberate government policy, Leo and company did not know, but evidently those on their side who still had contacts in intelligence advised them to beware of American agencies also.

In addition, none of the sources of supply—ships, nautical supplies, food, blankets (for refugees), etc.—wanted to be identified as bucking the British, nor as doing something which might be or might become against American policy (even unwritten, unspoken policy). Consequently, tracks were covered insofar as possible. The office was moved from time to time, and the new name was always different from the old name. The address at which Leo worked at first was the Weston Trading Company on Stone Street. Prior to that they were the Nautical Shipping and Supply Company, on Canal Street, and at present they were the Montrose Shipping Company, at a Wall Street address.

Even the ships that were bought ostensibly and legally changed owners several times before being sent out. The Haganah knew that the British were trying to get a line on the organization, its members, sources, etc., and knowing that the British intelligence service (at that time) was the best in the world, Leo was cautioned to be very, very careful. They were dealing with human lives, and getting a ship through to Palestine meant releasing hundreds, and perhaps thousands, of Jews from lives of misery and degradation. Even the ships that didn't get through took their human cargoes from the lands of concentration camps to relatively humane Cyprus.

One evening during this period Danny called Leo at home, and in his Palestinian accent, said, "I vant you should go immediately to a restaurant called 'The Mezzanine,' vich is on 56th Street between Second and Third Avenues. There you vill find Sammy Stockman having dinner vit Maureen Williams. Sammy vill tell you vhat you are to do."

Sammy Stockman was a legendary figure—a Broadway impresario, a man-about-town, the confidante of theatre and political figures, and an active Zionist. Maureen Williams was a widely-read columnist with world-wide sources of information, the female counterpart of Walter Winchell. The thought of joining their table excited Leo. Who knew what background and secret information they would be exchanging?

So he went to 56th Street, and went back and forth between Second and Third Avenues. He couldn't find a "Mezzanine Restaurant." He tried 55th Street and 57th Street. He tried 56th Street between First and Second and between Third and Park—no "Mezzanine." He finally returned to the designated block, and went into a restaurant to use the phone to get new directions from Danny. And there, sitting at a table right in front of him, were Sammy Stockman and Maureen Williams! He checked the name of the restaurant—it was "La Maisonette." Danny's Palestinian accent in French had led him astray.

Leo introduced himself to Sammy Stockman, who checked his watch, said there was still time to kill, and invited him to sit down and order something. Leo was almost too excited to eat. Leo couldn't believe it. Imagine! Leo Rabinowitz, from Moultrie, Georgia, sitting between Sammy Stockman and Maureen Williams. He tuned in immediately to their conversation, ready for all kinds of tit-bits of secret information. But he found, to his chagrin, that they were discussing whether Maureen Williams' niece, who had just been married, had been pregnant at the time. This was not exactly the world-shaking revelation he had been expecting, and besides, they couldn't even agree about the pregnancy.

After a while, Sammy said to Leo, "I want you to take down a telegram and send it off."

Now, telegrams to Leo were something you sent in an extreme emergency—death, dying, or a suddenly cancelled trip. He also knew that a telegram had to be ten words or less—the rate went up considerably for every word over ten. Consequently, he knew how to write wires that saved words (Western Union charged for each word in a combined word like "can'tcome," so you couldn't get away with that). One did not write things like "I cannot get there tomorrow but will try to make it the next day." Instead the wire would read, "Arrival deferred day"—three words instead of fourteen. Both Leo's experience and his own financial situation made him good at this kind of condensation.

So when Sammy Stockman began dictating a telegram to the head of one of America's largest fruit import companies, in New Orleans, Leo began rearranging the sentences. Stockman began, "Please forgive me for bothering you with a wire at this time of the night, but there is a severe emergency that I cannot commit to paper. I do hope you will forgive my temerity when you hear the facts—." Leo read back to him: "Severe emergency requires disturbance—."

"That's not what I said," snarled Stockman,. "Write exactly what I am saying."

So he dictated a very long apologetic wire letter, in essence saying that he was going to fly to New Orleans that night and that he hoped the recipient would cancel any appointments that stood in the way, etc., etc.

He ended by again apologizing profusely. Leo was shocked at the length of the wire, but made no further effort to cut it down. He was learning how big-time operators operate. After he filed the wire, he drove Stockman to the airport. Stockman had waited to send the wire until he was almost ready to leave, so he could not be told not to come, or that he would not be received.

Leo later learned the details behind the wire: There were refugees waiting in Malmo to be taken to Palestine, and although there was a ship ready to sail, the organization could not get flag papers from any of its usual sources. A dissident group, which took orders from no one and coordinated with no one, had sent a small yacht to Europe, ostensibly to rescue refugees, but with a great fanfare of publicity, in order to raise money for themselves. The publicity surrounding that ship had caused all of the Haganah's usual suppliers to back off and they were now fearful that their involvement might be publicized. Consequently, every country turned to refused to register the ship, and all consuls were suddenly unbribable, because of the publicity involved.

The refugees were getting desperate. Sweden, where they were waiting, did not want diplomatic incidents with the British, and wanted to get the refugees off before it was discovered that they were heading for Palestine. And the longer they stayed at their collection point the greater the fear of exposure by the British, and the greater the danger that the ship would be intercepted when it had picked up the refugees.

In desperation, Stockman flew to New Orleans and explained the situation to the head of the shipping line. The latter was not Jewish and had not been involved in the Zionist movement, but the story of survivors being in danger of being returned to the concentration camps moved him to action. He, too, had seen a camp while in the American army. He picked up the phone and spoke to the general who was at the moment (and for the moment) running one of the Central American countries—Nicaragua, Honduras, Guatemala, who knows? He informed the general that the price he would pay for bananas was being cut a cent a pound.

The general nearly had apoplexy. That would ruin the country—the total was millions of dollars. He screamed, he begged, he expostulated, and in the end he wanted to know why. He was informed that his consul in New York had refused to register a ship that the line needed, and without that ship, the market price on bananas could not be maintained.

The next morning Leo was told to visit a certain Central American consulate, where an envelope would be waiting for him, and this time he did not have to give an envelope in return. The refugees were picked up as scheduled, and the price of bananas remained the same.

One day Leo received a phone call from Akiva. "I have news from Palestine for you."

Leo's heart jumped. "I'll come right over."

"No need, Leo. You're a big boy and can take this. Naomi married a member of her kibbutz two months ago, and they're both on Cyprus, helping out in the refugee camps there."

Leo was silent for a moment, and then the incident began to take on its proper proportions for him—it was a vignette that had taken place in another country at another time, and was never destined to be fulfilled. But he still relived every moment of it in his memory.

With the thought of Naomi put into its proper perspective, Leo realized that he was a very lonely person. The daytimes were all right, but the nights were often spent alone in his room, reading. Sometimes the loneliness was so great that he would call his parents, just to have someone to talk to, although he had little to say. He couldn't talk about his work, and once they realized that, they didn't ask him. He decided that loneliness is the worst hell there is. He did not realize he was contradicting Sartre this time, because the latter had said that hell is other people, and Leo felt it was the lack of them.

He went to movies, he tried opera once, and he even went to a billiard parlor one night. The weekends were worse. He began taking long walks in the evening, getting to know parts of Manhattan that he didn't know.

One night on his way home from such a walk he passed the Jewish Theological Seminary, on the corner of Broadway and 123rd Street, which was very close to where he lived. It made him think of Rabbi Dubnoff, who had studied there. The windows were open and he heard conversation and laughter. On impulse he went in—he decided that if challenged, he would say he wanted to find out about the library.

However, what he found was three couples, laughing and talking in what was obviously a kind of reception room. They looked at him curiously when he entered, and then one of the men said, "Come in. Come in." Getting up, he continued, "My name is Mike, and this is my wife Shirley."

Leo introduced himself, adding that he lived on the next block, and the other couples introduced themselves. All of the men were last-year students for the rabbinate, but when it came to be Leo's time to explain what he did, he realized he couldn't say much. So instead, he mentioned that he had been discharged from the army recently and…. At that point he realized that as rabbinical students, all of the men in the room had probably been deferred, and he began to worry that they would take his comments about army service as an attack on them.

On the contrary, they wanted to know all about it, especially about the concentration camps and the attempts to get Jews to Palestine. As Leo warmed to his stories, they leaned forward, fascinated. The upshot was that they invited Leo to join the student body for dinner Friday night, although he would have to pay—in advance of Shabbat.

On Friday night he was very self-conscious as he entered, but Mike and Shirley waved him to a seat near them. Leo sat through the *kiddush*, and the blessing on the bread, and—at the end of the meal—the singing of the blessing after the meal. He found it an esthetic experience, although he didn't understand the words, and was disappointed to learn that he couldn't have real milk in his coffee because the dinner contained meat.

From that point on, Leo had Friday night dinners at the Seminary, and occasionally came in for holiday celebrations. He began to learn, and then to join in on, the *kiddush* and the post-meal blessing. He learned about the holidays, and some of the ritual. He met many of the other students, all of whom were fascinated by his adventures in Europe. And he, in turn, was fascinated by Shirley. He found her every gesture enchanting. It was hard for him to take his eyes off her. If Mike noticed, he never indicated it, but Shirley must have noticed.

At one point, Shirley brought her younger sister Esther to Friday night dinner, and after that it seemed accepted that Leo and Esther would make a pair whenever necessary. Esther was a coarser edition of Shirley, heavier, with larger facial features, and a particularly grating laugh. Her mannerisms and her speech were rougher than Shirley's almost inherently graceful behavior.

For a few months they were sort of thrown together, and during that time they went out together a number of times. Esther was more accepting and outgoing about Leo's petting and necking than any girl he had ever known, but she had one strict rule. As his hands began to explore her body she would say, "Only up to the edge of the panties," or "down to the edge of the panties," as the case might be—and he found out that she meant it. After some months of this kind of relationship, she began speaking in a matter of fact manner about wedding dates, housing, and future plans in general.

Leo was both frightened and worried.

When he managed to catch Shirley alone, he told her he wanted help. He didn't want to hurt Esther, but he also didn't want to marry her. He asked Shirley to find a way to intimate this to Esther. Shirley looked at him quizzically. "You were in the army, right?"

"You know it."

"You fought Nazis and fooled the British, right?"

"Yup."

"So you're not a coward. Either marry Esther or tell her you don't intend to. It's not fair to either of you to avoid the issue."

Leo knew Shirley was right—he had to put an end to it. But he found he was a greater coward than either of them knew. A face to face confrontation was more than he thought he could handle. And if it turned into tears, he knew he would give way despite his resolution. Suddenly, he realized how to do it.

In addition to the men studying at the Seminary, there were also some girls, mostly from Hunter and Columbia, taking some Jewish subjects. Leo had noticed Dora, a rather mousey little girl, not particularly pretty, who was evidently taking some courses, and who showed up for Friday night dinner from time to time. The next time she appeared, Leo managed to sit next to her. She seemed a rather placid girl, but agreed to Leo's request for a date.

To Leo's surprise, they had a nice, quiet evening of a movie and a bite. And to Leo's greater surprise, she was even more anti-religious than he was. Her father had died in a concentration camp after his rabbi had forbade him to leave the sanctity of the *shtetl* for another country, because he might become contaminated by living among Gentiles. At the last moment, the rabbi managed to escape.

Leo began seeing a lot of Dora. What had started as an attempt to free himself of Esther became a very pleasant relationship in itself. They never petted, or necked, or even kissed. Despite his own urges, he didn't want to get into his previous situation again, so holding hands was as far as their signs of affection went.

Leo learned that Dora herself was a refugee—after her father was taken she had escaped with the rest of her family from Poland, and all but she and her mother had died during the intervening serpentine travels. Dora was a nurse, somewhat lonely, and was taking some courses at the Seminary more to pass the time away than anything else, just like Leo. Leo felt very comfortable with Dora, and when, after several months of seeing each other fairly often, he almost off-handedly said, "How about getting married?" she replied, "Why not?"

Of course, there was the question of Dora's mother. When Leo felt he knew Dora well enough, he told her of his job, but he didn't feel he could reveal such secrets to her mother. Dora handled the matter for him. When her mother asked what Leo did, Dora simply said, "He's on Wall Street."

That was evidently enough for Dora's mother and any friends or acquaintances that she might have. The fact that the office had moved to an inconspicuous building at the end of Wall Street the previous week made this true.

Leo and Dora were married in a quiet ceremony by the Dean of the Seminary, with only Dora's mother, Mike and Shirley, and—to Leo's surprise—Akiva in attendance. Leo's parents couldn't get away from the store for a trip to New York, but Leo promised them he would bring Dora to meet them in Moultrie.

After he was married, Leo began to be a bit impatient with his job. It was all right working in the background, but, as usual, he wanted to be more active. At one point he learned that as a veteran, he could attend college on the GI Bill of Rights, having his tuition paid, and getting a monthly stipend. Further, he learned, through Akiva, that the Hebrew University in Jerusalem had been accredited for such studies.

Ever since Rabbi Dubnoff had insinuated that he was an ignoramus, it had been bothering Leo—way down deep somewhere—that he had never gone to college. Now he saw the way to become more active in the events taking place in Palestine and to study at a university at the same time—and perhaps even to see Naomi?

As a refugee who had knocked around from country to country, Dora wasn't keen on starting over in a new place. On the other hand, they weren't getting anywhere in the States and—if truth be told—her mother had become a bit of a *yente*, whining, demanding, complaining. So they decided to give it a try, and set May 8th, when there was a converted troop ship sailing for Haifa, as their departure date.

Leo's parents didn't really understand his motivation, and when he brought Dora to see them, tried to get her to dissuade him. But when it was clear that this was what he wanted, Leo's mother said, again, "If that is what you want, we want you to be happy." Dora's mother, on the other hand, just refused to listen to their plans, and brushed away with her hand their repeated mentions of May 8th as their sailing date.

Danny, however, was adamant that Leo couldn't leave. "You are doing more for Palestine here than you could possibly do there. I need you here. I don't have time to break in someone new. You can't go."

When Leo kept reiterating that he was leaving, and began to look for someone to replace him, Danny grudgingly accepted his decision, and at the end seemed to admire him.

They arrived in Palestine in May, 1947, and went immediately to Jerusalem, where they stayed in a student hostel until they found an apartment that they could share with another student couple from the States, Dan and Miki Marx. Dan and Miki had a bedroom; Leo and Dora had a bedroom; and they shared the kitchen and bathroom. Dan had been in the American army, too, but in the Pacific theatre. Coincidentally, he also wore a hearing aid, although his hearing loss came from an actual wound.

In the house in which they stayed there was another room, opening only to the outside, that seemed to be a small synagogue. It was dark, dusty, and had an ancient smell. Dora took one look, and said, "A *shteibel* in the *shtetl*," explaining that she meant the kind of prayer room that existed in small farming villages in Poland in the Middle Ages, and had continued to be maintained until the destruction of European Jewry.

Max, as a rabbinical student, was interested in this remnant of European Judaism, and when he saw a few old men entering on *Shabbat* he joined them. He wasn't exactly enthusiastically received. In fact, he was ignored—probably being seen simply as a voyeuristic tourist—until it turned out that he lived in the next room. After that, every time the group couldn't get the mandatory ten men together to make a *minyan*, they would tap on Max's window and beckon him to come.

He didn't have the nerve to refuse and, after all—as he explained to Leo—it was a *mitzvah*. However, on a few occasions when Max wasn't home, or when two men were needed, it was Leo's window that was tapped upon. Leo tried to ignore the summons, but the window-tapper would mouth, "*Minyan, minyan,*" not believing that someone would refuse to help make up a *minyan*. Leo would turn his back, whereupon the tapping would threaten to break the glass. At last Leo went outside and explained to the incredulous congregant that he was not religious, did not believe in God, and would not come to services. The old man drew back in fear. Someone who said he did not believe in God could only be possessed by the Devil—and certainly should not be living next to a synagogue. Leo was never approached again, but he felt a little guilty for causing the old man such pain.

Although the University didn't start its regular classes until after the High Holidays in the fall, Hebrew classes began at the beginning of summer. This just gave Leo and Dora time to see a bit of the country before classes began. Among other places, they visited kibbutz Yagur, at Leo's insistence, and after some discreet inquiries found that Naomi and her husband were still on Cyprus—at least, insofar as anyone would say.

Leo and Dora studied Hebrew assiduously, and began to make some headway. In the fall, when the University opened, Leo also arranged to take some courses in Judaica. They had, in the meantime, begun exploring Jerusalem. Almost every day they would take a walk—often a very long walk—to see and learn about their new city.

Late in November, 1947, they decided to pay a visit to a group whom they had met on the ship, now training in agriculture at a kibbutz in the Jezreel Valley. While they were there, they learned that the United Nations was going to vote whether to partition Palestine into a Jewish and an Arab state. The vote took place late at night in Palestine, due to the time difference. The group had a battery-operated radio in the one-room hut that served as their meeting room.

So all the members of the group clustered around the radio, listening to the speeches, and later to the vote. Behind them in the room were those members of the kibbutz who spoke enough English to under-stand what was being said on the radio. Outside the room, clustered around the one window, were all the other adult members of the kibbutz. As statements were made and positions stated, the group close to the radio repeated the statements to those further back. They, in turn, translated them into Hebrew for the benefit of those outside the windows. They then repeated it loudly enough for those on the fringes of the crowd to hear.

When the actual vote started, the hut sounded like a part song, with the country and vote being reported in turn by several voices: The radio, "Bulgaria, no." The near group, "Bulgaria, no." The far group, "Bulgaria, lo." In the meantime, the vote by Czechoslovakia was already being announced and passed on.

At the end, there was an expectant hush. Even those who had been keeping count weren't sure they were right, or that what they had heard meant what they thought it meant. When the vote was announced, however—39 for, 13 against, 9 abstaining—and the explanation was forthcoming that this was more than a two-thirds plurality, the kibbutz exploded with joy!

In their naivete the assembled people really believed that the Jewish state had been born. More than two-thirds of the nations of the world approved the plan to divide the land into Jewish and Arab states, and it didn't occur to anyone that this decision would not be accepted by everyone. It gave the Jews, it is true, very little land, and that was divided into little squares here and there. The very unfunctional nature of the division, however, appeared to guarantee peace, for neither state would be able to survive without cooperation with the other.

With this belief in the emergence of the Jewish state at last, and without a war, wine bottles appeared from several directions simultaneously; a bonfire was immediately prepared and lighted; everyone congratulated everyone else; and then the singing of Hatikvah broke out spontaneously. After a few minutes, the dancing started. The kibbutz members danced a hora around the bonfire. The Americans, who had learned their Palestinian dances abroad, thought they knew what a hora was, and usually danced it as fast as they could and joyfully, but the older Palestinians danced slowly with deliberateness, seriousness, and thoughtfulness of the steps, plus a linking of arms that signified more than just a dance. This created a whole new understanding among the newcomers. This was not just a dance, but a joining together of people who believed alike, had experienced alike, and who intended to stay alike.

The dancing by the older folks gave way to that of the younger members and the youth groups. The dancing became wilder, the wine flowed more freely, and by the time Leo and Dora went to sleep at midnight, there were already youngsters jumping over the fire as part of their dance.

They woke at three in the morning to catch the milk truck to Jerusalem. The embers of the bonfire were still smoldering, and a few couples lay on the ground wrapped in blankets. They walked across the yard with a light step—the state had been born, the goal had been achieved, and they already began to think of a return to America.

They bounced on top of the milk cans stacked on the flatbed truck until they reached the shortcut via Lydda for Jerusalem. At that point an armed man stood astride the road, and after a few words with the driver, sent them the long way around, through Tel Aviv. At one of the stops they asked why the change in plans, and were told that shots had been fired on Jewish traffic on the Lydda road, and all traffic to Jerusalem was being diverted through Tel Aviv. These were the first shots of what was to become the War of Independence, and although they didn't know that, they sobered up from their exhilaration with the

knowledge that the peaceful birth of the state had not yet occurred—
nor would it.

Back in Jerusalem, the wild celebrations that had taken place the previous night were already being seen in the perspective of the problems
that lay ahead. However, the University classes went on, and Leo and
Dora continued struggling with Hebrew.

It was in December that word was passed around that all American
students were invited to a meeting one evening. There, a Haganah officer, speaking English, outlined the military situation, and the need for
manpower. He was very clear—"We cannot force you to join the
Haganah, nor do we intend to. Anyone who wants to leave the country
is free to do so. Anyone who wants to stay here and not fight will be protected by us. But everyone who wants to take part in the fight for the
Jewish state is invited to volunteer for the Haganah."

Some students immediately began to plan to leave for home. Others
decided to stick around a while without volunteering, to see what
would happen. A few announced that they had come to study, and
would continue studying—military service was not what they had
come for. But the great majority of the small number of American students volunteered on the spot.

Although the Haganah was not the "armed forces of a foreign state"
within the meaning of the American law which deprived persons serving in such forces of their citizenship, a special oath had been devised
for those American students who had left their studies on Mount
Scopus and volunteered to help defend Jerusalem. The administrator of
the oath was the company commander, one Yosef, who, having been
brought to Palestine from Chattanooga by his parents when he was two,
spoke English with a very heavy Hebrew accent. (They later learned that
he had been given charge of the American students because "as an
American, you will understand their mentality," regardless of the fact
that he hadn't been an American since infancy.)

When the students finished taking the oath, the tension broke and they looked around at each other and exchanged whispered comments. They stood in three ranks: those with combat experience in the first row; those with army, but no combat, experience in the second row; and—later to become famous—Kitat HaRabbonim, the Rabbinical Squad, consisting of rabbis and rabbinical students who had been exempt from service in World War II, some of whom Leo knew from his visits to the Seminary.

As Yosef conferred with another officer, Ezra, a rabbinical student, leaned over from the back row and said to Leo: "Okay, veteran, what's going to happen now?"

"Oh," replied Leo casually, "all armies are alike. It'll take them a couple of weeks to do the paperwork, and another couple of weeks to call us into service, and some months to train us. I figure that if the war is still on at *Pesach*, we might get into it."

"By *Pesach*?" Ezra looked relieved. "The U.N. will have enforced the partition plan by then."

At that moment Yosef straightened up and said, "You vill report tomorrow morning vit two blankets and two mils. You vill be avay from home for several days."

Going down the stairs, Ezra kicked Leo in the behind. "Two weeks, huh? All armies are alike, huh? With such advice we could lose the war."

On the floor below, the female university students from the States, and the wives of the men who had volunteered, were being processed for various types of messenger and intelligence work. As the men joined them, the building buzzed with exchanged news, gossip and speculation.

"Imagine! Me, a member of the Haganah," Yoni's voice was incredulous. "No uniforms, no insignia, no saluting."

"And don't forget—no pay," his wife added dryly.

Not until a group of the students were on their way did someone wonder about the need for two mils. A mil was a small Palestinian coin with a hole in the middle, a hundred of which made up a Palestinian pound. One mil was practically worthless, and the need to be sure of two of them made a real mystery.

"Maybe we'll get our equipment from some sort of slot machine," ventured Ephraim.

Other genuises present decided it was for target practice—until they could shoot through the hole in the mil, they couldn't return home. Others had more prosaic explanations: Since they obviously wouldn't be paying their own bus fares to wherever they would be going the number of mils in the farebox would indicate how many fares the *Haganah* had to pay, going and coming. Others had still more lurid theories—mils in the farebox would indicate how many went out, and a smaller number on the return journey would indicate how many had fallen, since statistics were probably still pretty crude in the *Haganah*. In any case, they worried the detail, and tried to figure it out, and in some cases had difficulty rounding up coins as small as two mils.

It was about one o'clock in the morning when Max started pounding on Leo and Dora's door, doubled up with laughter: "I got it! I figured it out! I know about the two mils!"

When they quieted him down, he explained, still chuckling. "The two mils! The two mils! It was his accent. He meant to bring two meals! We are each to bring two meals for the first day's training. Think of the hungry Americans there will be in the *Haganah* tomorrow night!"

So at one o'clock in the morning they fanned out—none of them having telephones—to tell the others to bring two meals, or starve. Jerusalem was and is a daytime city, but that night it was the scene of wild activity. American students rushed through the streets, banging on each other's doors, shouting to each other, "Two meals! Two meals! He meant bring two meals."

It was late at night when bleary-eyed grocerymen were pulled out of bed by *meshugge* American wives, some in bathrobes and housecoats, to sell them frankfurters and salami and cans of sardines. Some of them figuratively shrugged—shopping at midnight. What did you expect of crazy Americans?

When they reported for duty in the morning, they were given some practice throwing rocks as make-believe grenades, and pointing sticks as make-believe rifles, and then told that they were to guard a rather isolated Jewish settlement in east Jerusalem, which clustered around the grave of, and was called, Shimon Hatzadik. The settlement was surrounded by Arab buildings and residents.

They were sent to a Well-Baby Clinic building on the edge of the city, to wait for dark to move forward without detection. As it began to get dark, some of the men began to move into an adjoining room. These were the religiously observant soldiers who were getting ready to say the afternoon and evening prayers. However, they were short one person for the necessary group of ten to make up a minyan, and Ezra came out to find a tenth man.

Leo was sitting leaning against the wall, his legs stretched out in front of him, reading a paperback novel about World War II and shaking his head at the errors he spotted. Ezra kicked the sole of his shoe and said, "Leo, we need a tenth for a *minyan*. Come into the other room, will you?"

Without lifting his eyes from the book Leo said, "Some people got religion. Some people ain't. I ain't," and went on reading. With such a response, Ezra gave up on Leo, and continued his hunt for a tenth man elsewhere.

When it got dark, the group moved across the street and across some fields to a small building where they were to spend the night. To Leo's surprise he found that they were in a synagogue. Some of the soldiers seemed embarrassed to be sleeping in a synagogue, which they felt to be somehow too sacred for such mundane things as taking off shoes, brushing teeth, etc., but Leo felt no compunctions.

While they discussed it, there was a knock at the door, and someone announced that the rabbi of the synagogue wanted to talk to them. The rabbi, a small bearded man with a heavy Yemenite accent, had sensed some discomfort, and said, in effect, "Do not feel that you will desecrate this synagogue by sleeping in it. On the contrary, you can only consecrate it because of your sacred mission to preserve Jewish lives." None of the men would admit it, but many of them, including Leo, seemed touched.

Just before first light they moved across another road and some fields, and took up hidden positions in Shimon HaTzadik. Their mission was to remain under cover, and to act only in the event of an Arab attack. Many of the houses, which faced the notorious Arab quarter of Sheikh Jarrah, had been abandoned, and were empty even of furniture. Since, however, Jews carrying arms were subject to the death penalty on the part of the British, they had to find places where their arms would be hidden in case of a search, but available in case of an attack. Not an easy assignment. Leo located a pile of rocks, and managed to remove a stone from the bottom of the pile, put his Parabellum pistol in the vacancy, and put a natural-looking stone over the opening.

They had evidently not hidden themselves as well as they thought, because one morning—without warning—a line of mounted British soldiers came riding into the area of Shimon HaTzadik, dismounted, and began searching for arms while questioning members of the group. Their cover story was that they had come to pray at the tomb of the ancient wonder-working rabbi, Shimon HaTzadik. It is doubtful whether the British believed them, but they didn't find anything to charge them with. They came close, though —

Leo had been posted in the small local synagogue, and when he saw the British come in, he quickly donned a prayer shawl and skullcap and picked up a prayer book. The British soldier who came to search the synagogue was small, weasel-like, with a narrow, pocked face. Of course, the British soldiers who had volunteered to serve in Palestine were hardly the intelligentsia of the country, and this youth evidently knew little of Jews or Judaism. When he saw Leo wrapped in a prayer shawl, with phylacteries on his forehead and arm, swaying back and forth, he stopped and stared.

Eventually, the soldier overcame his reluctance, and perhaps fear, and came into the synagogue, searching among the seats and in the corners, staying as far as possible from Leo, who was standing at the entrance to the cantor's raised platform. Finding nothing, the soldier had no choice but to approach the center, and the closer he came to Leo, the faster Leo began swaying and muttering in Hebrew.

At last the soldier noticed that there were hinges on the step leading to the cantor's platform, and drew his bayonet to flip it open. Leo, in desperation, said, in English, "I wouldn't do that if I were you!"

In his shock, the solder didn't realize he had been spoken to in English, and retorted, with mock bravado, "Why not?"

"Because that's where we keep our Holy of Holies, and nobody is allowed by God to touch it."

The soldier paused, and then said, "Ah, baloney." He flipped open the step with his bayonet, and there, covered only by a jute sack, was a machine gun and several grenades.

As he reached the point of the bayonet down again to flip off the sack covering, Leo looked up at the ceiling and said, "Father, forgive him. He knows not what he does."

Perhaps the phrase struck a half-remembered chord in the soldier's heart; or perhaps he was frightened enough to need only one more threat—in any case, he looked down at the jute sack uncertainly, and reaching the bayonet down, said, "Aw, t'hell with it," and flipped the step closed again.

When the British left and the group ran to the synagogue to see about the heavy arms, Leo was swaying back and forth, and fervently saying the prayer of thanks for escape from danger.. He looked up from the prayer book and said, "Some people got religion, and some ain't. Boy, have I got it!"

The situation in Jerusalem began to deteriorate during December, 1947, and January, 1948. Mail became sporadic. Train robberies became commonplace during that time. The train crews were Arabs, and trains were stopped in some of the deep valleys leading to Jerusalem, where the mail bags and freight were offloaded and reported as robbed. In addition, Arab-manned police stations were routinely robbed of their arms by other Arabs, with the British promptly replacing the munitions stolen.

The British began to operate openly on the side of the Arabs. For example, they would fire into Jewish crowds, claiming the crowd was belligerent, but when train "robberies" occurred, the British train guards fired into the air, "So as not to cause bloodshed."

Much of this situation did not get reported, since communications were virtually cut. At one time, the post-office was closed because the Jews refused to work due to the threats and attacks of the Arab workers; at another time it was closed because the Arabs refused to continue working alongside of Jews. Much of the news that did get reported was generally dismissed abroad as atrocity stories that were part of war-propaganda. In fact, outside Palestine many people could not overcome their image of the British as fair and impartial gentlemen in every situation, and nothing that the Jews could do would convince them.

The situation in Jerusalem became very bad. Many foods were short, prices went up every day, and Leo and Dora knew that unless something happened, they were going to be in for a bad time. No buses were running to the University or to the Hospital, and every night there was shooting in the outlying areas, and sometimes bombing in the daytime. Fortunately, they lived in the center of town, and their only danger was from a stray bullet, which was only likely to occur at night, so they stayed home most nights. They did go to a movie on some nights, but the heartache of walking home, scared every step, was no picnic. They ducked out of sight whenever they saw a British armored car or police car, since they were in more danger from these 'protectors' than from anyone else.

As it became apparent that a real shooting war was beginning to take place, some of the American students, including some of the rabbinical squad, began to leave the country. Every one had some urgent reason to go, of course. The climax was when the liaison person between the American students and the University, an American rabbi, announced that he was being sent to the States on a temporary mission, and would be glad to take letters and other messages to families, and bring messages back. In the actual event, however, he rushed away on the first available transportation, a few days before his announced date, so this method of communication was not available.

Of the students who remained in Palestine with the outbreak of open hostilities, many served in various capacities. Some of the women were on observation duty, some were armed guards, some were wireless operators and wireless interceptors, and some were messengers. Dora was put on duty at Patt's Bakery, then at the corner of HaNeviim and HaRav Kook streets, to stand on the balcony and alert the guards if any Arabs were seen going toward the Jewish sector. It is an indication of the pure luck with which Israel won the War of Independence that Dora didn't know how to tell an Arab from a Jew, but stood her post nevertheless. Later, when she mentioned this minor fact to the person in charge, she was used to deliver arms to outlying posts. Despite their general perfidy, the British were, at that time, still gentlemen insofar as ladies were concerned, and would not do a body search on females. Consequently, Dora long remembered the beauty of the countryside outside Jerusalem, as she carried hand grenades in her brassiere to Motza and other places—scared to death all the way.

Not all of the students stayed the course. Some, who had undergone training with a will, left the country when it became clear that the training was for reality. For some it was an intellectual decision, but for others, more traumatic. Leo went to visit one couple where the wife was pregnant, and they showed him the shell that had just come through the roof into their bedroom, but had not exploded. The dust hadn't settled and the shell was still revolving lazily on its side. They all got out of there pronto, and the couple left the country as soon as they could.

It was during this period that the whistled opening notes of *Hatikva* swung the attention of Leo, Dora, Max and Miki to the radio in the corner of their kitchen. For the first time all day the electricity was on, to enable Jerusalemites to hear the news from *Kol Yerushalayim*, the *Haganah's* station in the Holy City. Outside, a morter shell thudded in the distance, and over toward Sheikh Jarrah a light machine-gun chattered. The calm, cool voice of the announcer lined out the facts—another Arab attack on an isolated kibbutz; another British atrocity against unarmed Jews; the loss and recapture of Suba quarries on Castel Hill; Ben-Gurion's latest announcement and Bevin's splenetic reply. Then there was a pause, and in the same even, unemotional tone, the announcer said: "We have just received the following cable from America. The message follows: 'We, the thirty-two Jewish families living at twenty three hundred and eight Eastern Parkway, Brooklyn, pledge ourselves not to rest until Jerusalem is ours.' That is all for tonight. Shalom." The radio went dead.

"Good God," whispered Leo in amazement, "such nerve!" But then the humor of the message struck him, and he began to laugh. He dashed to the desk, scribbled something on a piece of paper, and headed for the door. A shell landed dangerously near.

"Where are you going?" shrieked Dora.

"Why, to the cable office," answered Leo, calmly. "I want to send a message to the thirty-two Jewish families in Brooklyn that the people of Jerusalem suggest that they at least take a short nap. It looks like a long war."

Had it not been for the fact that the civilian cable office had been closed for weeks, they might not have succeeded in dissuading him.

Although the situation in Jerusalem was not only difficult, but serious, official policy was to carry on with every normal activity possible, in order not to let the Arabs and the British succeed in disrupting Jewish life as they hoped. Leo interpreted this policy to mean that the daily sight-seeing walks of Jerusalem that he had begun before the war must be continued—by government order. Every day Dora pleaded and threatened when he started out, but decided she'd rather be with him than home waiting for news of him, so she always reluctantly and tearfully accompanied him.

They became a familiar and reassuring sight in the embattled areas of Jerusalem. Leo, in tweed cap and smoking a meerschaum pipe, walking calmly and slowly through the war-torn streets, pausing here to examine an historic site, there to view an interesting building, with Dora trotting protestingly alongside. Amid shellfire and mortar-bursts, they were a veritable symbol of Jewish Jerusalem—life as usual, despite the enemy's best efforts at disruption.

Often, on his return home, Leo would exclaim, "These are historic days. We are lucky to be here during these exciting times!"

Slumped wearily in a chair, Dora would echo, bitterly, "We are lucky to still be alive."

Few knew the secret of Leo's calm. His hearing aid, irreplaceable during the siege, was carefully left at home for safe-keeping during his daily walks. Consequently, anything short of point-blank fire or a direct hit sounded to him like a distant explosion, and distant explosions had become accepted as part of everyday life in Jerusalem.

Dora and Miki had other troubles with their spouses' hearing aids. In the middle of the night, when Arab shellfire in the distance had become monotonous, a much louder explosion, nearby, would cause Dora's elbow to find Leo's rib.

"Did you hear that?"

"No, honey, didn't hear a thing."

A moment later: "Surely you heard that one!"

"Can't say that I did."

Another moment, then, in a louder voice: "Miki, did you hear that?"

From the other room: "Yes, but Max didn't hear a thing."

"They—they're getting closer, aren't they?"

"I—I think so."

"Let's get these deaf men up so they can worry, too."

After a few moments of futile argument, Leo and Max would reluctantly arise, don bathrobes and hearing aids, and meet at the ponderous
iron door. When the door had slowly creaked open, they'd stand with
hearing aids in hand, listening. Invariably, at that moment, there'd be a
lull in the firing.

"Silly women," Leo would say disgustedly.

"Never again!" Max would agree, and back they'd go to bed, only to
be awakened in another half-hour with an elbow in the ribs, "Did you
hear that?"

This procedure became routine, until one night, after the usual argu-
ments, Leo and Max sleepily pushed the door open and stood yawn-
ingly regarding one another. There was a fluttering sound, and sliver of
shrapnel "pinged" against the door. Before they could pull the door
shut, a bullet ricocheted off the doorpost. Behind the closed door, Leo
and Max looked at each other in awe, having hastily acquired faith in
their respective wife's hearing and patience. In fact, every morning they
could pick up expended bullets, pieces of shrapnel, and other such
murderous debris that had landed against their walls or door overnight.

As the siege deepened and water was severely rationed, Max moped
around, muttering that if he didn't get a bath soon he wouldn't be able
to stand himself. Being a reasonable, logical thinker, he sat down to figure out where would be the last place in Jerusalem to run out of hot
water. Of course—the ritual bathhouse—the *mikveh!* And there was a
mikve for men in the Hungarian quarter of the city. But that section was
a long way off, buses no longer ran, and the longer one spent walking on
the street, the more danger there was from enemy fire.

The answer to this problem stepped into the house the very next
night, in the person of Reverend Lightman, the young, handsome
American Baptist preacher whose church was across the street. Rev.
Lightman had a motor-scooter, for which he received a gasoline allot-
ment as a religious functionary. The dream of his life was to establish a
kibbutz of Christians in Palestine, to exemplify in their own lives the

ideals they professed. He often dropped in to discuss his dream, and this time, Max broached his plan. Lightman was also suffering from lack of bath water, and readily agreed. Ten minutes later Reverend Lightman's familiar red motor-scooter was put-putting toward the Hungarian quarter, the minister on the seat and Max hanging precariously on behind, two towels streaming from under his arm.

Max reported later that the water felt wonderful (he didn't say how Lightman managed to conceal the fact that he wasn't Jewish), although a bit too hot for comfort. By staying as far as possible from the kerosene stove set in one side of the pool, he and the minister had their first real baths in weeks. They would have stayed in the water longer just for pleasure, although their skins were already red from the hot water, when an old man with a grey beard and earlocks came in, dipped one toe in the water, and muttered, "Es kalt, es kalt (It's cold, it's cold)." With obvious reluctance he managed to wade over to the hot stove, and turned the petcock wide open. As the flame roared in the stove, he turned to Max and the minister and apologized, in Yiddish, for their discomfort. He told them politely that if they would wait a few minutes, the water would be more comfortable—that is, much hotter. They didn't wait. It wasn't until much later that Max wondered whether the old Jew had realized that Lightman wasn't Jewish, and this was his way of getting rid of them. He decided he would never know.

After Leo had been on duty at Shimon HaTzadik and a couple of other places, someone noticed that he wore a hearing aid, and he was summarily transferred to the Home Guard. He was very upset—a decorated army veteran, giving out water rations and keeping the peace in public places! But all his appeals fell on ears more deaf than his.

The thing that irked Leo more than his assignment was the apparent disorder and lack of efficiency that he saw all around him. Things were, in fact, being done—food was rationed, water distributed, the wounded tended—but often in a haphazard way that he saw as symptomatic of the way things had been done in the rural Polish *shtetl*. His Boy Scout training and American army experience rebelled at the sloppy way things were carried out.

Thus, he was still grumbling when he got his orders one day to guard the block where the Jewish Agency was located. He was to be particularly careful about loiterers, since there had been rumors of another attempt to bomb the Agency headquarters, which had already undergone one such explosion. He reported early in the morning, only to find a lanky, morose, pimply-faced boy leaning against the Agency building, a suspicious bulge under his arm. Leo fingered his own pistol, took a deep breath, and sauntered up to the stranger.

"No loiterers on this block, friend," he said.

"Then why don't you move along?" responded the stranger, sourly.

"Look," Leo hesitated, "I don't want any trouble. Just go somewhere else and let's forget it."

"I don't mind trouble," said the other putting his face down into Leo's. "In fact, I just love it. And unless you take off, now, there's going to be trouble."

Visions of the King David hotel bombing, in which terrorists had killed Jews along with non-Jews, flashed through Leo's mind. He knew that, despite their propaganda to the contrary, neither the Etzel nor the Stern Gang hesitated to assault or attack Jews who disagreed with them, and he knew that officials of the *Haganah,* who were his commanders, had publicly disapproved of the terrorists, not only by pronouncements but by action. He took a deep breath and tried a new tack.

"I'm a member of a certain organization," he said guardedly, "that wants this block kept clear."

"And I'm a member of a certain organization," said the stranger, "that has ordered me to stay here. And here I'm staying."

Leo's orders didn't cover this situation, so he decided to bluff. "My organization is powerful and quick. Don't make me call them into action."

The stranger's hand darted inside his jacket. "Don't think you can threaten me, friend. My organization is more powerful and quicker."

Leo had a sudden suspicion. Seeking to keep the quaver out of his voice, he said, "Uh, which organization is that?"

"The *Haganah*," answered the stranger, "and you don't want to mess with them. What's your organization?"

Leo wiped the sweat from his forehead and breathed a deep and heart-felt sigh. "The inefficient, maladministered, don't-know-what-they're-doing *Haganah*. God bless their way of doing things."

By now Jerusalem was completely besieged, with only the remnants of occasional convoys being able to fight their way through from the coast. It was during this time, at about mid-night one night, that there came an authoritative sounding knock on the door. Dora jumped to let the visitor in out of the steel rain, and found a slight girl, in the inevitable khaki shirt and sweater, with a list in her hand, who asked: "Aryeh?"

When Leo identified himself by his Hebrew name, she said, "You will report to the Menorah Club in half an hour. Dress warmly. Don't be late." She slipped out the door and was gone.

Dora was terrified. Miki was sympathetic. Max was puzzled. But Leo was nonchalant. "B. G. probably has a special mission for a good man," he said. "Don't worry. After all, these are historic times. You wouldn't want to have missed this, would you?"

"Yes!" said Dora and Miki in one voice.

When Leo hadn't returned by dawn, Dora began to be really worried. By noon, she was frantic, and Max and Miki had run out of comforting things to say to her. By evening, she was distraught, and if there had been any sort of headquarters, she would have gone and demanded information, but the Menorah Club was deserted, and the location of Haganah (now army) headquarters was not known.

It was dark when Leo came limping in. "Oh, my aching back," he moaned, "and my poor aching feet."

"Where have you been?" asked Miki, as Dora clung to Leo.

"I don't know."

"What were you doing?"

"I'm not sure."

"Why were you so long?"

"Search me."

Finally, the story unfolded: "They took us out in a truck, dropped us off with shovels and picks, and said, 'Dig.' We dug all night and we dug all morning and when the truck hadn't come back by noon, we walked all the way back—ten miles. I've been on some pretty stupid training exercises in my army career, but this is the most stupid. I'll never go again."

They came for Leo again the next night. He gulped hard, and then straightened his shoulders. "After all," he said, "these are historic times, and someone has to build tank traps. Besides, it's safer out there in the hills—no shells or bullets to worry about."

Leo went out one more time, and then the messenger came no more.

When food and ammunition improved somewhat in Jerusalem, rumors ranged from parachutists to smugglers, until one night on the radio Ben Gurion announced: "Heroic volunteers, working at night, have secretly constructed a road through hills thought to be impassible. The road will be named The Road of Courage (*Kvish HaGvurah*), since it was within the sound of firing and at one point on the opposite side of the hill from an Arab military installation. The builders were in great danger all the way, but finished the road ahead of schedule."

"Hey," exulted Leo, "that must have been what I was doing on those nights. Did you hear that? I was being a hero! Yah, habeebi, we fixed that Arab siege all right. But, 'within the sound of firing'? My God, I wasn't wearing my hearing aid. I didn't hear the firing! I could have been hurt out there. I'll never go anywhere without my hearing aid again."

"Wonderful!" exulted Dora. "Then you won't be taking a walk this afternoon, will you?"

"Oh, I don't know," said Leo slowly, looking wistfully out the window. "These are historic times, you know. I hate to miss anything. Maybe I'll leave my hearing aid at home, and just this once…

It was in 1949 that the fighting seemed to be finally ended, so Leo and Dora returned to the States with newly-born Aviva. They decided against living in New York, nor did they want to live in Moultrie, so when a job as a publisher's representative opened up in Baltimore, they decided to make their home there. With help from the GI Bill, they bought a small house in a suburb.

Leo visited bookstores, department stores, shopping centers and churches, since his employer published both general and religious books. He went fishing for amusement; Dora played mah-jong with some neighboring women; and they had a son, Yoni. Leo's sales record was presentable enough to buy a house big enough for two children, and life was serene.

Walking home from the bus stop one day he saw a sign on what seemed to be a basement entrance: "Congregation Beth-El. Gigantic Bazaar and Fashion Show! Sunday, October 11th, all day." He hadn't even realized that there was a synagogue in the vicinity, and thought he might drop in and compare it with the synagogue in his house in Jerusalem. When he looked in his pocket diary, however, he discovered that October 11th, a month away, was the first day of *Sukkoth*, the Feast of Tabernacles, on which all work and commercial activity were prohibited. That would certainly include sponsoring a bazaar.

He knew that Reform Judaism rejected some of the tenets and ritual of more Orthodox Jews, but he found it hard to believe that during the time that he was in Israel it had moved so far as to reject one of the Biblically-ordained, as opposed to national, holidays. Consequently, out of curiosity he dropped in on Friday night services. He found about thirty men present. He was surprised to learn that there were so many Jews in the neighborhood. Leo still didn't believe in any transcendental being that controlled the world, but he was no longer as Jewishly ignorant as he had been before living in Palestine/Israel, and he was much more proud of being Jewish. Consequently, he was curious about such a desecration of a religious holiday—and by a synagogue, no less.

In conversation with his seat neighbor, he discovered that several members of the congregation were also disturbed, but that the president, who was the major financial contributor and only interested in his own prestige, had declared that nobody cared about *Sukkoth* any more now that the State of Israel was established. He had insisted that only on Sunday could a bazaar draw a crowd, and only this Sunday seemed convenient.

Leo was outraged. To use the emergence of Israel, for which he personally had fought and sacrificed, as a reason to abandon Jewish practice! For one man, who was obviously an ignoramus, to decide on his own that *Sukkoth* was no longer meaningful! He felt personally attacked. He had been an ignoramus, according to Rabbi Dubnoff, but he had come a long way since then, and anyway hadn't tried to exploit his own ignorance to change Jewish tradition.

Further questioning elicited the fact that the congregation as such was split on the question—those for whom it was primarily a social organization tended to go along with the president, while those for whom it had religious significance couldn't accept such a cavalier abandonment of a holiday mandated in the Bible.

"What do you plan to do about it?" asked Leo.

"What can we do? This is the only place we've been able to find for a synagogue, and it's owned by the president. Without this congregation we'd have nothing."

"Is a place to meet the major problem?"

"If we had another place, half the congregation would leave in a minute."

Leo thought about the basement of the house they had just bought. It was one large room, and had an outside entrance. They hadn't done anything with it yet, because they really didn't need it.

"Could you get some of the other people who are fed up to meet in my house Sunday night? We might be able to work something out."

The upshot was that a rump congregation was formed, and Friday night services, for which there was barely a ten-man *minyan*, were held in the basement. On Saturday mornings, when some wives and children came, the basement was respectably filled. Dora insisted on serving a *kiddush* after the service, in the new dining room of which she was proud. The basement was reasonably comfortable in the wintertime, when the heat could be turned on, but it got quite warm in the summer, since home air-conditioning was not yet common.

The new congregation rocked along for a year, and before the next High Holidays Leo had an inspiration. He went to a neighborhood bank that loaned out its auditorium to civic groups, and arranged for it to be used for High Holiday services. For the bank, it was good publicity and a chance to introduce new customers to the building; for the congregation, it gave them more room and comfort. However, the thing that Leo was counting on to attract a crowd was the fact that the bank auditorium was in one of the few air-conditioned buildings in the neighborhood.

Luck was with Leo. Both days of *Rosh Hashonah* were what in Israel would have been called *chamsin* days—not only hot, but sticky, with no breeze blowing, and the heat literally coming up from the sidewalks. On the first day, the congregants were delighted, and kept mentioning the air-conditioning to one another. On the second day, Leo recognized some of the Beth El members who had stayed with the original group.

Yom Kippur was even hotter, and the auditorium was almost full. The air-conditioning never felt better.

Of course, at every service there was an invitation for members to join the congregation, and during the following year the membership grew to the point that a fund-raising drive, plus a loan from the bank, plus a bequest from one of the original founders, made it possible for the congregation to acquire its own (air-conditioned) building.

During this time some administrative structure became necessary, for legal as well as internal reasons, and as the originator and moving power behind the new synagogue, Leo was elected president as a matter of course. Dora became head of the Sisterhood. As president, Leo felt that he owed it to the congregation to be present at services, and became a faithful attendant, participating in Torah reading and being honored by being given the first portion to read when the Torah began to be read over again at *Simchat Torah*.

As president, Leo participated in interviewing candidates for the post of rabbi of the congregation, and took some personal pleasure when Mike got the post, but saddened by the fact that Shirley had passed away.

Over the next ten years the neighborhood became more and more Jewish; the congregation became larger and wealthier; and Leo became an entrepreneur for the congregation, suggesting a pre-kindergarten program (which was eagerly accepted by young mothers as a wonderful Jewish baby-sitting service); then a kindergarten; and finally a full after-school educational program. He acquired both backing and help from the Conservative Movement, with which the synagogue had affiliated, and resigned as president in order to become unpaid educational director.

He continued his own Jewish education, auditing courses at Dropsie College, and doing an enormous amount of reading. He was invited to meetings of the Baltimore Jewish Education Committee, and became one of the leading members. As such, he became a member of the Conservative Movement's national education committee. He persuaded his employers, the publishers, to publish a number of books on Jewish subjects, and Jewish educational material for use in Sunday schools and day schools, which received positive reviews and satisfying sales.

Leo had some imaginative ideas about methods of Jewish education, and was gratified to learn that those schools that tried them were happy with the results. He was invited to lecture about his methods in a number of cities, and eventually became the chairman of the Conservative Movement's national education committee.

Still, it was with surprise and a thrill that he received a letter from the Jewish Theological Seminary, when he was sixty, that he was to be awarded an honorary degree as a Doctor of Jewish Letters for his contributions to Jewish education. The ceremony was a proud moment for Leo, and no less proud for Dora and the two children (who were now adults).

Leo's gratification with the ceremony was greatly heightened when he found that on the platform with him, also receiving an honorary degree, was Al Dubnoff, for his work in identifying and serving far-flung and exotic Jewish communities, like those in the Caucasian Mountains, in Cochin-China, and in Yemen.

At the reception following the ceremony Al and Leo caught up on the in-between times, and as they were getting ready to part—Leo to Baltimore and Al to South America—Dubnoff said, "You remember, Leo, I always said there was hope for you. You are living embodiment of the fact that experience, knowledge, and practice can bring even one-time agnostics close to God."

Leo thought a moment before he answered. "Rabbi—I still can't get myself to call you Al—we've always been honest with each other, so I won't stop now. Whatever I have achieved I have done myself, and with the help of others. If I had depended on God, I'd have died in the Ardennes Forest, or in the siege of Jerusalem. Jewish history has lessons to teach; Jewish tradition is rich and beautiful; Jewish identity can be made proud—but these do not depend upon a mythical, sometimes vengeful, sometimes jealous, sometimes benign, always remote chimera. I cannot be close to God, Al, because no reasonable person can really believe that such a being exists."

Al shook his head. "I can't believe that you really mean that."

Leo held out his hand. "Let's part friends, Al. You believe what you want to believe, and let me believe what I do—or don't."

They shook hands silently before parting.

My uncle Leo continued to visit Israel, and on one of his visits again went to Meshek Yagur to inquire about Naomi. It took a good deal of explaining, since Naomi was not an uncommon name, and he did not know her last name. However, he eventually learned that she had died some time previously, and her son was now in the Embassy in Sofia. He was delighted to meet Naomi's seventeen-year-old granddaughter, who was enthralled to hear Leo's version of the stories her grandmother had told her. When she rose to leave, Leo automatically took her light coat and held it open for her. She hesitated a moment, and then slipped it on. When he also opened the door for her, she gave him a lovely smile and said, "This must be part of that Southern hospitality that grandmother mentioned."

Despite the years and events that had intervened, the fact that Naomi had spoken about him so intimately and with such understanding to her granddaughter made Leo feel as though he were love with Naomi again for the first time.

Uncle Leo died on a visit to Israel during his seventy-second year. Dora had died some years previously, and there was no one in Israel to give instructions concerning his burial. Consequently, since he was known as a distinguished Jewish educator, he was buried among the Jewish greats on the Mount of Olives. Only learned, pious, and important Jews are entitled to be buried there because, according to a *Midrash*, in the end of days, when all the Jews roll underground from wherever they are to the Temple Mount to meet the Lord, those on the Mount of Olives will deserve the shortest journey.

Leo would have snorted in derision at this nonsense.

His tombstone reads, "Blessed be the righteous God, by whose word all things are done."

If there is a God, He must be chuckling. Leo must be fuming.

Uncle Monty

◆

UNCLE MONTY

My Uncle Monty refused an offer that would have made him the President of the United States. That seemed pretty stupid at the time, but it turned out to be the smartest thing he did. Or maybe it was the other way around.

The pattern of his life was to do stupid things that turned out to be smart; or to do smart things, and then learn that they were dumb. Like when he was in school and sent the teacher an anonymous note saying she was a harridan because he was so proud of having just learned the word. But he wrote it on the back of a page that had his name on it. She praised his vocabulary, but sent him to the principal just the same.

Or when he got terribly sunburned, and knew you were supposed to rub something on it. So when he saw a label that said "Rubbing Alcohol" he used it. Or began to. And like when he lucked upon a bunch of golf balls lying in the grass, and almost got brained by the next ball, because he was in a golf driving range.

But he must have been smart because he got good grades, and won a scholarship to the university. He couldn't decide between a course in psychology and a course in philosophy that were offered simultaneously, so he went one week to psychology and one week to philosophy for a whole year, and was proud of his cleverness until he failed them both. But he made it up the next year, because he went one week to philosophy and one week to psychology, making up the sessions he had missed. He was surprised to find that he had done well in both subjects, because for some reason they seemed awfully confused to him.

He spent a lot of time on a brilliant paper that proved that communism would never appeal to Cubans, and turned it in the week before Castro came to power. For his economics class he wrote a spirited defense of supply-side economics just as unemployment topped ten per-cent. The problem was that he was smart—his research was sound, his references were solid, his conceptualizations were novel, and his writing was good—but his timing was lousy.

He particularly liked a history teacher who would digress into other subjects at a hint from the students. For example, when someone mentioned marriage customs in the Middle Ages, the instructor said, "Some things don't change. You should never marry for money. But when you start dating, go with a rich crowd." He also taught such things as, "Everything costs more than the estimate," and, "Never sue for libel— they may prove it on you."

Uncle Monty was smart enough to take these things seriously. For example, about girls. He accepted the fact that you shouldn't marry for money, but he ran around with a rich crowd. It cost him all he earned as a salesman in a men's clothing store, but since he got a tuxedo and tails and a white linen jacket at a discount, he managed. He still had to pay for corsages and taxis and after-date refreshments, but he figured it was a good investment.

And sure enough, he fell for Ruth, a girl from the moneyed crowd who also liked him. She was smart, too, and didn't do the dumb things that Monty did. Like when he wanted to show off and told her to meet him in Sam's Saucy Restaurant downtown. She went straight to the Sans Souci—she knew his French accent was terrible. Once there, she ordered vichyssoise for both of them. He complained to the waiter that his soup was cold.

The waiter said, "Yes, sir. That is vichyssoise."

"I don't care what you call it, it is cold."

"Sir, vichyssoise is always served cold."

"I don't like my soup cold. Take it back and heat it up."

The waiter said, disdainfully, "Sir, you will get no warm vichyssoise in Sans Souci."

Monty realized he had done a dumb thing, so he drank his cold soup (and found it damn good) and ate his meal in silence. For dessert, Ruth recommended an ice-cream concoction for which the restaurant was famous. When Monty ordered ice-cream the waiter said, straight-faced, "You would like it heated, I presume."

Ruth kicked him, and he said nothing. But when she wasn't looking, he took back half the tip.

Monty and Ruth went out together for the better part of a year. By the time he found out that she was a poor girl putting on the same act that he was, it was too late—she was already pregnant. At first he figured he was just unlucky, but after they were married he changed his mind.

Not to worry. He was smart enough to see that with the advent of computers there would be an enormous market for punch-cards and punch-card operators. He began manufacturing the former and opened a training school for the latter. He did so well that he reinvested all his profits into a larger factory, a bigger inventory, and a larger building full of card punching machinery.

That was exactly when magnetic tapes began to replace punch-cards. He looked around for a market for his obsolete punch-cards, and figured that if he furnished old computers cheaply to developing countries who couldn't afford to buy newer ones, they would have to buy punch-cards. So he bought outmoded computers at factory prices wherever he could find them and practically gave them away to places like Paraguay, Peru, and Panama. Unfortunately, many of the computers that he picked up that way were Apples and Commodores, and he had forgotten that they could not use IBM punch-cards. He ended up with a warehouse full of blank IBM punch-cards. But he acquired a reputation as a strong supporter of developing countries.

He converted his factory for punch-cards into one for playing cards, and developed a profitable sideline producing decks of pre-marked cards, factory sealed, which he sold to magicians, casinos, and other carefully vetted purchasers. He found that a back design including the American flag was particularly helpful for marking, and as his cards found their way into developing countries, he began to build up a reputation as an American patriot.

He converted some of the card-punching machines and began punching out the sheet music for player pianos. There was a wave of nostalgia sweeping the country, and old player pianos were being picked up by the "in" group. However, there was a shortage of the punched sheets to feed into the pianos, and certainly none with modern tunes on them. As he negotiated the rights to current songs, he came into contact with musicians, composers, and music publishers. He liked the feel of being with such creative people, and since the player piano music brought in only a small income, he donated the proceeds to ASCAP, which gave him much publicity and good-will in musical circles.

The rest of his machinery that once punched cards was now punching holes in thin sheet metal for the armaments industry, and since no one seemed to care about the round pieces that were punched out, he had them made into junk jewelry. Unfortunately, it was so junky that it began to rust from body moisture a few days after it was put to use. But he never knew that, and as first-time purchasers also didn't know that, he sold a lot of jewelry.

Once he was in Turkey, on his way to Israel, and bought a ticket to the Holy Land on El Al, the Israeli airline, from the hotel travel agent. When he boarded he stupidly thought that Alia must be the Turkish way of spelling El Al. Not until he landed in Amman did he realize he was flying a Jordanian airline. Then he found that in those days the Jordanian authorities did not allow tourists to cross the bridge into

Israel. He had to fly back to Istanbul, and then to Tel Aviv. Those Jordanian entry and departure stamps on the same day in his passport aroused the suspicion of the Israeli authorities, especially since the same agent in Istanbul had booked him to Jerusalem, which had no international airport, instead of to Tel Aviv, which did. In the end he decided it would be smarter to just go back home, which raised the suspicions of the Israelis even higher. A clerk from the American consulate finally came and got him released.

He was smart at home, too. When he and Ruth decided to buy a house, he took a map and studied contours and distances, and made three estimates of where a new, more direct road to Candler Field, the Atlanta the airport would have to run. They bought a rundown house at the intersection of the three possible roads, and deliberately didn't fix it up. They figured to make quite a profit from having their property expropriated. Unfortunately, the mayor's brother-in-law, cousin, and crony all happened to buy houses along a much less desirable route, and that is where the road was put in.

Monty and his wife decided they'd better make their place livable, and Monty decided to do most of the work himself. He learned that you can't drive nails into steel-reinforced concrete, and that you can't hang heavy book shelves on lathboard and plaster walls. He also found out that if you measure heights from the floor, you'd better be sure the floor is level. He learned a lot more before he brought in a contractor, who— of course —charged them more than the estimate.

During a lull in local news the city newspaper decided to do a series on interesting citizens, and sent a reporter to interview Monty, the benefactor of developing countries and the distributor of American flags. Monty was preparing for a motor trip when the reporter appeared, and had maps spread out in front of him. The reporter opened the interview by asking what he was doing, and Monty told him he was studying road maps. The reporter smiled and said, "I guess that makes you a roads scholar." Monty thought that was funny, and said he guessed so.

In the interview Monty was smart enough to appear modest, and the reporter seemed impressed. The article portrayed Monty as a self-made man, who was terribly interested in and helpful to the developing countries; a consultant to arms manufacturers; a patriot who spread more pictures of the American flag throughout the world than anyone else (they didn't say on what the pictures were printed); a do-it-yourselfer; a supplier of beautiful but inexpensive jewelry to the younger generation; and one who deliberately lived in an out-of-the-way place in order to attract others like himself, thereby gentrifying rundown areas. Monty was very impressed when he read it—he hadn't realized what a great guy he was. Ruth was less impressed: "They want something," she said. The article incidentally called Monty a Rhodes Scholar, and although he thought of asking for a correction, he thought it would seem unduly finicky to do so.

It was the same reporter who told the local Democratic bigwigs that Monty might be willing to run for state senator, for despite his display of modesty, he was an ambitious person. He also told a few of them, in confidence, that Monty would probably be too dumb to realize that the Democrats had no chance in this election, and would take it seriously enough to contribute to the party.

Monty was sounded out, and was smart enough to realize that the first thing he should do was to contribute to the party, so he gave a hefty donation. He got the nomination, campaigned mightily, and was roundly defeated. When the victorious Republican state senator had a stroke two years later and withdrew from politics, to be replaced in the special election by a much weaker candidate, the Democratic politicos hoped that Monty would be smart enough to realize that this time they didn't want him, since they had a chance of winning.

But he wasn't that smart. He campaigned hard again, and ended up in the State Capitol. One of the first bills to come up after the election concerned legalizing gambling casinos in the state. Monty realized that if he voted for it, he could be accused of a personal interest, since he still manufactured playing cards. So he campaigned for the bill behind the scenes, and then had himself recorded as voting against it.

He hadn't realized that the casino syndicate would punish him for voting against them by not buying his cards. So he magnanimously apologized to them by donating all the cards they would need for at least five years. During that time he visited the casinos from time to time, never winning enough to make anyone suspicious, but getting further and further ahead of the game by little increments, until he figured he had made back the cost of the marked cards he had donated.

He intended to continue adding to his income with small wins, and even a contrived loss once in a while, but once when he picked up his cards and found he held four kings, he checked the back of the dealer's cards, and found that the dealer had four aces. Monty realized that he was being set up for a big kill. Ordinarily, a poker player holding four kings would bet his house, his wife, and his children on it. The chances of being defeated are infinitesimal. And since the dealer was also reading the back of the cards, that is how he expected Monty to bet, only to lose it all to the four aces. So Monty stupidly threw in his cards and didn't bet. The dealer looked surprised, and slowly turned over Monty's four kings, then looked at him with dawning comprehension. By not betting, Monty had indicated that he knew the dealer had a better hand—and he could not have known that legally. He was never admitted into any casino after that.

Monty realized that the church-going, conservative element of the electorate did not appreciate his atoning for his vote by giving cards to the casinos, and he searched for a way to seduce them. He went to church, he joined in the singing, he made a donation during the fund drive, but he didn't feel he had been forgiven, and began to think maybe he wasn't so smart.

Waiting in the car for Ruth to meet him one night (he had given her wrong directions), he got restless and walked up and down on the sidewalk. As he did, he saw a falling star, and then another. Just then two men joined him on the sidewalk, and in his excitement he said, "Hey, did you see that?" and pointed across the street. There was a flash from a camera, and one of the two men waved his arm.

From around the corner and out of parked cars jumped a covey of policemen. They surrounded the house across the street, and some of them broke down the front door. The morning paper headlined the storming of a notorious whorehouse, with a picture of State Senator Monty identifying the house for the police with his outstretched finger. Seduction of the church group became unnecessary.

A few days later a representative of the arms manufacturer for whom Monty did sub-contracts came to see him and showed him dummy models of the new weapons they were considering making. The dummies were in a foam-lined briefcase, each one in a setting molded for it. Monty promised to look at them to see if any parts seemed to lend themselves to sub-manufacturing.

Immediately after the representative left, two hefty types pushed their way into the office. One said, "You the guy that fingered our place, right?"

Monty instinctively ducked behind the open briefcase, turning it outward for protection as he did so. The two intruders stared in disbelief at the display of weapons they saw. Monty groped for something, anything, to hold onto in his fright, and as his fingers closed over the dummy grenade in the briefcase, he heard the door bang, and the room was empty. He never had another such visit.

It was a foregone conclusion that Monty would run for the House of Representatives, but he surprised the committee by announced for the Senate. They had a hard time finding an opponent who could match Monty's appeal as the supporter of the underdogs abroad, the crime fighter, the American propagandist via pictures of the flag, and—not least —as a contributor to the party.

In the Senate Monty followed the party line, voted regularly and conscientiously as instructed, and made a good impression on the voters. He kissed babies and wore Indian headdress, put on Stetsons, and ate at barbecues—even between elections, which made news. Slowly, he moved up.

Because of the positive way he was regarded in developing countries, he became the Senate expert on such areas. He was then given responsibilities concerning armament manufacturing, and he also became head of the committee investigating gambling.

Of course, he had his enemies. The reporter who had put him on the campaign trail at first never forgave him for not being as dumb as he had portrayed him to the local politicians, and seemed determined to get him. He conspired with two Republican senators to have Monty make a trip to London for a meeting concerning international cooperation against gambling—a meeting which had never been arranged. Then he had an amiable British racehorse owner offer Monty tickets to the Derby. He was all set to expose Monty, the Senator, on a junket to a non-existent meeting in order to attend a horse race. He had his photographers focussed and his witnesses ready.

Monty was to meet his host in the owners' section at the Derby, and had a special pass for that purpose. But Monty didn't know England, and didn't know where Epsom Downs was. As he drove in what he thought was the general direction, he stopped at a pub to ask directions. He wasn't sure how Derby was pronounced in Britain, so he spoke pure American.

The publican (bartender to Monty) had a hard time understanding what he wanted, since he was from Birmingham (the English, not the Alabaman). "You say you want Derby?" (He pronounced it Darby, of course).

"The Derby, sure," said Monty.

"Derbyshire? That's a long way from here."

By this time Monty was thoroughly confused. "I think so."

"Then you are certainly on the wrong road." And the publican gave him explicit directions to Derbyshire.

Monty couldn't believe how long he drove before he decided to ask again. The pub he entered was so similar he thought he might have driven in a circle, but this publican was small and dark, whereas the other had been tall and blonde, so he asked.

The publican had spent two years with American soldiers, and had no trouble with the accent. "If you want the Derby in Epsom Downs I'm afraid you won't make it. It's a long way from here and ready to start. But you can watch it on the telly if you like."

The only other person in the pub was a plump, white-haired man with red cheeks, who looked vaguely familiar to Monty. He waved Monty to a chair in front of the TV. "Racing fan, are you?"

"Actually, no. I was to meet someone at the Derby and got lost."

"Then you don't care who wins or loses?"

"Not really."

"A pity. Watching a horserace without caring who wins is boring. May I make it interesting for you? I have ten sweepstake tickets on the Derby. I will sell you half-interest in any one of them that you choose, and then you will find yourself rooting for a certain horse."

"That's sporting of you. I'll take you up on it."

When they became the joint winners of the sweepstakes, their pictures were in all the papers—Monty, the American Senator, and Sir Andrew Thompson, chairman of the Parliamentary Commission on Developing Countries. It was clear to everyone that Monty was in England on Senate business.

While he was there he was invited to dinner by a distant relative. Knowing that Monty hadn't found Epsom Downs, the relative was sure he wouldn't find Finchley, so gave him minute directions. He was to take the Tube to Golders Green, and then the Number 21 bus. He was to get off at the fifth stop. That stop was marked by a statue of a naked lady pouring water into a fountain, which would be how he would know he was right. Monty carefully found the Underground line to Golders Green, and got on going in the right direction. Once there, he carefully took the Number 12 bus, and began counting the stations. At what he was sure was the fifth stop, there was only a drugstore and a supermarket. He kept looking for the statue. They rode and rode, and he saw no statue, so when the West Indian conductor checked his ticket, Monty said, "Have we passed the naked lady?"

The conductor's eyes popped. "What did you say?"

"I was told to look for a naked lady. Have we passed her yet?"

The conductor backed a few steps away from him, and then turned and shouted down the coach, "This man wants a naked lady. Anybody here know where to find one?"

Every eye on the bus focussed on Monty, and the woman sitting next to him quickly moved across the aisle. The conductor turned back to him. "You sure you want a naked lady, mister?"

Monty wanted to dive under his seat, but couldn't, of course. Instead, he got off at the next stop to call his relative. He found a pay-station telephone, but it required a tenpenny piece, which he didn't have. It was a deserted neighborhood. He didn't know where he was; he didn't have the money to make a phone call; and he realized he hadn't brought his relative's phone number with him.

He cursed his own stupidity, and with little choice, rang the bell of one of the houses on the corner. A small girl came to the door, looked through the half-window, and ran screaming into the back of the house: "It's a strange man!"

A burly man in an undershirt came to the door, a hefty poker in one hand. Through the window Monty tried to explain his predicament. The man stared at him, and then looked surprised. He opened the door and said, "Ain't you the bloke that won the sweepstakes? A 'Merican senator, aintja? Saw your photo on the telly. C'mon in."

Not only was the family awed by such a distinguished guest; they sent the kid out to tell all the neighbors. In a short time Monty was surrounded by people. It took a long time before he could again explain his situation, and then people vied with one another to find his relative's name in the telephone directory. His relative offered to come for him, but his new host would have none of it. He would drive him there himself. But first, of course, he would have a cuppa, wouldn't he?

So the couple and the child, another couple from across the street and Monty piled into what seemed to be a fourth-or fifth-hand car, and after only one tire (actually, tyre) was changed, arrived at his relative's house. Dinner had been set for eight, and it was now after ten. His relative graciously invited the accompanying party in, but they bashfully refused.

Monty was truly grateful for their help, and thanked them profusely, mentioning that he rarely had a chance to visit normal, working-class people in their homes, and had learned a lot. They parted friends.

In the course of the evening, Monty mentioned that he was looking for a part for the British-made food processor he and Ruth used, and for some reason, was having a hard time locating it. His relative promised to try and help him.

Evidently the family to whom Monty had turned for help was inordinately proud of their visitor and talked about him a good deal, for it got to one of the London papers, and there was a feature story about the American Senator who plays Haroun al Raschid, visiting people at home to understand how they live and what their problems are.

Monty knew good publicity when he saw it, even if it was mostly for a foreign audience. He would see to it that it got back home. Consequently, he decided to build on what he had started. He moved out of the posh hotel in which he had been staying, and checked in at a small, no-star hotel. The building had once been a home, and was now run by an Indian family. They did not recognize Monty, nor his name. His room was in a basement, with a small, high window. He ate curry in the small dining room, and before going to bed used the pay-station phone in the hall to call his relatives. He didn't tell them where he was staying, but just left the number.

He was awakened early in the morning by hearing his name called. He looked around, recognized where he was, but couldn't find the source of the call. Finally he realized that there was a loudspeaker near the ceiling, and a voice with a heavy Indian accent was telling him there was a call for him on the phone in the corridor. He could find no way to acknowledge the message, so he jumped into his pants and went to the phone.

His relative was calling to say that he had located the part that Monty needed, and was going to dictate the address. Monty had neither paper nor pencil with him, so he asked his caller to call back later, but the latter said he was on his way out and wouldn't get another chance to call, so Monty asked him to hang on, and turned back to his room. The door had locked on a spring lock, and the key was inside. Holding his pants up with one hand, Monty sprinted barefoot up the stairs to the desk, asked for paper and pencil, and ran back downstairs, to the amazement of the early risers in the lobby.

In the corridor, he tried to hold up his pants with one hand, hold the receiver with another hand, and write the address with a third hand. He found he didn't have three hands. He finally found that if he buttoned the top of his pants, ran his hand through the fly from the inside, and crooked his leg, he could hold his pants up and simultaneously write against his leg, which he proceeded to do, although it wasn't easy.

Three separate couples on their way to the dining room for breakfast passed him, but with true British reticence, said nothing and looked away. When he hung up the phone, Monty had to again go upstairs, barefooted and holding his pants up, to get a key for his room.

The American Ambassador was a bit stiff the next day as he told Monty that if he wanted to pay visits around London, to homes or to hotels, he might do well to let the Embassy staff arrange it for him. And he handed him a plain brown envelope in which there was a picture of

Monty talking on the telephone, trying to hold up his pants and write with the same hand. Monty didn't know whether to be impressed with the American security service in England, or with the British CID. He was always sorry, however, that he never did see the naked lady.

Back home, Ruth asked him one day how long he was going to keep closets piled full of IBM punch-cards. She had used a few to make notes of various kinds, but he had thousands, and she needed those closets for other things. Monty said he would try to find a use for them, and when his ten-year-old nephew came over, Monty asked him if he could use some IBM punch-cards for notepaper. His nephew asked him what an IBM punch-card was. He stared at his nephew. His ignorance gave Monty an idea.

A few days later he showed his twenty-year-old computer operator a punch-card and asked her if she knew what it was. She turned it over and over in her hands and said, "I give up. What is it?"

He tried it on a thirty-year-old aide, who asked, "Does it have something to do with time clocks?"

Around age forty, people not only recognized the card, but invariably said, "Gee, I haven't seen one of those in years."

So Monty got in touch with the manufacturer of Trivia games, and had most of his cards inserted into the sets. He figured that older people deserved some advantages. The cards, incidentally, had a logo printed on them that indicated they had been manufactured by him. Thus, his name got into a lot of houses, and before a lot of eyes. And that's all a politician wants.

As Monty acquired seniority in the Senate, his advice was called for by numerous people in various circumstances. In some cases he offered advice without being asked. Thus, he advised President Nixon not to hand over the tapes, because the whole matter would blow over and be forgotten in a few weeks. He practically promised President Carter that the Shah had the full support of all Iranians; and later assured him that a military rescue operation to free the hostages could not fail. He also warned Carter that Begin and Sadat would never agree with each other; and he advised Prime Minister Begin that a massive invasion of Lebanon would finally bring about peace in the Middle East.

Knowledge of the number of his consultations, and the people with whom he consulted, added considerably to his prestige. However, it was clear that for security reasons the public could not know what advice he gave. Fortunately.

Only once in Monty's political career did he come close to disaster. In 1969 the reporter who had been dogging him all the time finally prepared a full brief on Monty. He dug up Monty's university papers, which had misjudged events so badly. He verified that Monty had sent old, outdated computers to developing countries—computers that couldn't use the software that was available to them. He accused Monty of taking and using army surplus material, in the form of circles cut out of munitions parts; he documented the fact that this "stolen" material was sold as jewelry—jewelry that rusted and became a health hazard. He showed that the American flag on the back of playing cards had not kept up with the times, and hadn't been changed to include Hawaii and Alaska until long after the fact. And he made a big deal about Monty untruthfully claiming to have been a Rhodes Scholar. The reporter would have had a field day if he knew that Monty manufactured marked playing cards—and profited from them—but this was one bit of information he didn't unearth.

The reporter prepared a complete dossier, designed to end Monty's political career, and probably his business one as well. In fairness, the editor let Monty see the article before publishing it. Ruth told Monty to ignore it—as the old political adage goes, there is no such thing as bad publicity; just make sure they spell your name right. But Monty decided to reply to the article on TV. Ruth pointed out that this would spread the story to an enormous number of people who would otherwise not have read it, but he pretended he didn't hear her.

Monty prepared his defense brief. He intended to refute the facts one by one, to call for various people to witness the truth of what he said, to defend himself, to recount what he had done for others, to wrap himself in the American flag and to almost tearfully call upon the public to support him. In other words, he was preparing to make a complete ass of himself. Ruth kept telling him that for a smart man, he was acting awfully dumb.

The night before the story was to appear, to be followed by Monty's TV appearance, President Ike Eisenhower died. The paper was full of eulogies, reminiscences, pictures, history, and discussions concerning Ike. The accusations against Monty were cut to ten lines and buried on page thirteen. However, he decided to use the TV time already allotted to him, which Ruth insisted was stupid, but instead of refuting the accusations, he used his time praising the memory of Ike, which added some Republicans to his supporters.

At the next round of Democratic Presidential primaries, Monty's name kept coming up. The third-world supporters were for him; the law-and-order people were for him; the entertainment and media world lined up for him; the munitions people were for him; and his name was well-known to the average voter. A number of groups asked him to run. That scared the professional pols to death. They didn't want him. They didn't think they could control him.

So a delegation visited Monty and explained to him that he didn't have a chance of getting the nomination, but that if he would throw his support to their proposed candidate, he could have the Vice-Presidency for the asking. He did his own polling, tested the wind with some trusted friends, and weighed the situation. It would be a hard battle for the Presidency, and he might not make it. But win or lose, his background would be thoroughly examined. The old accusations of the reporter would be dug up and investigated. And he couldn't sue for libel—they might prove it on him.

He talked it over with Ruth. She said, "You know, Monty, you really are smart. You would learn everything you lack—economics, social welfare, defense, in fact, everything—very quickly. But every now and then you do something really dumb, like giving away computers that don't use your punch-cards; or flying Alia instead of El Al; or obviously throwing away four kings. Remember the advice you gave Carter and the others? One dumb move like those and either you'd wipe out a foreign country, or we'd be wiped out. I think you owe it to the future of this country not to run for President. And I say it because I love both you and this country."

"You know, Ruth, you are pretty smart yourself. I think you are right. I have made some whoppers. And I'm not at all sure that I'd get the nomination or be elected. But if I can't be President, I don't want to be Vice-President. What did John Garner say after he was Vice-President, that the office isn't worth a pail of warm spit? I don't want to be a figurehead. And if I don't become Vice-President, I'll have gone as far as I can in politics. I think I'll just get out of politics and enjoy life."

"That may be the smartest thing you ever did."

"Or maybe the dumbest."

And that's what he did.

When the President was about to be impeached and resigned, and the Vice-President became President, Monty felt that he had again done something dumb. But when the new President was shot dead by a teenager who wanted attention, Monty felt he had been lucky. Ruth insisted he had been smart.

I visited my Uncle Monty after Ruth had died, when he was old enough to be writing his memoirs. He said, "You know, one thing keeps bothering me. When I read what I wrote, I can't figure out whether I was a smart fellow who did dumb things, or a dumb person who occasionally did something smart. Or if I was just lucky. It makes a difference to me. You're a historian. Would you read what I've written and give me your opinion?"

So I read it, and I told him what I thought.

Uncle Alan

◆

UNCLE ALAN

When my Uncle Alan was poor, everyone called him a nutty inventor and made fun of him. When he got wealthy, they called him an inventive eccentric and were respectful of him. He didn't care much one way or the other.

In school he invented things to frighten girls and embarrass teachers—mostly female teachers. His was the first balloon that gave off a sound like a person passing gas when it was pressed, and he put it under the cushion on the teacher's chair when he was still in third grade. He had a whinnying laugh that carried through the class when the teacher sat down. Of course, it carried him right down to the principal's office, too.

His next-door neighbor, Rivon, made the most fun of him, and thus became the target for many of his inventions. For example, when he was twelve Alan built an elaborate burglar alarm, with glass eyes and antenna sensors, and coils of wire running around the cabinet, a siren, and all kinds of exotic looking instruments visible in the box. He built it on the front porch where Rivon could watch him, and explained to his family and people who asked that this was a new kind of burglar alarm. Once plugged in, it was so smart that it would call the name of the person getting close to it.

He knew that Rivon was so proud of his unusual name that he wouldn't be able to resist the temptation, so he left the burglar alarm on the porch, with an electric cord and plug prominently displayed. He watched from his upstairs window as Rivon looked cautiously around and prepared to plug the cord in. Alan hadn't anticipated this. He thought Rivon would take the whole gadget to his own house to try it out there, in secret. He rushed down the stairs just in time for the flash as the electricity shorted out in the neighborhood. Alan enjoyed the sight of Rivon frantically trying to put out the fire which ensued from the ungrounded and disconnected wires. Alan's whinnying laugh sounded through the neighborhood. Unfortunately, Rivon couldn't stem the flames, and since the burglar alarm was on Alan's porch, it was the front of his house that burned down.

It was hard for the family, the fire department, and the insurance company to fix the blame. Alan had made the machine, but hadn't plugged it in. Rivon had plugged it in, but didn't know it would cause a fire. In the end, it was decided they were both to blame, and they both thought that was unfair.

Alan was not handsome, not the smartest boy in school, on no athletic team, and was thought of as somewhat peculiar—but he was a boy. So as he grew up he had his share of dates, mostly with the girls that the popular boys didn't date. You'd think the girls would be grateful to Alan for dating them, but on the contrary, they seemed to resent the fact that they had to go with him instead of one of the more desirable boys. But they went.

Alan was not a great conversationalist, so he always took with him some little trick or funny gadget that he could show off to his date and thus at least start a conversation. He was surprised when, at about age sixteen, girls would ask him with real interest what he had brought or what he had made. This caused him to think seriously about what had been gadgets up to then, and eventually led him to study mechanical engineering in college.

Alan's parents were Orthodox Jews from Poland, but when they learned about the horrors of the Holocaust, their belief in a benign, just, supernatural being began to waver. When they heard about the Society for Secular Humanistic Judaism they went to some meetings to learn more about it, and were immediately convinced. They were quite active in the Society, trying to bring some of their friends in, too.

However, over time, they had difficulty distinguishing Jewish ethics from purely humanistic ethics, and in an effort to resolve this intellectual dilemma, went to some meetings of the Society for Ethical Culture. There they found many Jews like themselves. They also found a number of wealthy and important people among the members, and were not above enjoying this, their first contact with public figures.

Eventually, however, they found that ethics were not enough to answer their questions and needs. They felt there must be some power that made order out of chaos in the universe, and, in addition, they began to want a framework of at least semi-ritual for themselves. The Unitarian Church seemed to be the answer—a belief in One God, without the complexities created by a Trinity.

In the end, they found the Unitarian Church colorless. Perhaps they subconsciously missed the ritual and the ceremony of Orthodoxy. They examined Jews for Jesus and abandoned it as consisting only of Jews who didn't have the courage to convert. They dabbled in Theosophy, Bahai, and even looked into Rosicrucianism, insofar as they could. Finally, when they were invited to join the Masons they found a substitute for religion, with ritual, a hierarchy, a moral code (to be subscribed to, if not practiced), and enough worthy causes to fill in their retirement time, which they had now reached.

Alan dropped out of the search when it reached the Ethical Culture Society. He found he didn't need a belief in a higher power, nor ritual. Ethics seemed to him enough of a belief system, and he didn't try to elaborate on it, other than determining to try to be an ethical person.

Consequently, when Alan went to the university his entire attention was on his studies. He didn't bother his head with anything more ethereal than his assignments. His instructors noted immediately that he had a natural bent for things mechanical. They also noted that he would never accept the simplest way of doing things, but would invent elaborate procedures for doing the same thing. One instructor tried to explain Occam's Razor to him, which holds that one should use the simplest possible explanation that fits the facts. Alan understood the law, but didn't understand what made it correct, and continued to elaborate on the simplest activities.

He also continued his reputation as a nut. He showed the other students in his class the reading machine he had built. It had a mirror, that he claimed was an optical sensor, that moved visibly across the page, line by line, reading—as Alan explained—every word in the book.

"And then?" asked several students.

"And then, what?"

"What does it do with what it has read?"

"Nothing."

"What do you mean, nothing? Does it summarize it, or read it out loud, or print it out? What does it do?"

"Nothing."

"What do you mean, nothing?"

"Just that, nothing."

"It just reads, and that's the end of it?"

"Sure."

"Then what good is it?"

"I didn't say it was any good. I just said I invented it."

Alan was forcibly escorted to the bathroom and put under the shower. It wasn't the first time.

He became quite interested in a girl named Sorrel, who all but threw herself at him, but he dropped her because whenever he began explaining the things he was doing or trying to invent, she would yawn and begin to freshen her makeup. He sometimes thought that if he could invent a new method of sexual intercourse, he would finally have her attention—at least for a few moments.

A while later he met a girl named Heather but she hung on his every word, batted her eyelids at him, and said, "That's fascinating. That's wonderful. That's interesting," no matter what he said. Once he made up some gobbledygook and spouted it at her and she responded, "You make everything so clear." Since they hadn't even made love, he dropped her, too.

Alan tried to find another girl friend. He dated a number, but found no chemistry with them. One girl, Rosemary, to whom he was particularly attracted, kept rebuffing him, and as he persisted, she finally said, "You are wasting your time. Don't you realize that I am a lesbian?"

He never found out if that was true, or just an effective put-off. In any case, it worked.

At a New Year's Eve party a lovely young lady, seemingly attracted to Alan and obviously very sure of herself, sidled over to him and said, very confidently, "We met at the same party last New Year's Eve. Remember me?"

Alan eyed her, tried to remember last year's party, thought a moment, weighed a white lie, and finally answered, ethically, "I'm afraid I don't."

"Well," she said, obviously miffed, "what a memory you don't have!"

"Yes," said Alan, gently, "and what an impression you didn't make."

She turned on her heel and walked away, and he never saw her again. "Why do I kill my own chances like that?" he thought.

Alan suddenly realized that all the girls with whom he had bad luck had the names of herbs. He didn't understand it, but began instinctively to steer clear of girls with names like Angelica, Bella, Rue, or Cicely. When he met a girl named Marjie, he felt his jinx was broken, so they began to date. But Marjie turned out to be a gold-digger—she wanted gifts for her birthday, for Valentine's Day, for Christmas, for the weekly and monthly anniversaries of when they met, and "just-so" gifts; she wanted to go only to expensive places; she wanted him to buy amusing things that they saw when they were together (usually expensive things) and give them to her. He began to be chronically short of money. It was quite accidental that he learned that she called herself Marjie, but that her name was really Marjoram—"Isn't that a ridiculous name?" she caroled. He found he could manage quite well financially after he dropped her.

In his senior year Alan became a research assistant to a faculty member who was trying to invent a blood-fractionating machine. At that time there was no such machine, and medical science felt the need for one. With Alan's help, the machine was finally operational, and he was very proud. But Professor Roebuck wouldn't put it on the market. He wanted to perfect it. Alan pointed out to him, as respectfully as he could, that even in its present shape it would probably save lives, but the professor was a perfectionist, and refused to allow the machine to be shown or duplicated, for fear someone might point out an improvement he hadn't thought of.

At that time Alan was going with a girl named Rose Upton. When he met her at a party and learned her name, he said, "Nobody ever promised me a herb garden, but a rose garden, that's different."

"What are you talking about?" she asked.

"Nothing. A private joke."

"Do you always tell yourself jokes?"

"Sho. I'm the nutty inventor. Didn't anyone tell you about me?"

"No. You must not be as famous as you think."

"Oh, I'm not conceited. I don't think I'm half as good as I really am."

She laughed. "That's funny. Do you really invent things?"

"Yep."

"Like what?"

"Well, I just helped invent a blood-fractionating machine."

"A what?"

So he explained to her how the machine worked and what it was used for.

"Why, that's wonderful. Will you get rich?"

So he had to explain what "helped invent," meant. And then he couldn't stop himself—he complained bitterly about the professor's refusal to make the machine available.

"Why, that's awful. Can't the law or something make him let people use it?"

"Seems not. He can sit on it the rest of his life, I guess."

"But you say lives can be saved…"

"Only if it is available."

They began discussing plans for prying the machine away from the professor, and Alan suddenly realized that Rose not only understood what he was saying, but had made his problem hers. This was the beginning of their relationship.

As their dating became more frequent, and as each one stopped dating others, Alan's natural instincts began to exert themselves, and he became more and more amorous, but Rose kept resisting. They were necking in a parked car outside the University chapel one night when Alan became quite insistent, and when Rose refused, he said, "Why not, for God's sake? We love each other, we're not children, we know enough to take precautions. C'mon, Rosie."

Rose was fighting her own impulses, and couldn't find a logical explanation, but looking up at the archway over the chapel's entrance, she began to giggle. "That's why," she said, pointing to the arch. On it was carved, "Virtue is its own reward."

Her giggle helped Rose to regain her perspective, and the rest of the evening was a blank for Alan.

It was a few months after this that Rose's father came down with a perplexing disease. As she explained it to Alan, it had to do with his blood, and the doctors were trying various combinations of drugs to stem the condition. Alan again remembered the blood-fractionating machine, and could not shake off the feeling that had the machine been available—either for research or for treatment—it might have offered some hope for Rose's father.

He again spoke to Roebuck about making the machine available in its present state, and Roebuck again refused. Alan shared his frustration with Rose. Talking about it, she suddenly said, "Has Professor Roebuck patented his machine?"

Alan thought. "No. He is afraid to even let the patent office see his unperfected machine, lest they criticize it."

"Could you build one?"

"Jesus! Do you mean what I think you mean?"

"Could you?"

"If I could afford the materials I could. But that would be unethical. After all, it was his idea."

"And withholding help from dying people is ethical?"

"Well…, Look…, Geez, I don't know what to say. Anyway, it is probably illegal to build such a machine. It is theft of an idea, at least."

"My father's firm uses a lawyer. His name is Ron Carter and he is the patent specialist in one of the most prestigious law firms in town. I talked to him about it. Patents are only granted for physical, material things. Ideas can not be patented. Theft of an idea only applies to things like books or plays. My father has money. There couldn't be a better use for it than to save his life—and maybe that of others. I'm not saying you should patent it or make money out of it. Just build one and release it for use by anyone who needs it—or even only by my father. Will you do it?"

"Rose, please. It was Professor Roebuck's invention. I just helped with it. If I were to steal that idea my name would be mud in academia for perpetuity. Nobody would hire me."

"First it was your ethics and now it is your future. My father isn't going to have a future if he dies."

"But we can't be sure such a machine would help him, and anyway, it would take months to build."

"Start."

"Rose, I don't like Professor Roebuck, and I think what he is doing is wrong, but if I stole his idea I'd feel like a thief."

"First your ethics, then your future, and now your self-image. And what about my father?"

In the end, Alan couldn't bring himself to undertake what to him was a completely unethical course of action and Rose stopped seeing him or talking to him. Her father did die, and she never forgave him. He, on the other hand, couldn't bear to keep working for Professor Roebuck, forever tinkering with the same invention, for he was constantly reminded of Rose. One day he just quit. He told Roebuck he wouldn't be back, and left without even collecting his final salary.

He was hired by an architectural concern as an engineer, and began a rather routine period in his life. He dated some girls from the office, and some of their friends; he went to plays; he was invited to parties; married women began "fixing him up" with unmarried girls; in short, he was just sort of rolling along. So between sporadic and short-lived romances—which sometimes became temporary affairs—he finished the university and took a second degree. When he thought of Rose at all, he wryly remembered that she had been the only girl he went out with for some time that was not named for a herb.

One day he took home the model of a skyscraper that was no longer needed in the office, and began to tinker with it. He put in a small elevator, and when it got to the 14th floor the light on one of the rooms went on. A moment later the window opened and a doll—a figure of a man in pajamas—was catapulted through the window and floated down holding an opened umbrella, landing in the swimming pool, creating a wave…In short, Alan was constructing a Rube Goldberg machine, in which each action led to another. He worked on it for weeks, and had great fun with it.

He showed the gadget to people who visited him at home, including his occasional date, Frances, who came in for what was euphemistically referred to as a night-cap. When she saw it she induced him to bring it over to the new Museum of Kitsch, where she worked. The Curator liked it, and put it on display. Alan didn't want to appear too grateful to her, because he had learned that her mother's maiden name was Pepper, and he was afraid her interest might lead to something more serious.

He thought that with his item in the museum, people might treat him more seriously, and that he might be invited to invent other pseudo-art items. But he was wrong on both counts. He was still thought of as a gadget-maker rather than an inventor, and his museum piece was considered what the British call a one-off. He also steered clear of Frances, and she made no effort to see him.

Walking down the main street one day he saw two men unloading a truck. One carried boxes from the truck to the sidewalk-opening of the cellar, and in the cellar another man reached for and took the boxes lowered to him and stored them away. As Alan watched, a boy on roller skates approached the opening, suddenly saw the danger, and veered away, banging into the man who was carrying a box. The man yelled at the boy, the boy stuck out his tongue and darted away. And Alan had an idea.

Thinking of the wheels on the roller skates, and the difficult time one man had handing the boxes down, and the other had in lifting his arms for the boxes, Alan went home and drew a sketch of a set of rollers in a frame, that could run from the sidewalk down into the cellar, on which boxes could roll down under their own power. In the office he made a scale model, and it worked perfectly. He could already see room for some improvements, but put that idea out of his mind at once.

Alan knew that he had better patent his new invention as soon as possible, but didn't know how to go about it. He remembered Rose mentioning a patent lawyer, and he looked up the address of Ron Carter and made an appointment. At the last minute, however, he decided he'd better not have anything to do with anything that Rose was connected with—after her father's death her regard for him had turned into palpable hatred.

Alan simply looked in the phone book for a patent lawyer, and took his idea to Bob Carlsson. Carlsson looked over the drawings and the model and nodded. "Yes, it is certainly patentable, even though it is a bit crude. Are you sure you don't want to perfect it a bit more before you apply for a patent?"

"What's your middle name, Roebuck?" asked Alan, with some asperity.

"Roebuck? What do you mean? I don't have a middle name. What are we talking about?"

"Never mind. What's the next step?"

"We could file papers immediately. However, let me give you some advice. I have been in this business for some time, and I've seen what can happen. You have only a scale model. You don't know if it will work in real life. You don't know how heavy a load it will carry, whether the rollers will lock under too much weight, whether the package will gain so much speed it will burst open at the bottom, what are the maximum lengths and inclines—there are lots of bugs yet involved. If you try to patent it as it is, the application may be refused. An item must be demonstrably useful to be patented. One which cannot produce the intended result cannot be patented. In addition, someone else can take out a patent on an improvement—yes, they can do that—and the improver may make more money than the original inventor.

"My advice to you is to have some prototypes made, and have them tested under various conditions. Add improvements that will become obvious to you. According to the law, any use or distribution that you do within a year of applying for a patent will not affect the patentability. Use this year to test and improve your invention, and then we'll apply for a patent for a tested, useful machine that can hardly be improved upon."

Makes sense, thought Alan. Nobody will be hurt if this machine is patented next year, and in the meantime I probably will be able to change it and find other uses for it.

Alan went to a machine shop and had the parts made for his roller conveyor, and put together his first full-scale model. He had trouble finding any store that would let him test it, since they were afraid it would result in breakage. Bob said he knew a lawyer with a department store as a client, and got that lawyer to persuade the owner of the store to give Alan permission to install his prototype. Sure enough, he found some bugs and spent time straightening them out. At a later time, he found that if he put a rubberized material over the rollers, they would carry small items as well as large ones, and even awkward objects would not get caught between the rollers. He was awfully glad that Bob had suggested he continue experimenting.

He kept Bob in touch with what he was doing, and about six months after his first approach he felt that he was ready to apply for a patent, but just before he did he had an idea as to how he could get his conveyor belt to turn corners, and spent some months on that. Finally, he realized that the basic machinery could be used for moving walkways, obviating the long, long distances that travelers were beginning to walk in airports, among other places, and he went to work on that.

It was almost eleven months from the time he first approached Bob that he was able to report that he was through experimenting for the time being, and was ready to apply for a patent. Bob showed him the file he had, and together they extracted the various drawings, explanations, photographs, and the affidavit as to usefulness from the store where he had experimented. He watched Bob put this material in a sealed envelope, and took it to the postoffice himself, where he mailed it registered. Then began the waiting period.

In the meantime, Alan went back to his hobby, and constructed a number of Rube Goldberg inventions. They were wacky, but they were pretty, and could keep an audience interested for a long time. He made enough on these to live well, but his reputation as a nutty inventor grew. People smiled at whatever he said, humored him, but backed away when he became serious. He found his social life was becoming restricted, since when he was asked out he was expected to put on a performance—to play the clown.

At the opening of an exhibit including one of his contraptions Alan ran into Frances again. He was delighted to see a familiar face, and even more delighted when she seemed genuinely interested in him as a person, and not as an oddity. They began to see each other, but when she introduced him to her mother, he was very distant and withdrawn, which puzzled her. She pressed him for an answer, but he was embarrassed to explain why he had a phobia against names drawn from nature, and didn't attempt to.

It seemed like a very long time to him, but it was two months later when Bob called him and asked him to come in.

"Did you get an answer?"

"Yes, come in tomorrow morning."

"Did I get the patent?"

"It's not something to discuss on the phone. Come in tomorrow."

Alan had a sense of foreboding, and in the morning Bob said, "There is no way I can soften this. You have been preempted. Such an invention has already been patented."

"By whom, when?"

"They don't give us that information in their reply. It is a form letter. Here. I could go to Washington and dig it out, if it is important to you."

Alan was crushed. "Please do," he said, subdued.

Frances was supportive. "You'll invent other things. This isn't the end of the world." But it didn't help very much.

Bob called him again a week later. "I have the information. I can give it to you on the phone."

But this time Alan preferred to do things face-to-face, so went to Bob's office.

It had been a routine search, but had taken time. "The patent was granted about six months ago to the Southside Mercantile Company. They are a small conglomerate that owns department stores, a trucking line, a dress factory, and other things."

Alan's ears pricked up. "Department stores? Do they own the store in which we demonstrated our prototype?"

Bob stared at him, then picked up a list from his desk. "By God, they do!"

Alan couldn't believe what he was going to ask, but did: "What was the name of the lawyer who arranged for the demonstration to be there?"

"The lawyer? Oh, he wouldn't have anything to do with that. He's a well know patent lawyer—upright and ethical."

"Does his name happen to be Ron Carter?"

Amazement. "How did you know?"

"Ethical, huh?"

"Why, sure."

"Who owns Southside Mercantile?"

"It's a stock company."

"Can you find out the name of the majority stockholders?"

"Sure. That's a matter of public record."

Bob called his broker, and holding the phone, recited three names to Alan. The third was a Rose Ginger Upton.

"Rose Ginger Upton, huh? I should have known it!" Alan was furious. "She stole my idea! I want to sue the pants off of her!"

"Alan, I know how you feel. But you don't have a case. Let me first call Ron Carter and find out what I can."

"I don't care what you find out. I want to sue."

Carlsson picked up the phone and got through to Carter. "Ron, what do you know about the Southside Mercantile Company, and about an R. G. Upton there?"

His eyes opened wide, and he controlled himself with a visible effort. Quietly, he put the phone down.

"Rose Ginger Upton is the maiden name of his wife. They're newly married."

"Then it's collusion, it's conspiracy, it's unethical behavior, it's theft of an idea! I want to sue them!"

"Unfortunately, you can prove none of those. I'll guarantee you that Ron Carter is too smart to have handled the patent application himself. They probably used the manager of the store as the applicant. You couldn't even prove unethical professional behavior to the Ethics Committee of the American Bar Association, since you'd have to prove that Ron deliberately suggested that store with malice aforethought, and you can't do that."

"So what do you suggest?"

"They've beaten you, Alan. Hog-tied you, hornswoggled you, outwitted you. There's nothing you can do. So cut your losses, see the whole thing as a learning experience, and go to work on something else. If you sue and lose—which you will—you'll be tagged as litigious, and investors and co-workers will shun you."

Alan tried hard to resist the advice. He got a second opinion from another lawyer, he studied law books himself, and he brooded night and day, but in the end he had to admit that Bob was right. There was nothing he could do.

Frances tried to console him. "It's only money, Alan. It isn't your good name, or your health, or your dignity. You still have your inventiveness, you still have your job, in fact, you still have me. It's only money."

"Yeah," he said, "that's the point—it's money."

He decided that he needed some no-thinking time to get over it, and decided on a cruise to the Virgin Islands as the kind of thing he needed. To his surprise and immense delight, Frances agreed to go with him, although she insisted on paying her own way.

They had a lot of fun. On the ship they drank Cuba Libres and Margeritas, dunked in the bathtub-size swimming pool, played shuffleboard, danced the rumba, and wore costumes to the masked ball. On shore they walked to the few places of interest on each island rather than taking the tourist sightseeing buses, and went swimming in relatively uncrowded coves. On one beach Alan was sitting in a beach chair thinking back on recent events, and felt he needed a Margerita, which he had.

He liked the taste so much he had another. He forgot that he hadn't eaten since breakfast and it was now mid-afternoon.

When the world began to seem far from him, and spinning, and he was floating above it, he heard a familiar voice say, "Did you see what happened to me?! What an undertow! I was in water just up to my knees when a wave knocked me down and began to carry me out. If it hadn't been for two men who saw what happened, I would have drowned. I lost my sunglasses and my watch—that's how strong the undertow was!"

"That's nice," he replied, dreamily.

"Nice?! That's all you have to say? I tell you I actually almost drowned. You…, You…, Why, you're drunk! You are absolutely blotto! I've never seen you like that before." He heard a crystal-like sound that he recognized as laughter, and tried to respond, just before he passed out.

Strangely, he felt better about himself after that episode. It was as though he had purged himself of his bitterness. Both he and Frances were sorry to see the cruise end, but he felt he had regained his natural balance.

Consequently, it was quite unexpected when, on going through his accumulated mail, he found an unsigned postcard that said: "You have your ethics, and I have the patent. A fair exchange."

He was thrown right back into his depression, which alternated with fury and frustration. Frances watched what was happening, and one day said, "Alan. It's time to pull yourself together. What happened happened. Now you have to look to the future, and do you know what that future holds? I'll tell you. Me. Let's get married, Alan."

Since he had been proposing to her at least once a week for the last several months, he couldn't believe his good luck, and popped out of his depression like a jack-in-the box.

Alan had no idea that wedding preparations required so much driving around. It wasn't the driving that was draining, it was finding a parking place, waiting for a parking place, fighting for a parking place, parking illegally hoping not to get a ticket, double-parking and waiting in the car, without end. While double-parked on Columbus Avenue, waiting for Frances, he idly watched a mobile Luna Park across the street. The characters in the Ferris Wheel seemed to be enjoying themselves, and suddenly he had an idea.

That night he began doing the calculations and the sketches that would eventually result in his newest invention: A parking garage that picked the cars up on a gigantic wheel. The rotating wheel was between several stationary wheels, and a hydraulic mechanism lifted and moved the parked car from the moving wheel to the stationary wheels. He also found that cars did not have to be only at the ends of the arms of the wheels—they could be all the way down the arms. Computerized, the wheel could move cars up and down to open parking spaces, and then return them to the ground via the rotating wheel. He figured that three times the number of cars could be parked in the same space as a conventional garage, the need for parking attendants was minimal, and—best of all—the cars could not be stolen.

This time, with Bob's help, Alan deposited sketches and models every step of the way, and in time received his patent with no strings attached. Then came the job of merchandising the new invention. He eventually persuaded one of the architectural firm's clients to build such a garage next to a new shopping center. The garage was the center of attraction for some time, and gave rise to a number of newspaper feature stories, as well as news stories.

Alan sat back to wait for the money to roll in. And waited. And waited. One garage was built in Minneapolis; another in Los Angeles; two in Dallas; and one in Atlanta. Four were built overseas. And that was all. He could never figure out why the idea didn't catch on, although, it was true, the initial expense was high. He made a decent amount of money from the nine that were built, and that, together with the publicity, caused him to be looked upon as a wealthy eccentric. He felt he was more eccentric than wealthy, but didn't tell anyone that. In the end, he sold the rights to his invention to a Japanese firm for a sizeable sum, and watched his garages go up all over urban Japan.

Alan kept his job with his company, and Frances developed a name for herself as an interior decorator. They had no children, although both wanted them and they went through a period of fertility treatment to no avail.

A few years after the garage episode, they went to the opening of a new sculpture exhibition at a museum. Alan was startled to see that the feature attraction was an enormous contraption that looked very much like his original Rube Goldberg. In conversation with the sculptor, the latter thanked Alan profusely for putting him on the right track. He had admittedly acquired the idea of kinetic sculptures from Alan.

The idea of kinetic sculpture grew rapidly. It became the "in" thing to have such a contraption, usually very large, in the foyers and reception areas of public buildings. Alan watched the profusion of "knock-offs" of his original idea with amusement and amazement. Frances was less charitable. She wanted to sue each sculptor for stealing Alan's idea, and he patiently explained to her, over and over, that ideas cannot be patented.

She was somewhat mollified when, at one opening, the catalogue referred to Alan as the "seminal inventor," and was not amused when Alan said that could be interpreted as fucked up. As time went on, Alan was glad he had not made a fuss about his kinetic work being copied. He felt some pride at having at least been partly responsible for the beginning of a new art form.

They had been married over twenty years when they decided to dine in a new, much-talked-about, restaurant. After they were seated and had ordered, Alan looked around the room and then did a double-take. Professor Roebuck and some companions were sitting a few tables away. He quietly explained to Frances that this was the man whom he had refused to betray so many years ago, and that the refusal had caused him to lose his first and most profitable invention.

"But you felt good about yourself, didn't you?"

"Yes, I must confess that I felt very righteous."

"Isn't that of some importance?"

"What are you, a member of the Ethical Culture Society?"

On their way out they passed Roebuck's table, and on impulse Alan stopped and said, "Professor Roebuck, I wouldn't expect you to remember me, but I worked for you many years ago—when you were perfecting your blood fractionating machine."

Roebuck peered at him through thick glasses, and then said, "Oh, yes. Young Alan. Do you know that your leaving me so suddenly put the perfection of my machine back by almost six months? I wonder how many people died during that time because of your selfish behavior. Have you no ethics?"

Outside, Frances said, "Alan, what's the bottom line?"

"Well," said Alan, "it must be: 'Virtue is its own reward.' But believe me, it's damn poor pay."

Uncle Jim

◆

UNCLE JIM

My Uncle Jim was unlucky enough to get into the *Guinness Book of Records*, and he's thoroughly ashamed of it.

Jim came from a hard-luck family. His father bought ten-percent of the original IBM stock, and bragged to the family a year later that he had unloaded that stock without losing a dime. Jim's uncle was an inventor—he spent all his time and money trying to invent a money maker, and came exulting to the family one day that he had finally done it. He had invented a fountain pen that held twice as much ink as any previous fountain pen. "Do you know what that means?" he bragged. "You only have to fill the pen half as many times."

That was the year that ball-point pens first came onto the market.

During a short, experimental period as a geologist, Jim pinpointed the place where a small-time but hopeful prospector should begin drilling for oil. Within a few feet of digging they were showered with oil and nearly fainted from excitement until one of the more knowledge-able workmen pointed out that this was refined oil, not crude. They had drilled into a Texaco pipeline, and were sued for an enormous sum.

He was with his family in Italy when his young nephew complained of a headache and nausea. He wasn't wearing a hat, and they realized he had simply been exposed to too much sun. Seeing a sign saying "*Albergo*

Diurna" nearby, they went in and found that they could rent a small—almost cell-like—room by the hour, and the matron said she would look in on the boy. So they left their son to sleep for a few hours, after which he felt fine.

An hourly hotel was a new idea to them, and when they got back to the States Jim borrowed some money from friends and opened such a hotel in the heart of Philadelphia. He did well. People—mostly men and young women—came and went at all hours of the day and night, although most of them stayed for only an hour or so. Some came so often that he recognized them. He also recognized the two policemen from the beat who were with the vice-squad lieutenant when he was arrested for running a brothel. It took the services of a good—and expensive—lawyer to convince the police that he was not living off the earnings of prostitutes, but simply (and ignorantly, they pleaded) renting space to them. They advised him to quit, which he did. He was offered a miserly price for the hotel, but sizing up the two gorillas who made the offer and deducing where they came from, he decided he'd better accept.

When Jim came back to Jacksonville he realized that there were no bowling alleys in town. He had not only seen how crowded bowling alleys were in Philadelphia, he had impatiently waited his turn at an alley a number of times. He proposed to his brothers and sisters that they open a bowling alley in Jacksonville. They divided the work between them: One priced equipment, one priced labor, one scouted around for the best location, one got estimates from builders, one worked out the costs and income of the drink stand and equipment sales, and when they had all the information together, they went to their mother, who controlled the family finances.

They explained the investigations they had made; how bowling alleys in Savannah, in Charleston, and in Tampa were all doing well; what the initial costs would be, the expected income, the return on investment—everything.

Their mother looked at the documents, looked at them, and asked, "What's a bowling alley?"

They realized she had never seen a bowling alley in her life, so they explained to her the equipment, how the game was played, the rules, the scoring, again—everything.

She summarized. "People roll balls down a wooden path and try to knock over wooden dolls. That's all there is?"

They assured her that people got hooked on the game, couldn't play it enough, formed teams, had tournaments—everything.

She thought it over and then announced: "No."

"But Ma, why not? It's a sure money maker. Every city has them except Jacksonville. We could get in on the ground floor."

Again: "No."

"But why not, Ma?"

"Because comes a depression, there is nothing on the shelves you can eat. You gonna eat bowling balls?"

Nothing they could say would move her. Her life experience said that you needed assets you could use to stay alive, like cans on the shelf of a grocery store.

Later that year a New Yorker opened the first bowling alley in Jacksonville, which rapidly expanded into a franchised set of neighborhood alleys all over town. When the kids pointed this out to her, their mother simply said, "Wait. He won't be able to eat those balls."

It was just a hard-luck family. Their uncle Jake invented a new type of TV antenna with a much wider range than the previous ones, but before he could get it patented TVs were being linked to cable. He invented an inkjet ribbon for typewriters as computers were taking over, and then a razor-edged gadget to cut the perforated margins off computer paper while single-sheet printers were becoming popular.

They were a hard-luck family in little ways, too. Before the days of compensation for being bumped from airplane flights, they were invariably the ones who had to wait for the next flight; but when the law required compensation to be paid, they always had a seat. Even when my uncle's grandfather bought one of the first automobiles in Jacksonville, and the mayor bought the second, these two cars—the only ones in a hundred mile radius—crashed at an intersection in the middle of town. And who do you think was charged with causing an accident? Not the mayor.

So when my uncle Jim began to be interested in flying, the family mentally prepared to visit him in the hospital, if not in a more somber place. The only ray of light was the fact that nobody in the family, nor all the family together, could afford an airplane or even flying lessons, so they bought him some model planes. He promptly cut off the tip of his thumb putting a model together.

It was the draft that changed his life. He decided that if he waited to be drafted, he wouldn't have a choice of services, so he volunteered for the army airforce. He did his basic training at Keesler Field, in Biloxi, Mississippi.

Keesler Field was a wide expanse of hot sand, not even within sight of the waters of the Gulf of Mexico; it consisted of a center of wooden buildings ringed with tents. The recruits were assigned to the tents, of course, and their first experience with the Air Force came within a few hours when a PFC (private first class), small, somewhat disheveled, evidently without much schooling, arrived and called them out to learn how to make hospital corners on their beds. Pulling a bed into the company street, he reached the point of making the first corner when he got confused. He began to paw through his pockets, and seeing everyone watching him, explained: "I got a diaphragm somewhere here."

Somebody snickered, and he looked up suspiciously. As luck would have it he caught Jim smiling, since Jim was thinking of the headquarters staff in Europe all bending over a diaphragm on which the enemy forces had been sketched. Really, not a bad spy device, he decided.

"Forty pushups," the PFC said to Jim.

"Why? I didn't do anything."

"For what you were thinking—whatever it was."

And luckless Jim lowered himself to the ground.

They had been in Keesler Field three long weeks of drilling, calisthenics and lectures when it was announced on a Friday that after lunch on Saturday they would be given weekend passes—that is, Saturday afternoon until Sunday night—but one of the conditions of leaving the base was that one wear the "class-A" (that is, khaki) uniform, instead of the green drill fatigue uniforms they had been wearing since they were inducted. Now, when clothes had been thrust into their arms at the induction center in Jacksonville, they were in the usual army sizes: Either too large or too small. Jim's were much too large. It didn't matter too much about the fatigues, because he could roll up the cuffs and sleeves and slop around in oversized pants and shirt. Consequently, like most of the others, he hadn't bothered to do anything about his khaki clothes.

With the weekend pass announcement, however, there was a mad dash to the post tailor. The line was long, but the first soldiers came out pleased—their uniforms would be done in time to go to town. Later, soldiers came out angry and frustrated: "That fucking tailor won't do mine until next week." Which meant no weekend pass, of course. Consequently, many of those still in line just faded away. Those who remained were those who either felt that could talk the tailor into doing their uniforms earlier, or those—like Jim—who decided to just take a chance.

Directly ahead of Jim in line was a soldier who shared the tent with him; Jeremiah Bottlenose, a lawyer from Boston who preferred, for obvious reasons, to be called J.B. They had, in fact, become good friends. They discovered the same tastes in literature and music, they reacted the same way to many army experiences, and there grew up enough affinity between them to help each other in the myriad ways that soldiers need help from each other. J.B. was tall, well-built and handsome. He always spoke in a resonant voice, as though he were arguing a case before the Supreme Court. He had "presence," and looked as though he should have been a general, at least. It was obvious that he came from a wealthy family and was used to getting his way. He now watched the departing soldiers with amusement. "They just don't know how to argue a case," he told Jim, smiling.

Then, through the half-open door, Jim heard J.B. say to the tailor who was marking his uniform, in his usual resonant and impressive voice, "I am invited to dinner with the base commander, who is my wife's cousin, tomorrow night. I would appreciate your having my uniform ready tomorrow morning."

The tailor, mouth full of pins, looked up from the cuffs and said, "Tuesday."

"You don't understand," said the lawyer, very clearly and slowly. "If I don't show up for dinner the base commander will want to know why, and I'll have no choice but to tell him that my uniform wasn't ready."

"Maybe Tuesday, maybe Wednesday," said the tailor. J.B. changed his would-be impressive manner and put on a sincere and man-to-man attitude: "Look, this dinner is important to my future in the army. Do me a favor, yes?"

The tailor raised an eyebrow and said nothing. Finally, J .B. leaned down and became very confidential. "We are both men of the world. We understand each other. I'll make it well worth your while to finish my uniform tomorrow."

At this the tailor stood up, about two heads shorter than the lawyer, and looked up into his face. "No sooner than next Friday," he said, conclusively.

J.B. strode out angrily. Jim almost thought he was going to say, "You'll hear from my lawyer," but he didn't.

Jim was still smiling at the exchange as he entered. As the tailor began to mark the necessary adjustments on his uniform Jim gave him his name and unit number. Perhaps it was his Southern accent, in contrast to the Bostonian English he had just heard, or perhaps it was just to relieve his own anger, that the tailor muttered, "Goddamn Yankee."

Then, as though sorry at being overheard, "Where are you from?"

"Jacksonville," he replied.

The tailor glanced up for a moment, and then—eyes still on his work—said, "Do you happen to know an Eva Thorngold?"

"Of course," he said. "We went to the same high school and worked at the same lunch counter."

"Where was that?" the tailor asked, suspiciously.

Jim named the high school, and added that she had begun to work at the lunch counter a few months before he joined the army.

Still a little suspicious, the tailor asked, "What did she look like?"

"Tall, rather thin, blonde, glasses, rather shy with other people. And, oh, a very nice smile."

The tailor stood up straight and shook Jim's hand. "Well, this is really a nice coincidence. You really were her classmate? And you worked together? You'll spend the weekend with us. She's my wife's sister."

And so it was arranged. Jim took the tailor's address in Biloxi, and he did Jim's uniform to perfection while he waited—and the remaining line outside the door fidgeted and complained.

Jim couldn't resist wearing his class-A, beautifully-fitting uniform back to the tent. He passed J. B.'s bunk, where the latter was smoldering, trying to read a magazine. J. B. sat straight up. "How in the hell…?"

"Oh," Jim replied, nonchalantly, "I told the tailor that I was having dinner with the base commander Saturday night, and he broke his neck to get this uniform done for me."

"I don't believe that," said J. B., emphatically.

"Well," Jim explained, kindly, "one just has to know how to argue a case."

Unlucky Jim was assigned guard duty for Saturday night, of course, and couldn't use his pass.

During basic training, Jim's particular pain in the ass (literally) was (or were) calisthenics. He was in pretty good shape, or, at least, better than he had ever been before, but the early morning calisthenics, in particular, were torture to his luxury-loving body. Although Biloxi was very hot during the day, it could be quite cold in the hours before dawn, which is when calisthenics were performed. Consequently, when an announcement appeared on the bulletin board that soldiers taking part in organized sports would be excused from calisthenics, he and J. B. sped over to the enclosed, warm gymnasium to see what they could do in place of cold outdoor calisthenics. There was wrestling, which was not for him. There was boxing, which was not for him. There was weight-lifting, which was not for him. There was high-jumping and broad-jumping, marathons and dashes, swimming and gymnastics (involving flying rings, trapezes, wooden horses, and other equally uninviting equipment).

About to give up, his eye lighted on "Fencing." Now, that was the answer. The epee weighed very little, the face was protected by a mask and the body by padding. The total movement was a few steps back and forth, and the swinging of arms. Both of them signed up for fencing on the spot, and in the first lesson were taught how to hold the epee, and the basic strokes. It seemed just what they were seeking. Douglas Fairbanks, Errol Flynn, move over. They reported to the calisthenics instructor that they were training for the fencing team, and he took their names off his list.

The next time they went to the gym for their fencing lesson the instructor told the class to squat down, rump almost on the floor between their legs. Uncomfortable, but possible. He then passed behind them, urging many of the soldiers—Jim included—to get their butts closer to the floor. More uncomfortable. In fact, almost impossible. Then, in that position, he ordered the group to waddle completely around the gym, keeping close to the wall. These were the muscles they would have to strengthen to be able to duck and sway, bob and dance, while fencing. The waddling was pure murder to Jim. His thigh muscles screamed. His leg muscles gave off lightning flashes of pain. Every time he eased up, the instructor would shout, "Butt to the floor!"

He couldn't keep it up. He couldn't get all the way around the gym. Or halfway. Before they covered one side he tumbled over, and had a hard time standing up, much less squatting again. He told the instructor, regretfully, that he would go back to calisthenics. He couldn't waddle around that gym even once, much less the three times that were included in every lesson. The same was true for J. B.

The next morning J. B. reported for calisthenics, but Jim decided to take a chance. The army being the army (and this was before the day of computers), he didn't believe his change of plans could have reached the calisthenics instructor so quickly, so he didn't report for calisthenics. Instead, he went to the small Red Cross lounge, which was open all night for people working various shifts. With a cup of coffee, a doughnut, and the morning paper that was furnished there, he managed to keep busy until breakfast time. The next day during calisthenics time he was back. His friends reported that his name wasn't called at calisthenics roll-call that day, so he decided to take a chance on another day. Then he decided he would wait until he was marked absent, and make up some excuse. He was not called in for missing both calisthenics and fencing that day. Or the next. Or the next.

He wasn't sure what the Red Cross girls took him for, but he was there every morning after that, reading the paper, writing mail, or reading a book from their library. He realized that the calisthenics instructor thought he was fencing, and the fencing instructor thought he was at calisthenics. It made his life a lot easier.

At last basic training was over, and he eagerly awaited his posting to a pilot training base. All the soldiers were wondering about their next post, and he learned the army saying: There are only two good posts in the army—the one you used to be at, and the one you hope to go to. Keesler Field began to look better and better as he got closer to leaving it, but he was sure that a pilot training base would be even better.

One of the afternoons while they waited was quite hot and sultry, although it was already the end of November. Having nothing else to do, J. B. and Jim went to the beach in Biloxi. They swam out to Dog Island and back, and then lay on the sand, shooting the breeze. There a rather shapely young lady, not able to determine their ranks from their bathing trunks, tried to find out if they were officers. They did not want to be charged with impersonating officers. On the other hand, she made it rather clear that she was interested in, if not available to, officers only. They evaded her indirect questions, but gave enough (false) hints to keep her interested. At last, she decided she was wasting her time, and started to walk away. Anxious to keep the game going (it was the only game in town), J. B. followed her. When he was about twenty feet away, Jim called, "Major, let her go. She's not interested in us."

It was comical the way she spun on her feet and headed back toward them. They, of course, walked away, deep in conversation, completely ignoring her. They laughed all the way back to the barracks. They stopped laughing when they learned she was the base commander's daughter. In fact, they began to stay indoors and look up and down the street before emerging.

Suddenly, soldiers began to get their travel orders. One by one other soldiers would come back from the bulletin board excited: "Los Angeles!," or depressed, "Harrisburg." J. B.'s orders sending him to Chanute Field came while Jim was on guard duty, and when he returned, J. B. was already gone.

Jim checked the bulletin board three times a day, but instead of orders, he saw an announcement that chilled his heart. The organized sports teams that had been training for three months were going to put on an exhibition on Tuesday, and all calisthenics were cancelled so soldiers could watch the exhibition. There would be boxing and wrestling, weight lifting and gymnastics but the *piece de resistance* would be the opening exhibition—the famous Keesler Field fencing team would perform. He saw visions of the guardhouse, because certainly the calisthenics instructor would be there to cheer the soldiers from his unit on—and where would he find Jim, who had been practicing for three months?

Now it became an urgent necessity that he get shipped out. But his orders never came. On Monday, he decided on desperate measures. He began to do what they were forbidden to do while waiting for

travel orders: He sent his dirty clothes to the post laundry, which usually took five days to return clothes; wrote all his correspondents to
keep writing him at the same address; made a date with a waitress for
the following Saturday night; and took a one-day pass into Biloxi, just
to get off the base. The army would certainly ship him out, now that
he had arranged to stay.

The ploy didn't work. He didn't go to the exhibition that night, and
was not terribly surprised when the calisthenics instructor showed up
in his barracks the next day. "You've been screwing me," he announced,
"and I'm going to fix you."

Jim felt a tremor of fear. His visitor was not an instructor in physical
education for nothing.

"I'd charge you and have you put in the guardhouse, but I'm shipping out tomorrow and there isn't time. So I'm going to make sure you
do double calisthenics, wherever you go. Where are you going?"

Jim didn't dare say he didn't know. The instructor was waiting with
clenched fists, and wouldn't have believed him. Jim remembered J. B.'s
orders and croaked, "Chanute Field."

The instructor grinned wolfishly and stood up. "Now isn't that nice?
I happen to know the calisthenics instructor at Chanute Field, and I'm
going to write him right now to have your name put on the double calisthenics list. Teach you to fuck around with me."

Jim figuratively wiped the sweat from his forehead, but that evening
he got his travel orders—to Chanute Field, Illinois, of course

.Jim embarked on the troop train still wearing his summer khakis,
and stepped off the next day into sixteen inches of snow and a blizzard
blowing off the prairies of the mid-West. The cold came as a shock to
his system—a shock that never wore off the whole time he was in
Illinois. The first barracks they were taken to was patched all over with
cardboard, and the blower on the heating system was out. He shivered
all night under the two army blankets issued them, plus his overcoat,
other uniforms, and duffel bag.

As he knew, Chanute Field was not a pilot training base—but they were there to learn the basic functions of an airplane, since the training there was basically aircraft mechanics and maintenance. In later memory, the thing that typified Chanute Field for Jim was the constant roar of airplane engines. It wasn't from planes constantly flying, but from tens of airplane motors mounted on blocks, their propellers being tested night and day without ceasing to try to detect when metal fatigue would set in.

A typical day included morning and afternoon instructional sessions, which included the basic elements of weather observation, navigation, radio, and emergency repairs. Jim was surprised at how much a pilot was supposed to understand before he even saw a whole airplane. For Jim the day also included calisthenics—twice.

One afternoon in the mess hall he saw a familiar figure. He and J. B. had a back-slapping reunion, and in the course of the conversation that followed, J. B. said, "How about coming ice-skating tonight? There's a rink in Rantoul. We'll have a good time."

"Ice-skating? I'm from Jacksonville. I've never ice-skated in my life. If I tried, I'd probably break my leg."

"Don't be ridiculous. You won't break your leg. Ice-skating is easy. Everyone in Boston, even little children, can ice-skate. Come to think of it, maybe it is the only thing that goddamn-Yankees can do that you Rebs can't."

Jim knew that J. B. was pulling his leg, because the Civil War had long ceased to be anything but romantic history in the south, but he felt more bored than challenged. "Okay, what's the drill?"

"I'll come by your barracks at eight. Some of the local girls skate there, too. Who knows, we might get lucky tonight."

By nine that night Jim was in the post hospital. It wasn't his leg—it was his left arm that was broken. "At last," he thought, "a bit of luck. I can't do calisthenics with this arm."

The stay at Chanute Field lasted only three months—the longest, coldest, most uncomfortable three months of Jim's life. When he arrived at the army air base in San Angelo, Texas, he felt that he had come home. It was March, the sky was clear, some wildflowers were already in full bloom, there was a warm breeze, and he wondered why anyone would voluntarily live up north.

When he arrived at the base, Jim went by the luggage room to pick up his duffel bag, only to discover that it had not arrived. He checked backwards and forwards, until he was sure that it was missing. He had only the clothes he was wearing—in the duffel bag were not only the rest of his clothes, but his toilet kit, his address book, and his chess set. He located the day room and went over, where, after a short wait, he got in to see the sergeant-major.

The sergeant-major was a tall rawboned man with a very clear Chicago accent. "What's your trouble, soldier?" he asked, his accent grating on Jim's ears like a buzzsaw.

Jim explained his predicament, and the sergeant noted down the details and said, "Okay. We'll write to Chanute Field and try to locate your duffel bag."

"Write!?" exclaimed Jim. "That'll take a week or so. I tell you, sergeant, I can't even shave. I don't have anything. How about sending a wire?"

"Soldier," replied the Chicagoan, "you're down south now. We do things our own way down here. You're going to have to get used to that."

Jim knew when he was licked. He bought another pair of undershorts and a razor at the PX, and bumbled along until his duffel bag, which had been off-loaded at San Antonio instead of San Angelo, showed up.

Jim felt that he had already spent a lifetime in the army and was anxious to get into a plane, but the first weeks were spent in lectures, simulations, and other exercises, as well as a seemingly never-ending series of psychological and personality tests. He sometimes thought it would never end. But at last came the bright, wonderful, exciting day when he was buckled into the second seat of a two-seater Auster training plane—and it actually left the ground!

Jim took to flying as though he were born with wings. His enthusiasm seemed to communicate itself to the plane. He was one of the most eager, gung-ho, heads-up pilots in his course. The family jinx seemed to drop off when he got into the sky; not only was he not unlucky, in a number of instances he was damn lucky. When the first wash-out took place, with about a quarter of the course members dropped from further training, he wasn't even worried.

In the second section of the course Jim moved on to soloing in more advanced aircraft, and always did a little more than the standard exercise required. He was always respectful of the plane, and never violated safety regulations, but if the exercise called for a figure eight, he did a closer figure eight than the others; if it called for a dive, he waited a second or two longer to pull out; he was, in the eyes of the rest of his group, becoming a hotshot, crack pilot. He became facile at filling out the questions on the psychological tests, which continued from time to time.

When the results of the second wash-out were posted, Jim practically swaggered up to the bulletin board where anxious trainees were congregated. He didn't see his name on the list of retained trainees at first, so he read the list more carefully. Then he looked to see if his name had been misspelled. Finally, he went down the names on the list one by one, and realized that his name had been inadvertently omitted.

He was a little embarrassed to be seen scanning the list of wash-outs, but just to be sure, he did so. His name seemed to stand out on that list as though it were written in red capital letters. He couldn't believe it! He was the hottest pilot in his group—perhaps on the whole field. He wanted to gallop to company headquarters to straighten things out, but felt that didn't befit his status. So he forced himself to walk leisurely to the white building, seething within.

His commander did not seem surprised to see him, and kept him waiting only a few moments while he finished talking to one of the other wash-outs. Jim controlled both his anger and his disappointment, and managed to say, "Is that list correct, major?"

"Tough luck, soldier. I'm afraid it is."

"But...but...I don't understand..."

"There are many reasons why a soldier is not permitted to continue pilot training. Sometimes he is too cautious; sometimes too reckless; sometimes too careless; sometimes he punishes his aircraft; sometimes he doesn't relate properly to the ground crew. There can be many reasons, but the most common reason is usually not obvious— it has to do with basic personality traits that show up on the psych tests. We are not always sure of what we want, but we are always sure of what we don't want.

"You will continue in the airforce, and you will continue to be a pilot—but only on the type of aircraft you have been checked out on so far. I'm afraid there'll be no further training."

Jim saw his visions of flashing through the wild blue yonder in a gleaming saber-like fighter plane go glimmering into that same wild blue yonder. In its place came a picture of slow, lumbering training planes ground-hopping from place to place. "Can you tell me where I went wrong, major?"

"You didn't go wrong, soldier. It is nothing you did—it is just the way you were born and brought up. Who knows how much is nature and how much is nurture? The psych people say you're just not right for a fighter pilot. Look at it this way—most happy, successful people in the world are not fighter pilots; and not all fighter pilots are happy successful people. Most happiness and success are matters of luck. Good luck to you."

The major rose and the interview was over. Jim saluted smartly and turned on his heel. He had never been more depressed in his life. Then he felt anger replace his disappointment—the airforce was wrong, and he knew they were wrong, and he would prove it to them some way!

Some day, some way, he would make the army say, "We were wrong about that guy."

Jim was not transferred out of San Angelo immediately. First, he received his commission as second lieutenant. Then he was permitted to book some flying time by touring around to other airbases in the vicinity on a variety of missions. He flew to Lubbock, Big Spring, Abilene, and Midland. He found, not entirely to his surprise, that army life was better for officers than for enlisted men. Of course, second lieutenants were the lowest of the officers, but they were still infinitely higher than the highest of the enlisted men.

In preparation for shipment overseas Jim was transferred to an embarkation camp in Santa Ana, California. The time spent there was just waiting time. The camp was full of soldiers getting ready for embarkation. It was pretty boring, and one night he went to the large amphitheater where a variety show was being presented, courtesy of the USO.

The first act was a magician, whose act evoked both cheers and jeers. Jim thought that as an obvious amateur, he wasn't bad. The next act consisted of acrobats, and several soldiers near Jim groaned as they were reminded of calisthenics. Then, in a fanfare of music and light, a blonde bombshell appeared in a silver costume. The men went wild with appreciation even before she opened her mouth. Her voice was slight and—probably aware of it—she made no effort to really sing; she sort of chanted the words of "Don't Sit Under the Apple Tree" until the audience joined in. She was called back for two encores.

Suddenly she pointed in Jim's direction and said, "Gorgeous, would you come up on the stage with me, please?"

Before he could move five soldiers from all around him elbowed him back and began loping to the stage. Jim didn't even bother to *think,* "Just my luck."

It was the next day at noon that orders came to prepare for embarkation. On the ship he shared a cabin with three other officers. They lay around swapping rumors until dark, when the ship got underway. None of them knew where they were going, of course, and any little incident that seemed to offer a hint was eagerly discussed.

When he woke the next day he could see nothing but blue ocean in every direction. He searched for other ships in the convoy, or for protective warships, but saw nothing. The ship plowed through the water, and from the sun they deduced that they were, at least, not heading right for Japan, but heading southwest. During the first day a large map was strung up on a bulkhead, and some of the airforce navigators aboard plotted the course of the ship with their sextants and marked it on the map. The next day the map was gone—evidently higher echelons had decided it was dangerous for the troops to know where they were. Perhaps, thought Jim, they were afraid the location would be given away to the enemy by carrier pigeon or by an Olympic swimmer, since there was no other way that a soldier could get a message off the ship.

They saw nothing on their journey—no land, no other ships, not even sea birds. The ship was evidently depending on speed and secrecy to make its run without protection. They threaded their way further and further south, avoiding all sight of land and other ships. The weather, which had been sweltering on the equator, got cooler and cooler. After three weeks of such travel, Jim woke one morning to the realization that the engines were no longer operating. Looking out the porthole, he realized that they had reached their destination, and along with thousands of others he made his way to the deck to discover where they were.

It took a long time, and the help of some powerful binoculars, before he found an advertising sign that indicated they were in Hobart, Tasmania. He hadn't the slightest idea where Tasmania was—to his mind the word brought pictures of grass-skirted natives, but what he saw were warehouses and factories, and men in work-clothes on the dock. He learned that Tasmania is an Australian island lying south of the mainland. They had sailed around to the south of Australia, and were now lying at dockside in the main city of the island.

What luck! thought Jim. Service in Australia seemed like a dream come true. A civilized country where English was spoken, where the climate was like the south of the United States, and where the bulk of the manpower was off fighting the Japanese in the north, leaving all those lonely women—even if they did drive on the wrong side of the road.

However, as Jim's usual luck held, the orders to debark that some officers received did not include him. Instead, he was among those who were formed up and marched through the main street of Hobart, and then back, just to give them some exercise. On the march, Hobartans threw apples—which was the main crop of the island—to them, and some of the soldiers began to throw American coins back. The Australians, not to be outdone, threw out Australian coins.

The march took about two hours, after which they re-embarked and after dark, sailed out again. A day or so later they again made port, this time Freeport, the port city for Perth, on the Australian west coast, and here, too, a group of soldiers and officers debarked. But not Jim, of course. And then began the second long voyage of their journey. They sailed north, again dodging all sight of land, and being very much on the alert for Japanese submarines, for they were sailing up the Indian Ocean, which was practically a Japanese pond by now.

Over time, Jim began to develop an obsession. All the food served on board was cooked in enormous steam vessels. They had steamed potatoes, steamed vegetables, steamed meat, steamed fruit, boiled eggs, and soft bread. He needed something he could sink his teeth into, something fried, something brittle—but he couldn't find any. He dreamed of fried chops, toast, fried hamburgers—anything that couldn't be steamed. He decided the first thing he would do when he had a choice was to eat a meal of nothing but fried foods.

It was an early morning, exactly six weeks after they had embarked at Santa Ana, that a smudge appeared on the horizon. The smudge slowly resolved itself into land, and by afternoon the Gateway to India—that large monument on the dockside in Bombay—became visible. Before

they landed, representatives of the Red Cross and of the Bombay
Chamber of Commerce appeared on board, brought out by the pilot
boat, and gave out pamphlets about India—mostly, how to behave to
stay out of trouble in India.

Sacred cows were to be treated as sacred; women were not to be whistled at; traffic ran on the left; and a number of other warnings, plus
invitations to visit Red Cross and other official installations. In addition
to the material thus given out, the army issued its own set of instructions: Food was to be eaten only in army messhalls and PX's. Anyone
contracting amoebic dysentery from eating in an unauthorized place
would be considered personally responsible, sent back to the States, be
tried, and have the entire episode—hospitalization and jail time—considered "bad time," which would have to be made up after normal
enlistment was over.

As the ship approached the shore, hundreds of rowboats, canoes,
dinghies, and other vessels approached. In all of them people were
standing, shouting "Boxes! Boxes!" Not understanding the reason for
such a shortage of boxes in India, the soldiers began throwing overboard every kind of box they could lay their hands on. People—mostly
young men and children—dived off the boats to retrieve the boxes.

As the four cabin-mates made their plans to leave the ship, three of
them, including Jim, decided their first stop would be at a restaurant
where they could get fried steak, french fries, toast, and crisp cookies.
One man looked at them with some concern. "Didn't you read the
warning about dysentery?"

"Oh, c'mon. We're not going to spend our whole time in India eating
in army establishments. There's a whole wide new world out there."

"Well, you can do as you want, but I am going to eat only in army
establishments."

So as they left the ship, they split up. At least, they tried to, but they
found themselves ringed with young beggars. A crowd of children
blocked their way, each of them crying, "Boxes!"

Jim was bewildered, but suddenly he remembered what he had read about India, and grinned. "They're not saying 'boxes,'" he informed his friends. "They are begging. 'Baksheesh' means charity—alms." They all felt rather foolish for the boxes they had thrown overboard when the requests had certainly been for more meaningful things.

Almost in retribution they all reached into their pockets and found whatever American coins they had, and threw them as far as they could to draw the pack off. They were then surrounded by another group of youngsters. These each had a brush and a rag, and insisted on cleaning their shoes. The loner tried to stride through the crowd, but a child, not more than four by his size, attached himself to one leg like a limpet, and as he strode away, he carried the young shoeshine boy with him.

Eventually Jim and his two friends found a Chinese restaurant that looked clean, and that was frequented by a number of other uniformed Americans. At his first bite into the fried steak, Jim thought that his teeth would come out. He was so used to soft foods that he had to relearn how to chew his food. The entire time they were in Bombay, Jim never went near an army establishment, let alone eat there.

At the end of a week, their orders were to embark on a train, and as they gathered at the station, the three looked for their fourth cabin-mate. Not finding him, they inquired, and learned that he had been diagnosed as having amoebic dysentery on his fifth day in Bombay, and was already on his way back to the States. Jim felt that he had at last broken the family hard luck jinx.

From Bombay they went by slow train through the Great Rann of Kutch to Karachi. After a few weeks there, they were sent—again by slow train—across country, via Delhi, to Calcutta. At the stop in Delhi, Jim and his two friends hired a gharry and were driven to Agra, where he got his first look at the Taj Mahal with a full moon at his back, shining directly on the reflecting pool and the pearl-colored building. The sight etched itself indelibly on his memory, and he never saw anything the rest of his life that he thought more beautiful.

From Calcutta he went upcountry, again by train, to a stop on the Brahamputra River. There followed a three-day boat ride up the river to Dibrugarh. In addition to the Indians who were on the lower deck, packages, goats, chickens and all, there were thirty enlisted men and ten officers on the upper deck, and one Oriental-style toilet, which consisted of footplates and a hole in the floor. A bout of diarrhea broke out among the army passengers, and not only was there a constant line at the door—the floor became ankle deep in excretory matter. They ended up sitting on the rail and excreting into the river—not a very dignified position for an officer in the United States Army Airforce, as Jim found out. They then transferred to a narrow-gauge railroad that ended at Tinsukia. From there by truck to an airforce base called Dinjan, deep in Assam tea country.

At Dinjan, Jim learned that he was to be, in essence, a courier. There were small airbases scattered around upper Assam, and it was neither economical nor convenient to use fighter planes to deliver papers, messages, or passengers. So he flew a Piper from Dinjan to Chabua, to Ledo, and to other local airfields. The work was neither dangerous nor difficult, and he was frequently bored when on the ground. But in the air, he was always thrilled, as he had always been.

Life in Dinjan was far from exciting. He managed to hitch air-rides to Calcutta twice, ate at Firpo's, went to a ballet, saw the sights of Calcutta, including the largest banyan tree in the world, the Victoria monument and the ivory museum. He played poker a good deal, occasionally winning small amounts, but more often losing larger ones.

Dinjan was a fighter base, and after Jim had been there long enough to make friends with some of the pilots, he persuaded one or two to let him sit in the cockpit, and they explained the various instruments to him. From there it was an easy step to accompanying them on practice runs, and twice (although it was strictly unauthorized) they let him take the controls for a short time. He again felt very much at ease flying the fighters, as though he had a knack for it.

This encouraged him to make friends with some of the pilots at Chabua. This was a transport plane base, and he studied the controls and talked about the differences involved in flying fighter and transport planes. He never got to fly a transport, but he was confident he could if given the chance.

The news was that the Japanese were moving through Burma faster than had been anticipated, and advance units were even said to already be in Assam. One day a general meeting was announced, and while the soldiers and officers stood (separately) on the parade ground, a box was brought out to the middle. A moment later the commanding officer of Dinjan and a tall man wearing a spotless white navy uniform entered the area. The commander introduced him as Lord Louis Mountbatten. He was a handsome man, made more striking by the contrast between his white naval uniform and his dark suntan.

He mounted the box and in a surprisingly casual voice said, "Fellows, the Japs are getting quite troublesome. They seem to think they can do whatever they want around here. In fact, little groups of them seem to be infiltrating here and there. You know, they can live for a week on the handful of rice that they carry in their pockets, and they cover ground quite rapidly. Do me a favor, will you? If you see any of them, kill them."

Lord Mountbatten got an amused round of applause, but afterwards every soldier was required to carry his weapon with him at all times, even to go to the latrine.

June 24th was Jim's birthday, and he celebrated by going with some friends to a Chinese restaurant on the Chabua road and getting drunk, which he rarely did. He remembered that birthday, because years later he found a book on the war in Burma on a used bookstand, and leafed through it. The book was by General Slim, and one passage caught his eye:

"We had been told that morale in Dinjan was very low, so on June 25th, 1944, the Pipes and Drums of the Royal Highlanders marched into Dinjan and performed their famous drill on the parade ground. Morale improved immediately."

The thing that interested Jim was that he had been in his quarters nursing a hangover all of that day, and although his window opened on the parade ground, he neither saw nor heard the pipes and drums. It was, he mused, the difference between the war as seen from a general's head-quarters and the war as seen by the soldiers on the ground. The Pipes and Drums may have performed somewhere else by mistake; or they may have simply stopped at a bar and become drunk; or Slim may have mis-taken the date. But in any case, at that moment Jim felt he knew more about the war in Burma than the British commander did.

There was a Red Cross hut on the base that served coffee and dough-nuts, had some old magazines from the States, and hosted visiting per-formers as well as amateur performances, when such were offered. The staff consisted of three women—an older, gentle-faced woman who was everyone's advisor and comforter; a very efficient dark girl with a nasty temper; and a jolly, heavy girl who was fast at repartee. Although the staff had made attempts originally to be seen as a service for the enlisted men, the latter were inevitably frozen out by the officers, since the sol-diers found it uncomfortable to be together with officers.

There were the usual latrine rumors about the Red Cross staff. The "matron" was said to be sleeping with the base commander; the dark girl was suspected of being a lesbian, since no one had been able to seduce, or even interest, her; and the heavy girl was said to be a nymphomaniac, although no one had slept with her himself—he just knew others who had.

It was a few days after Mountbatten's appearance that a rumor swept through the officers' quarters that the lesbian had been arrested, and a new girl had taken her place. Some of the married officers dropped in to meet the new girl out of curiosity, although some of them saw marriage in a different light under the circumstances. Most of the single officers found an excuse to visit the Red Cross, and even some of the more self-possessed enlisted men developed an interest in old magazines.

The new girl, Judy, was pleasant, but quiet. She had no gift for smart talk, and just smiled at many of the things that were said to her. She rapidly and efficiently discouraged any attempt to touch her, other than a curt handshake. After the first wave of interest, she became more-or-less a fixture of the hut. It was after the excitement over the new girl had died down that Jim was asked to come down to the hut. There the matronly woman took him into her office and said she had some bad news for him. His mother had died, suddenly but peacefully. She showed him the cable.

Jim was thoughtful. He hadn't seen his mother during the last two years, but her presence in the house was something he had taken for granted. He could hardly imagine home without her. He was glad she had suffered no pain, but found he was not overwhelmed with grief as he might have thought he'd be. He had a sudden thought. "Does this mean I can go home for the funeral?"

"I'm afraid not. The army doesn't grant compassionate leave for such a reason, and not for many other reasons, either."

Jim went out to the reading room where he leafed through a magazine while trying to compose his thoughts. Judy watched him from behind the counter and then came over. "Bad news?"

"Well, yeah. My mother died, but…"

."I saw the cable. She lived in Jacksonville, yes?"

"That's right."

"Are you from Jacksonville?"

"Uh huh."

"Me, too."

"What! Really? Where did you live?"

"Fourth Street."

"Hey, I lived on Fifth!"

"Where did you go to school?"

And they were off and running. They had been in the same grammar school and high school. He tried to tell himself that he recognized her, but he knew he didn't. She had been two years behind him, and to an eighteen year-old boy, sixteen year-old girls are just somebody's little sisters. They swapped memories of places and people in Jacksonville, including the string of bowling alleys that Jim's family didn't own. She laughed out loud at the story.

When he got up to go he said, "Can I see you again?"

She smiled. "I'm behind the counter every day."

"But I mean, would you go out with me?"

"Where would we go?"

"Oh, yeah. I forgot where we are. Well, can I come to see you at the planter's house that you live in?"

"Nope. Nobody visits us there." She looked at him with amusement. "We have our reputations to protect, you know."

He was nonplussed. Then he had an idea. "When you get tired of army food, would you go with me to a very good Chinese restaurant that I discovered on the road to Chabua?"

This time she grinned. "Is that the same restaurant that all the rest of the officers tell me they've discovered?"

"Oh, hell, Judy. There just isn't anything else to do here."

"Why don't you drop in for coffee and doughnuts from time to time? Maybe I'll let you walk me home."

He felt like a quivering adolescent—imagine, being excited about walking a girl home. But he was.

He thought about Judy that night, and he planned to come in again the next night. For the first time in months he found he was excited about something.

That morning a meeting of junior officers was called, and the commander informed them that he had orders to second one officer to Myitkyina, in Burma. Merrill's Marauders—that rag-tag, undisciplined, wild group of jungle fighters—had taken an airfield in central Burma from the Japs, and the intention was to send troops in to protect and enlarge the perimeter until it was safe enough to be used as a forward airbase against the Japs operating in Burma, Siam, and China.

An airforce officer was needed to liase with the ground troops, who were under the command of General "Vinegar Joe" Stillwell. The commander looked at his junior officers, evidently weighing their various assignments in his mind. Jim had no question as to how it would end, and it did. After he was picked he found he was excited. After so long a period of doing courier work he would now be where the action was—and in charge of airforce operations! He almost forgot to tell Judy good-bye.

He was flown into Myitkiyina in a transport plane that landed, discharged its troops—including Jim—and turned around and took off. He found that they had landed in a lull in the almost constant mortar barrage by the surrounding Japanese, and before he could get his bearings the thud of mortar shells landing surrounded him. Seeing a slit trench, he dived in. Four soldiers playing poker in an underground bunker greeted him without excitement. "Stud, draw, and seven card. You want in?" The fact that he was an officer was obviously of no interest to these jungle fighters.

With the help of an experienced sergeant from Merrill's Marauders, he had a Burmese native dig him a foxhole, cover it with a tent, dig a deeper hole for protection from mortars, and dig him a separate latrine. He paid him with five cigarettes, at the sergeant's direction. He had brought with him a shortwave radio sender and receiver, and he set these up in his foxhole. He was in business.

He found that the majority of defenders of Myitkiyna were Chinese soldiers, with more Americans arriving every time the shelling and the weather allowed. Once, when mortar shelling began, he looked over the edge of his foxhole and saw a Chinese soldier relieving himself at a latrine, which was simply a hole in the ground. When the shelling ended, he was horrified to find the upper part of the soldier's torso in front of his tent, and the lower part in the latrine. This was the first time that Jim really realized that he was at war, and could be killed.

The second time occurred when he was standing in front of a plane parked on the tarmac with a soldier whom he had discovered was from Jacksonville—rank meant very little under the circumstances. Suddenly, he saw a small hole appear in the fabric covering the airplane's wing. When he saw another hole appear, a bit closer to him, he pointed out the curiosity to the soldier.

"My God, a sniper," shouted the soldier, and started for his foxhole on the run.

"A sniper?" mused Jim. And then he realized what was happening. He ducked under the plane just as a third hole appeared in the fabric, behind where he had just stood.

Within a few weeks the American presence on the airfield had increased to the point where it was decided that counterattacks were in order. American soldiers then fanned out from the perimeter in the direction of the Irrawaddy River. There were pitched battles fought in the underbrush. The Japanese seemed determined not only to stay in Burma, but to push on to India.

During this period, Jim received information that General Stillwell had ordered an air strike against the Japanese between the airfield and the river. Jim knew that American troops were in that area, and that an air strike into the jungle would not be able to distinguish between the Japanese and the Americans. Rather than risk American lives, he countermanded the order for the airstrike. As he wrote out the countermanding order, he decided he had better keep a copy for himself. Not often, in the course of the war, would there be an order signed by General Joseph Stillwell marked "Countermanded" by a second lieutenant.

As he expected, Jim was relieved of his post as liaison with the ground troops the next day. The airstrike was delivered; American soldiers did die from it; but the enemy was pushed back across the river.

Once back in Dinjan, Jim found that his action in trying to protect American lives was not exactly appreciated. On the contrary, his commanding officer was dressed down for sending a liaison person who tried to exceed General Stillwell's authority. Jim found orders posting him to Barrackpore, an airbase about eighteen miles from Calcutta. He went looking for Judy. There was no Judy. She had been posted elsewhere, and then posted again, so no one knew where she was.

Settled in Barrackpore, Jim decided to make the most of his new locale, and went into Calcutta as often as he could. He kept abreast of concerts, movies, ballet, and even the horse races. One night he went to the performance of a visiting ballet group, called the Four Seasons Ballet. He was not highly impressed, and at the intermission his eye happened to catch that of his seat neighbor—a portly Indian gentleman. Without thinking, he shook his head sadly, and his neighbor gravely shook his. Then they both laughed. Jim said, "My idea of ballet consists of small, dark Russians on tip-toe; not big-boned blondes walking flat-footed."

His neighbor said, "I'm afraid this group is misnamed. One season, perhaps, or even two, but certainly not four." Again they both laughed. The neighbor introduced himself as Mr. Singh (which is like Mr. Jones in the States), and Jim introduced himself. The upshot of this encounter was that he was invited to the home of Mr. Singh for tea.

When Jim came to tea, he asked Mr. Singh what he (the inevitable American question). Singh said he was a government employee. Jim looked around the white house, which was almost a mansion, and pressed Singh further. Singh finally admitted that he was the Treasurer-General of Bengal. They continued talking, Singh on the sofa and Jim in a deep easy chair, when a young lady entered the room. Jim immediately rose, and Singh, without rising, introduced his youngest daughter. She delivered the message that she had come to impart, and left.

When she was outside, Singh said to Jim, "In India, a man does not get up when a lady enters the room."

Jim replied, "I didn't know that," and they continued talking. A few moments later another, somewhat older, lady entered, and Jim automatically came to his feet. Singh introduced his oldest daughter, and when she left, he lectured Jim: "If you want to identify with us, or even honor us, you must behave according to our traditions."

Jim apologized, and resumed his seat. At that point Singh had to leave the room to take a phone call, and as Jim sat there, an older woman came in, stretched out her hand to Jim, and said, "Hello. I am Mrs. Singh."

Jim was halfway up when he remembered what Singh had said, so he forced himself to sink back into his chair and he shook hands with her while sitting down. He nevertheless felt uncomfortable, and explained, "My mother taught me to always stand up when a woman enters the room, but your husband has explained to me that this is not proper in India."

She looked in the direction that her husband had gone and said, severely, "Don't listen to my husband!"

Jim felt that he had now begun to understand the struggle between the traditional India of the Raj and the new independent India trying to emerge.

One day Jim was invited to a tea at the Singhs', whose purpose was to raise money for Indian War Relief. There was a raffle, and a cake sale, and some Indian art was auctioned off. Also present during the afternoon was a group from the army's Special Services Unit. This was the unit that ran the army radio entertainment service, published the army newspaper, arranged for visits by entertainers, and were in general in charge of morale-lifting activities. The unit had been together for some time and made up a tight in-group. They considered themselves intellectuals, and as such a cut above common fighting soldiers, including low-ranking officers. They had their own inside jokes, code words, and internal culture. They also treated all Indians, regardless of rank, class, or caste, as rather dull-witted natives; making fun of them behind their backs, mimicking their accent, and sometimes making fun of them to their faces, secure in the knowledge that the natives wouldn't understand.

As that group gathered around Mr. Singh and began to talk to him, laughing understandingly to each other as they did so, Jim was amazed to see how Singh became what they pictured. He seemed to become smaller, more hesitant, with a much more pronounced Indian accent. Knowing that Singh owned racehorses, one of the leaders of the group said, "Tell me, Mr. Singh, why do horses in India run the wrong way?"

"Wrong way?" asked Singh, puzzled.

"In every civilized country horses run counterclockwise and here they run clockwise. Does that mean that horsemen in India don't know whether they are coming or going?"

The members of the group grinned at each other and Singh looked at the floor.

"Races in India are always fixed, aren't they, Mr. Singh?" continued the interlocutor. "As an owner, can you give us a tip on the Derby this afternoon?"

Singh looked from one to the other, smiled uncertainly, and said, "Well, I am putting a few rupees on Adonis II."

"But that's not your horse."

"I know."

Members of the group looked knowingly at each other. For the next few moments there were hasty consultations among the group, and then two members started for the door. It was clear to Jim that they were rushing to the track with all the money that the group could get together. He was sure the odds on Adonis II would begin shrinking soon.

The afternoon wore on, with more people coming and others leaving. The Special Services unit all trooped out to the track, and Jim saw that Singh again became the man he knew. It was amazing, he thought, what that group did to Singh's self-image.

It was at the tail end of the afternoon, almost six, when the Special Services soldier who had asked about the race reappeared. He went right over to Singh and said, "That was a bum steer you gave us. We had over a thousand rupees on Adonis II, and your horse won."

"Did he?" said Singh, surprised, in a very thick Indian accent. "Did he really? What to do? What to do? I lost two rupees on Adonis myself. What to do? What to do? So Adonis lost. Tsk-tsk."

Jim noticed that Singh had neither shrunk nor become hesitant. Suddenly, across the room, Singh grinned at Jim. And Jim then understood.

Later, when they were talking, Singh said, "Would you like to come out to the Indian Flying Club?"

"Very much. I didn't even know there was an Indian flying club."

"Yes. It is very small. A friend and I own two planes, together. Perhaps you'd like to fly them?"

To his surprise he found that one of the planes was a large, four-engined seaplane, and the other was an eight passenger plane often rented by the government. With Singh's agreement, the pilots of both explained their planes to Jim, but they would not let him fly them.

"Why don't you get a license?" one of them asked him.

"Could I?"

"No problem," and to Jim's surprise, he winked. "I am the examiner."

So, without reporting it to the army, Jim took the requisite instruction and won pilot's licenses for both types of planes. He was never happier than when he was in the cockpit and in the air, but he never mentioned this on the base. He wasn't sure whether he was allowed to fly as a civilian, and he didn't want to ask.

Jim became a frequent visitor at the Singh's. He did not know why they were so nice to him, but they practically adopted him. One day, sitting on their verandah, he noticed that "Arsenic and Old Lace" was playing at the theatre near the big market. Since Seemah, the Singh's youngest daughter, was also on the terrace, he said, "Seemah, would you like to see 'Arsenic and Old Lace'?"

"I sure would," she replied.

"Then how about Friday night? I'll pick you up at about eight."

She looked at him in alarm. "I'll speak to mother," she said, and left the verandah.

Jim realized what had happened and felt like a fool. When he asked her if she wanted to see the movie, and she replied yes, she was just being truthful. She did want to see that movie. But she hadn't realized that this meant going with him. He didn't know what to do, or what to say.

In a few moments Mrs. Singh came out and said, "Seemah has asked my permission to go to the movies with you. I'll ask my husband when he comes home." She went back into the house. He had never seen her so severe.

When he called the next day, Mrs. Singh motioned him into a corner of the big room and said, "Seemah is only twenty. She has never been 'out' with a man. Dating, as you know it in America, isn't done here. Girls go to the movies with another girl, or a group of girls; boys do the same. Only certain types of girls go out alone with a man. However, we realize that times are changing, and American influence will be here for a long time. Seemah's father and I have decided that she can go to the movie with you, but only because we feel that we know you well. We would never let her go out with an Indian boy, and certainly not with any other American soldier. Do you understand me?"

Jim gulped. "I certainly do. Would you rather I didn't take her?"

"Well, I wish you had asked me first, but now I don't want to disappoint her."

Oh boy, thought Jim. If I had ever had anything else in mind, I'm boxed in now.

They went to the movie, and enjoyed it. They laughed when the crazy nephew thought the stairs were San Juan hill, drew his sword, and yelled, "Charge" before running up the steps. Jim was careful not to touch Seemah, even inadvertently, but he couldn't help feeling a bit proud when soldiers waiting in line, none of whom were with girls, ignored his rank and wolf-whistled at Seemah.

When they got back to the stairs leading up to the verandah, it was dark under the tree and Jim touched Seemah's arm to delay her a moment. She jumped away, stark terror in her eyes. When she realized, however, that Jim had stopped her so that he could pretend to draw his sword, and then say "Charge!" before starting up the steps, she laughed hysterically. Jim knew it wasn't that good a joke, and her laughing was release from the tension she had been under all evening. He never invited her out again.

V-E day, when it came, was not entirely unexpected, and the forces in the Far East dug themselves in for what they expected to be a long and bitter period. Until now theirs had been a holding action; now they would go on the offensive against an enemy who had sworn to defend every inch of his territory.

When Jim had some leave coming, Mr. Singh advised him to spend it in a mountain resort called Nanital, on China Peak. He made all the arrangements and reservations for Jim, who flew as far as he could, and then took the train up the mountain. When he checked in, he found that the hotel had a main building, and bungalows set in the mountain woods. He was given a bungalow, and came down for his first dinner.

In one corner of an enormous dining room were two British colonels, eating together. Jim was the only other person in the entire hotel. He resigned himself to a lonely vacation, and the next day confirmed his fears. For recreation, Nanital offered a couple of swayback horses who walked around a stagnant lake. However, for a comparatively enormous fee, one could rent a real horse and ride to the top of the mountain. Jim had never ridden, and had no desire to start now.

He was awakened at seven in the morning by his bearer, who put a cup of tea and a piece of toast on his bedside table, and said, "Chota hazri" (Small breakfast). He was surprised that such a famous hotel served such a small breakfast, but found that at nine there was an enormous spread—for the three guests!

While at lunch, he saw a flash of color at the door, and Judy walked in, stopping dead when she saw him. "Jacksonville! What are you doing here?"

Judy was on vacation from her Red Cross duties, and had also had Nanital recommended to her. She was now stationed at an army rest and recreation facility in Srinigar. She had come to China Peak to get away from too familiar surroundings.

Judy's presence turned the whole experience around for Jim, and they rode both the swaybacked and the good horses, saw China Peak, took long walks, and talked and talked and talked. They also kissed, and petted, and came close to making love. It was on the fourth night of his scheduled two weeks that Jim proposed to Judy. She was much more practical.

"This is an unusual experience for both of us. We may be like passengers on a cruise ship, who swap addresses and swear fidelity and then never see each other after they dock. We're not going to decide anything until we are both in our normal surroundings. Then, if you still want to propose, I'll give you my answer."

Among other things, Jim asked Judy what had happened to the dark Red Cross girl from Dinjan. He repeated the rumor that she had been arrested as a lesbian. Judy laughed so hard she could hardly stop, and told Jim that Mimi had been transferred to Bangalore, had married the commanding officer, and was expecting a child. "So much for army intelligence," said Jim.

One evening at dinner Jim and Judy felt a presence near their table and looked up to see both British Colonels, who had previously never acknowledged their presence, waiting to talk to them.

"Lieutenant," said one, "may we talk to you a moment."

"Sure," said Jim grandly. "Sit down, Colonel."

The officers ignored his invitation and the one who had spoken said, "We have just heard on the wireless that you Americans have dropped some new kind of bomb on Japan. I think it is called an atom bomb. As an American, do you know anything about it? Do you think it will shorten the war?"

"Colonel," replied Jim, grandly, "you know as well as I do that for every new weapon invented a new defense is devised. A new bomb will mean a new defense. This war won't end until we land in Japan and pry every last Japanese soldier out of his foxhole."

"Well, General," said Judy when they were out of earshot, "you do make a persuasive case. But I hope you are wrong. I want to get home and try to make sense of my life. With you or without you."

On the last day of their stay in Nanital, where they had been substantially cut off from the world, Jim got a telegram from Mr. Singh. The telegram read simply: "The war has ended and the share market has crashed."

Judy thought the wording as hilarious as the news, and that night they made love.

Jim got back to the States in a returning airforce bomber, and as usual, took as much instruction as he could from the pilot en route. Judy was already in Jacksonville, and they were married almost at once.

Jim knew only that he wanted to keep flying, but with all the discharged airforce pilots, he didn't know whether he would have a chance. To his surprise, he found that light plane pilots were in demand—fighter and bomber pilots were applying to the airlines for jobs as pilots, but crop-dusting companies, small passenger airlines, corporations with company planes, and others were looking for pilots experienced in light planes, short hops and rough airfields.

Jim worked for a crop dusting company, spraying cotton fields all over northern Florida and southern Georgia. When the opportunity presented itself, he bought into the company, and kept them on the cutting edge of the industry by always buying the very latest equipment and gadgets. Eventually he became the majority stockholder in the company, which branched out into charter flights, short hauls, and instruction. As he prospered, he did less flying himself, and more instructing.

He also began acquiring pilot's licenses for every type of plane he knew about—single engine, twin-engine, four engine; land planes and sea planes; gliders and STOLs. He heard about a new type of superlight helicopter that he felt could be used for cropdusting, and had himself checked out on it. While at the factory, he took lessons and acquired licenses for both autogyros and helicopters, and when the latter became ram-jets, he was ready. Jet planes had been developed during the war—indeed, they were being tested while he was at Chanute Field—and this was a problem for him. He heard that the army was using civilian instructors in Dothan, Alabama, so he went there and applied for an instructor's job for all the planes he was licensed for. He used the opportunity to take lessons on the jets, and in a couple of years was licensed to fly single, two-engine, and four-engine jets.

Jim kept looking for new fields to conquer. His business was running itself, and was quite profitable. His attention turned to lighter-than-air craft, and he became an instructor for blimps and hot-air balloons. He could never figure a way to get a pilot's license for a dirigible, but not because he didn't try.

When ultralight planes were invented, Jim was right there, instructing. When planes were used to pull water skiers, Jim was one of the pilots. Nor did he depend on aircraft. He made over fifty parachute jumps, and when he was sixty, he took up free falling.

Judy was concerned with Jim's obsession. When he was flying he was fine, but between flights, or waiting for arrangements to be made, he just moped around the house.

"You need another interest for in-between times," she told him.

"Like what?"

That was a stickler. He didn't like to play cards, he wasn't interested in athletics, he took no pleasure from reading, and chess frustrated him because he didn't have the patience to plan far enough ahead.

One day Judy looked out the back window and said, "Jim, our back lot is a mess. Nothing but weeds. That's something you can do—clean up the lot and plant some flowers."

"I'll hire a gardener."

"No. You do it yourself. It'll keep you out of my hair and…Tell you what, plant vegetables. Then we'll have fresh salads."

Grudgingly, Jim went out into the yard. It was a relatively small plot, and right in the middle was a concrete slab, slanting down to a small hole in the middle. It took him some time, between flights, to level the ground and plant flowers around the edges. Just to be perverse, he planted the vegetables all around the concrete slab.

He did a desultory job of gardening, mostly because Judy kept him at it. The carrots didn't get very long, the cabbages often had worms, and the spinach didn't get very leafy. He had no hesitation neglecting the garden whenever he had a chance to fly. There was no question as to where his first love was.

Once he noticed that something had sprung up in the hole in the slab. As he watched it over the weeks, it seemed to be healthiest thing in the garden. His neighbor took a look and said it seemed to be either squash or pumpkin. They both began to check on it after that, and when it began to fruit, it was clear that there was a little pumpkin.

"That'll be great for Halloween," said Judy when he told her.

The growth of the pumpkin fascinated him, because it was untypical of his garden. His elderly neighbor on the other side laughed when he mentioned it. "That slab was part of the floor of an abattoir that stood here when this was still out in the country. That hole caught the excess blood and drew it underground. Then the building was used for chickens, and I guess a lot of chicken droppings went down that hole. That may be the most fertile piece of land in the county."

The vine held only the one pumpkin, but that began to grow rapidly. Judy complained about the quality of the other vegetables he had set out, but Jim brushed it off. "Hell, I'm a pilot, not a gardener. What do I know about vegetables?"

Jim continued to accumulate flying and instructor's licenses, and one day he felt he had reached his goal. He couldn't think of another license he had a reasonable chance of acquiring. In fact, he couldn't think of any more aircraft but a space capsule and the dirigible license, which continued to elude him. He checked all the records that he could find, and then compiled his own record, with notarized transcripts of all his licenses, which now amounted to sixty-two different varieties of aircraft in nine of eleven F.A.I. Commissions. He sent this record to the Guinness Book of Records, indicating that his investigations indicated that he held more flying licenses than any other person alive.

He told the remaining members of his family about this, and all his friends. They all waited to celebrate Jim's entry into the record book. Only Judy, who knew his history, realized that he was seeking neither fame nor money. He was proving to the American Airforce that they had been wrong about him. During all those years, this had been the thing that motivated him.

In the meantime, the pumpkin continued to grow. Judy decided it was already too big for a Halloween lantern—too hard to carry—and began digging out recipes for pumpkin pies, cookies, and other goodies.

The local newspaper sent a photographer to record the pumpkin growing on concrete—which was the way they titled it, and that's the way it looked in the picture. Jim's neighbor suggested that he enter it in the state fair for a prize, but Jim answered, rather stiffly, that he really didn't want to be considered a farmer. He was, in fact, much more interested in hearing from Guinness. The letter from Guinness, when it came, reminded him of his washing out of pilot training so many years ago. They simply informed him that they had no category that covered his accomplishments. Period.

Jim was furious. "So let them open a new category!" he shouted. He wanted to sue, but Judy convinced him that he had no case.

Jim was anything but a quitter. If they wouldn't recognize the number of his licenses, he'd do something more unusual and more exciting. He'd *make* them recognize him. He revisited Dothan; wrote to airplane manufacturers; and got in touch with airlines. He proposed to fly more different types of aircraft in one day than anyone had ever done before. Over a period of months, they all agreed to help him by putting aircraft at his disposal on a given day. The publicity this would create was, of course, a prime factor in their considerations. The newspapers picked up the story; he was interviewed on radio and television; the day and the site were announced; and there was a surprisingly large crowd to watch Jim set a record.

The rules Jim had set for himself was that he had to be airborne in each of the aircraft, alone, for at least fifteen minutes. Fortunately, the day dawned bright and clear, and at first light Jim took off in a Beechcraft. The moment he returned, and the plane stopped rolling, he was off at a run for the next plane, which had been lined up on the tarmac for him. Jim managed to fly thirty one different types of aircraft ("types" were defined as requiring a specific license) in the thirteen hours that the effort lasted. The day ended with his hot-air balloon landing just at dusk, whereupon Jim set off a row of fireworks that he had arranged beforehand. As an extra publicity gesture, TWA immediately flew Jim's notarized, witnessed record to Guinness in England.

Again, a period of impatient waiting. He realized that in the meantime, even without tending, the pumpkin had become truly enormous. He could almost picture Cinderella riding in it. People began to come by to look over the fence, and a stringer for a national newspaper syndicate had the story and picture published as a feature in a number of papers.

People asked permission to enter the yard, and many took pictures, measurements, and even tried to weigh the pumpkin. (Jim thought of charging admission, but dismissed the idea at once—he wasn't in the carnival business). Once a group of three men, who seemed to be officials of some sort, carefully measured and weighed the pumpkin, even checking the vine to make sure it wasn't a fake. He assumed they were from some agricultural organization.

His neighbor kept urging Jim to enter the pumpkin, which was still growing, in various kinds of contests, and he consistently refused. The neighbor even offered to make the arrangements for him, but Jim wasn't interested in being known as a pumpkin-grower.

So much time had passed since Jim had sent his flying record to the Guinness Book of Records that he began to wonder if they had ever received it, but one morning he received a registered, special delivery letter from the publishers. He was afraid to open it, and first went in and sat down. He slit the envelope and peeked at the opening sentences: "We are pleased to inform you that we have checked the records, interviewed witnesses, and undertaken independent investigations, and we are convinced..."

He put the envelope down, breathed a deep sigh, and exulted. It had taken him almost all his life, but he had shown the airforce that they had been wrong to wash him out. He had flown more different kinds of aircraft in one day than any one else ever had—in the airforce or out of the airforce. What had the commander said when he washed out—"Good luck?" Well, he had proved that luck wasn't important. He wished he knew where that commander was so he could make him eat his words. He was almost crying with joy as he continued reading his vindication.

He did cry when he read on: "We are pleased to inform you that we have checked the records, interviewed witnesses, and undertaken independent investigations, and we are convinced that you have grown the largest pumpkin on record. That fact will be contained in our next issue."

He was consumed with mortification. He burned with shame. A hot-shot pilot, the focus of a nationally-known flying exhibition, the holder of more pilots' licenses than anyone alive or dead, the man who flew more planes in one day than anyone in history—to be remembered for an accidental pumpkin?

He crumpled the letter in his hand, and as he did, he found another sheet underneath, also addressed to him. It said, simply, that as they had informed him previously, the Guinness Book of Records had no category covering his accomplishments in flying different types of planes. Period.

So Uncle Jim had finally made it into the Guinness Book of Records. But although he had flown more different types of aircraft in one day than anyone else ever had, that's not why he was in the Guinness Book of Records.

Uncle Jim hung his head. He slowly walked into the kitchen and picked up a short, sharp knife from the counter. He tested its sharpness against his thumb, and then put the tip to his wrist and tested it again. He walked out into the backyard and made a deep hole in the top of the pumpkin. Unzipping his fly, he urinated into the hole. He felt better as he walked back to the house.

Uncle Cat

◆

UNCLE CAT

My uncle Cat was either a true-blue American patriot or a nefarious Communist spy. Or both. Or neither. I don't know, nor does anyone else.

Cat's mother, Aunt Rosita, was a Barcelona beauty when my great-uncle, Cat's father—Phil—met her. Phil had opened a tobacco store at Five Points, with great ideas how to make it the center of Atlanta smokers. Although he made a modest living, he could never be as enterprising as he would have liked. He had ideas about promotions, advertising, loss-leaders, contests, and other ways to get ahead of the competition. However, the first time he announced a cut-price sale of cigarettes, the wholesalers threatened not to sell to him.

He then realized that the price of cigarettes from the wholesalers would go up from time to time—they never seemed to come down—and he would have to adjust his prices accordingly. One day he woke up to the fact that every brand changed its price the same amount on the same day. It was apparent that a cartel was operating, in violation of the anti-trust laws.

Phil not only had guts; he was an imposing figure of a man—tall, broad-shouldered, and good-looking with his Spanish-style moustache. He began to visit other cigarette shops, and pointed out the pricing phenomenon to them. This was before the days of class-action suits, but he managed to collect a war-fund with which he hired a lawyer and charged the tobacco manufacturers and the wholesalers with violation of the law. It would be nice to say that he won the suit and changed the situation, but the tobacco lobby was much more powerful. However, to get rid of this nuisance, they made him a member of the board of one of the companies, as representing retailers. In short, he was co-opted.

As a member of the board, with all its privileges, he became part of the tobacco establishment. Phil read all the reports, went to all the meetings, asked many questions, and began to get an education in corporation financing. He learned about debentures—stocks and bonds; stock options and stock splits; buy-outs and takeovers; dividends and deductible expenses. He also learned about insider trading, which was neither called that in those days, nor was it illegal. As a result of all this, he began to accumulate some capital. Then he learned that a big merger was in the offing, and he borrowed all the money he could from everyone he knew and bought stock. The result of this and similar maneuvers was that he became a rich man.

Since the outcome of the big merger was to the detriment of the retailers whom he ostensibly represented, he decided to take a trip abroad until the repercussions died down. A trip to Spain to learn about Spanish cigar-making was tax-deductible, so he went to Madrid. There he was taken by a local tobacco dealer to a performance of *Carmen*.

Phil had never been to an opera. Although he liked the set, which was a small Spanish village, the music meant little to him until the Toreador Song, which he recognized, and remembered to his delight that he had heard it many times. That made him feel comfortable, and from that point on he enjoyed the opera. Carmen herself seemed a bit old and a bit fat for a seductress, but he was struck by the beauty and by the voice of Micaela. In mentioning this to his host, he learned that she was his niece, and that her name was really Rosita. The upshot was that Phil was invited to an after-theatre party, including the cast.

Rosita was only mildly interested in him until she was told that he was in the tobacco business, and then she asked him, "In the opera, do we act like the girls in your cigarette factories?"

He was amused by her naivete, but assumed she was anxious to improve her acting. "There are no girls in American cigarette factories," he said gently.

"What? Only men? What sex discrimination!"

"Well, actually, no men either."

"Don't you manufacture cigarettes?"

"The cigarettes manufactured in America are practically untouched by human hands. Machines do almost all the work."

"God, it's good that Bizet doesn't live now, isn't it? Imagine the difficulty of writing an opera about a machine seducing a soldier."

He suddenly realized that she had been teasing him, and he found it charming. He groped for something to say to keep the conversation going. "Are you a full-time member of the cast," he asked, "or do you do other things, too?"

"Oh, many things." she said flippantly.

"Such as?"

This time she looked at him evenly and said, very seriously, "When I know you better, I might tell you."

He couldn't believe that she was indicating interest in seeing him again, but he hastened to take advantage of the opening, and she acceded.

As they began to see each other, he found that she considered herself a liberated woman, and as such had no patience with the Spanish custom, which still existed in some families, of having a chaperone along when meeting a man. On the contrary, she sometimes seemed to disappear for days at a time, and to reappear without notice. She often went out at outlandish hours, evidently coming back in the early morning. He had bitter bouts of jealousy, when he was sure she was with other men—and even more terrible feelings when he thought about what she might be doing with them. He was elated when he was with her, and depressed when he wasn't. He realized that he was in love.

She seemed to pity him, and more than once urged him to go home to America, but he resisted. He was living on his investments, and didn't need to be in the States to protect them. Slowly, their relationship grew closer, and there were times when he felt she loved him, too.

The denouement came one night when they were in a restaurant. She looked around, seemed to spot someone she knew, and with a word of apology approached a man sitting by himself at another table. After a few words they left together, leaving John's father sitting alone, feeling like a fool. Rather than tear out after her, thus attracting attention, he finished his meal—seething but quietly—and was just asking for the check when she reappeared. He controlled himself, took her home without a word, and turned to go.

She called him back. "Are you really furious?"

"I'm more than furious. I'm through."

"Come in, my dear. I guess the time has come to talk to you."

He debated refusing, but she had never called him "dear" before, so he cautiously entered her apartment.

"Do you remember when we first met, and you asked me what I did with my time?"

"Yes."

"Do you remember what I answered?"

"That when you knew me better you might tell me."

"Well, I don't think I need to know you any better than I do now, and I think you deserve to know more about me. What do you know about Catalonian history?"

This switch from the personal to the academic caught him by surprise. "Very little," he said, still cautious.

So she explained to him that she was an ardent Catalonian separatist, and this is what she felt she was doing with her life. She went to meetings, she spoke at meetings, she arranged meetings. She was part of a secret group that made decisions about political moves, and when a slight degree of home rule had been given Catalonia in 1913, there had been general agreement that she had been one of those who had brought it about. But, she explained, there was still opposition in the government to the idea of Catalonian autonomy, and always the danger that their plans would be betrayed. Hence, her unexplained absences and oddly-timed meetings.

Cat's father was so relieved to learn that her behavior was political rather than personal that he proposed marriage on the spot. She, in turn, was shocked. She was so wrapped up in her cause that she hadn't realized that he was in love with her. But as she thought about it, she realized that she was in love, too.

Cat's mother was torn between her desire to stay in Barcelona and agitate for more independence, and her love for his father, which—carried to its ultimate conclusion—would mean living in Atlanta. Fortunately, Cat's father was able to point out that he was quite wealthy, which meant that frequent trips back and forth would not be too difficult; and that she would be able to give some financial help to various Catalonian projects. To prove his earnestness, he bought a house in Sitges that had once been a Duke's palace and furnished it with old Catalonian (not Spanish) pieces that would have done credit to a museum.

When the baby was born he was named Juan, and his mother imported a nursemaid and a tutor from Barcelona to Buckhead. She declared that only Catalan would be spoken in the house. But this was a problem, since Juan's father spoke little Catalan. The result was that young Juan learned both English and Catalan. However, his mother's fierce pride in being a Catalan was instilled in him.

When he was eight, his father insisted that he go to school, for social reasons if nothing else. They chose a private school, run along European lines. On his first day there a classmate referred to him as John. He patiently explained that his name was Juan, pronounced Huan.

"You're a Spick? You don't look like one."

"What's a Spick?"

"A Spaniard, of course."

"I am not a Spaniard. I am a Catalan."

"What? What's a Catalan?"

He drew himself up and said, proudly, "I am from Barcelona."

"Then you are a Spick."

Juan was frustrated that he couldn't make the other boy understand what it meant to be a Catalan, and infuriated that he insisted on referring to him as a Spaniard. He launched himself at the unsuspecting boy, who drew back with a bloody nose. Before the incident could develop into a real battle, Juan was escorted to the master's office, where he was lectured on the rules of gentlemanly battle. If he felt insulted he was to challenge the other boy, and they would fight with gloves in a ring, under supervision.

Despite these rules, Juan fought a number of unauthorized battles as the boys learned that the new boy was insulted by the term "Spick." He kept insisting that he was a Catalan, and eventually his nickname became Cat, which satisfied both sides. By the twelfth grade Cat was well accepted by his peers, in great part because of his soccer prowess. He was the captain of the team and won a letter, although even he realized that soccer was a foreign sport in America.

When Catalonia became a republic in 1931 Cat's mother's joy was so great that she insisted that the entire extended family, both on her side and her husband's side, spend a week in Sitges, where she rented houses for them. When, the next year, a compromise with the central government in Spain gave Catalonia autonomy instead of complete independence, she felt betrayed by her former comrades and declared she would never go back to Barcelona until Catalonia was an independent state.

Perhaps it was well that the expensive celebration was held when it was, for as the Depression in the States deepened, Cat's father's financial position became more and more precarious. The value of the stocks that he held dropped precipitously, and as he maneuvered to shore up his fortune, he lost even more money. They gave up the house in Buckhead and moved to Marietta. They held on to the house in Sitges, however, on the one hand because nobody was buying Spanish real estate, and on the other because it had such strong emotional value for both of them.

When the Civil War broke out in Spain in 1936, Cat's mother was beset with ambivalence. It was clear that if Franco were successful he would wipe out all vestiges of Catalonian independence or autonomy. On the other hand, supporting the very Spanish government that had refused to give Catalonia independence seemed like a betrayal.

Cat had no such conflict—he was twenty years old and had finished two years at Harvard. He immediately joined the International Brigade and fought in a number of engagements, falling back as Franco moved forward. He was in Madrid when the fall of that city seemed inevitable, but Franco's troops moved on Toledo to rescue a besieged garrison there, and Madrid had time to prepare.

The fact that Juan (whose name caused him no trouble in Spain) spoke Catalan, Castilian (which he picked up easily), and English; was an American; and a Harvard student, were plusses for him. It was felt that he would be wasted as an infantryman. Consequently, Juan became, in effect, the administrator-cum-public relations officer and spokesman for his unit. He took foreign newsmen around, wrote press releases, and made an occasional radio broadcast. He visited the various fronts in Madrid in order to keep in close touch with what was happening.

On one of his visits he stopped in at a Madrid hospital where he interviewed an American volunteer nurse, Joyce. He learned that she also came from Atlanta, but not from Buckhead, where he had lived, or even from Marietta, to where his parents had moved, but from Jonesboro, which was a long way from Marietta, physically and socially; and even further from Buckhead. However, in short order they began to see a lot of each other between their various assignments.

The siege of Madrid lasted twenty-eight months. In the early days morale was high. Food stocks were sufficient, water was no problem, and the defenders were sure they would be victorious in the end, particularly with the help and material which was arriving from both Russia and Mexico. As Franco's troops were victorious elsewhere, however, some doubts began to run through the defenders' minds, and when the effects of the blockade began to be felt, a siege mentality took hold. Every piece of resistance elsewhere was blown up into a major victory; there was talk of regrouping, of foreign help, of a turn of the tide, and so forth. Nobody really believed that Madrid would fall to Franco.

Cat was visiting Joyce in the hospital on one particularly tense night when a shell falling very close by sent her rushing into his arms. As he wrapped his arms around her he found the zipper on the back of her uniform under his hand. Almost without thinking he began pulling it down. Just as automatically she began to resist, then suddenly melted back into his arms and said, "Oh, Cat, let's, let's. Who knows how much longer we have?"

They made love on an operating table in a storeroom. It was impulsive, frantic, with little foreplay and no restful period following. The urgency of the situation seemed to communicate itself to them. He was apologetic when it was over, but she clung to him, "I love you, Cat. I really do."

After that they made love whenever they could, but no longer with such intensity. There was foreplay, and laughter, and teasing, and a feeling of satisfaction—which never lasted long enough for either of them.

In Madrid food began to be rationed, gasoline for transportation became a luxury item, and even fuel was a problem. Despite their pride in the beauty of their city, Madrileneans began cutting down trees for firewood. In the third year of the siege the situation was desperate.

One day Cat looked in on Joyce in the nurses' quarters, and found her crying. She explained that she had been on duty in the tuberculosis unit, and due to a shortage of help, was serving lunch. The food situation in

Madrid was already very bad, and in the hospital they were reduced to serving black bread, jam, hard-boiled eggs, and ersatz coffee. When she offered this to an elderly patient, he erupted: "Don't you know that I have tuberculosis? Don't you know that I need soft, rich foods? What kind of lunch is this for a tubercular man? Go back to the kitchen and bring me the kind of food I need!"

Joyce tried to explain to him the facts about the siege, but he wanted none of it. In desperation, she went back to the kitchen, but all she could bring him was another hard-boiled egg. He took one look at it, turned on her, and said, "Do you speak Catalan?"

She said she did not, so he began to curse her. He cursed her, her mother, her family, wished death on her, and said it would have been better for her to have died rather than become a nurse. She broke down and ran.

Between her tears Joyce said to Cat, wonderingly, that she had understood every word the man had said, although she knew no Catalan at all. As she thought about the incident, she couldn't explain to herself how she understood all his curses, unless—and she said this seriously—that under so much stress, she suddenly could understand Catalan.

She was impatient to return to the ward the next day to unravel the mystery. When she approached the patient, he immediately apologized for his ranting the day before, and said that he had been under a lot of stress, realized that Joyce wasn't responsible for the food, and that he should have controlled himself. Timidly, Joyce asked, "Didn't you ask me if I understood Catalan?"

"Yes, I did," he said.

"Then how did I understand what you were shouting?"

"Oh," he replied, "I asked if you understood Catalan, and you said no, so I spoke English. I wanted you to understand every word I said."

Cat thought that Joyce's instant Catalan facility was hilarious, but Joyce wasn't amused.

At this time the defenders of Madrid were scraping the bottom of the barrel for soldiers. Cat no longer had the luxury of being a public relations officer, and had been put in charge of a group of very young draftees. One night, as he assigned individuals to various points along the perimeter, he found he was instructing a teen-ager dressed completely in black. On inquiry, it turned out that the youngster was an apprentice to his uncle who was—of all things—an undertaker; hence the black attire. The young man spoke in a highly affected way—a flutey voice that carried distances, careful diction, very proper pronunciation, and pompous words. Cat realized that he was practicing speaking the final words at funerals.

Cat gave him two grenades, which was all he would have as weapons, and started to move away, but the young man motioned him to stay and said:

"Let us say, as might well be the case, that twelve enemy soldiers approach my position. What would you say would be the appropriate action for me?"

"As I showed you, you pull the pin, release the handle, and toss the grenade overhand in their direction."

"The ultimate result of such a procedure on my part would, I take it, be the demise of some unfortunate souls. Am I correct in my assumption?"

"Yeah, you'd probably knock off about five with one grenade."

"And it would therefore follow that I should repeat the same procedure with the second defensive weapon. The result to be expected?"

"You'd probably knock off another five."

"Now, let us look into the heart of the matter. Five and five total ten, and there were twelve soldiers approaching. Put your faith in Jesus, sir. Good night."

And he disappeared in the darkness before Cat knew what was happening.

This time it was Joyce who found it hilarious.

When it became obvious that Madrid could hold out no longer, a decision was taken to make a supreme effort to break out of the siege, in order to move the pick of the fighting forces to Barcelona. Casualties from this operation were high, but Cat and a few hundred other soldiers managed to reach Barcelona. In the operation a shell had landed very close to Cat, and he thought he felt something hit the side of his head, but whatever it was didn't incapacitate him, nor did it break the skin.

When Barcelona fell, early in 1939, Cat joined the troops who crossed the border into France. Although the early refugees were turned back, by the time he arrived policy had been changed and internment camps had been set up. After a few weeks of internment an official of the American consulate visited the camp and arranged for the Americans to be repatriated to the States. Cat tried to refuse, since he wanted to return to Spain to look for Joyce. When he learned that he would be held in the camp indefinitely if he did not agree to repatriation, he gave in.

His plan was to use the opportunity to get out of the camp, and then to return to Spain. However, the American officials had arranged for a train from the camp to the dockside in Calais, and immediately onto a ship. It seems that the French government wanted no problem of American mercenaries wandering around the country, or crossing the borders.

From Atlanta, Cat made a bee-line for Jonesboro, and found Joyce in a terrible state of anxiety about him. She had been among the first Americans repatriated direct from Spain, and had been unable to get word of him by any means. She had already met his parents, who were equally worried, and Cat and Joyce had no further courtship at all—it was just a question of a date for the marriage.

Although both Cat's family and Joyce's family were willing to sacrifice other things to give an enormous wedding for the courageous hero and his selfless bride, Cat and Joyce decided that after what they had seen in Spain this would be conspicuous consumption, and they had a small wedding followed by a modest reception. Then came the question of what Cat should do.

Cat solved the problem by announcing that he wanted to resume his studies. He knew he was a bit older than his classmates would be, but he also realized that regardless of experience, without at least a first degree he would be handicapped in many areas. However, he did not want to go back to Harvard. Both because of the difference in tuition and because he wanted a less elitist school, he enrolled in Emory University.

Joyce worked as a nurse, at first in the Emory University infirmary, then in Piedmont Hospital, and finally as a private duty nurse, where night shifts and weekend work added considerably to their meager income. In the summer they worked at camps—Joyce as a nurse, and Cat as a sports instructor.

Of all his courses, Cat found that he liked the psychology courses best, so he took all that were allowed: Introduction to Psychology, Advanced Psychology, Individual Psychology, Applied Psychology, Group Psychology, Social Psychology, Selected Issues in Psychology, Schools of Psychological Thought, Psychological Testing and Psychological Counseling. As graduation approached, he met with the head of the Psych department and told him he would like to continue for a Master's degree in psychology.

"Can you support yourself for the next two years?" asked the professor.

"We have a baby on the way," replied Cat, "and it won't be easy, but I think we can swing it."

"And after that."

"After that I'll go to work."

"No, no. I mean, can you support yourself and your family through an additional two or three years while you study for a doctorate?"

"Oh, I have no intention of doing that—at least, not at first."

"Son, you don't seem to understand. A master's degree in psychology is just permission to study for a doctorate. Without a Ph.D. you're dead in psychology. You won't get a job, have a career, or be able to succeed in private practice. If you can't finance yourself through to a doctorate, I suggest that you pick a field where the master's is the terminal degree."

"Like what?"

"Oh, like social work, for example."

Social work didn't seem too far from psychology to Cat, and if he could begin a career with a master's degree, why not? So Cat began to apply to schools of social work. His first choice was what he thought of as one of the better schools—Columbia University.

The interviewer for the Columbia School of Social Work was evidently a new graduate of that school, presently on the faculty of Oglethorpe University. Cat met with the interviewer. He found the interviewer quite young, and rather supercilious. The interviewer kept pressing him as to why he particularly wanted to go to Columbia and, perversely, Cat wouldn't give him the answer that he obviously wanted: that he understood it to be one of the best social work schools in the country. Instead he spoke of his own career plans, what a degree from Columbia would mean to possible employers, and so forth.

At last the interviewer said, "Sir, I don't know whether you are aware of the impression you are giving. I feel that you just want to get that piece of paper in your hand, regardless of anything else."

Cat replied, "Mister, I really don't expect Ultimate Truth to be revealed to me in a blinding flash of light at the Columbia University School of Social Work, but nevertheless I would like to study there."

He was not accepted.

Cat realized that he had not been accepted because of his attitude, but he was more amused than chagrined. He felt that as a star athlete (although in a very restricted field), and with three years of fighting a war on foreign soil, and a very respectable average in psychology, he shouldn't have to lick the ass of a beginning academic to be able to study.

Among the other schools that he considered was Atlanta University's school of social work. "But that's a Colored school!" exclaimed one of his classmates. (This was when being called black was still an insult, rather than being beautiful).

"Well, the way I figure it," explained Cat, "most of the underclass in America—the people with problems—are colored, and most social workers are white. I'm not sure they really understand their clients. Two years of study amid colored students should give me a better understanding. And although the colored clients might relate better to colored social workers, my studies in psychology lead me to believe that they may aspire to be more like whites. In any case, I'd like to try."

So Cat applied to Atlanta University, and received a very warm and very frank refusal. Although the university did not believe in practicing discrimination, and although his record was good enough for admittance, inquiry had indicated that if they accepted a white student, their State financing would be immediately cut off. This would result in the school closing, and colored social workers having one less school to which they could go. So Cat became one of the very first victims of reverse racism.

In the end, Cat decided on the School of Applied Social Science (which was the rather pretentious name of the school of social work) at Western Reserve University. He went to Cleveland, registered, and began classes. The plan was for Joyce to join him after the baby was born, in January.

But they reckoned without Hirohito and Tojo. On Pearl Harbor day Cat was ready to enlist, but Joyce pointed out that he was no longer a carefree college student. He was married, with a child on the way, and deferrable as a student. Intellectually, Cat realized that she was right, but emotionally, he was unable to live with the feeling that he was hiding behind his status. He remained uncomfortable until a new program, called Voluntary Officer Candidates, was announced. Under that plan, anyone who had been deferred from the draft as the sole support of dependents could volunteer for six months training. At the end of that time, they would either be officers, and thus presumably able to support their dependents; or they would be returned to civilian life. With Joyce's consent, he enlisted in the VOC program.

As the first step, he was given a complete physical. The doctor who examined him did a thorough job; looked at the results; and said, "I'd like you to repeat some eye tests."

"Why? There's nothing wrong with my eyes. I was practically a sharpshooter in Spain."

"Nevertheless."

After the re-examination, the doctor said, "You might still be a sharp-shooter..." and Cat almost said, "I told you so," but the doctor continued "...but you'll never be an officer. Did you ever have any injury to your eyes, or even your head."

Cat thought a long time, and gradually dredged up from his memory the "ping" he thought he felt outside Madrid.

"You have very little peripheral vision in your left eye," explained the doctor, "possibly from whatever blow that was. It doesn't affect your sight as such, but you do not see things out of the corner of your left eye. In many areas that isn't important, but for an officer in any active service, a slight movement on the periphery might be extremely impor-tant. I know that you might end up with a desk job, where this wouldn't be important, but we can't guarantee that, so my responsibility is to dis-qualify you as an officer. Sorry."

Joyce sympathized with his mixed feelings. She was glad, of course, that he wasn't going to be a soldier again, but she realized that a physi-cal reason could make him feel like a cripple. Cat moped around the house for some months, and suddenly there was a phone call from a friend he had known in Madrid. The friend was now a minor official in the State Department, and told Cat that he had recommended him for a job. He was mysterious about the job, and Cat had visions of the OSS, or some other secret outfit.

However, when the call came it was to see someone in the Interior Department. Cat went with a feeling of curiosity. His friend met him before Cat went in for the interview and said, "Don't be put off by this guy's manner. He is the original Colonel Blimp. He has done nothing, and knows nothing, and therefore affects a 'This is a war, can't you see I'm busy?' attitude."

Cat's file was open on the official's desk. "You were recommended by someone in State, yes? You were in the army in Spain, yes? Had administrative experience, yes? Were in an internment camp in France, yes? Know how things are done there, yes? And" —his tone changed to one of more respect—"your brother is a Senator, yes?"

Cat realized these weren't questions, but statements, so he just nodded.

"Okay. Your country needs you. You will be in charge of one of the internment camps for Japs on the West Coast. Good luck."

"But, sir…, wait a minute. I don't speak Japanese. I never ran an internment camp. And we haven't even captured any Japanese."

"These are Japs living in America. Probably traitors, all of them. Long life to the Emperor and all that junk. Anyway, we are packing them all in. Can't take chances. McMillan will fill you in on the details. Oh, by the way, you won't have to worry about the draft. This is considered an essential job."

Rounding up Japanese-Americans on the West Coast and shipping them to tent camps inland was done more quickly than Cat's orientation and preparation took. When he got to the camp he was to command, it was in a state of wild disorder. He found that his army experience—and especially the disorder that existed in the Spanish Republican forces—made him more capable than he realized. He also found that most of the Japanese living in the United States spoke at least some English, so that Japanese as a language was less important than he had anticipated—there was no lack of translators among the Japanese themselves. Nevertheless, he embarked on a crash course in Japanese.

Cat was troubled by his job. He realized that most Japanese in the States were no less loyal to their new country than any other immigrants. On the other hand he also knew that there must be some among them who still revered the Emperor or, at least, had some loyalty to Japan. But how to sort them out? The West Coast was already rife with rumors of Japanese submarines off the coast of California; of signal lights being sent them; of sabotage in munitions factories, etc. The internment of all Japanese was a symptom of mass hysteria, and he knew it; but he also didn't know what else could be done, especially in view of the crushing blow at Pearl Harbor, and the imminent threat of another such blow on continental America at any time.

As Cat got to know some of the groups in his camp, he became even more aware of the paradoxes. The Nisei, who were born in America of Japanese parents, tended to be extremely patriotic, and from this very patriotism came their reaction to being interned. As loyal Americans, no one had a right to treat them this way, and they reacted against the restrictions of internment as Americans. On the other hand, the Issei, born in Japan, tended to maintain some respect for the Emperor and some pride in the successes of the Japanese armed forces, although they had come to America for what it offered. They were torn in their reactions, and many simply retreated into themselves and their families, waiting for events to determine their future for them.

In any case, the camp was a pretty horrible place—much worse than the one in France. In good weather it was a flat, hot place without trees, and a sea of mud during and after rainy periods. Cat tried to make individual contact with some of the thousands of Japanese in his camp, but found the Issei apathetic to his approaches, while the Nisei were outright hostile. However, he learned that some of the Nisei were organizing the camp inhabitants. They divided them into groups, had them elect leaders, who then elected leaders of groups of leaders—in short, a bureaucracy in civilian terms, or a chain of command, in military terms.

With this organization they took charge of many aspects of the camp, from digging drainage ditches to organizing kindergartens. They dealt with Cat only through their elected leader, one Saigo Ito. Saigo had been a teacher under his Americanized name Sam Attel, but in the camp he reverted to his Japanese name and insisted that it be used. Cat recognized in Saigo a gifted leader, and made use of him to see that the camp ran efficiently and quietly. Although Saigo resented having been interned—especially since in all his teaching he had emphasized the positives of the American way of life—he and Cat wanted the same thing, that is, as decent a life as possible for the internees, so they found a modus operandi.

Saigo went to Cat only for things he couldn't handle himself—supplies needed, for example, or more telephone lines, and things like that. Cat was always respectful of Saigo, and a guarded friendship grew up between them. Saigo began to realize Cat's ambivalence about his assigned job, and Cat understood Saigo's desire to help his peers without assigning legitimacy to the policy of internment. Over time they began to have real conversations about subjects broader than the governance of the camps.

One night Cat looked from his quarters outside the perimeter toward the camp, and saw that it was completely dark. There were neither street lights nor lights in the tents. He assumed there had been an electrical outage of some sort, and knowing that the maintenance men on his staff were very capable, waited for the lights to go on. They did not. The next day, he learned that the electrical system had been sabotaged in a number of places.

He asked Saigo to meet with him the next day, but before that meeting took place he was informed that the water in the camp had also been cut off—again, sabotage. In the meeting with Saigo he asked what was taking place. Saigo thought a few moments as to how much he was willing to share, and then told Cat that a dissident element had organized itself in the camp—an unelected element made up of some of the more adamant Nisei, who decided that the current policy of cooperation with the camp authorities was not acceptable. They had decided to oppose everything the authorities suggested or required, even if it created physical and other difficulties for the internees. They planned to continue to cut telephone wires, douse streetlights, block the sewage lines—in short, to create chaos.

"This is a political move," explained Saigo, "to make the camps so uninhabitable that humanitarian organizations will demand abolition of the camps. I am opposed to their method of making people suffer to achieve the ends they want, but I would accept it as a difference in viewpoint if it had been decided upon through voting or elections, or in any other way that indicated that the people involved were willing to undertake such sacrifices in hope of results. What I can't accept, however, is that this small group is taking these actions without any reference to what the majority might want. It is a form of terrorism, and my problem is that there is nothing I can do to stop it. As you know, we have neither police, courts, nor jails—we have only consensus and moral pressure, and these mean nothing to the dissidents. So now it becomes your problem."

Cat thought a moment. "If people are really suffering from lack of electricity, water, and so forth, they will rise up against these self-proclaimed leaders in their own self-interest. If the camp authorities take action against the dissidents, it might rally the people behind them as a protest measure. I have faith in the power of the people."

Saigo sighed. "You sound like an old-line communist. Life isn't that simplistic. Okay, play it your way—there is nothing I can do about it anyway."

The sabotage continued, was repaired, happened again, and Cat waited for the people to disavow the group that caused them such discomfort. One day while walking through the camp Cat saw a young man with a classical case of a black eye—really ringed with a black bruise. Looking closer, he saw that he also had blue bruises on his arms. When Cat tried to question him as to what had happened, he looked around fearfully and ran away. This aroused Cat's curiosity. He was afraid the guards were using physical coercion on the inmates, which was strictly forbidden. To indicate his awareness of this possibility, he asked the guards to report to him any signs of physical violence they found.

Several of the guards laughed when he made this remark, confirming his fear that they were abusing the internees, but when he raised the question, they informed him that the bruises were inflicted by organized gangs within the camp. Cat began investigating and found that although the dissident group reported to him by Saigo was still organizing sabotage, they had also realized that there was no restraining power in the volunteer society in which they lived, so some of the members became, in a way, dissidents from the dissident group and became, in effect, outlaws, engaged in stealing, extortion, and physical beatings.

The internees would not report the outrages committed on them by these gangs. On the one hand they were afraid of reprisals, and on the other their resentment at being interned caused them to boycott all dealings with the administration. Cat asked the guards to try to prevent such acts, and/or to report anything that could be used as evidence, but they were cut off from the inner life of the camp by language barriers as well as by the hostility of the internees toward them.

One day Saigo came to Cat and said, "You have a problem."

Cat was surprised, because ordinarily a problem in the camp would be referred to as "our" problem. Saigo explained that the policy of hands-off was not working. "When democracy abdicates its responsibility, the result is fascism. The camp is now being run by a small group of outlaws, concerned only with their own welfare. 'The only thing necessary for evil to triumph is for good people to do nothing'," he quoted.

"Maybe a little more time…" temporized Cat.

"There was a gang rape last night," said Saigo. "A fifteen year old girl. If it isn't punished, there'll be others."

In the camp Cat was judge, jury, and executioner. The normal rules of American democracy did not apply. Consequently, he had the guards name for him all the internees whom they thought to be members of the terrorist group, and he imprisoned them in a small tent camp built a few hundred yards from the main camp, ringed with barbed wire fences and constantly guarded.

Saigo commented that he didn't see much difference between the dissidents being in the little camp or in the big one.

Cat explained, "Imprisonment has three aims: rehabilitation, punishment, and protection of society. I don't expect this step to rehabilitate the gang members, nor is it a very severe punishment, but by God, it protects the rest of the camp from them."

With the removal of the terrorists, camp life settled back to normal. The sabotage movement brought no results—the United States government would simply not let the Japanese out of the camps, and living as best one could proved more popular than continuing protests. Gradually the situation changed—a Nisei unit in the American army proved itself under very difficult circumstances, it was clear that America was no longer in danger of a Japanese invasion, and the camps were eventually abandoned.

Cat's record as a camp commander was commendable, and at the end of the war he could have had several posts—head of the prison services in several large cities, director of a large humanitarian and aid organization, and even the vice-presidency of a bank. However, he and Joyce decided that it would be wise to build on the strengths that he had, so he applied for an administrative post with MacArthur's occupation forces. He was, indeed, an ideal candidate—he spoke Japanese, he had been in charge of a Japanese population, and he came from a respectable Atlanta family. His only condition for accepting the post was that Joyce and the baby be with him, which was accepted with some surprise that he had even questioned it.

The four years in Japan were good years for Cat and his family. Their son learned to speak Japanese, just as Cat had spoken Catalan, and they had a daughter before the assignment was over. Joyce insisted on working as a nurse whenever she could, and became more or less an expert on the use of Japanese herbs of which she had never heard. Since MacArthur insisted that the Americans eat only foods grown by hydroponics, Cat developed an interest in growing exotic houseplants without soil. The only minor discomfort they experienced was that their son seemed to be allergic to fish, and Japanese diets seemed to be based on sea-food.

On their return to the States Cat was made chief aide to the Undersecretary of State for Pacific Affairs. He was rather amused that for someone who still considered himself a Catalan, his assignment was on the other side of the globe. He acquitted himself well, and at the end of his first year his responsibilities were widened. He himself became an Undersecretary without a specific title, and was given responsibility for information concerning minority groups and political refugees. His first thoughts on being informed of his responsibilities were of Japanese-Americans in the States, and Catalans in Spain.

Joyce and both sets of parents decided on a celebration for Cat's appointment as Undersecretary of State. They arranged a buffet dinner in the Georgian Terrace Hotel on June 9th, 1950, for all the extended families and their friends. It was a light-hearted affair. Cat's career seemed settled; Joyce had taken a degree in nursing education and was now teaching nurses in Grady Hospital; Cat's mother and father were in reasonably good health—he was consultant to the tobacco lobby, and she maintained a lively interest in Spanish affairs. Joyce's mother had died, but her father was present, beaming with pride at the position his daughter's husband had achieved. In all, a successful party.

On the same day, in Wheeling, West Virginia, an obscure Senator from Wisconsin named Joseph McCarthy was saying to the audience, "I have here in my hand a list of two hundred and five members of the Communist Party who are working and shaping policy in the State Department."

There was no tape recorder present, and the few reporters there did not make careful notes, so it was later never clear whether he said two hundred and five, or twenty-five, or fifty seven, or some other number. In McCarthy's subsequent accusations to different audiences, the number constantly varied, and the list—if it actually existed—was never shown to anyone. However, the accusation was picked up by the national media, and the era of McCarthyism began.

It took only a few months until there were shown into Cat's office in the State Department Senator McCarthy's two falcons, Roy Cohn and David Schein. They were falcons because they roved out ahead of their master in search of prey, and then left their victim figuratively dying on the ground. They used the full weight of Senator McCarthy's delegated influence to silence, to intimidate, and to destroy whomever they centered in on.

They entered Cat's office with a stenographer, and sat down without invitation. Cat bristled, but controlled himself.

"You fought for the Commies in Spain, didn't you?" asked Cohn.

"I fought to defend the legally constituted government of Spain against forces seeking to overthrow it," answered Cat, carefully. He noticed that the stenographer was not writing.

"Yeah. So you were with the Reds. Make a note of that," he said, turning to the stenographer.

"I didn't say that," commented Cat, trying to be equable.

"Mister, this record is for my use, not yours. It will contain what I think it should contain. Now, the nurse that you took up with—she was a Commie, too, wasn't she?"

"My wife worked in a government hospital." He emphasized both words.

"Married a communist," Schein instructed the stenographer.

"Now, wait a minute," interjected Cat. "If you want a record, let's get it straight. I fought in Spain for three years against fascism—the same kind of fascism the United States fought in the Second World War."

"But the government you call fascist didn't fight against the United States in that war, did it?" asked Cohn. "In fact, it helped stem the tide of world communism. You think you know history? Well, do you know that Franco said, 'Yesterday, today and tomorrow, for the countries of

Europe there exists only one danger—Communism'. And that's the man you fought against."

"Speaking of fighting against fascism," added Schein, "I notice that you did not run to enlist when America entered the war. My notes say you waited several months."

"I volunteered…" began Cat.

"Yeah, but only if you could be an officer. And if you couldn't be an officer you wouldn't stay in—I'm familiar with that kind of patriotism." Cohn again signaled the stenographer.

Suddenly, Cohn started a new tack. "Ever hear of Saigo Ito?"

The name brought back many memories to Cat. "Sure," he said. "He was the leader of the interned Japanese during the War. We worked together for some time."

"Worked together? You mean you and he set up a special camp for his friends. And don't try to tell us that you don't know that he is now one of the leaders of the Communist Party in Japan."

"What are you talking about? He was a teacher."

"What was your contact with him after you left the camp?"

"I never saw him again."

"Did you write to him, get messages from him, counsel him?"

"Of course not."

"Not even during the long stay that you wangled in Japan."

"I didn't 'wangle' a stay there. I was posted there. And I never saw Saigo again."

"Oh, you still call him by his first name, do you? Okay," said Schein, "we can't waste much more time on you."

To the stenographer: "Read back what you have."

In an unemotional voice she repeated, "Fought for the communist side in Spain; married a communist; tried to avoid army service; trained Japanese communists in a special camp; admits knowing present head of Japanese communist party; arranged duty in Japan; denies continuing contact with Japanese communists or their head." She shut her notebook.

"This is absurd," said Cat. "Not one of those things will stand up in a court of law."

"There isn't going to be any trial in a court of law," said Cohn, almost gently. "We'll give you a break for cooperating. You can resign from the State Department with just a small note in the newspapers; or you can be fired, with nationwide publicity. Frankly, the Senator would prefer the latter—it will indicate how adamant he is about getting the communists out of the State Department. You decide."

They left Cat in a daze. He had seen what McCarthy had done on more flimsy evidence—or none at all—to others. The State Department, in particular, was paralyzed. McCarthy worked on the Hitlerian principle of the great lie. If the lie was big enough, and repeated often enough, people would inevitably believe that where there was smoke there was fire, and McCarthy's repeated accusations about the State Department had resulted in enough forced resignations to give credence to his thesis.

Cat decided to resist. He first contacted Monty, in his senatorial office, and told his story. Monty sucked on his pipe, looked a bit embarrassed, and said, "I may not be smart, but I am not stupid enough to fight with Senator McCarthy for my own brother. The press would make mincemeat out of me for such nepotism. It would be the worst thing I could do for you. Besides, I've been told that a reporter is about to publish a so-called expose of my career, and even a recommendation from me might not be helpful. I suggest you take it up directly with the Secretary of State. I'll make the appointment for you if you like."

So Cat visited the Secretary of State, who listened to his story respectfully, but without surprise. He sighed. "If the Boss (which meant Eisenhower) were willing to fight, we'd fight tooth and nail. But he isn't. Several times he has been persuaded to include a paragraph in some speech condemning McCarthyism, or at least defending the State Department, and he has invariably skipped that paragraph when delivering the speech. The message is clear to McCarthy and to us. He won't back us. And we are, after all, an instrument of the Presidency. I can't help you, Cat. I will accept your resignation and make no public announcement about it, but that's all I can do. If you don't resign, and I don't fire you, there'll be a public flap from McCarthy that will reflect on the President and his appointments. I might have to resign."

Suddenly he grinned. "If it's a question of your resignation or mine, I think I'd prefer yours. That's pretty selfish of me, isn't it? Or let's put it another way: I only fight battles I have a chance of winning. On this one, I have no chance, at least without the Boss' backing. So I'm not going to fight."

When Cat resigned there was no announcement from the State Department, but Cohn and Schein saw to it that at least a mention was made in the Washington papers.

Again, just as when he was rejected for the army, Cat moped around the house and the neighborhood. When he got over the shock and the rage, he began to apply for jobs—mostly administrative positions in relief and rehabilitation organizations, since he wanted to put both his experience and his basic idealism to work. From the responses he received, he realized that something was wrong. His credentials for the jobs were good, and after they rejected him they kept advertising the positions.

Finally, the chairman of the board of a Boston organization who had known his father confided to him that he was ticketed as a communist. Cohn and Schein, true to form, had not kept their promise to simply let him resign without fanfare, but had put him on a list of communists that they circulated to every organization that depended upon or participated in government funding; and to many that did not.

Their finances were in a precarious position. Cat had never made much money in any of his posts, and nursing, as Joyce would have been the first to point out, was one of the most highly underpaid professions that existed. In addition, before Cat's father had died his terminal illness had eaten up most of the money that he had left. Cat's mother was in a sheltered housing project for the aged, which was also very expensive.

Cat went to work in a local community center as a group leader, but the pay was minimal.

Uncle Bernie showed up one day, and in a very secret two-man meeting made Cat a very lucrative proposition. Cat rejected it out of hand, and never even told Joyce that there had been such a meeting. Uncle George offered to help out financially, and Cat thanked him sincerely, but said he'd rather make his own way.

They were already talking about moving to a less expensive part of town—perhaps back to Jonesboro—when a phone call led to a visit from a very well-dressed Japanese business man. He bowed to Cat, who bowed back with the proper degree of modesty, and they made the small talk that was a necessary preliminary in Japan to doing business. Joyce served tea Japanese style and left them alone. It seemed that the visitor had come from Saigo Ito who, true enough, was in Japan.

The visitor explained that Ito had many interests in Japan, among them a steel factory. There was a severe shortage of steel in America at the time, due to a series of strikes in the coalmines and on the docks. In short, Ito had several hundred tons of steel that he wanted to be sold in America, and he wanted Cat to be his agent.

Cat was astounded. "I don't know anything about steel. I wouldn't even know how to describe it. I wouldn't know where to begin."

The visitor smiled. "Mr. Cat," he said, "(Ito told me I could call you that), you don't need to know anything. American industry is gasping for steel, and all you have to do is to offer it for sale. They'll snap it up. You get five percent for your efforts."

"Look," said Cat earnestly, "I appreciate that Saigo wants to help me, and that this is a way that wouldn't insult me or hurt my pride, but I couldn't take money this way. I'd be fooling nobody, least of all, myself."

The visitor rose. "I am sorry, Mr. Cat. I will convey what you have said to Mr. Ito. He will be sad, too, since you are the only person he really trusts in America. However, I am the more disappointed, for now I have to find someone else to sell this steel for Mr. Ito, and I have little time, and know almost nobody else. Could you recommend someone, Mr. Cat?"

"Wait a minute," said Cat. "You mean you really are looking for someone, almost anyone, to sell the steel for you? You have no organization, no representation, no agent in the States?"

"That is right."

"Well, now…"

The upshot was that Cat took a piece of paper to a steel warehouse in Pittsburgh, talked to the owner for a few minutes, and came away with another piece of paper. Money was deposited in escrow. He repeated this several times, in Allegheny, in Etna, and in Youngstown. When the steel was delivered, and the money in escrow sent to Ito, Cat found himself with a very substantial bank account.

As a piece of poetic justice, he invested his money in steel stocks, and with the Korean War and the Vietnam War and the threat from the Soviet Union, his investments grew very nicely indeed. When his capital was great enough, he decided to go into the manufacture of high tech components. However, he wasn't sure he had enough money to survive through the starting-up period, and he was afraid to borrow from banks, for fear that in the end they would own his company. It was a banker himself, an acquaintance from his student days at Emory, who explained to him, "The bank doesn't want your company. We aren't set up to run companies—we don't even know how. We want your company to be successful. We want you to expand. We want you to borrow more and more money from us, because we make our money on interest—not on owning companies."

So he borrowed the money, and opened his high tech component company on Route 128 in Boston, among others of the same type. His chief technician was a metallurgist, who insisted as part of his work conditions that he be enabled to continue research in metallurgy. Because he had acceded to this request, Cat found that his company was becoming a leader in a certain section of the high tech industry—that which used newly composed metals for highly specialized jobs.

At one time it became necessary for Cat and his metallurgist to visit New York, and since they wanted a long time to talk, they decided to drive. All the way to New York they discussed business and general problems, but on the way back, after dark, the metallurgist turned to Cat and said, "What do you know about metal fatigue?"

"Not much," admitted Cat.

"Well, I'm going to tell you about metal fatigue. You see, the way I stay awake while driving is to talk. You talk to me and I fall asleep, but if I talk to you I stay awake. Now, the first thing you have to know about metal fatigue is that nobody knows anything about it."

And with that opening, he spoke solidly all the way to Boston about how metal seems to suddenly become tired and break, with no previous warning. Aircraft manufacturers test propellers for years, for example, to see when they will break, but one may break fairly early and another seemingly never breaks. As they turned into the driveway of Cat's house, four hours later, the metallurgist ended, "So you see, nobody knows anything about metal fatigue."

Cat was amused by the exercise, but the more he thought about it the more he became interested in metal fatigue. In the end, his company became one of the nation's central points for research into metal fatigue. It was for this fact that Cat was first invited to Soviet Russia as a guest of the metallurgy industry there. With the agreement of the State Department, he set up a joint research project with the Soviets on the problem of predicting metal fatigue.

As the years passed Cat's company grew into a conglomerate, and his visits to Soviet Russia became almost routine. He was introduced to all of the country's leaders, and served as a volunteer arbitrator in a number of American/Russian industrial disputes.

On Cat's seventy-fifth birthday the Soviet Government decided to honor him with a decoration devised especially for foreigners who had been helpful to Soviet industry. A young aide to the Prime Minister placed the ribbon around Cat's neck, and when the ceremony was over, fingered the ribbon for a moment and said, with a smile, "I guess now I can call you a Communist."

Cat figured the young man's birth-date as around 1960. Remembering his induction into the International Brigade in Spain in 1936, and the visit from Cohn and Schein in 1950, he said, "Son, I was being called a Communist long before you were born."

I was present at the ceremony in Moscow at my uncle's invitation (and expense). When I heard his comment to the young aide, I realized how his being branded as a Communist so many years ago still rankled. Later, in his hotel room, I said , "Uncle Cat, you've experienced so much in your lifetime. You've contributed so much, done so much. Why does that old, false accusation still bother you? Everyone knows that it wasn't true."

He looked at me for a long time, then looked at his drink, and I thought I saw a twinkle in his eye for a moment. "Ever see Rashomon?"

"Sure. The story of a rape that is seen differently by different people. Why?"

"Which story is true?"

"Why, all of them, or none of them. It depends on the observer, I guess."

"Know your Bible?"

"Uh, not much."

"What did Pontius Pilate say?"

"I don't know. What did he say?"

"He said, 'What is truth?'"

"I don't get it."

"You're the family historian, right?"

"You know it."

"Then you know what a revisionist historian is—someone who takes things that everybody knows is true, and either denies it, or puts another slant on it. I'm going to give you a chance to be a revisionist historian."

"What?"

Uncle Cat smiled mischievously. "You know the story of my life as history. Now I'm going to unfold an alternative history for you, and you'll decide which one is true. Ready?"

"I'm listening."

"During my first two years at Harvard I joined the communist cell there. It was, to be sure, harmless. We got together through the use of secret passwords, drank beer, talked about Marx, Trotsky and Lenin, and had great sympathy for the working classes, of whom we knew not one member. It was exciting—no, thrilling. It was especially thrilling for me, because I had led a cloistered childhood at home, and in a private school. This was my first, rather delayed, adolescent revolt.

"I joined the International Brigade at the urging of our cell leader, a young instructor—who himself never went to Spain. I officially joined the Communist Party while in Madrid. I had met many Russians, was predisposed to believe in their ideal state, and it made no sense to risk my life for something I was unwilling to join.

"Joyce urged me to join the Party. She had been active in the Atlanta cell even before she came to Spain.

"Back in Emory I lay low. The activities of the college chapter seemed childish to me after what I had seen and done in Spain. The opportunity to run an internment camp was a God-given gift (even though officially I did not believe in God). There were enough Japanese-Americans who were bitter at their internment to offer a fertile field for recruitment activities. Saigo Ito was, of course, their commissar. The second camp we set up was for training underground communists.

"In Japan with the occupation forces I was able to use Saigo's contacts to strengthen the party there considerably, and my appointment to a State Department job could not have been stage-managed better by

Joe Stalin himself. I did not think of myself as a spy while in the State
Department. I passed on information that would be helpful to the
Party, and warned them of impending dangers, but I don't think that
helped Russia as such very much.

"Saigo arranged the money for me to start the high tech business. It
was Russian money, I am sure, but how he did it I never knew. The ultimate goal was to share high tech secrets with Russia, and that is what we
did, beautifully. Russian industry, including the munitions industry,
would never have reached the heights that they did without our
secrets—incidentally, especially concerning metallurgy, since our metallurgist had been recommended to me by Saigo.

"And now my lifelong efforts have been recognized by the Soviet
government."

I both gasped and gaped.

Uncle Cat enjoyed my confusion for a few moments, and then he
said, "And what if all of that was true, but I was employed by the CIA
and reported every Russian move to them?

"Okay, which story do you believe? The lady or the tiger? God or the
Devil? Tell me, nephew, what is truth?"

That was the last time I saw my uncle Cat, who was an American
patriot. Or a communist agent. Or a double agent. Or all of the above.
Or none of the above. He's dead now, and I'll never know the truth.

Uncle Sam

◆

UNCLE SAM

My Uncle Sam was born to be a doctor. Not that he had any innate talent, or a calling, or even a desire in that direction. In fact, he had nothing at all to do with it. The family decided that my Uncle Sam would be a doctor even before he was born. Sam's parents had come from the old country, but the children were all born in America, and were part of the "Aw, Maw" generation—"Aw, Maw, you don't understand;" "Aw, Maw, none of the other kids do that;" "Aw, Maw, that's old country stuff." In short, they were still trying to affirm their Americanism.

Consequently, Sam—as the youngest —was going to be a doctor. No matter what it cost, no matter what sacrifices had to be made, Sam was going to be a doctor. Not just for the money involved, and not just to be able to refer casually to "My brother, the doctor," but to reflect respectability on the whole family—a respectability that the parents' activities did not exactly reflect. A family that contained a doctor—a medical doctor, not just a Ph. D.—had made it.

Sam had no objections to these plans for his future. Indeed, being rich, famous and admired did not seem like a destiny to be dodged. So Sam, too, decided that he would be a doctor, and that having been determined, didn't feel the need to put himself out too much.

The result was that his high school grades were just average, but fortunately that didn't really matter. With Georgia Tech, University of Georgia in Atlanta, Emory and Oglethorpe to choose from, he figured he would get in somewhere. Since both Sam's father and mother had died in quick succession while he was in high school, his six siblings got together to make the necessary decisions and plans.

Insofar as pre-med programs were involved, however, it was the University of Georgia in Athens, Georgia, that had the best reputation and the largest number of successful graduates. However, it wasn't feasible to live in Atlanta and study in Athens, so a small inexpensive room in a boarding house near the campus was found for Sam. A budget was drawn up enumerating all the expenses that Sam would have and contributions were figured on the basis of individual incomes and expenses. A bank account was opened in Sam's name, and monthly deposits made by every brother and sister.

Sam began to feel the burden of these sacrifices, and for the first time began to study seriously. The result was a slight improvement in his grades, which the family greeted almost ecstatically. At the same time, at college Sam for the first time felt freedom from the constant family presence, and began experimenting with his new sense of liberty. He attended some parties hosted by other students, and learned to drink beer.

It was at an end-of-semester beer party that Sam found himself standing at a urinal, along with several other party-goers. He was still holding a beer bottle in his hand and, already feeling slightly drunk and not wanting to increase the feeling, he carefully poured the remaining beer into the urinal, announcing, "Gentlemen, this is what is meant by 'cutting out the middleman.'" The fat boy on his right laughed so hard that he wet his pants with a few drops, and several others smiled.

When Sam returned to the party, the joke was evidently making the rounds, because several people looked in his direction and smiled. This was the beginning of Sam's reputation as a wit. People began to expect jokes and bon mots from him, and although he tried to oblige, even to the extent of buying *America's Best-Loved Jokes,* he often had to work hard to maintain his reputation.

Glancing through a comic book while waiting for a haircut, Sam saw an ad for a magician's kit, with "accompanying explanations that will let you mystify your friends." Feeling that this might enhance his reputation as an entertaining person, he sent away for the kit, but when it came, he was very disappointed. It was not even a child's kit, but a sleazy collection of a false moustache, a magic wand, a magnet, a round piece of glass referred to as a crystal, and similar pathetic artifacts. Even the so-called book of explanations was badly printed on cheap paper, and consisted mostly of directions to send for other, more expensive, materials.

The book angered Sam, but it also piqued his curiosity, and on his next trip to Atlanta he went to the Carnegie Library and took out a book on magic. He sat in the library and read for three hours, and then went back to his room and began practicing. To his own surprise, he was good. He could palm even relatively large objects, and thus take not one, but several, coins out of his own ear. He had no difficulty palming the coins and producing a silk handkerchief from his sleeve. He was intrigued by his own success.

Sam did some research, and when he finally felt that he had located the best how-to book concerning magic, bought it. In a way, Sam had found his metier. He practiced assiduously, although he lacked an audience. For his school work, he borrowed books, used the library, and copied the notes of others, while he shamelessly extracted money from the family for the books he supposedly needed, using it for magicians' equipment—trick hats, capes, pockets, etc. He even branched out into juggling, but didn't practice enough to become really expert at it.

Sam was still keeping his new-found skill to himself, not sure how to begin to use it, when he met Jo. She was the first Scandinavian girl that he had ever met and talked to face-to-face. His social life on the South Side of Atlanta had been mostly with Jewish girls whose parents were from Central Europe. Her straight blonde hair and deep blue eyes intrigued him. Theo, who was with Jo, introduced Sam as the class clown, and Jo looked Sam in the eye and said, "I like clowns," before Theo whisked her away.

Sam fantasized about Jo in a way he had never been able to bring himself to think about other girls, and when he saw an announcement of the Barnum and Bailey Circus, which was opening the following week, he decided this was a sign sent from somewhere—he wasn't sure where.

Theo was more amused than surprised when Sam asked him how to get in touch with Jo, but Jo took it seriously when Sam said, "You said you liked clowns. How about going to the circus with me?"

She half-smiled and said, "I like some clowns. I'm not sure I'll like the circus clowns. But to see a clown watching clowns might be fun. Sure, I'll come."

They had a ball at the circus. They ate popcorn and cotton candy, had their fortunes told, gasped at the trapeze artists and cheered the bareback riders. During the tense moments, they held hands. Sam thought the clowns awkward, but Jo didn't take her eyes off them, and on the way out she said, "The other clowns were okay, but did you see that juggler! Balls and bottles and feathers and firebrands, all at one time! That's not easy. He was good!"

Sam felt ridiculous being jealous of a circus clown, but before he thought about it he heard himself saying, "Juggling's easy. I can juggle."

"You really can?"

"Sure. Come up to my room and I'll show you."

Jo shrieked with laughter. "What, no etchings? No paintings? No nightcap? Just juggling? Is that how you get your way with women?"

Sam blushed. "I really can juggle," he said.

Jo turned and looked at him pensively. He couldn't figure out her face. "Okay. We'll go to your room, and you'll show me how you juggle. If you can, we will. If you can't, we won't. That's fair, isn't it?"

Sam was so astounded he couldn't answer. He had never heard a girl talk like that—and certainly not to him. He thought maybe he had misunderstood her meaning, but she squeezed his hand and started for the bus.

In his room Jo sat on the edge of the bed while Sam picked up two tennis balls and began juggling them—not too high, and not too fancy.

"Oh, c'mon," Jo said. "Anyone can handle two balls. I bet you handle yours all the time. I've even handled some myself. That's not juggling."

Sam nearly dropped one of the balls on hearing this, but managed to capture it, and picked up another tennis ball without losing his rhythm. By keeping the three balls at exactly the same height each time, not varying directions, and maintaining the same speed, he was able to keep them all in the air.

"Now," proposed Jo, "let's see some real juggling—over the shoulder, between the legs, off to one side."

Desperate to prove himself, Sam tossed one ball further to the right than he had previously—and promptly lost it. He retrieved it and tried again, but again it eluded him. After two more tries Jo got up, and Sam panicked that she was leaving. But she captured the balls, pushed Sam down on the bed, and began juggling. She didn't start with two balls, but with three, and kept them all in the air—over her shoulder, between her legs, off to one side and then off to another. Spotting two beer bottles on the table she dropped two of the balls without losing a beat and began to juggle two beer bottles and a tennis ball—faultlessly.

Sam was riveted to the bed, alternating between anger and humiliation. Suddenly, Jo put down the bottles and the ball and strode over to the bed, where she stood between Sam's legs. "You're a lousy juggler," she said, "but maybe you're a better lover. Let's see." She began to unbuckle his belt.

Later, in bed, when Sam had finally come down to near normality and felt he could converse casually, he asked Jo about her juggling. "My mother died when I was ten, and my father raised me. I was an only

child, and whenever I became depressed or angry or hurt, he would juggle anything he could get his hands on to amuse me. When I got older,
that wasn't enough, so he taught me how to juggle. I do it now just to
cheer myself up sometimes—whenever I need to prove to myself that
there is something I do well. That's how I knew," she smiled at him
provocatively, "that the circus clown was really very good."

This time he overcame his pang of jealousy by pulling her over to
himself once more. Toward morning he asked, "Am I a better lover than
a juggler?"

"For an amateur in both fields, you're all right. You'll learn. This was
your first time, wasn't it?"

Sam had to admit that she was right. "You see, I grew up in a strait-
laced atmosphere—my family, my house, my neighborhood, were all
very, well, I guess moral. We were all inhibited, naive, religion-bound,
afraid of what our parents—and even more important, what her parents—would say if they found out. But mostly we were scared. And I
guess the girls were, too.

"I can't believe that you never had a chance. You're not Clark Gable,
but you're not bad. You must have done something other than talk
about morals when you went out with girls."

"Oh, yeah, but it was just petting and necking…"

"Until you came in your pants. And then you got very uninterested
and she got very insulted."

"How'd you know?"

"Because I'm a girl, and I've dated lots of boys like you. Come here
before you insult me."

Sam fell into a deep sleep later, probably from exhaustion, and when
he woke up, Jo was gone. That was okay with him. He wasn't ready for any
more sexual exertions, nor was he sure where she lived, or whether he was
supposed to take her home, so he lay in bed fondling his memories and
luxuriating in his new-found role of seducer of beautiful women—or, at
least, that was how Sam tried to remember the day before.

He looked for Jo on campus the next day, but didn't see her. On the following day, when he saw her, she was with a crowd that he didn't know. The next time, with Theo again. He never seemed to be able to catch her alone. In fact, he began to get the impression that she was avoiding him. She would smile, or wave, but then begin talking to someone else, or move in another direction.

It took two weeks of actual physical stalking before Sam was able to meet her face to face. Before he could say anything, she said, "Play the field, Sam. Don't get tied down. That's the only way to enjoy life. When you begin going with lots of girls, maybe I'll be one of them, but until then, I'm playing the field, too. I don't want to be your girl friend, and I don't want you to be my boy friend. It was great, but it's finished, over, done. Good-bye. Oh, don't forget to practice your juggling."

And that was the end of it for Jo. It took Sam a helluva lot longer to get over that first affair.

When Sam graduated the University of Georgia, slightly above the middle of the class (which the family promptly announced as, "In the top of his class"), the family laid on a celebration. It was a sit-down dinner, and Uncle Bernie was in one of his flush periods, because he provided a bottle of wine for each table. There were speeches, mostly about Sam, although Marilyn mentioned their parents and the sacrifices they had made for all of them, but especially for Sam. Sam was somewhat embarrassed, and thought it in bad taste, but he saw the other family members applauding and realized that they were all sharing in the glory of the moment because of their own contributions to the evening and to Sam.

When it was time for Sam to respond, he had a sudden moment of insight. He realized how much his success meant to them, and how they had sacrificed for him. None of them had risen much higher than they had started—money was still a problem for all of them—but in him they saw their own aspirations fulfilled. He was suddenly very grateful to them, but he felt that if he tried to say it he would start to cry. To gain some time, he pulled a nickel out of Marilyn's ear, and was gratified by the smiles that Marilyn's surprise brought to the people at the tables. He walked over to Phil and shook hands with him, then stood back so everyone could see the dollar bill now gracing Phil's breast pocket. To his surprise, someone started clapping, and then others joined in.

He picked up Sophie's white napkin, passed it behind his back, and put it back, red. The applause mounted. Sam was in his element—he had found an audience! He was warming to his act, with everyone waiting for the next trick, when he looked at Leo. He shot a glance at Willie, and then at Buck. They weren't smiling. Sophie's lips were compressed and Marilyn looked like she was trying not to cry.

Sam wished he was good enough a magician to make himself disappear. The family was showing off their scholastic, academic, intellectually successful member, and he was responding with cheap parlor tricks. With everyone watching him, he silently took out of his sleeves and pockets the paraphernalia that he usually carried with him, and laid it all on the table. Then Sam began to speak:

"To graduate college, one must become somewhat of a magician. You have to juggle hours, classes, library time and tests, and still find enough hours for eating and sleeping. The happy, carefree days of college that we see in movies are a myth. College students are generally anxious, harassed, and above all—busy. So everyone must find a way of relaxing from time to time. Some drink; some go to movies; some go to ballgames; some even play ball; some do things I won't mention here"—a few men in the audience smiled knowingly—"and I do magic tricks."

Buck was glowering and Sophie looked apprehensive, but the others began to look interested. "Why magic tricks?" Sam was ashamed of what he was going to say next, but plowed ahead, trying to exude sincerity.

"I hope to become a doctor. A doctor's hands are his major instrument. With them he probes, he feels, he takes the pulse, he manipulates other instruments, and"—smiling—"he makes out the bill." Laughter.

"Keeping hands nimble and healthy is important to me, and it was"—he gulped before pulling this one out—"a surgeon who visited our class who said he did magic tricks to keep his fingers in shape. So I began. I'll admit it has other usages, such as impressing certain"—pause—"people." A man laughed out loud.

"But all of that is incidental. What I really want to say is…" and from here on Sam honestly praised and thanked his family for the magic they had worked for him, their faith in him and their support. He hoped he would be worthy of it, and he was only sorry that his parents wouldn't be there when he reached his goal. When he finished, his brothers and sisters were looking at him almost in adoration. Only Bernie looked over the top of his glasses at him, deadpan.

When the party was over, Marvin began to move from table to table, filling half-empty wine bottles from other half-empty ones. "Let it go," called Bernie. "I paid for it."

"I know you did," said Marvin, "and that's why I don't want the waiters to have it. We'll each take several bottles home."

Sam again felt deep guilt. Parsimony was so ingrained in the family members that they couldn't let go, and he felt that some of it must come from having to sacrifice all their adult lives for him. His guilt was not diminished when Phil walked over on his way out and said, "Nice performance, Sam. You really have become quite a trickster."

The question of what medical school to choose was the subject of a family meeting. Sophie pressed for an Ivy League school, and Sam was infinitely relieved when Marvin, instead of dwelling on admission difficulties, pointed out that the entire family together wouldn't be able to pay the terribly high tuition, let alone the living costs. Louis thought maybe a mid-Western school would be cheaper, but Marilyn had been studying catalogues, and she took charge.

"What we need is a small, not exclusive, private medical school, not necessarily university connected. They are cheaper, give more individual attention, and are easier to get into."

This was the first indirect mention of Sam's not-so-brilliant grades, and he wondered whether he was blushing. Marilyn went on quickly, "I think something like Middlesex College in Waltham might be the answer."

"What? Where? Waltham, where's that?"

Marvin: "Wait a minute. What kind of reputation does that school have? What would people think of a doctor who graduated there?"

Marilyn: "You saw the doctor last month about your gall bladder. What school did he graduate from?"

Marvin: "I don't know."

Marilyn: "Hessie, where did your gynecologist train?"

Hessie: "Never thought about it."

"You see," summed up Marilyn, "once you're a doctor, nobody asks where you went to school. Are you well recommended, are you reasonable, are you convenient? That's all that counts."

So Sam went to Middlesex. The main building had once been a castle, built by a whimsical millionaire who aspired to be a European. Other buildings, including living quarters, were houses scattered haphazardly over what had once been farm land. There was a train once a day from and to Boston's Back Bay Station, and a bus once every two hours. Waltham itself was a company town, devoted to making watches, and the word amenities would have puzzled the inhabitants.

Sam found Middlesex more demanding than the University of Georgia, but not terribly so. He found time not only to practice his magic, but to give performances at student affairs. Twice he was invited to appear at the Veterans' Hall in Waltham, for which he received a token payment, and once he won third prize at an amateur night in a Brookline theatre.

As the months and years passed, Sam found the theoretical material more and more difficult and the practical work more and more interesting. His hands seemed to make up for what his brain lacked, but it wasn't enough. He had difficulty remembering the names of the bones, but he bought a skeleton and hung it in his closet, and by running his fingers over each bone, he was able to retain most of the names. But he couldn't do that with the nervous system, the blood supply, and certainly not with symptoms and diseases. His time devoted to magic diminished, and he became a typical medical student, nose figuratively worn away on the grindstone.

As graduation time began to be perceived on the far horizon, the family gleefully informed Sam that if he thought his university graduation was a celebration, wait until he heard about the plans for this party! Sam begged them not to go ahead with the plans until he had a chance to talk with them, and that chance came during the spring break.

Again the siblings got together. The agenda had become a ritual by now. Wine and cake on entering, exchanging news about spouses, children, grandchildren, jobs, vacations, whatever. A delicatessen spread— whitefish and lox, salami and bologna, corned beef and pastrami, various kinds of pickles, three or four salads. Then coffee and cake, or maybe mandelbrot. At last, the siblings would move into the living room, while the spouses—some now with children in carriages or portable playpens—played penny ante in the kitchen, and Louis' wife kept knitting on an apparently endless afghan.

This time Sam took the floor in the living room immediately. "I know you are all planning for my graduation from medical school. You are looking forward to the moment when I am supposed to get that marvelous piece of parchment in my hand. The party you are planning will be an extravaganza, I know. But I have some important—and to me, wonderful—news for you: I won't be present to receive that parchment. I won't be at the ceremony, and I won't be at the party."

The silence was absolutely complete. Not a paper napkin crinkled; not a chair creaked. The family sat motionless, every eye on Sam. He waited until it looked like someone might want to say something, and—with a big smile—began again.

"I will be on my way to Sweden."

Still no reaction.

"The Swedish government has offered me a very well-paid internship in the hospital in Malmo. An internship that will allow me to specialize in almost any field that I choose. But—and here is the bad news—I have to get there in time for their academic year to begin, and that means I will have to leave here before the graduation ceremony. Would you mind terribly if the graduation celebration was turned into a bon voyage party for me?"

The dam broke. "Sweden? Why Sweden? So far away! It's so cold there! Why not nearer home? Wow, the travel costs alone…Why, Sam, why?"

Sam quieted the noise. "Every year several European governments offer internships to American graduates, like Rhodes scholarships are offered for political scientists in England. Middlesex was offered two internships, one in Paris and one in Malmo. Everyone who was interested in a scholarship applied for Paris. I figured that would happen, so I applied for Malmo, and was accepted."

Patiently he explained that the hospital in Malmo was noted for its all-round excellence; that he could work there using English, instead of having to learn a foreign language; that the travel costs were part of the internship; and that in the United States foreign-trained doctors commanded higher fees.

"That's certainly true," said Hessie. "Marjie Dugan is always bragging that her gynecologist trained in England—and does he charge!"

Gradually, alarm turned to pride. No one in the family had ever been abroad, or even dreamed of going abroad, and now it would not only be, "My brother, the doctor," but "My brother, the doctor, who studied in Sweden."

So when the party was held it was a bon voyage celebration, and Sam took the train to New York and the S.S. Gripsholm to Sweden.

For two years there were cards, notes, and sometimes little gifts from Sam. Not always from Sweden—it seemed that on his free time he traveled all over Europe. His nieces and nephews saved his stamps, and his siblings wrote to him—when they did, for none of them were easy letter writers—to his postoffice box in Malmo.

Sam's return was to be triumphant—at last the family had a doctor! But they reckoned without Hitler. When Poland was invaded and England declared war, travel to the States was still possible, although dangerous. However, Sam wrote that he was now badly needed in Swedish hospitals, but not to worry—there was very little chance that Sweden would be involved in the war. Sam did not mention, nor did the family make reference even among themselves, to the fact that if he returned to the United States he would probably face army service very shortly.

During the next few years even Sam's postcards ceased arriving, and with America's entrance into the war, the postal service to destinations abroad made contact almost impossible. The mail that did get through was returned, months later, marked, "Address unknown." Sam had evidently disappeared from Malmo. The family worried, of course, and after the war they tried to trace Sam through the American Embassy in Stockholm, the hospitals in Malmo, and even the Red Cross.

Consequently, when Sam showed up in Atlanta without advance notice several months after V-J Day, his greeting was overwhelming. After an interval of making the rounds to catch up on family, and explaining that he had been working in hospitals up and down the length of Sweden—which is why he hadn't been in Malmo very much—the time came to discuss future plans.

A week before the proposed family meeting, Sam went to an office in the Whitehall Arcade and spoke to a red-faced pudgy man with a loud voice. "Sarasota. Next week. Glad to have you with us," the man said, closing off the conversation.

The family gathering took place in Uncle Jim's office, complete with photos of Uncle Jim in a pilot's outfit standing next to various kinds of planes. Some family members were clearly apprehensive of what was coming. They were not unmindful of the costs of outfitting a doctor's office, not just with furniture, but with all of the modern and expensive equipment that modern doctors used. Nor did they—and especially their spouses—feel that they should have to resume supporting Sam after all these years.

Sam led right into this. "You know how grateful I am to all of you for helping me become a doctor. I know how you made real sacrifices for many years, and I thought that my return from Sweden would be the beginning of my making it up to you. But as you know, things have changed in the world. Opening a private office has become immensely expensive, and building up one's practice until one is self-sustaining can take years. This is a burden that I refuse to load onto you.

"In addition, more and more medicine is going to be government run and administered. We already have Medicare and Medicaid, and this will probably spread into some sort of national health service, as they have in England. Doctors are increasingly going to end up as government employees, and the government is never going to match the income that private practitioners made at one time. In short, we are going to see a lot of relatively poor doctors in government service simply trying to get along. That's not what I want to be, and not what you want to see me become.

"The most prestigious and well-paid doctors are going to be those who work for large international organizations—privatized and globalized. They will have prestige, and power, and income. So that is the kind of position I propose to seek. I will no longer need your financial help, and I hope that I will shed credit on the family."

Buck said, "Makes sense to me."

"Have you made any inquiries?" asked Sophie.

"As a matter of fact, yes. Some positions are very chancy; some don't pay well; many won't give me a final answer for months. There is only one that has offered me an immediate well-paying job."

"And that would be?"

"An international entertainment and exhibition company."

"Wow! Warner Brothers?"

"No, not exactly. Look, I'll give it to you straight. The best offer I have had—in fact, the only real offer—is to head the medical services of the world's largest and most successful circus—Ringling Brothers and Barnum and Bailey."

"A circus doctor! My God!" breathed Marilyn.

"You're crazy," said Monty, flatly. He had never talked like that to Sam before.

"Do you know what we've given up for you; how we've supported you; what we've gone through for you? I didn't buy a new pilot's helmet I needed once in order to support you." That was Jim, shouting.

"How could you, Sam? How could you?" Hessie was out of her depth.

Phil looked at him intently. "Is that the best you could do?"

"Believe me, Phil, the best of the offers. And there were only two of them."

Phil turned to the family. "What's the matter with you people? You think he wants to do this? You think he wants to be a circus doctor? A Swedish trained doctor working for a circus! He's doing it for us. He wants to get off our backs. He doesn't want us to have to support him any more. Give him a little credit. Give him a little thanks. Give him a little love."

Hessie began to sniff, but Marilyn stood up and started for the door. "My brother, the circus doctor. Big deal! What'll I tell people who ask about him? That he's taking care of Bozo the Clown, the fat lady, and the wild man from Borneo? He isn't doing this for us—he's doing it for himself. I think he likes the circus."

Willie started for the door, but suddenly came back and put out his hand. "If that's what you want, okay. Take care and good luck."

Louis didn't look at him. "C'mon, Hessie, let's get to the car," and they were gone.

Phil stood looking out the window as Hessie and Louis drove away. Without turning he said, "I don't think you're being straight with me, Sam. I don't think you've been straight with the family for a long time.

But it's your life and you have to live it. God knows I'm not the one to throw the first stone, but I live by my intuition, and my intuition tells me you're not being completely honest. Are you really being hired by the circus?"

Sam was delighted that Phil had put the question that way. "I really am going to work for the circus, Phil. And I appreciate your having defended me…"

"Cut it, kid. You live your life and I'll live mine. Still," reflectively, "I think that what you are doing takes guts. Good luck." And he was gone.

In March Sam reported to the circus in their winter quarters in Sarasota, and fitted into the routine with a minimum of fuss. He was not, of course, the circus doctor. His sideshow was emblazoned, "Stan, the Magic Man," with a stylistic drawing of a man in top hat and tails, pulling a rabbit out of a hat.

He wore top hat and tails, of course, but he also wore a false nose under which there were several compressed scarves and handkerchiefs. His glasses had thick frames, and held other small props, as well as being magnetized. He wore a wig, and that, too, was for ulterior purposes. He seemed taller than he really was, for the high heels held other goodies. And, of course, there was the red-lined magician's cloak and the hollow ebony cane. In short, Sam the doctor became Stan the Magic Man with very little apparent connection between them.

The circus toured the United States all spring, summer, and fall, with occasional side trips into Canada. When they played New York, the Hippodrome was no longer in existence, nor was the Winter Garden, so they performed in Madison Square Garden (which he found to his surprise was neither on Madison Avenue, square, nor a garden). In New York, Sam scanned the audience at his sideshow from behind the curtains every night, and once he thought he saw Phil near the rear, but the lights were already going down, and he wasn't sure.

Sam was friends with Chuck who had hired him for the circus, and it was in New York that Chuck made his proposition to Sam. "You can stay in Sarasota all winter; or you can take a vacation; or you can make a lot of money."

"I'll take the money. What's up?"

"You take part of the show, and you go below the equator where it is summer, and you travel."

"That's what you call a lot of money?"

"As the man said when he was asked where he got the black eye: 'I was standing up talking when I should have been sitting down listening.' Now sit down and listen.

"You, the magician; the strongman; and the female contortionist travel in South America and Africa. You don't play the cities. You go out into the jungle, and you amaze the natives—for a price."

"Are you nuts? What kind of price?"

"Come here."Chuck led him down the hallway from his small office and opened the door of a museum. Or so it seemed to Sam. There were wooden statues on the floor, ivory statues on stands, and unidentifiable things hanging down from the ceiling. There were brilliantly woven scarves and some beautiful miniature paintings. Chuck stood back smiling as Sam wandered through the room, picking up a small statue here or an intricately carved box there. Finally, he looked his question at Chuck.

"South American and African native art."

"And what do we do with this, uh, art?"

"We hoard it. We let it go, piece by piece, very slowly, over a long time. We get lots and lots of money for it, because this is authentic primitive art that is disappearing. Some of it is from tribes that are hardly known to exist. You wouldn't believe what some of this is worth to collectors. Tell you what, go over to the Metropolitan and see their African collection, and compare it with some of these pieces. You'll be surprised."

"And where do you sell this stuff?"

"I told you. Go over to the Metropolitan. Three of their pieces they bought from me—see if you can identify them."

"I'll take your word for it. But where do I fit in?"

"Your magic will wow 'em. And the pieces you pick up by bartering other things—magnets, mirror illusions, whatever—are yours to sell. But I get ten percent. Deal?"

"Wait, wait. Why are you cutting me in? Why aren't you doing it yourself?"

"Sam, I can't get from place to place—not those places—anymore. I have diabetes and a heart condition. I need to diet, to exercise regularly, and to take insulin that has to be kept cool. But I know what I'm talking about, and I'll give you all the backing you need. A magician, a strong man and a female contortionist will be in like Flynn in those places. Are you interested?"

Sam thought for a moment. He was cut off from his family, who wanted nothing to do with a circus doctor, and would want even less to do with a doctor who had become a circus entertainer. He wasn't married. He wasn't rich. He didn't even have any plans for the summer. He decided. He was in.

Chuck's small troupe spent a month in the Amazon jungle. They flew from Lima to Iquitos, and then took the steamer south. They debarked where Peru, Brazil and Colombia meet, and hired a guide to take them deep into the rain forest. After two days of walking they came to a clearing beyond a rude wooden bridge over a stream, and the people in the three houses came to the banisters of their bungalows holding out what looked like small dolls, weapons, hats, and woven baskets, shouting to the guide. He shook his head no, and continued past the village.

Sam touched his shoulder and raised his eyebrows to indicate a question. The guide searched for the proper word in his meager supply of English, and said, "For touristes." Sam was surprised that tourists would take the walk they had taken just to buy what looked like assembly line-produced artifacts, but from the behavior of the natives, he realized the guide knew his jungle.

Eventually they got deeper and deeper into the forest, and when the guide was satisfied that they were in what Sam had begun to call "authentica," he attracted a crowd by simply tapping a small glocken-spiel. It looked something like Papagano's instrument in "The Magic Flute," and he only played three notes, waited a moment, played three other notes, and continued that until a crowd gathered either to see the instrument, to see the travelers, or simply to see what was doing.

The rest, as historians would have it, is history. The strong man bent double a pipe that none of the audience could even curve; the contortionist touched her head to the ground behind her back; and Sam pulled a large spearhead out of a tree that no spear had touched. And then the bartering began.

From the entire month in South America, Sam contented himself with two small but very beautiful carvings of an animal that he could not identify. The wood was not smooth to the touch, but actually velvety, and the animals were so lifelike that he was tempted to put them in cages. He had been offered a lot of crude art, and the strong man and contortionist had loaded up on it, but when he fondled it he got no satisfaction. From his two animals he got a sensuous feeling.

The traveling company then spent two months in Africa, part in South Africa where they performed for money which supported them during their jungle period, and the rest deep in the interior of East Africa. Again, Sam collected very little—three pieces in all, but each of them a gem.

During the beginning of the trip Sam slept twice with the contortionist, but he kept having the uncomfortable feeling that she was trying out a new act with him. Consequently, he wasn't completely surprised when she proposed that they organize a travelling sex-show when they finished the jungle trip, but he declined. She didn't seem to mind, and contented herself with the strong man from time to time.

Sam worried how the company would get through customs when they arrived in Miami, but Chuck met them and said, "Not to worry."

They walked through with no problem, since they were carrying only their personal belongings, and then they went to the mercantile shed, where their props and collection was waiting in a wooden lift.

"Barnum and Bailey, Sarasota," Chuck told the customs inspector, breezily. "Props, costumes, and stuff," and he started to walk away.

But the inspector pried open the lift, and Sam had a vision of prison—without his statues. Sure enough the first thing the inspector saw when he looked into the case was one of Sam's small animal sculptures. "What's this?" he began, and Chuck motioned to Sam.

"Why, nothing at all," he said. "Sam, do you see anything here?"

"Where? Here? No, but look over there."

The inspector automatically looked to where Sam pointed, and when he looked back the statue was gone. "Well, I'll be damned," he said.

"Do you mean this statue, inspector?" asked Sam, lifting it out of the inspector's open briefcase.

"Yeah, that's the one."

Sam swept it behind his back, and felt Chuck lift it away. "Oh, I thought you meant this one," and Sam lifted a costume off the other statue. They looked enough alike to make the inspector think that it was another of Sam's magic tricks, and he began to laugh. "C'mon, you do it with mirrors. I know it is really behind your back."

Sam made a complete turn to show that his back concealed nothing, and then dropping the costume back over the second statue, he took the first out of the inspector's briefcase again.

"Inspector, I think you have been concealing things in your briefcase," he said severely.

"Ah, you circus folks. Don't forget me when you give away those complimentary tickets," and he closed the lift.

"Be my guest," said Sam suavely, pulling two passes from under the inspector's tie.

And they were home safe.

Sam sold one of his animals to a gallery on Fifth Avenue for what he thought was a handsome price, but Chuck said it was a giveaway. He couldn't bear to part with the other one.

The African artifacts he priced very high, and while traveling with the circus sold one to a dealer in Dallas, one to a museum in Chicago, and one to a gallery in Waltham, the latter for a sentimental price. (That gallery had never aspired to a one-of-a-kind piece of authentic African primitive art, and they couldn't believe their luck. They never knew the reason).

Sam went to South America and Africa—and once to Australia—another four times. Then he decided he was tired of travelling, and as he thought about it, he was tired of circus life, too. He had enough primitive art to open a gallery, and so he rented a small place near the high Museum of Art and put a few of his pieces on display. He was an instant success.

Primitive, and particularly African, art had become the rage. Every sophisticated and noveau riche person needed a piece in their reception room or entrance hall. Sam kept raising his prices, and high society kept buying. His gallery was mentioned in art notes, and he himself was invited to openings, post-opening parties, and finally to receptions and parties for his own sake. He was decent-looking, he was unmarried, and he was rich. That was a heady combination for hostesses.

At the opening of a post-modernist exhibition in New York (which Sam couldn't understand), he ran into Chuck, whom he hadn't seen in two years. They had a joyous reunion, and Chuck said, "Come on up to my place. We'll have a party to celebrate old times. Just you and me and my wife."

Sam found that Chuck had also done very well in the last few years. His diabetes and heart condition didn't seem to keep him from living well. His apartment was lavish, and he had a butler. Just to celebrate their rise to their present positions, they ate nothing but caviar and drank nothing but champagne while waiting for Chuck's wife to come back from what Chuck called her "gender equality—formerly 'women's lib'—meeting".

Sam was half-drunk when she entered the room, but he froze. Blonde hair, blue eyes, trim figure—older, but still Jo. He thought Chuck had deliberately set him up, but Chuck was busy getting ready to offer more drinks, and said, almost perfunctorily, over his shoulder, "Sam, Jo. Jo, Sam."

Jo looked from Chuck to Sam, and then she froze in turn. "Sam?" she asked tentatively, and then she was certain. "Sam! How nice to see you again." She came over to him as though they were meeting unexpectedly on the street and kissed him lightly on the cheek.

He tried not to show any emotion, but he kept looking from Jo to Chuck as though seeking an explanation. Jo understood. "I guess we'd better talk," she said, and putting her hand under his elbow she moved him toward the bedroom door.

"Hey, not so fast, Sam," shouted Chuck, a bit high and laughing. "That's my wife and that's my bedroom. Don't you have any manners?"

Jo motioned to Chuck that this was serious, and he quieted down immediately, although he looked puzzled. Jo closed the door and pushed Sam into a chair. She found another chair, placed it backwards in front of him, and sat down, facing him over the chair back. "Sam, first things first. Chuck and I are not married. We've been living together for two years, and we are very happy, and he would love to get married, but I won't."

Sam looked at her somberly. "Will you marry me, Jo?"

"What?! Oh, my God, you don't understand. I won't marry you, I won't marry Chuck, I won't marry anybody. I need to feel free. I've always needed that. I need to know that as a woman I can do whatever I want to, that there are no strings tied to me. You can't understand that, can you? Well, put it this way—I need to juggle with my life."

"I love you. I've always loved you, Jo. Marry me."

"Jesus! You're not listening. I'm very happy with Chuck, at least so far. I don't want to shock your Biblical morals, Sam, but he isn't even the first man I've lived with. And if I ever do decide to leave him, it won't be to get married."

She thought about whether to say more, and then went on. "And certainly not to marry you. We had one fun evening; I enjoyed seducing you and taking your virginity, especially since I did it by juggling. I think my father might even have been proud of me. But to tell you the honest truth," she paused again, "from what you told me about how your family made all your plans for you, pushed you around, and insisted that you study medicine although you were interested in other things, I knew you were not for me."

Chuck opened the door, with a tray of drinks, just in time to hear Sam say again, stubbornly, "Marry me, Jo."

"What the hell is going on here?" Chuck shouted. "You're trying to steal my girl in my own house? What kind of friend are you? Out! Out!"

He threw one of the drinks at Sam, and although the glass missed him, he was spattered with alcohol. Jo tried to quiet Chuck with one hand and pushed Sam toward the door with the other. On the sidewalk, Sam was in a daze. He walked toward the river, and as he did so, he realized that he was not only cut off from his family—he had now lost the only girl he ever cared about, and made an enemy of his only friend.

But the thing that hurt him deepest was the accusation that he had never done anything on his own.

Sam never married. He continued with his gallery, buying as well as selling, and although he didn't need the money, it piled up. Once he thought he saw Phil looking in the window, and when he rushed outside he saw that it was Phil, trying to make sense of the primitive art displayed.

Sam made Phil come in to the back of the store where there were easy chairs and a sofa. "I've been hearing about you and your gallery," Phil explained, "and I just wanted to know what it was that made you rich."

Sam eagerly told Phil the story of Chuck and the travels abroad. Phil nodded sagely, "I never believed you were going to be a doctor for the circus. A magician? Okay, that I could believe. By the way, I saw your act once. You were good."

"So it was you? I thought I spotted you, but I was never sure."

Phil gave Sam details about the family. As in all families that grow older, two had died, one was deteriorating, the children and grandchildren were proliferating. Only George and Monty had become rich, but after the war everyone's kids went to college, everyone had homes and cars—the American dream was still being played out.

Gradually, tangentially, Sam broached the possibility of helping anyone in the family who needed it. "After all, Phil, it is a paying back, although God knows I could never pay back what you all did for me. But I have so much, and I'd like to share…"

Phil shook his head. "They won't take it from you, Sam. They don't want to know about you."

"They still hate me so much?"

"Sam, you betrayed them. They needed a doctor in the family that they could point to, talk about, look up to. Your becoming a doctor became a family fixation. And you became a doctor. They were so proud. They bragged about you while you were abroad. All their friends were waiting to meet the famous doctor. And then, suddenly, you became the kind of doctor they couldn't talk about, couldn't brag about, couldn't look up to. Even if you had become an abortionist, you would still have been a doctor with an office, an address, a calling card. But a doctor with a circus? No way."

Sam started to speak, had second-thoughts, and asked Phil if he wanted a drink. "Boy, do I want a drink. I could sure use one right now. But I can't drink. A liver problem. You understand, doctor."

Without being able to control them, tears came to Sam's eyes. "You are so accustomed to calling me doctor that even knowing the truth can't stop you. Believe me, I do understand how badly you all wanted me to be a doctor, and I do wish I could have. But no, although I've been many other things I was never a doctor."

"Good-bye, Sam," said Phil. "I won't be back. The family would find out somehow and then I would be the outcast. But I truly wish you well."

Sam lived to be ninety-one, and died painlessly in bed, all alone. He left his money, and the proceeds of his gallery, to be divided equally among his nieces and nephews, all of whose parents were by then dead, which made it difficult for them to object. When I got my share, it was just in time to pay my son's tuition to medical school, which I thought was poetic justice, in a way.

Some time later my son's wife was on a "roots" kick, wanting to know all about the family's past. By chance, she found some of Sam's documents, including a diary, thrown in with other old family papers by someone.

She was puzzled by several things. For one, Sam ended his diary by saying, "Jo said I never did anything on my own. She'll never read this, but I wish she could."

"Who was Jo?" she asked, but nobody knew.

Then there was Sam's Middlesex Medical School record. She showed it to me and I finally began to understand the family legends, puzzles, and theories that had grown up around my uncle.

Sam had never graduated medical school. He flunked out of Middlesex in his fourth year, failing almost all of his theoretic studies, although his practical work was fine. He joined a small Swedish circus as a magician and toured Europe with them until the war ended. He performed as a Swedish magician in all the neutral countries of Europe, and some of the warring ones. Early on he was approached by Allied intelligence and during his travels he picked up information and served as a courier for them. He even devised and proposed some strategies based on his background in illusions.

Gradually, he became more active in the Resistance movement, being involved—among other things—in the escape of the Jews of Denmark to Sweden. By the end of the war he had become one of the leaders of the Resistance in the Baltic States, with the cover name of Magician.

After the end of the war he became active in the *Bricha*—the movement of Jews from Europe to Palestine. He not only helped a group of Jewish women refugees to get from Ravensburg to Palestine, but as one of his last feats, he arranged for a group of concentration camp survivors to gather in Malmo, from where they were to be taken by the "illegal immigration" organization to Palestine. There was some delay due to a problem with ship's papers, but they eventually made it.

When Sam returned to the States, it was with the firm intention of telling the family that although he wasn't a doctor, he was in actual fact something historically more important: an American secret agent and a leading member of the Resistance, whose cover name would be mentioned in history books. But their certainty that he was a doctor, their pride in him, their belief that their sacrifices had paid off, made that impossible. He couldn't do it.

When he traveled through South America it was actually for Shin Bet, who were looking for Mengele. In Africa, it was partly with the connivance of, and to be of help to, the CIA, who were trying to assess the strengths and loyalties of many native groups. None of this could he tell the family.

So it seems that my uncle Sam was an accomplished magician, a very successful business man, a pioneer in bringing primitive art to America, a prominent Resistance leader, a help to Shin Beth, and a CIA member. But his family never forgave him for being the wrong kind of doctor. And he wasn't even that.

About The Author

◆

David Macarov grew up in Atlanta, and served three years in the United States Airforce, two of them in China, Burma and India. He went to then-Palestine in 1947 and was a Lieutenant-Colonel in the Israel Air Force. He lives in Jerusalem with his wife, four children, and eleven grandchildren. He is a fair folk-dancer, a better lawn-bowler, and a pretty good amateur gardener. He has written twelve professional books and is an Emeritus Professor of Social Work at the Hebrew University in Jerusalem. He can be reached at:

Nayot 8

Jerusalem, Israel
Tel: 972 2 679 2873
Fax: 972 2 679 3169
e-mail: DavidMacarov@huji.ac.il

3107239

Made in the USA